ALSO BY ÅKE EDWARDSON

Sail
of
Stone

Åke Edwardson

TRANSLATED BY RACHEL WILLSON-BROYLES

Simon & Schuster Paperbacks

New York   London   Toronto   Sydney   New Delhi

Simon & Schuster Paperbacks
1230 Avenue of the Americas
New York, NY 10020

Originally published in Sweden in 2002 by Norstedts Förlag in the Swedish language as the
title *Segel av sten*.

Published by arrangement with Norstedts Förlag.

First Simon & Schuster trade paperback edition March 2012

For information about special discounts for bulk purchases, please contact
Simon & Schuster Special Sales at 1-866-506-1949 or business@simonandschuster.com.

The Simon & Schuster Speakers Bureau can bring authors to your live event.
For more information or to book an event contact the Simon & Schuster Speakers
Bureau at 1-866-248-3049 or visit our website at www.simonspeakers.com.

Designed by Akasha Archer

Manufactured in the United States of America

10   9   8   7   6   5   4   3   2   1

Library of Congress Cataloging-in-Publication Data

Edwardson, Åke, date.
   [*Segel av sten*. English]
   Sail of stone / Åke Edwardson; translated by Rachel Willson-Broyles.—1st Simon &
Schuster trade pbk. ed.
      p. cm.
   Summary: "In *Sail of Stone* Chief Inspector Erik Winter and one of his female detectives
find themselves separately pursuing two unusual missing-person cases. *Sail of Stone*
is an outstanding psychological thriller, a character study of great depth and skill, by
internationally bestselling author Åke Edwardson."—Provided by publisher.
   I. Willson-Broyles, Rachel. II. Title.
   PT9876.15.D93S4413 2012
   839.73'74—dc23   2011028497

ISBN 978-1-4516-0850-2
ISBN 978-1-4516-0854-0 (ebook)

To Rita

I

In the harbor the ebb had put the boats ashore. They lay crooked, stems pointing at the steps in the wall.

Pointing at him.

He saw the bellies of the boats shining in the twilight. The sun was curving behind the cape to the west. The gulls cried under a low sky; the light thickened into darkness. The birds were pushed toward the surface of the water by the sky, which was stretched like a sail over the horizon.

Everything was pushed toward the sea. Pushed toward the sea, pushed down under the surface, pushed . . .

Jesus, he thought.

Jesus save my soul! Jesus save *my soul*.

So foul and fair a day I have not seen.

He heard sounds behind him, footsteps on stone on the path back to the church, which seemed to be carved out of the mountain, pounded out of stone by a hammer, like everything else here under the sail of the sky. He looked up again. The sky had the same tint of stone as everything else around him. A sail of stone. Everything was stone. The sea was stone.

Here I have a pilot's thumb,
Wrecked as homeward he did come.

The people moved behind him, on the way to a moment of peace in the Methodist church. He didn't turn around. He knew that they were looking at him; he felt their eyes on the back of his neck. It didn't hurt; they weren't that sort of eyes. He knew that he could depend on the people here. They weren't his friends, but they weren't his enemies either. He was allowed to move about in their world, and he had done so for a long time; so long, actually, that he had become something more than them, he had become like a part of the stone, the cliffs, the walls, the steps, the houses, the breakwaters, the sky, the sea, the roads. The ships. The trawlers.

The ones that lay here.

The ones that lay buried under the waves that moved in all those rolling quarries between the continents.

Jesus. Jesus!

He turned around. The footsteps had quieted and disappeared into the church, which was shut, closed up. The few streetlights down here were lit, and their only effect was to intensify the darkness too soon. The light thickens into darkness with time. He thought that thought as he began to walk. A darkness, before it was time. Every late afternoon. Before time and after time. I am living this life in after time. Way after time. I am alive. I am someone else, someone new. That other someone was a loan, a role, a mask like this one. You cross a line and become someone else and leave your old self behind.

There were children's clothes hung to dry in the yard next to the steps up to the road. The small arms waved at him.

He stood on the street. The viaducts towered over him like railways built to the heavens. Here is the streetcar that goes to heaven; Jesus drives and God is the conductor. But there had never been streetcars here. He had ridden the streetcar, but not here. That was in another life, a life far away. Far away. *Before* before time, before he crossed the line.

The viaducts cut through the sky all the way across this part of the city. The trains had roared along up there, but that was a long time ago. The last train departed in 1969. Maybe he had seen it.

The stone road in the heavens was built in 1888. Had he seen that, too? Maybe he had. Maybe he was a part of the viaduct's stone.

And nothing is but what is not.

They brought him here, and here he stayed.
No.
He stayed, but not for that reason.
He walked across the street and continued on to North Castle Street

and went into the pub at the crossroads. There was no one there. He waited, and a woman he'd only seen a few times before came out into the bar from the back room, and he nodded toward the taps on the bar in front of her.

"Fuller's, right?" she said, and took a pint glass from the clean stack beside the register. She hadn't yet had time to put the glasses on the racks.

He nodded again. She filled the glass and set it before him, and he watched the haze in the glass clear slowly, like the sky after a storm, or the bottom of the sea after a squall.

He ordered a whisky. He pointed at one of the cheaper brands behind her. She set the whisky glass before him. He drank and shivered suddenly.

"It's gettin' to be a cold night," she said.

"Mmhmm."

"It calls for somethin' warming, eh?"

"Hmm."

He drank some beer. He drank some whisky again. He felt the cold warmth in his stomach. The woman nodded in farewell and disappeared again into the back room.

He wondered if *she* would come this afternoon.

He heard the sound of a TV through the wall. He looked around. He was still alone. He looked around once again, as though for figures he couldn't see. He was what he'd always been, alone. A lone visitor. He was the visitor, always a visitor.

He was not afraid of what would come.

Present fears are less than horrible imaginings.

The whisky was gone, and he finished the beer and got up and left.

The sky had become black. The silhouettes of the viaducts were like animals from a prehistoric time. Before time. A north wind blew in his face.

He walked on the road again. There were no cars. The city glittered under him. There was no light on the sea. He stopped walking, but he saw no light out there. He waited, but all was dark. A car drove past behind him. He didn't turn around. He could smell the sea. The sharp wind was like needles in his face. He felt the weapon in his pocket. He heard the scream of the sea in his head, other screams.

Jesus!

He knew now that everything would come to an end.

2

It was two hundred and twenty yards to the sea, or two hundred fifty. They walked across a field where no one had trampled any paths. It can be us, he thought, we can make paths here.

The sky was high, space without end. The sun was sharp, even through sunglasses. The sea moved, but nothing more. The surface glittered like silver and gold.

Elsa shouted out toward the water and began to run along the edge of the beach, on the small stones, hundreds of thousands of them, which were mixed with the grains of sand, millions and millions of them.

Erik Winter turned to Angela, who was crouching and running sand through her fingers.

"If you can guess the number of grains of sand in your hand right now, a lovely prize awaits you," he said.

She looked up, raising her other hand to shield her eyes from the sun.

"What kind of prize?" she asked.

"First say how many grains of sand you have in your hand."

"How can you tell how many there are?"

"I know," he answered.

"What kind of prize?" she repeated.

"How many!" he said.

"Forty thousand," she answered.

"Wrong."

"Wrong?"

"Wrong."

"How the hell do you know?" She got up and looked at Elsa, who was fifty feet away, collecting stones. Angela couldn't see how many she had. She moved closer to the man in her life before he had had time to answer her question with "intuition."

"I want my prize. I want my *prize*!" she said.

"You didn't answer correctly."

"*Prize, prize,*" she shouted, falling into a clinch with Winter; she tried to put a reverse waist hold on him, and Elsa looked up and dropped a few stones, and Erik saw her and laughed at his four-year-old daughter and then at the other woman in his life, who was now trying to do a half nelson, not too bad, and he felt his feet starting to slide in his sandals and his sandals starting to slide in the sand and now he really started to lose his balance, and he slowly fell to the ground, as though he were pulled by a magnet. Angela fell on top of him. He kept laughing.

"*Prize!*" Angela shouted once more.

"*Prize!*" shouted Elsa, who had run up to the wrestlers.

"Okay, okay," said Winter.

"If you know, admit that I guessed right," said Angela, locking his arms. "Admit it!"

"You were very close," he answered. "I admit it."

"Give me my prize!"

She was straddling his stomach now. Elsa sat on his chest. It wasn't hard to breathe. He raised his right arm and pointed inland.

"What?" she said. "What is it?"

He pointed, waving with his hand.

"The prize," he said. He felt the sun in his eyes. His black sunglasses had fallen off. He could smell salt and sand and sea. He could see himself lying here for a long time. And often. Making those paths across the field.

From the house.

From the house that could stand over there in the pine grove.

She looked across the field. She looked at him. At the sea. Across the field again. At him.

"Really?" she said. "Do you really think so?"

"Yes," he answered, "you're right. Let's buy the lot."

Aneta Djanali was still producing her police ID when the woman closed the door that had just been opened. Aneta hadn't had time to see her face, only a shadow and a pair of eyes that flashed in the disappearing daylight, which seemed to be the only light in there.

She rang the doorbell again. Beside her stood one of the local police officers. It was a woman, and she couldn't have had very many months on the job behind her. A rookie. She looks like she came straight from high school. She doesn't look afraid, but she doesn't think this is fun.

She doesn't think it's exciting. That's good.

"Go away," they heard through the door. The voice was muffled even before it came through the double veneer or whatever it was between her and the long arm of the law.

"We have to talk for a minute," Aneta said to the door. "About what happened."

They could hear mumbling.

"I didn't understand what you said," said Aneta.

"Nothing happened," she heard.

"We have received a report," said Aneta.

Mumbling.

"Excuse me?" said Aneta.

"It wasn't from here."

Aneta heard a door opening behind her, and then closing immediately.

"It isn't the first time," she said. "It wasn't the first."

The officer beside her nodded.

"Mrs. Lindsten . . . ," said Aneta.

"Get out of here."

It was time to make a decision. She could stand here and continue to make the situation worse for everyone.

She could more or less force Anette Lindsten to show her face. It could be a battered face. That could be why.

To force herself on Anette now, to force her way in, could be more or less irreparable.

It could be the only right thing to do. It could be settled here and now. The future could be settled here and now.

Aneta made her decision, put away the badge that she still held in her hand, signaled to the girl in uniform, and left.

Neither of the two policewomen saw anything in the elevator down. They could read the walls if they wanted to, a thousand scribbled messages in black and red.

Outside, the wind had started to blow again. Aneta could hear the streetcars down at Citytorget. The massive apartment buildings marched along, in their particular way. The buildings covered the entire area;

sometimes they also covered the sky. The buildings on Fastlagsgatan seemed to stretch from horizon to horizon.

Some were being torn down now; there was a crater just over the hill. Buildings that had been built forty years ago were torn down and the sky became visible again, at least for a while. Today it was blue, terribly blue. A September sky that seemed to have been collecting color all summer and was ready now. Finished. Here I am, at last. I am the Nordic sky.

It was warm, a ripening warmth, as though it had accumulated.

Indian summer, she thought. It's called *brittsommar* in Swedish, but I still don't know why. How many times have I meant to find out? This time I'm going to; as soon as I get home I'll check. Must have something to do with the calendar. Is there a Britta Day in September?

And as though by chance she caught sight of the street sign on the street they'd swung into earlier: Brittsommar Street. Good God. They'd parked on All Saints Street. You could quickly wander through all the seasons of the year here. Season Street itself ran to the south. All time was gathered, placed in a ring north of Kortedala Torg: Advent Park, Boxing Day Street, Christmas Eve Street, April Street, June Street.

She didn't see a September Street. She saw Twilight Street. She saw Dawn Street, Morning Street.

One could be battered by all the hours of the day and all the seasons of the year here, she thought as she steered away, toward a different civilization to the south. It was like crossing a border.

Arabic-speaking children were playing on Citytorget. Women with covered heads came out of Ovrell's grocery. On the corner was a video-game store that also sold vegetables. Across from it was a flower shop. The sun cast shadows that divided the square into a black part and a white part.

"Have you met Anette Lindsten?" she asked the police officer in the seat next to her.

The girl shook her head.

"Who's seen her?"

"Do you mean out of our colleagues?" the officer asked.

Aneta nodded.

"Do you mean met her?"

Aneta nodded again.

"No one, as far as I know."

"No one?"

"She hasn't let anyone in."

"But someone has called five times and reported that she's been assaulted?"

"Yes."

"Anyone who identified themselves?"

"Uh, a few times. A neighbor." The girl turned toward her. "The woman we spoke to."

"I know."

Aneta drove past the factories in Gamlestaden. The inner city came nearer. The first houses in Bagaregården became visible. They were built for a different civilization. Beautiful buildings, for just one family, or two, and you could walk around the building and enjoy the fact that you lived there and had the money necessary for it to be Saturday all week long. She wondered suddenly if there was a Saturday Street in the area they had left behind them. Maybe not, maybe the city planners stopped at Tuesday, or at Monday, Monday Street. That's where that line was drawn. Monday all week.

"This can't continue," said Aneta.

"What are you thinking about?"

"What am I thinking about? I'm thinking that it could be time for a crime scene investigation."

"Can we do that?"

"Don't you know the Police Act?" Aneta asked, quickly turning her head toward her young colleague, who looked like she'd been caught out, like she'd flunked a test.

"It falls under public prosecution," said Aneta in a milder voice. "If I suspect that someone has been assaulted I can go in and investigate the situation."

"Are you going to do it, then?"

"Go into the Lindstens' home? It might be time for that."

"She says that she lives alone now."

"But the man comes to visit?"

The officer shrugged her shoulders.

"She hasn't said anything about it herself," she said.

"But the neighbors?"

"One of them says that she's seen him."

"And no children?" asked Aneta. "They don't have any children?"

"No."

"We'll have to look him up." That bastard, she thought.

"That bastard . . . ," she mumbled.

"What did you say?"

"The man," said Aneta, and she could feel that she was smiling when she turned toward the young officer again.

It was evening when Aneta opened the door to the house and smelled the familiar odor in the stairwell. Her house, or her apartment building, to be exact, or even more exactly: the building she lived in. But it felt like her own house. She enjoyed living in this old patrician house on Sveagatan. It was centrally located. She could walk to almost anything. She could choose not to walk. And change her mind again.

The elevator lugged itself up. She liked that too. She liked opening the door and picking up the mail from the wooden floor. She liked dropping her coat where she stood, kicking off her shoes, seeing the big old shell that she'd always kept on a bureau, seeing the African mask that hung over it, walking in her socks to the kitchen, heating the water in the kettle, making tea, or sometimes having a beer, sometimes a glass of wine. Liked it.

She liked the solitude.

Sometimes she was afraid because she felt this way.

You shouldn't be alone. That's what others thought. There's something wrong when you're alone. No one chooses solitude. Solitude is a punishment. A sentence.

No. She wasn't serving any sentence. She liked sitting here and deciding to do whatever she wanted whenever she wanted.

She was sitting on a kitchen stool now, of her own free will; the kettle worked itself up to a climax. She was just about to get up to make tea when the telephone rang.

"Yes?"

"What are you doing?"

The question was asked by Fredrik Halders, a colleague, an intense colleague. Not as much anymore, but still really very intense compared to almost everyone else.

Two years ago he had lost his ex-wife when she was hit and killed by a drunk driver.

She's not even still here as an ex, Halders had said for a while afterward, as though he were only half conscious.

They had been working together when it happened, she and Fredrik, and they started seeing each other. She had gotten to know his children. Hannes and Magda. They had begun to accept her presence in their home, truly accept it.

She liked Fredrik, his character. Their preliminary banter had developed into something else.

She was also afraid of all this. Where would it lead? Did she want to know? Did she dare not to try to find out?

She heard Fredrik's voice on the phone:

"What are you doing?"

"Nothing. Just got in the door."

"You don't feel like a movie tonight, do you?" Before she could answer he continued: "Larrinder's daughter wants to earn some extra money babysitting. She called me herself. He asked me today and I told him to have her call." Bo Larrinder was a relatively new colleague in the criminal investigation department. "And she called right away!"

"A new world is opening for you, Fredrik."

"It is, isn't it? And it leads to Svea."

The Svea cinema. A hundred yards away. She looked at her feet. They looked flattened, as though they had been pressed under an iron. She saw her teacup waiting on the kitchen counter. In her mind's eye she saw her bed and a book. She saw herself falling asleep, probably soon.

"Fredrik. I'm not up to it tonight. I'm exhausted."

"It's the last chance," he said.

"Tonight? Is tonight the last showing?"

"Yes."

"You're lying."

"Yes."

"Tomorrow night. *Bien*. I'm already mentally preparing myself so it will work to go out tomorrow."

"Okay."

"It's okay, right?"

"Of course it's okay. What the fu—What do you think? What were you doing this afternoon, by the way?"

"Possible wife beater in Kortedala."

"They're the worst. Did you get him?"

"No."

"No report?"

"Not from the wife. Not from the neighbor, either, it turned out. But it was the fifth time."

"How does she look?" Halders asked. "Is it really bad?"

"You mean injuries? I haven't met her. I tried."

"I guess you'll have to go in, then."

"I thought about it as I was driving away. I went back and forth about it."

"Do you want company?"

"Yes."

"Tomorrow?" said Halders.

"No time tomorrow. I have those café burglaries in Högsbo."

"Say the word and I'm ready."

"Thanks, Fredrik."

"Now get some good rest and mentally prepare yourself for tomorrow, babe."

"*Bonsoir,* Fredrik."

She hung up the phone with a smile. She made tea. She went into the living room and put on a CD. She sat on the sofa and felt her feet begin to recover their shape. She listened to Ali Farka Touré's blown-apart desert blues and thought about a country south of Touré's Mali deserts.

She got up and changed the CD, to Burkina Faso's own great musician Gabin Dabiré: his *Kontômé* from 1998. Her music. Her country. Not like the country she had been born in and lived in. But her country.

Kontômé was the idol found in every Burkinian home. She had hers in the hall, above the bureau. The icon represented the spirits of the ancestors, who were the guiding light for the family and for the entire society.

The light, she thought. Kontômé lights the path. We thank Kontômé for what we are and what we have, now and in the future. And Kontômé helps us when fate unfolds on that path.

Yes. She believed in it. It was in her blood. That was as it should be.

*   *   *

Aneta Djanali had been born at Östra Hospital in Gothenburg to parents from Upper Volta. The country's name had changed to Burkina Faso in 1984, but it was still the same impoverished country, filled with wind, like the music she listened to, steppes that became deserts, water that didn't exist.

It was a vulnerable country.

Dry Volta. Impoverished Volta. Sick Volta. Violent Volta. Dangerous Volta.

Her parents came to Sweden in the sixties, a few years after the country's independence, fleeing persecution.

Her father had been in prison for a short time. He could just as easily have been executed. Just as easily. Sometimes it was only a question of luck.

The former French colony inherited terror and murderers from the Frenchmen who had murdered there since the end of the nineteenth century. Now the Frenchmen were gone, but their language remained. The people were African but out of their mouths came words in French, the official language.

She had learned French as a child, in Gothenburg. She was the only child in the Djanali family. When she wasn't little anymore, when she had been with the police for a long time, her parents chose to return to their hometown, Ouagadougou, the capital.

For Aneta, it was an obvious choice to stay in the country she was born in, and she understood why Mother and Father wanted to return to the country *they* were born in, before it was too late.

It was almost too late. Her mother had come back with two months to spare. She had been buried in the hard, burned red earth at the northern fringes of the city. During the funeral, Aneta had watched the desert press in from all directions, millions of square miles in size. She had thought about how there were sixteen million people living in this desolate country, and how that wasn't so many more than in desolate Sweden. Here they were black, incredibly black. Their clothes were white, incredibly white.

Her father mulled for a long time over whether the journey back had caused the death, at least indirectly.

She kept him company in the capital as long as he wished. She walked with big eyes through streets that she could have lived on her entire life, instead of returning to them as a stranger. Ouagadougou had as many citizens as Gothenburg.

She looked like everyone else here. She could communicate in French with the people—at least with those who had gone to school—and she could speak a little Moré with others, which she did sometimes.

She could keep walking, without attracting attention, all the way out to the city limits and to the desert, which assailed the city with its wind, the harmattan. She could feel it when she sat in her father's house.

She heard the wind, the Swedish wind. It sounded rounder and softer, and colder. But it wasn't cold out. It was *brittsommar.*

Right. She got up and went to the bookshelf along the far wall and got out the Swedish Academy dictionary. She looked up the word:

A period of beautiful and warm weather in the fall—named after Saint Birgitta's Day on October 7.

She didn't know much about the holy, but she suspected this was true for most Swedes, white or black. October seventh. That was a while from now. Did that mean it would get warmer?

She smiled and put back the thick volume. She went to the bathroom and undressed and ran a hot bath. She slowly lowered herself into the water. It was very quiet in the apartment. She heard the telephone ring out there, and she heard the machine pick up. She didn't hear a voice, only a pleasant murmur. She closed her eyes and felt her body float in the hot water. She thought of a hot wind, and of the luxury of running a bath. She didn't want to think about that, but now she did. She thought away the water, the luxury.

She saw a face for a few seconds, a woman. A door that opened and closed. A dusky light. Eyes that shone and disappeared. The eyes were afraid.

She kept her eyes closed and saw water, as though she were swimming underwater and was carried along by the current, the wind of the sea.

3

Winter biked west on Vasagatan, for the thousandth time or more. He needed to oil the chain. He needed to put air in the front tire.

Along the boulevard, the cafés were open. He had read somewhere that this street had more cafés than any other in Sweden. And likely northern Europe. That particular expression was often used in comparisons. He had thought about that sometimes, as he did now. Where did the boundary of northern Europe run? Through Münster? Antwerp? Warsaw? He smiled at the thought. Maybe through Gothenburg.

But there *were* a lot of places. Thousands of people were sitting in the outdoor seating areas.

Winter tromped across Heden. He thought of the sea and the sky, suspended like a sail over the bay where he might live his life. A new life, a different one. Yes. Maybe it was time. A new era in his life.

They had talked about it in the car while Elsa slept in the backseat. The sun had been on its way elsewhere. Angela had driven with one hand behind his neck for a little while.

"Isn't it dangerous to drive like that?" he had asked.

"Don't ask me. You're the policeman."

"Are we doing the right thing?" he asked.

She understood what he meant.

"We haven't done anything yet," she had answered.

"It *is* only a plot of land," he said.

"Yes, Erik," she said. "You don't need to be worried about anything more."

"We *do* have a nice flat," he said.

"It's a nice bay," she said.

"Yes," he had answered, "it's nice, too."

"It's wonderful," she had said.

The police station greeted him with a full embrace. The façade was as welcoming as always. The entryway smelled the same as usual. It doesn't matter how many times they remodel it, he thought, nodding at the woman at the reception desk, who nodded toward him but also farther, past him. She opened the security window.

"There's someone waiting for you," she said with a gesture.

He turned around and saw the woman who was sitting on one of the vinyl sofas. She started to get up. He saw her profile reflected in the glass case where the police command had placed caps and helmets from police forces all over the world. As proof of the global friendship among police. There were also a few batons, as though to hit home the friendship message. He had said those exact words to Ringmar one time as they walked by, when the case was new, and Ringmar had said that he thought the Italian pith helmet was the nicest. It's from Abyssinia, Winter said, you can bet your life on it. Perfect protection from the sun while they killed all the blacks.

The woman was about his age. She had dark hair but with a light sheen that might have come from the summer sun. She had a broad face and an open gaze, and he had the vague feeling that he'd seen it before, but in another time. She was wearing jeans and some kind of fisherman's sweater, which looked expensive, and a short jacket. Now he recognized her.

He extended his hand.

"We've definitely met before," he said.

She took his hand. Her hand was dry and warm. She fastened her eyes on his and he remembered that too.

"Johanna Osvald. From Donsö."

"Of course," he said.

They sat in his room. It still smelled like summer in there, the stuffy kind, dry. He still had last season's documents on his desk. There was a smell to those documents, too, and it was death.

He hadn't wanted to touch that damned pile since it happened.

He wanted only to forget, which was impossible. He must learn from his mistakes, his own mistakes, but it was painful, more painful than anything else.

He would ask Möllerström to take everything down to the basement.

He looked at the woman. She hadn't said anything as they walked here, as though she wanted to save it until they were alone.

It must have been twenty years ago.

He knew that he knew nothing about her, nothing more than that she had a birthmark on the left side of her groin. Or the right side. That she bit his lip once. That he had felt the stones drill into his back when she sat on him and moved faster and faster and finally exploded when he exploded, when he threw her off in that glowing instant.

The stones had stuck in his back. She had laughed. They had dived into the sea. He had rowed home to the islet. It was only one summer, not even that. One month. He hadn't learned much about her, hardly anything. Everything was a mystery that he sometimes thought he had dreamed.

In some way, that's a summary of youth, he thought. Dreamed mysteries. Now she's sitting on the chair. I haven't seen her since that summer. That's a mystery too. Now she's saying something.

"Did you remember my name, Erik?"

"Yes. When you said it, I remembered."

He saw that she intended to say more, but stopped, and started again:

"Do you remember that we talked about my grandfather?"

"Yes . . ."

It's true. Now I remember her grandfather. Even his name.

"John," said Winter. "John Osvald."

"You remember."

"It's not so different from your name."

She didn't smile; there was no smile in that face, and he remembered that too, that expression.

"Do you remember that he disappeared during the war?"

"Yes."

"You're not just saying that?"

"No. Your grandfather had to take shelter in some harbor in England during the war. I remember you told me that. And that he disappeared at sea later. During a fishing trip from England."

"Scotland. He was in Scotland. They had to seek shelter in Aberdeen at first."

"Scotland."

"My dad wasn't even a year old when he left," she said. "The last time. It was in the autumn of 1939."

Winter didn't say anything. He remembered that too. The teardrop that suddenly burned on his shoulder. Was that how it was? Yes. He had felt it. She had told him about it then and there were still tears. Perhaps they were her father's tears most of all. He could understand but he couldn't really *understand,* not then. It would be different now, if he had heard it now. He was someone else now.

"My dad's brother hadn't been born when they made the final journey. He was born three months later."

A brother. He couldn't remember that. They hadn't spoken about a brother.

"He died of rickets when he was four," said Johanna. "My little uncle."

Suddenly she opened the small pack she had carried on her back and took out a letter. She held it up expectantly. A distance. She kept that letter at a distance. Winter had seen it many times. Letters that flew to people, like strange birds, black birds. Letters with messages no one wanted to have. Sometimes the addressees came to him with the message. Who said that he wanted to have them?

"What is it?" he said.

"A letter," she answered.

"I see that," he said, and smiled, and maybe she smiled too, or else it was just the light that moved around the room in an unpredictable way. The Indian summer out there was starting to worry about the future.

"A letter arrived," she said. "From there. This letter."

"From there? From Scotland?"

She nodded and leaned forward and placed the envelope in front of him on the desk.

"It's postmarked in Inverness."

"Mmhmm."

"There's no return address on the back."

"Is it signed?"

"No. Open it and you'll see."

"No white powder?" said Winter.

She might have smiled.

"No powder."

He took the letter out of the envelope. The paper was lined, thin and cheap; it looked as though it had been torn from an ordinary notebook. The words were printed, two lines in English:

THINGS ARE NOT WHAT THEY LOOK LIKE.
JOHN OSVALD IS NOT WHAT HE SEEMS TO BE.

Winter looked at the front of the envelope. A stamp with the British monarch on it. A postmark. An address:

OSVALD FAMILY
GOTHENBURG ARCHIPELAGO
SWEDEN

"It made it to you," he said, and looked at Johanna Osvald. "All the way out in the archipelago."

"Clever mail sorters at the terminal."

Winter read the message once more. *Things are not what they look like.* No, he was aware of that; it practically summed up his opinion of detective work. *John Osvald is not what he seems to be.* Seems to be, is thought to be. He is thought to be dead. Isn't he dead?

"He has never officially been declared deceased," she said, although he hadn't asked. "At least not by us."

"But by the authorities?"

"Yes."

"But you thi—"

"What are we supposed to think?" she interrupted. "Of course we hope, we've always had hope, but the boat sank out in the North Sea. No one has been recovered, as far as I know."

"As far as you know?"

"Well, it was during the war. They couldn't search without risk, or whatever you say. But we . . . my grandmother, Dad, none of us have ever heard anything about Grandfather being alive. Or that anyone else from that boat was found."

"When did it happen?" asked Winter.

"The accident?"

"Yes."

"Not long after they had to seek shelter after they made their way through the mines to the Scottish coast. The war had begun, of course. And the boat disappeared in 1940. It was in the spring."

"How old was your grandfather then?"

"Twenty-one."

"Twenty-one? With a year-old son?"

"Our family marries early, has children early. My dad was twenty-two when I was born."

Winter counted in his head.

"In 1960?"

"Yes."

"That's when I was born, too."

"I know," she said. "We talked about it, don't you remember?"

"No."

She sat quietly.

"I broke that trend."

"Sorry?"

"Marry young, have children young. I broke that."

"I didn't know that."

"I didn't get married and I didn't have children."

Winter noticed that she spoke in the past tense. But she looks younger than she is, he thought. Women today have children when they're older. I know nothing about her life now.

"How are things with your mom?"

"She's gone. She died three years ago."

"I'm sorry."

"Me too."

Her eyes slid toward the window. He recognized that look. In profile, she looked like that young girl on the slab of stone, in the sunshine.

"When did you receive this letter?" he asked, holding up the envelope. He thought about how his fingerprints were on it now, along with tens of others from both sides of the North Sea.

"Two weeks ago."

"Why did you wait until now to come here?" And what do you actually want me to do? he thought.

"My dad went there ten days ago, or nine. To Inverness."

"Why?"

"Why? Is it so strange? He was upset. Of course. He wanted to know." She looked at Winter now. "He took a copy of the letter and the envelope with him."

What did he think he would find? Winter thought. A sender?

"It isn't the first time," she said. "He . . . we have tried to investigate, of course, but it hasn't led anywhere."

"But how would he be able to find anything new with only this to help him?" asked Winter.

She didn't answer, not at first. He saw that she was considering her next words. He was used to seeing that. Sometimes he could even see the words that were on their way, but not this time. She moved her eyes from him to the window and back to him and then to the window again.

"I think he got a new message," she said now, with her eyes turned away from him. "Maybe a telephone call."

"Did he say so?"

"No. But that's what I think." She looked at the letter, which Winter had put back on the desk. "Something more than that."

"Why do you think that?"

"It was his decision, sort of. He didn't say anything in particular when the letter arrived. Other than being upset, of course. We all were. But then, suddenly, he wanted to go. Right away. And he went."

"And you say that was ten days ago?"

"Yes."

"Has he found anything, then?"

Johanna turned to Winter.

"He has contacted me three times. Most recently four days ago."

"Yes?"

"The last time, he said he was going to meet someone."

"Who?"

"He didn't say. But he was going to contact me afterward. As soon as he knew more." She leaned forward in Winter's guest chair. "He sounded, well, almost agitated."

"How did it go, then?"

"Like I said, it was the last time I talked to him. There's been no news since." He saw fear in her face. "He hasn't contacted me since then. That's why I'm here."

4

Aneta Djanali was back in Kortedala. It was a rainy day, and suddenly it was colder than early spring. Maybe autumn had arrived.

It seemed like the masses of houses on Befälsgatan and Beväringsgatan were marching away in the fog, or maybe it was like they were floating. They're like battleships of stone, she thought. It's like a living drawing, a film.

She suddenly thought of Pink Floyd, "Another Brick in the Wall." The walls enclosed the people here, led them into the fog.

We don't need no education.

But that's what everyone needed. Education. A language. Communication, she thought.

She parked on one of the season streets, maybe spring, maybe autumn. She didn't see a street sign. She walked toward one of the walls. Anette Lindsten lived behind it. It was a name that somehow fit in here, in this environment. *Lindsten,* "linden stone." It was a very Swedish name, a compound of things in nature. That's how it is with most Swedish last names, she thought. Everything has something to do with nature. Something soft and light, along with something hard and heavy. Something compound. Like the hovering houses. Stones in the wind.

She thought of the eyes in the crack of the door; they had also been like stone. Had she spoken with her husband? Really had a conversation? Had it been possible? Did he have a language? A language to speak with? Aneta knew one thing: A person who lacked any other method of expression often resorted to violence. Words were replaced by fists. In this way, violence was the ultimate form of communication, the most extreme, the most horrible.

Had he hit Anette? Had he even threatened her? Who was "he," really? And who was she?

Aneta went in through the doors, which were propped open. A pickup with something that looked like a rented cover stood parked outside. She could see the corner of a sofa in the truck bed; two dining chairs, a bureau. A paper bag that contained green plants. Someone is coming or going, she thought.

A man in his sixties came out of the elevator with a packing case and walked past her and put it on the truck bed. Someone is going, she thought.

The man walked back and into the elevator, where she was waiting with the door open.

"Fifth floor for me," he said.

"I'm going there, too," she said, and pushed the button.

There were three apartments on the fifth floor. When they came out into the stairwell, she saw that the door to Anette Lindsten's apartment was wide open.

That was a change from last time.

She realized that the woman was on her way out.

The man went in through the door. She could see boxes in the hall, clothes on hangers, more chairs. Some rolled-up rugs. She heard faint music, a radio tuned to one of the local commercial stations. Britney Spears. Always Britney Spears.

Aneta hesitated at the door. Should she ring the bell or call out? The man had turned around in the hall. She could see into the kitchen, which seemed completely empty. She didn't see anyone else.

"Yes?" said the man. "Can I help you with something?"

He wasn't unfriendly. He looked tired, but it was as though his tiredness didn't come from lugging things down the stairs. His hair was completely white and she had seen the sweat on the back of his shirt, like a faint V-sign.

"I'm looking for Anette Lindsten," she said.

A younger man came out from a room holding a black plastic bag with bedding sticking out of it.

"What is it?" he said, before the older man had time to answer. The younger man might have been her own age. He didn't look friendly. He had given a start when he saw her.

"She's looking for Anette," the older man said. "Anette Lindsten."

Aneta would later remember that she had wondered why he said her last name.

"Who are you?" asked the younger man.

She explained who she was, showed her ID. She asked who they were.

"This is Anette's father, and I'm her brother. What does this concern?"

"I want to talk to Anette about it."

"I think we know why you're here, but that's over with now so you don't need to talk to her anymore," the brother said.

"I've never talked to her," said Aneta.

"And now it isn't necessary," he said. "Okay?"

The father cleared his throat.

"What is it?" said the brother, looking at him.

"I think you should lower your voice, Peter."

The father turned toward her.

"I'm Anette's dad," he said, nodding from a distance in the hall. "And this is my son, Peter." He gestured with his arm. "And we're in the process of moving Anette's things, as you can see." He seemed to look at her with transparent eyes. "So, in other words, Anette is moving away from here."

"Where to?" asked Aneta.

"What does that matter?" said Peter Lindsten. "Isn't it best that as few people know as possible? It wouldn't really be so good if all the damn authorities came running to the new place too, would it?"

"Have they, then?" said Aneta. "Before?"

"No," he answered in the illogical manner that she had become used to hearing in this job. "But it'll fu—" the brother began, but he was interrupted by his father.

"I think we should have a cup of coffee and talk about this properly," he said, looking at her. He looked like a real father, someone who never wants to relinquish control. At that very moment, at that second, she thought of her own father's shrinking figure in the half light in the white hut on the African desert steppe. The darkness inside, the white light outside, a world in black and white.

He wasn't letting her go. She was the one who had relinquished his control.

"We don't have time," said Peter Lindsten.

"Put those things down and put on the coffee," said the father calmly, and the son put down the sack he had been holding during the entire conversation and followed orders.

*　*　*

Winter got two cups of coffee and placed one in front of Johanna Osvald. She seemed determined and relieved at the same time, as though she had triumphed over something by coming there.

"I didn't know where I should go," she said.

"Do you know where he's staying over there?" Winter asked.

"Where he was staying, at least. I called there and they said he had checked out. Four days ago." She looked up without having taken a drink from her cup. "It's a bed and breakfast. I don't remember what it's called right now. But I have it written down." She started to look in her backpack. "I have the notebook here somewhere." She looked up again.

"Where is it?" Winter asked. "The bed and breakfast?"

"In Inverness. Didn't I say that?"

Inverness, he thought. The bridge over the river Ness.

"And he hasn't contacted you since then?" he asked.

"No."

"Did he tell you he was going to check out?"

"No."

"What did he say, then? When he called the last time."

"Like I said before. He was going to meet someone."

"Who?"

"He didn't say, I told you."

"Did you ask?"

"Yes, of course I did. But he just said that he was going to check something and that he would call later."

"What was he going to check?"

"He didn't say, and no, I didn't ask. That's how it is with my dad; he hasn't ever said much, especially not on the phone."

"But it had to do with his disappearance? That is, the question of your grandfather's disappearance?"

"Yes, I assumed it did. It's obvious, isn't it? What else could it be?"

"What else did he say?" Winter asked.

"What do you mean?"

"You must have talked about something else. Other than that he was going to meet someone who might have had a connection to your grandfather."

"No. I asked how things were going in general. He said it was raining." Winter thought she gave a small smile. "But that's not really unusual for Scotland, is it?"

"Was he calling from a cell phone? From the hotel? From a bar or a café?"

"I don't actually know. I assumed he was calling from . . ." She had a notebook in her hand now; it was open. ". . . from this place, it's called Glen Islay Bed and Breakfast." She looked at him. "Ross Avenue, Inverness. The street is called Ross Avenue. I assume he was calling from there."

Glen Islay, thought Winter. It sounds like a brand of whisky. I recognize it, but it's not whisky.

"Why do you assume your father called from there?" he asked.

"He might have mentioned it, now that I think about it. And anyway, he doesn't have a cell phone."

So there are still people who aren't cellified, Winter thought. In my next life I'll be one of them.

"I tried to send my cell along with him, but he refused," said Johanna. "Said that it wouldn't work and then he'd just get frustrated on his trip."

"He had a point there," said Winter.

"In any case, he hasn't made any sort of contact since then," she said.

"Is it really that long a time?" Winter asked.

"How do you mean?"

"Four days. After all, you did wait four days to become worried. It could—"

"What do you mean?" she interrupted. "Like I wasn't worried the whole time. But as I just said, my father is not the type to call every day. But finally I became worried enough on top of my normal worrying that I called Glen Is . . . Glen Is . . ." She broke off and started to cry.

Winter felt immobile, like a stone. I'm an idiot, he thought. And this is something I can't really handle. It suddenly feels personal. Now I have to find a way out.

"What is your dad's name?" he asked gently.

"Ax . . . Axel," she answered. "Axel Osvald."

Winter got up, took her cup and his own, put them away to create a distraction, another way of thinking.

He went back to his chair and sat down.

"What do you think?" he said. "What could have happened? What are you thinking right now?"

"I think something has happened to him."

"Why do you think that?"

"There's no other explanation for why he hasn't contacted me by now."

Winter thought. Thought like a detective. It felt like an effort after all his other thoughts this summer, all his other plans.

"Did he rent a car?" he asked.

"I don't know."

"But your father has a driver's license?"

"Yes."

"What kind of work does he do?"

"He's . . . a carpenter."

"That took you a moment," said Winter.

"Yes. He was a fisherman before, like everyone else in the Osvald family. And like almost everyone else on the island. But he quit."

Winter didn't question this further. He continued:

"Maybe he found something, met someone, and maybe it was somewhere other than in Inverness and he'll contact you soon."

"Oh, it's such a relief to hear you say that," she said with sudden irony.

"Well, what do you want me to do?" he asked.

"I don't know," she answered. "Forgive me. I just thought that you would know."

"We can register a description of him with Interpol," Winter said. "If you want to do that, I can help you."

"Interpol—that sounds so formal. Will it really get results? Isn't there something else you can do?"

"Listen, Johanna. It hasn't been very long yet. There's nothing to indicate that your dad is in danger. He could—"

"How do you explain that letter, then?" she interrupted, nodding toward the letter that was still on the table.

"I can't explain it," said Winter.

"You think it's some nutcase?"

"Is that what you think?" asked Winter.

"I don't know what to think. I only know that Dad took the fact that he was going very seriously. Or maybe he learned something new, like I said before. And that it's weird that he hasn't contacted me."

Inverness. Winter got up and walked over to the map of Europe that hung on the wall facing the hall. Inverness, the northern point of the Highlands. He had been there, twenty years ago. Only one time, on his way through from north to south. He thought of the woman who was sitting behind him. It must have been the same summer . . .

He considered this as he looked at the map. Yes, it could have been that summer, or right after it. An Indian summer like this one, in September. He had been on his way somewhere in his life, but he didn't know where. He had decided to quit studying law after the survey course, because that survey was quite enough, thank you very much.

He had worked as a sorter at the post office. That was before the inheritance from his grandfather, which changed a lot. He had said *adiós* to the letters and decided to travel in Great Britain because he had never been there. He wanted to do it right. He took the ferry to Newcastle and the northbound train all the way to Thurso and out to Dunnet Head, which was the northernmost point of the island nation, and then he traveled south by train and bus and thumb to the southernmost point, Lizard Point; it was a mission he'd assigned to himself, and he realized that this was what his life would be like forever after: He was on his way, but he never really knew how, and yet his uncertainty was methodical and planned.

I haven't allowed myself to have confidence in my uncertainty until now, he suddenly thought, and he looked at the name "Inverness" on the map again. He had stayed there for one night, at a B and B.

There was one particular memory. He thought of that place. He remembered it now because he had gone from the station to the streets where all the B and Bs were, and it had been a long way there, at least that's how he remembered it; longer than they'd told him at the tourist bureau at the station, and they had called a place he didn't remember the name of and gotten him a room and then he walked, walked through the city center and over a bridge and through a new city center that looked like it came from a different civilization and into a neighborhood of small houses, houses of stone, granite, and to the left and to the right and straight ahead and to the left and right and right and right and left. *You can't miss it, dear.* It was one of his first experiences with the peculiar people of Britain.

He had looked for the name of the street his B and B was supposed to be on for so long that the name was forever archived deep in his memory. He also remembered it because he had been looking for a fancy avenue but hadn't seen one, especially not when he found the right street: Ross Avenue. A street like any other.

Winter turned to her with a feeling of wonder in his body.

"Didn't you say that his B and B was on Ross Avenue?"

"Yes."

He turned back to the map.

"I've been there," he said. "I stayed in a B and B on Ross Avenue. For one night."

"How strange," he heard her say.

Winter didn't want to say that it was *then,* that it was after *that* summer. He turned to her again. He had been struck by another thought.

"I know someone from the Inverness area," he said. "A colleague, actually."

Anette's dad poured her a cup and placed it in her hand. His son had been standing by the window looking out, and then he left and continued carrying things.

Aneta sat on a stool in the bare kitchen. The table was folded up and leaning against the wall.

"Why did you decide to come here now?" Lindsten asked.

"I was here the other day, and it didn't look so good," she answered.

"What didn't?"

Aneta sipped her coffee, which was hot and strong.

"The situation."

"Did the neighbors call?"

"Yes," she answered. "And it wasn't the first time."

"But it was the last," he said.

"At least from here," she said, looking around the kitchen. "From this place."

"No," said Lindsten, and she saw the resolve in his face. "There will be no more times." He drank from his cup, with the same resolve. She could see that the hot coffee hurt his throat.

"Where is Anette now?" Aneta asked.

He didn't answer at first.

"In a safe place," he said after a bit.

"Is she staying at your house?"

"For the time being," he said, and looked away.

"Do you know where her husband is?"

"No," he answered.

"What we're discussing now is very important," said Aneta. "From a general perspective, too. There are many women who are afraid of their husbands. Or their exes. Who try to stay away. Who must go into hiding. Or who sometimes hope for a change. Who stay."

"Well, that's over with in this case," said Lindsten.

"Who rents the apartment?" asked Aneta.

"It's always been in Anette's name," he said. "There are two months left on the lease but that's our treat, if I can say so. It will be empty."

"Have you spoken with the husband? Her husband?"

"That damn bastard? He called yesterday and I told him to stay away."

"Will he?"

"If he shows up at our house, I'm afraid I won't be able to stop Peter from beating him up, and then we'd really have to deal with the police, wouldn't we?"

"Yes. That's not a good way to go about it."

"He'd be getting a taste of his own medicine," said Lindsten. "His own bitter medicine."

They heard a box thud in the hall, a curse from Peter Lindsten. The dad motioned toward the hall with his head. "The difference would be that that devil would be dealing with someone his own size."

Forsblad, Hans Forsblad. That was the man's name. Aneta had seen the name in the papers at the dispatch center, and later with her colleagues in Kortedala. The matter was on its way to the coordinator for the violence against women program.

Forsblad's name was very Swedish too, she thought—"rapids leaf"—it came from nature, and just like his wife's it linked something with great power to infinite lightness. An airiness. Who stood for what? Should it be interpreted physically?

"Doesn't he have the keys to this place?" she asked.

"We've changed the locks," said Lindsten.

"Where are his things?"

"He knows where he can collect them," said Lindsten.

Somewhere where the sun doesn't shine, thought Aneta.

"So you've made him homeless."

Lindsten laughed suddenly, a laugh without joy.

"He hasn't stayed a night in this apartment for a damn long time," he said. "He's been here, it's true. But only to . . . to . . ." And suddenly it was as though his face cracked and she saw his eyes fill and how he suddenly turned toward the window, as though he were ashamed of his behavior, but it wasn't shame.

"She didn't have a restraining order," said Aneta. "Unfortunately."

"As though it would help," said Lindsten in a muffled voice, with his head lowered.

"He could have been issued a restraining order if Anette had reported him," said Aneta. "Or someone else. I could have made the decision myself, for the short term. I was prepared to do it now. That's why I came here."

He looked up, his eyes still glistening.

"It's not a concern anymore," he said, "none of it."

Suddenly it was as though the father didn't believe his own words. She heard another thud in the hall, another curse. It was time for her to go. These people had a move to undertake, a departure that would lead to a new era in their lives. She truly hoped that it would be so for the woman whose face she had seen for only three seconds.

"You know someone from there?" asked Johanna Osvald. She looked like she was about to get up. Winter remained standing by the map. "From Inverness?"

"I think so."

"A colleague? You mean a policeman?"

"Yes. He lives in London but he's a Scot."

Winter thought, searched the archives of his memory. There were many corridors. He saw London, an inspector his own age with a Scottish accent, a picture of a beautiful wife and two beautiful children who were twins, the inspector's face, which perhaps couldn't be called beautiful, but was probably attractive to one who could judge such things.

The face had an origin. A farm outside of Inverness. That's what

Steve had said. Winter looked at the map; it was of an impossibly large scale.

"Steve Macdonald," said Winter. "He's from there."

"Do you mean that you could ask him?" said Johanna.

"Yes," said Winter.

"He could probably check if Dad rented a car?" she said.

"We can do that," he said. "You can do it yourself."

"Yes, but if your colleague is from there maybe he knows someone who can . . . oh . . . check if it . . . no, I don't know." Now she was standing next to Winter, in front of the map. It seemed as though she didn't want to see it, didn't want to see any of the country that had played such a large and tumultuous role in the Osvald family's lives. And might continue to do so, he thought.

He felt her nearness, heard her breathing. At that second, he thought of how the years go by, a completely banal thought, but true.

"If you want to know more, maybe Steve knows who we should ask," said Winter, turning toward her.

What am I getting roped into here? he thought. In normal cases, this conversation would have been finished before it started. Now it has almost become a case. An international case.

5

He stood at the summit. The church lay below him. He had prayed there sometimes, in earlier years, prayed to Jesus for his soul. The church was the only thing from the really old days that was still there in Newtown.

When Lord and Lady moved the village in 1836, the church was allowed to remain where it was. It was from the 1300s, after all. That sounded like before all time, before the great sailing voyages. The great discoveries.

Still, what a brutal story it was! Lord and Lady moved the village. They didn't want it next to the castle.

They didn't want the railroad next to the castle.

He could see the viaducts down there, clanging in the air from the bite of the wheels. They had to be built down there, far away from Lord and Lady. A superhuman act, but possible.

Lord and Lady were gone now, like so much else here. The sea remained, but even that seemed to pull away, little by little each year. The trawlers ended up farther away during ebb, their shining bellies like jaws in the twilight, as though a school of killer whales had started to attack the city but had gotten stuck in the ebb.

He stood above the docks. There was sulfur in the air. In the air, he thought: What seemed to be physical floated away in the wind.

His hips hurt, more each day. He shouldn't have walked, but he did. It was his body, after all. This was nothing. He knew what was something. He knew.

When he came there for the first time, the city was the primary harbor for fishing fleets along this part of the coast, south of Moray Firth.

Bigger than Keith, Huntly; even bigger than Buckie.

The Buckie boys are back in town.

He didn't stay long that time. It was when he still didn't know who he was or where he was. That's how it had been. Like a blindness. He knew now that he had walked and stood and talked then, but he hadn't been aware of it.

It could make him scream at night. He could be awoken by his own screams and discover that he was sitting straight up in bed in the ice-cold room with his own breath like a white cone before him. The scream was caught in that breath. It was a dreadful feeling, dreadful. His whole throat felt mangled, as though it had been squeezed in an iron grip. What had he screamed? Who had heard him? He had gone out into the street but hadn't seen any movement behind the black windows in the house on the other side.

No one had heard him.

He had seen the light from the city above, only a few lights.

He had thought of her then, briefly.

He had seen the telephone booth that shone in the fog. It never rang.

He would ask her.

She would do it.

She had done as he'd asked.

Now he was no longer certain.

She had looked at him last time with an expression he didn't recognize.

He hadn't asked.

He left the harbor behind him and walked through Seatown. The houses clung to one another, squatting under the viaducts. He walked toward his house through the streets that didn't have names. This is where the streets have no names, he thought. He often thought in English, almost always.

Sometimes there might be a fragment of the old language, but it was only when he was very upset. There were only two other places where the streets had no names, and those were heaven and hell.

He had been to both places. Now he was traveling between them.

The houses had numbers, apparently without any order. Number seven stood beside number twenty-five, six beside thirty-eight. He lived in the black house, at the southern gables. It was number fourteen. That meant that the house had been the fourteenth one built in Seatown. That was the system here. His was the only black house.

6

Fredrik Halders lay on the sofa with his feet on its arm. An odd lamp hung from the ceiling above the sofa. Or maybe it was his perspective.

"Have I seen that lamp before?" he asked, pointing up.

"That's a question you probably have to ask yourself," said Aneta Djanali from the floor, where she was sitting and leaning over some photographs.

Halders giggled; at least that's how it sounded to Aneta's ears.

He tried to turn his head from his supine position, but that was a mistake. His neck would never be the same again. He had taken a blow once when he was being a bigger idiot than usual, and it could have been his last mistake. He would never regain his original bull neck. That was just as well. Everyone knew what happened with bull necks in the end.

"Is it from Africa?" he asked.

"What do you think?" she asked, without looking up.

He studied the underside of the lamp again. It had a pointed base and something else above that was green.

"It's from Africa," he said.

"Good, Fredrik."

He applauded himself. That was called Chinese clapping.

"Can you guess from which country?" He heard Aneta's voice from the floor. "And to make it harder I want to know what the country was called before what it's called now."

"*That* is a tricky question," he said.

"I realize that."

She was aware of the level of difficulty. They had talked about her homeland only three times per hour every day since they started working together and since they started to see each other during their free time. Speaking of talking. It was Fredrik who kept on talking about her exotic origins and her wonderful homeland, which he pretended not to be able to find on any map of the world, but which he, under all the talking, kept close tabs on, just as he actually kept close tabs on most things, under his tough exterior.

"This country's former name starts with the letter *u*," she said.

"Uuuuuh . . . ," he said.

"Yes, that's a good start," she said.

"Ukraine," he said.

"That's not in Africa," she said.

"Well, shit."

"The second letter is *p*," she said.

"Uuu . . . Upper Silesia!" he shouted at the ceiling.

"Where's that?"

"In Africa," he said.

"Not in my Africa, anyway," she said.

"Isn't that a film?" he said. "*My Africa?*"

"To get you on the right track, I can tell you that this country's name is made up of two words," she said.

"Uuu . . . Upper Soppero!"

"One of them is right," she said.

"Lower Soppero!"

"But it started with *u*, didn't it?"

"Shit, right."

"Now I'm done helping you," she said.

"If we talk about something else maybe I'll think of it," said Halders. He propped himself up on his elbow. He could feel it in his neck. "What are those pictures?"

"From last summer," she said.

"Am I in them?" he asked.

She held up a photo that she'd developed and copied herself. She and Fredrik were standing behind Fredrik's children, Hannes and Magda. She could see the cord of the shutter cable coming from Hannes's hand. He looked like he was concentrating, but happy. Everyone looked happy in that photograph.

They looked like a family.

"Where did we take that?" Halders asked from the sofa.

"Guess," she said.

"Don't start that again," he said.

"Do you see the waves behind us?" she asked.

"Yeah, yeah, but which sea is it?"

"The North Sea, of course."

"The Old North Sea, it roars and rooolls," said Halders.

"Not that day," she said. "There wasn't a single ripple."

"Do you think an African would dare to jump in the North Sea no matter the season?"

"I will refrain from answering," she said.

"Have you heard about the African who came to Sweden as an exchange student for a year and went home afterward, and his friends asked him how the weather was up there, and he said that the green winter was okay but the white one was horrible?"

"No, I haven't heard that one," said Aneta, "please tell me."

"Uuuu . . . ," said Halders.

"I hear you're still working on the name of that country."

She looked at the photograph in her hand again. That day had been perfect. *Such a perfect day.* Fredrik had played Lou Reed in the evening. Lou Reed sounded like Fredrik looked.

The perfect family.

She thought suddenly of Anette Lindsten, safe in a secret location, maybe her childhood home or some other secret place.

Somewhere there must be a wedding picture. The perfect day. A light across their faces. Anette and Hans, their origins in nature, linden, stone, rapids, leaves . . .

Do you take this woman . . . to love her in sickness and health . . .

To beat her in sickness and health.

Nature to nature, dust to dust.

"Did you ever want to hit Margareta?" she asked.

Halders's jaw dropped, it *dropped*.

"What the hell kind of question is that?"

"Don't be so shocked. You know what I was doing yesterday. I'm just trying to imagine how it can happen. How things like that can happen."

"Jesus, Aneta, this is like a parody of the question 'Have you stopped beating your wife?' It's a question you can't answer yes or no to."

"That's not the question I was asking."

He didn't say anything. She looked at him. He was a violent man; she had always seen him as an *intense* man, but in a literal sense. I take down the bad guys literally, as Halders put it. He almost always did. He was a desperate man, and he wasn't alone in that. He could control his rage. He walked through life angry, but he could control it. Many others could not.

"There was one time during the divorce," he said slowly. "Or before. One time, or a few. I would get so angry that I wanted to . . . wanted to . . ." He looked straight at Aneta. "Wanted to hit *something,* but there was never never *ever* the slightest risk that it would be her. Never."

"What was it, then? Or who?"

"Dammit, Aneta, you know me. Not a person . . . well, some thief once, but you get what I mean. No one close to me. At home." He started to rub his neck, suddenly, a nervous gesture. "I would bang my fist into a cupboard door. It happened. I kicked a leg off a kitchen chair once."

"My God."

"It was a *chair.*"

"My God again."

He stopped rubbing. She saw that his eyes had taken on a different light, as though they had turned inward. It was as though he, all of him, had turned inward.

"And at the same time, I knew it was my fault. Do you understand? That I was the cause of my own rage, or whatever it's called. That I was the biggest reason that we had ended up in that situation. That I was the one who was splitting up my family, was just about to do it. And that made me so desperate that I lashed out." He seemed to snap back from inside himself and now he was looking at her. "There's a paradox, huh? You hit your way out of your own responsibility."

She didn't answer.

"But those few times I'm talking about, when I hit something, it was dead things."

Dead things, she thought. There's another expression.

She had seen dead things. Halders had seen dead things. It was part of the job. Part of the *routine* of the job. Routine: What was a body that no longer had a life?

Calm down, Aneta. This evening isn't part of the routine. There's a man lying on your sofa and you're sitting on the floor with pictures of summer happiness and soon you'll both be sitting at the kitchen table eating and drinking something good. There's a light in here, in this room. You don't need to drag in the shadows right now. Kontômé is lighting up the room, lighting the way.

"*Try* to hit your way out of responsibility," she said. "You can't escape."

"There are so many people who try," said Halders.

She got up. The photographs still lay on the floor like a sunburst. *That* was a good expression. It summed up the content and mood of these pictures.

"And are going to try again," she said.

Winter turned around in the doorway and watched the sleeping Elsa. She held her arm tight around her stuffed animal, Pelle, a black and white panda whose head was bigger than Elsa's. Pelle studied Winter as he stood there. Pelle never dropped his gaze. Pelle's face expressed a belief in the future.

"She knows all the books inside and out," he said. Angela was sitting on the sofa with *Femina* magazine in her lap. "She recites them for me. Like an actress." He was standing in the middle of the room. "Until she falls asleep." He stretched his arms upward; they had become stiff in Elsa's bed. "I think Pelle knows them all too, but he doesn't say anything." He brought his arms down. "But Elsa talks enthusiastically until she crashes in the middle of a sentence."

"Or you do."

"Not tonight," he said.

She looked up.

"Can't you fix something?" she said.

"Something? What kind of something?"

"Something. Something good."

He walked across the hall to the kitchen.

There was phyllo dough and eggs and dill and butter, and a little smoked salmon left over from last Sunday. White pepper.

He drank a glass of white wine while the packets were in the oven. They smelled good. He listened to Wynton Marsalis on the little Panasonic in the kitchen. Or Marsalis was on, but he wasn't really listening. He watched the multilayered blanket of dough rise up over its contents.

He carried the tray into the living room. Angela was sitting with her legs tucked under her and she was looking out at the sky, which was clear and dark above Vasaplatsen.

"Mmm," she said.

He poured some wine.

"It is Tuesday, after all," she said, raising her glass.

"Tuesday all week," he said, toasting.

She sliced into her packet and inhaled

"Ahhh!"

"I try my best," he said. "I try to make the most of my limited abilities."

"I like you anyway, Erik," she said, smiling.

"You haven't tasted it yet."

They drank coffee in the dark. The only light was the nighttime light of the city, outside. It was constant, like an eternal day.

"This used to be called 'sitting twilight,'" said Angela. "One of the nurses on my ward says it sometimes."

"Good expression."

"Mmhmm."

"Is that what it's called in German too?" asked Winter. "Is there an expression like that?"

"No idea."

Angela was originally from Germany, old East Germany actually, *die sogenannte DDR,* Leipzig, an old, devastated center of culture according to her father, and that was why he took his wife and their only child at the time, a son, and moved to Berlin, East Berlin. Soon after, he had seen the wall, *die Mauer,* rise up against the free sky; that was in 1961. Surgeon Günther Hoffmann had seen this from one of the large windows at the hospital that had ended up in the shadow of the wall; the lower floors were already dark in the early afternoon.

The next year they had made it across, hidden in the chassis of two VW Beetles. Günther Hoffmann had been sure that his wife and son would manage; the arrangement was based on that. He came later, when it was dangerous but possible.

He tried to live in West Berlin but felt that the city pushed him away with its gaudy Western neon lights. This wasn't his country. These were not his fellow citizens. He wasn't even the cousin from the country. In the light of the advertising signs, even black Leipzig began to glow like some sort of memory of loss. It was an insane thought.

Doctor Hoffmann felt like a stranger in both of his homelands, and he suffered the consequences. He spoke with his wife and son again. They journeyed north across the sea.

He removed the final *n* in his last name and became Hoffman. He saw it as yet another consequence. A new era of life.

He got a job at Sahlgrenska Hospital in Gothenburg and found peace. His daughter Angela was born in 1967, in the summer.

"Known as the Summer of Love," Angela had said once, in the beginning, and explained to the free-form jazz nut Winter what had happened in the Haight-Ashbury district of San Francisco in the summer of 1967—the flowers; the people just hanging around, which still seemed to have been something special to experience; the music: the Grateful Dead, Jefferson Airplane, Peanut Butter Conspiracy. She had bought records from that time; it was her year, after all. Erik had laughed at Airplane but listened to the twin guitarists in Quicksilver Messenger Service on the live album *Happy Trails* with some interest. "These guys could have been something on the jazz scene," he had said. "They sure can play." She had put on "Eight Miles High" by the Byrds once, and Erik had flown out of the easy chair during Roger McGuinn's intro: "But that's Coltrane!" Later she had found that he was correct. In an interview she'd read in *Mojo,* McGuinn had said that he had been looking for John Coltrane's particular atonal tenor sax in that guitar solo. The guy could play.

She got up and turned on a floor lamp near the opposite wall. The light was warm.

He was going to call Steve Macdonald soon.

He needed to say something to Angela first.

"I had a visitor from my past today," he said.

"That sounds ominous," she said.

"An old girlfriend."

"I don't know if I want to hear this," she said.

"With emphasis on 'old,'" he said.

"Well, what did she want?"

Her tone was not exactly warm, not like the light from the lamp.

He explained.

"He hasn't been gone for that long," said Angela.

"No."

"But I would probably have gotten worried myself," she said.

"Mmhmm."

"What can you really do?" she asked.

"We can put out a missing person notice and issue a description of course, internationally. Interpol, as usual."

"Are you going to do it, then?"

"She wanted to wait a day or two."

"She? Does 'she' have a name?"

"Johanna."

Angela didn't say anything. He could tell she was thinking. He wasn't sure what she was thinking.

"Johanna Osvald," he said.

"Okay, okay," she said.

She got up and took her cup out into the kitchen without saying anything.

He followed her. She was standing at the sink and looked like she didn't know why.

"I haven't actually seen her in twenty years," he said.

"That's too bad," she said.

"Please, Angela," he said.

She dropped the coffee cup on the counter. It bounced off the steel but didn't break. It spun on the counter.

I will have to try to get out of this. Help her to get out of it too.

"Do you think I should call Steve?" he asked.

Angela turned around.

"What can he do?" she said. "And you said yourself that she wanted to wait."

We'll release it, he thought. Her dad will contact her in the morning. The letter to the "Osvald Family" is some kind of joke from the past. Maybe they've gotten some letters since the war, more of them. You never know.

He looked at the cup.

"It should have broken into a thousand pieces," she said.

"Have the countertops gotten softer or have the coffee cups gotten harder?" he said.

Aneta Djanali drove to Anette's former apartment before seven. Maybe she would have been named Anette herself if her parents had gotten it right. Was it Anette you were trying for? she had asked her mother once.

Her mother had smiled in her African manner, a manner that Aneta had never really understood.

Her mother came from Koudougou, not so far from the capital. She could dance the *hagra,* alone when there really should have been a group of women singing and dancing to the *tira* flutes. It was wedding music, a wedding dance. Maybe that was why her mother had danced it. Aneta! We're waiting for your wedding!

Aneta had records with *hagra* music; she could hardly keep moving with it. It was in her body, as it had been in her mother's. She had a *koso* at home, the double-skinned drum, and the dried calabash filled with sand, the *niabara,* and the finger rings that were struck against each other in an eternal rhythm, *boyo.*

The houses shone in the remaining light of dusk. It had rained during the hour before dawn, and puddles had formed in the uneven asphalt. She saw women and children on the way to day-care centers or schools. She didn't see any men. A delivery van went through a crossing on its way to a shopping center she couldn't see.

She had a hunch.

She parked illegally on the cross street directly opposite the entrance. Her car was as anonymous as everything else before the morning begins in earnest.

The elevator mirror was missing. Despite that, she made a motion to fix her hair.

There was a smell in the stairwell from some kitchen or another.

The nameplate was still on the door.

She pushed down the door handle and the door slid open toward her. She could suddenly feel her pulse.

She opened the door a little more and saw a shadow. Then darkness.

7

It took a few seconds for her to understand. No one had touched her. The darkness was part of the room, the hall.

He had shut two doors, a sound she hadn't heard. The light had suddenly disappeared when the doors closed. She heard him on the other side of the bedroom door. It wasn't a pleasant sound. She felt the SIG Sauer in her belt, its weight against her hip, security.

He had no business there. That was the law and it was on her side; it stood here next to her in a black robe and white wig, an orb in its hand.

A fat shadow.

She just wanted to turn and leave this house. Leave quickly.

These people's problems were not hers. And the problem wasn't there anymore. The two of them had split up and gone their separate ways, or paths, to find happiness. There was happiness somewhere, maybe everywhere, like a promise to everyone: The grass is greener here, the sky is bluer.

Now she could hear a scream from inside. He hit the door, one, two, three. Soon she would be able to see the axe through the chips of plywood. After that, something that might look like Jack Nicholson's crazy face. But there was no one here who could yell "Cut!"

If someone could, it would be her.

He opened the door, wild eyes, blank, no focus, until now.

"Who are you?"

"Police," she said, and held her identification so he could see.

"Po . . . police? What are you doing here?"

"What are *you* doing here?" she said. "This isn't your apartment."

"My apartment? I *lived* here. I *lived* here, for fuck's sake!"

"Not anymore," said Aneta. "I must ask you to leave."

Yes, she thought. I'll do it this way. It could get messy otherwise. Unpleasant.

"I have no intention of going," said Hans Forsblad.

"Do you want to come with me?" she said. "I could arrest you."

"*You?*" He tried to laugh but it was a weak attempt. "How the hell would you manage that?" He took a step forward.

"*Stand still!*" shouted Aneta. Her weapon was in her hand, her arm straight out in front of her. No. But she was on her way there.

"Are you crazy?" he said.

He was close to her; he towered up over her like a shadow that was bigger than the shadow of the law, which was no longer visible. The only thing that was visible was the damned pistol she had been forced to draw. Or hadn't been forced. She hoped that he wouldn't see that it was trembling in her hand.

She waited for his next step. God, make me disappear. I don't want to shoot this man. I don't have time for that kind of investigation. He doesn't have time. The health care system doesn't have time. Only the funeral industry has time, eternal time.

She had him in her sight.

He sat on the floor, just collapsed.

He cried.

It was a loud noise, the same one she had heard through the door a moment ago. He lifted his head. They were real tears. His face was naked, his hair was like an ill-fitting wig, she could see now that he was wearing a suit that seemed expensive, of a label that managed to look more fashionable when it was wrinkled.

He blew his nose with the handkerchief that had been sticking out of his breast pocket. He's not even missing that, she thought.

"You don't know how it feels," he said. "You don't know what it's like."

Aneta had lowered her SIG Sauer but hadn't replaced it in her holster.

"What?" she said.

"Being shut out of your own apartment," he said, sniffling, "from your own home."

"I heard that you haven't lived here for a long time," she said.

"Who said that?"

She didn't answer.

"It's them," he said, focusing his gaze on the door behind her. "They're the ones that said it. But they don't know anything."

"Who is *they?*" she asked.

"Surely you know," he said.

She put away her weapon. He followed her movement with his gaze.

"So I'm not under arrest anymore?" he said.

"Get up," she said.

"You don't know what it's like," he repeated

Now he got up, swaying.

"May I leave?"

"How did you get in?" she asked.

He held up a key.

"The locks have been changed," she said.

"That's why I have this," he said, waving the key in his hand. The tears were gone now.

"How did you get hold of it?" she asked.

"You must be able to figure that out," he said. He had suddenly grown, straightened out.

He was someone else now.

This is too weird, she thought. I can see him changing before my eyes.

"She lent it to me, of course," he said. "May I go now?"

He turned around and walked into the room and immediately came back with a briefcase that looked expensive, expensive like the suit he was wearing.

"I needed this," he said.

"Give me the key," she said.

"She let *me* borrow it," he said, with a childishly defiant voice. He made a disappointed face. This man is a raving lunatic, she thought. Dangerous, he's very dangerous.

He looked at her furtively. Now he was smiling. He threw the keys across the room at her. She let them land on the floor next to her. She wasn't totally nuts.

He put the briefcase under his arm.

"May I go now? I have some work to take care of." He held up the briefcase. "That's why I came here. I need it to take care of my work."

Go, just go, she thought. She moved, stood by the wall.

"Nice to run into you," he said; he bowed and walked out through the door and she stood still and heard him mumble something to himself as the elevator creaked its way up, and then he went in and it clattered away and she could feel the sweat on her back now, and between her breasts, in her groin, her hands. She knew that she had been close to something awful. She knew that she never wanted to be alone in a room again with that man.

Suddenly she understood the woman, Anette Lindsten, at the same time as she understood less than ever. She understood the silence. And the running away. She didn't understand anything else.

She locked the apartment door after her.

When she came out, the sky had grown lighter and opened up in different shades of brown. The rows of houses looked like they were ready to take off, like spaceships of stone, and sail away through the leathery sky, to a better world.

A routine set in, unrelenting in its indifference to people's misfortunes. What else could have happened, he thought as he sat at his desk. This desk, worn down by papers and by photographs heavy with blood. Yes. Heavy with blood.

Worn down by elbows, thoughts, murmurs, outbursts, interruptions. Break-ins. Once someone had broken into his office. The thief had lowered himself down from the jail and gotten in through the open window and stolen the Panasonic and was nabbed out in the corridor, of course. But what a thing to happen! Winter had tipped his hat. The guy is in on suspicion of theft and he breaks out of the unbreakable and immediately breaks in again and commits another theft! In the police building! Touché! He had long been a role model in the mire of gangsters in the southeast side of the city, where even the sun kept its distance.

Southeast. He thought of southeastern London, below Brixton. Croydon. And above: Bermondsey, Charlton, shady districts southeast of the river. Millwall, the soccer team that God forgot. We are Millwall, no one likes us.

His colleague who investigated murders there. And who had solved all but one, and that failure always left him without peace.

They had accompanied each other down into the abyss, back then, on those streets, and later here, too, in Gothenburg. Winter hadn't gotten over it, never would. He was still human, in the middle of all the routines. No, on the contrary: The routines helped him to retain his humanity.

He looked at the clock and picked up the phone and dialed the number.

"Yeah, hello?"

"Steve? It's Erik Winter here."

"Well, well."

"How's it going?"

"Going, going, gone. Counting the days to my retirement."

"Come on. You're still a young man," said Winter.

"That's just wishful thinking, man."

Winter smiled. Macdonald was referring to Winter's age, which was exactly the same as the Scottish inspector's.

"Do you know that song, oh thou Erik the rock 'n' roll wizard?"

"What song?"

"It's been a long, long, long time."

"Sure. It's by Steve Macdonald and the Bad News."

"It's George Harrison. Heard the name?"

Macdonald was quiet for a second.

"When members of the Beatles leave the world, the world is not the same," he then said.

"I think I can understand," said Winter.

"Did you feel that way about Coltrane? Or Miles Davis?"

"In some way. And then again, not. If I understand what you're feeling."

"Shall we leave that topic?" said Macdonald.

"I met someone from the past," said Winter.

"I'm listening."

Winter described his conversation with Johanna Osvald.

"Might be time to put out a missing person alert soon," said Macdonald.

"I'll talk about it with her again," said Winter.

"If the dad doesn't turn up soon, maybe I can ask around a little," said Macdonald.

Winter knew that Steve was from a little town a short way from Inverness. He didn't remember the name right now.

"Did you work in Inverness, Steve?"

"Yes. I was even a detective inspector. I moved there from the police station in Forres, which was the nearest big city."

"Where was that, again?"

"Home? A little Wild West hole of a town, called Dallas."

Winter laughed.

"It's true," said Macdonald. "Dallas, the mother of big Dallas in big Texas. And my Dallas consists of one street and a row of houses on either side and that's all, except for the two farms on the southern slope, one of which is ours."

Right. Winter knew that Macdonald was a farmer's son.

"My brother still works on the farm," said Macdonald.

"Are your parents still living?"

"Yes."

Winter was quiet.

"I also have a sister, and she actually lives in Inverness now," said Macdonald.

"I didn't know that," said Winter.

"I didn't either, six months ago," said Macdonald. "Eilidh lived down here in the Smoke, up on the regular-people side of Hampstead, but something happened between her and her husband so she headed back, and within twenty-four hours or something she had established herself at a new office up there."

"New office?"

"Eilidh is a lawyer. Everything but criminal law. Now she runs a little office with another woman of the same age. Macduff and Macdonald, Solicitors. They've made the whole farm in Dallas proud."

"Prouder than they are of you?"

"Jesus, Erik, no one has ever thought of me with pride."

"That's good," said Winter.

"But Eilidh is a Scottish dame worth admiration."

"How old is she?" asked Winter.

"Why?" asked Macdonald, and Winter thought he heard a smile.

"I was asking out of politeness," said Winter.

"Thirty-seven," said Macdonald. "Five years younger than you and me."

"Mmhmm."

"And ten times more beautiful than you and me."

"I'd call that beautiful," said Winter.

"But I don't think she'll be much help with this," said Macdonald.

"Depending on what happens, is it okay if I call again and ask you to check around with your colleagues up there?" asked Winter.

"Of course."

"Good."

"Maybe I should run up and check it out myself," said Macdonald.

"Sorry?"

"Nah, I was just thinking out loud. But it would be nice to have a change of scenery. What do you say? Shall we plan to meet in Inverness and solve a new mystery together?"

Winter laughed.

"What mystery?"

Four days later he would not be laughing at Macdonald's joke because it would no longer be a joke. The joke would become a mystery.

Aneta Djanali was in her own little world, a better world. She drank a glass of wine in silence. It was red wine. Burkina Faso ought to have been a good country for wine. The grapes were big and terribly sweet. There was nothing to grow in, but they grew anyway. Not many people drank wine in the partially Muslim Burkina Faso. Maybe that was why. No one could afford wine, either. Few had seen a bottle of wine. She had seen one at a hotel in Ouagadougou, carried to a fat and loud French family who were eating lamb and couscous with their sleeves rolled up. The waiter had carried the bottle as though it contained nitroglycerin.

Her father had been sitting across from her, and he had observed the Frenchman like an African who can see farther than the end of time. Her father was no longer a European, not a Swede; all of that was gone when he traveled back, never to return. He no longer practiced medicine. Aren't you going to open a small practice? she had said. There are only three hundred doctors here. God knows you're needed. Which one of them? he had answered, and she realized that it wasn't a joke. She had realized so much about her father, and about her mother, when she returned. Her father's gods had been many, and they still were. They waited out there in the light and the dark, during the horribly hot days and the dreadfully cold nights. He spoke with the gods, sometimes with the spirits, but the difference between gods and spirits seemed to be gratuitous.

Some spirits were strong and powerful, like a lion that kills.

Others were weaker, more diffuse, like the spirits of trees.

Everything we encounter has power, her father had said. A lion, a snake, lightning, a river. All of them can kill people, and therefore they must be inhabited by strong spirits.

The sea can kill people, she suddenly thought now. Why did she think of that? There was no sea around Burkina Faso.

Her father had spoken about language. The most important art form in Africa was the art of speaking. In each language there are more than one thousand sayings, he had said.

Dear God, she had thought on the Air France plane home, where do I come from? *Where* do I come from? Who am I?

What will I become?

She took another little sip of the wine, which was heavy, with a scent of oak and leather.

What will I become?

I am over thirty, and black as sin. There are other people like me in this white, innocent country. The people are white, and it's white on the ground. Mom would have wanted to see me together with a nice black man. She did get to for a little while, but not as long as she wanted. Now none of that is interesting anymore.

She thought of the dinner in the hotel restaurant again, the last one she and Dad had had together. The colonial clatter in the big room. The sand that refused to leave, despite determined appeals from the staff and guests. The wind that came in through the openings in the gigantic wooden blinds in the ridiculously big windows; ridiculously big because they offered no protection.

The gods know that *you* are needed, Aneta, her father had said, and he had had a smile that only his daughter could see. Competent detectives are important in a modern country. Haven't people had enough of police in this country? she'd asked. Those aren't real police, he answered, and he knew everything about that while she knew nothing. Those aren't good police. A proper society needs good police; then it will be a society that contains goodness.

Had he been joking? It hadn't sounded like it. What did it mean? In recent years, even before he returned, his speech and thoughts had begun to resemble aphorisms and riddles, as though he could see something no one else could see, or remembered things that were no longer to be found in anyone else. She had found it fascinating, and frightening. Her mother had found it crazy. Or pretended that it was not worth listening to.

A proper society needs good police; then it will be a society that contains goodness. Suck on that, Aneta. Perhaps she would make a motion to the police conference suggesting that the sentence be engraved in gold or silver, maybe on their caps, even the ones on exhibit in the police build ing: a sentence everyone could rally around. Goodness. We all strived for it, and we caught those who didn't in our arms and took them to a better place.

That's what our duty here in this world amounts to. She took another sip of wine. It's nothing to joke about, nothing to become cynical about. And still it looks silly as hell in print, and sounds even worse out loud. Goodness looks sillier than evil in print and out loud.

Evil is you and I. That's what she thought now. It was a true thought, and it was her own.

At night she dreamed of doors that closed and never opened. She saw faces with one side that laughed while the other cried. Faces became icons. Someone spoke to her and said that she couldn't trust anyone. Not even you? she asked, because she was feeling secure at that point in the dream.

Her father said to her that there were gods that no one knew about in the desert. How can they be gods, then? she asked. That shut him up for a second.

She flew over Kortedala on Air France and had a stopover in all the seasons without leaving the plane.

She flew in a castle that was also a house.

She dreamed all her thoughts and experiences from the past few days, and she understood everything as she dreamed, as though she were simultaneously devoting herself to dream analysis.

Then she dreamed something she didn't understand, and her own scream woke her up.

8

When he felt the wind in his face, the memories came. It was always like that. It could be light or dark. The memories. Out there, there was no day, no night. The sea was its own world. His work revolved around the trawling, the winches, the work deck, up and down, every five hours, seldom at night, at first, but he had wanted it to be otherwise. It was still hell to try to sleep up in the forecastle along with seven others, everything sour, wet, always nights without sleep. The work ached like a shadow in his body. No warmth, no feeling of dry skin. He would dream about it during the weeks out there. The dry skin.

The wind changed on the night when Frans went off the back with the trawl net. He never heard the scream; no one did. Frans was gone without a scream. Yet another gray stone on its way to the bottom, but not really. Whatever fell into the North Sea here, between Stavanger and Peterhead, came ashore again up in northern Norway. A lonely journey through the black currents. Frans.

Was that what had happened?

They prayed during their journeys back, and they went directly to the pub from the harbor. He remembered when he walked in, but never when he walked out. He had had so many similar nights there; all those nights ended without memories.

At sea it was never possible to wash away the tiredness, and when they came ashore again he did his best to get it to pass.

The evening he got caught by the trawl door could have been his last. He became more careful with the drink after that, for a while.

He sat outside his house. He could see the old church from there. He saw cars on their way to and from the church, and to and from the golf course that was on the point behind the church. The idiots hit their balls into the water and didn't understand why.

The westernmost viaduct ran in from the left, in his field of vision, and became part of the church, or maybe it was the church that became part of the viaduct. He had studied this image many times. They belonged together. The viaducts were cathedrals of another time, the time that came after, and it was natural that they should converge with the churches.

He spit toward the church. He regretted it. He dried his mouth and got up. He walked on the street that didn't have a name. A child passed but didn't look up at him. He was invisible to the child, too.

When children don't see the invisible, there is no longer any hope.

A middle-aged couple came down the stairs, and they didn't see him. He stepped aside so that they wouldn't pass right through him. He heard their voices but didn't understand the language, or maybe he didn't hear it over the wind.

He ordered his ale at the Three Kings. He sat for a long time in front of the glass that no one else could see. He signaled to the woman behind the bar, and she looked in the other direction. He had spoken with her on other days, he knew it.

She knew.

He couldn't tell what she was thinking now.

She had tried to talk to him but he hadn't wanted to listen. She had said one word, but he didn't want to hear that word. She had said another word; it was the word "lie." She had said the word "life." She had said the words "lifelong lie."

She had said too much.

The couple he'd met on the steps came into the pub and sat at one of the two tables by the window. The woman behind the bar stiffened, as though she dreaded taking an order. No, it wasn't that. The couple looked around. The man said something and he heard what he said this time, and he recognized the language. He carried remains of it inside himself. He didn't think about it anymore, but he heard the words and could still put them together if he had to.

He wouldn't have to.

He ordered another glass from the woman, who couldn't see him. He drank with his back to the couple, who sat by the window and looked out over the viaducts and the sea.

Frans hadn't been the first.

In the currents, the bodies embraced each other.

Jesus. Jesus!

* * *

When he came out he passed a truck filled with fish. He knew where it came from and where it was going. The truck raced down, on its way west. He smelled the odor of fish through the diesel fumes, or he thought he did. Naturally he only thought so.

The truck disappeared down into the tunnel, a danger for anyone coming the opposite direction. He waited for the crash but didn't hear anything, not this time. He only heard the familiar roar as the motor forced itself up the hills on the other side.

He would never go there again. Never again!

He walked east. He had a meeting.

9

Aneta Djanali made breakfast with her bad dreams winding around in her head like a lingering fog. She put water in the kettle but forgot to turn on the power and waited in vain, standing at the kitchen counter, until she realized what had happened and looked around to see if anyone was standing there smirking.

No one was standing there.

Sometimes she missed having someone there to let out an indulgent laugh at her absentmindedness. Who was always there. Sometimes Fredrik was there, and there was nothing wrong with his indulgent laugh, but he wasn't always there.

And she wasn't always in his kitchen, at his counter.

Was this what being a live-apart couple was?

No. That presupposed a relationship that could be called a *relationship,* something accepted and . . . and, well, confirmed, established.

Something obvious. For both people. They weren't there, she and Fredrik. Why weren't they there? Or were they on their way there without needing to confirm it, or even think about it?

Life is complicated.

She toasted two pieces of bread at the same time. It was more complicated than toasting one slice, but compared to other parts of her life it wasn't particularly complicated. She spread butter on the bread, sliced some cheese, spooned some blackberry marmalade on the cheese. Simple, easy actions, like brewing tea: milk in the bottom of the mug, pour in the tea, two sugar cubes, stir, let cool.

Drink the tea. Eat the bread.

Empty the brain.

For fifteen minutes.

The moon was still up when she came outside, but it was lingering, pale, behind thin clouds, like in a fog. Her car was in shadow from the sun, which shone happily in another part of the sky. The car was cold when she got in, the scent of night still in the leather. Everything from the night was lingering this morning. That's what she thought.

She drove south. There was a line of cars at Linnéplatsen. Three lanes, keeping time. Some idiot kept revving the engine, stared at her, revved it again, staring from his Audi.

Should she throw open her door and show her ID?

The light turned green and the idiot flew away, on his way to Le Mans, the Nürburgring, made it seven yards, swerved to the left, accelerated, on his way to a late start in Monte Carlo, roared past a few asphalt mixers and the road worker farthest out lost his cap in the rush of wind.

Aneta lifted the phone and called the officer at dispatch and gave him the disappearing license plate number on the car up ahead.

No goal today for Audi.

She had seen the flash of racism in his eyes.

You soon became sensitive to such things. A sunburn from Africa always caused reactions, no matter the year, decade, century, millennium. You know, of course, that all humans have their origins in Africa? she said once when Fredrik was playing racist. Yes, *playing*. That was at first; then he had stopped.

She passed Sahlgrenska Hospital going up the hill. She drove into Toltorpsdalen, which sounded like it belonged in a fairy tale. She turned left at the church and crept over the damned speed bumps, fifty yards between each one. Workers in vehicles hated the speed bumps: bus drivers, taxi drivers, delivery people, police. She looked around. The people in the neighborhood hate the speed bumps sometimes; the more accelerations, the worse the air. Fair Toltorpsdalen already had the city's worst air even before that; it was among the worst in north Europe.

In Krokslätt everything sloped downward. She rolled without accelerating off of Krokslätt's Parkgata and parked behind Sörgård School.

It was idyllic. The city was of two minds here, on the boundary between the crude downtown of Mölndal and the abyss of the big city that began at Liseberg. It was quiet here, Fridkullagatan ran like a protective arm to the west and the north; here it was calm like the eye of a cyclone. A person who stayed here found peace.

Anette Lindsten had not stayed here. Why she had left the protective pocket of Fredriksdal for the condemned Kortedala was a question that only love could answer. Anette had moved to the windswept district of seasons for the sake of love, a district where the authorities were now blowing up their own buildings, and when even love had been smashed to pieces, Anette had returned here, home again.

Aneta stood outside the house, which was hidden behind a hedge that would be difficult to climb over or chop your way through. The house was wooden, like most houses here, built between the wars, expanded during the welfare period, well cared for in less fortunate times, these times. Aneta hesitated outside the iron gate, which had recently been scraped and would soon be painted again. Why don't I leave these people alone? What answer do I want? I am tired of this shit, tired of women having to live long lives of fear, in exile in their own country, worse than that, living in protected places like refugees, hidden from state entities and their verdicts, and from the powers that be, which is me, us, the police. Them, she thought. I wouldn't haul children out of a church on order. It has been done before and those pictures are not in the most beautiful albums of humankind's time on earth. Now Anette is hiding here at home. Is that enough for her?

She saw her hand ring the doorbell. All I want is to see that Anette is okay.

Her hand rang again. She could hear a dog barking inside; maybe it had been audible before. The door was opened and within it she saw jaws opening, and not to smile. The dog growled. She knew a Rottweiler when she saw one. In most cases it was a matter of striking first.

"*Quiet,* Zack!"

She could see the top of the man's head as he bent toward the muscular monster down there. What did the people of Fredriksdal say about them when they were out for a walk?

The man turned his face to her.

She didn't recognize him.

"Yes?"

He had opened the door halfway.

"I would like to . . . have a word with Anette," said Aneta. She felt caught off guard. She didn't understand why.

"She isn't here," said the man.

The dog growled in agreement and turned and disappeared.

"But she moved home," said Aneta.

"What? What do you mean? And who are you, by the way?"

She finally showed her ID and said her name.

"What do you want with her?" said the man, without looking at what she was holding in her hand.

Aneta felt something horrible inside, a feeling of dizziness.

She tried to see past the man into the hall, and she saw the dog waiting for her, or for some part of her. The monster was already licking its lips.

She felt the feeling again: a lost foothold. She made her voice stronger than it was.

"I would like to speak with her father."

"What?"

The man looked truly surprised.

"Sigge. Lindsten," said Aneta. "I would like to speak with him."

She saw doubt in the man's face. He sneaked a look at the ID, which she still held in her hand.

"Is that a real badge?" he said with a tone that said "Are you a real police officer?"

"Is her father home?" said Aneta. "Sigge Lindsten? Is he in the house?"

"*I'm* Sigge Lindsten, for God's sake," said the stranger in the door. "*I'm* her dad!"

She saw the other face in front of her, the other Lindsten dad who had worked calmly in Aneta's apartment, removing everything that was there. The dad, the nice and collected one. And the brother, the dismissive brother.

"Pe . . . Peter," said Aneta, the feeling of dizziness more and more marked.

"What? Who are you raving about now?" said the man.

"Peter Lindsten. Her brother. Anette's brother."

"Anette doesn't *have* a brother, dammit!" said the man.

Bertil Ringmar was hanging around the window, gazing out at the river, Fattighusån. The buildings on the other side were new, private residences for the privileged. The poorhouse for which the stream was named was gone now. They're gone all over now, he thought. The houses are gone but the poor are still here.

"Don't you get depressed, looking out over Fattighusån every day?" he said, turning to Winter, who was sitting at his desk doing nothing.

"I do."

"Do something about it, then."

Winter let out a laugh.

"That's the point," he said.

"It's the point for you to be depressed?"

"Yes."

"Why?"

"Then everything is so much easier when you leave here."

"Is that why you leave so often?"

"Yes."

"Mmhmm."

"I have thought about it," said Winter, "about this damn office."

"What have you thought?"

"That I don't want to be here anymore. Sit here anymore."

"You don't?"

"I'm going to set up an office in the town."

"Are you?"

"In a café. Or a bar."

"Your office in a bar?"

"Yes."

"Interrogations in a bar?"

"Yes."

"That's brilliant."

"Isn't it?"

"Have you talked to Birgersson?"

"Do I have to?"

Ringmar smiled. Birgersson was a chief inspector and the chief of the homicide department. Winter was a chief inspector and deputy chief. Ringmar was only a chief inspector, and that was enough for him. He knew that nothing worked without him anyway. Look at Winter. Look at him! Sitting on his chair and doing absolutely nothing, and it would stay that way if Ringmar weren't there. If, for example, he didn't keep this conversation going.

Look at this room. There was a sink in one corner, where Winter could shave if he was restless. There was a map of Gothenburg on one wall. There were some mysterious circles and lines from past investigations. There were lots of lines. Winter—and he himself—had redrawn the map of the city. Their map showed the criminal Gothenburg. That city stretched in many directions, to unfamiliar points. No such points existed in the official map of Gothenburg.

Winter was sitting in a chair that was entirely too comfortable, too new. He had recently rewallpapered the office. He had put in new bookshelves, different lamps from the ones that shone the way for other colleagues in other rooms in this beautiful building. He had lugged in his own little furniture arrangement.

It was time to get out of here. A café. A bar.

On the floor, a yard from Ringmar, stood the eternal Panasonic and the eternal tenor sax wailing atonal blues. Coltrane? No. Something else, from our time. It was good. Depressingly good.

"What is it?" said Ringmar, nodding toward the portable stereo.

"Michael Brecker," said Winter. "And not just him. Pat Metheny, Jack DeJohnette, Dave Holland, Joey Calderazzo, McCoy Tyner, Don Alias."

"Alias? What's his real name?"

Winter laughed again and lit a Corps. The thin cigarillo made a bobbing motion in his mouth.

"You listed a whole investigation squad," said Ringmar.

"If you want to look at it that way."

"May I borrow it?" said Ringmar.

Winter turned around in his chair and reached for the CD rack and took out a CD case and tossed it like a Frisbee to Ringmar, who caught it with an elegant motion. He saw a man's back, clad in a black coat, wandering along a river. It said "Tales from the Hudson" at the bottom. Ringmar thought of the sluggish river behind him and thought of something else.

"The Hudson River," he said.

Winter knew what he was thinking about.

"How is Martin?" asked Winter.

"Good."

"Is he still in New York?"

"Yes."

Ringmar's son Martin worked as a chef at a good restaurant in Manhattan. Third Avenue. He had a complicated relationship with his father. Or maybe it was the other way around. Winter didn't know, but he had his own idea of what had happened. He hadn't asked, not about everything. And Ringmar had reestablished contact with his son. They spoke to each other, before it was too late. For Winter it had been too late, or almost too late. He had spoken with his father days before his death. Bengt Winter had died at Hospital Costa del Sol outside of Marbella and Winter had been there. It was the first time they'd seen each other in five or six years, and the first time they'd spoken to each other. It was a tragedy. Worth crying oneself to sleep over night after night.

"Have you thought about going over and visiting soon?" asked Winter.

"Thought about it."

"Go, for fuck's sake."

Ringmar moved his head in time with the piano music that streamed through the room. He rubbed the bridge of his nose.

"They had some sort of catering job for a firm in the World Trade Center," he said.

Winter didn't answer, waited.

"Martin was there sometimes; he was in charge of getting the buffet set up or something."

"When did he tell you that?" asked Winter.

"When do you think? After nine-eleven, of course. There was no reason to before."

Winter nodded.

"But he wasn't there that day." Ringmar walked away from the window and sat on the chair on the other side of the desk. Winter took a drag. It sounded like the volume had been turned up, but the music had just changed tempo, become even more nervous. Desperate. Tales from New York. "Good God. He was supposed to have been there *that day* but that consulting firm or whatever the hell it was changed the reception to the next day." Ringmar rasped out a rough sound, like half a laugh. "There was no reception the next day."

"How did Martin react?"

"He's thanking God, I think."

"Mmhmm."

"He's started to visit the church next door," said Ringmar, and Winter thought that his face brightened. "He says that he sits there without praying or anything. But that he feels peace there. And thankfulness, he says."

"Go over," said Winter.

"I've been about to," said Ringmar. "But now he's coming home."

"Is he?"

"Just a break. For a few weeks."

Winter left early and walked by way of Saluhallen, the indoor market. He bought a pound of farmer cheese from Brittany and two Estonian flatbreads; that was all.

A bar on Södra Larmgatan glowed invitingly. It was new and he didn't see a name. He went in and ordered a beer from the tap and sat at a window table. A man was sitting alone at the bar. The bartender was preparing glasses and olives and plates and bottles and doing all the other pleasant things bartenders occupy themselves with during the hour of blue twilight before guests arrive. Winter lit a Corps. This was the best time in a bar, as good as empty, a sense of anticipation before the evening, an unidentifiable serene sound. He looked around. The twenty-first century had introduced new trends in bar design. It was no longer mini-mini-minimalistic, the kind of design that gave the impression that you were sitting in a deserted hangar.

There was leather and wood and a warm light here. No bare light-bulbs hanging from the ceiling.

He could have his new office here. Here, by the window. During interrogations you could hold the candle a little closer to the person being interrogated in order to see the play of his eyes. The video camera could stand on the windowsill.

His colleagues from the jail could wait at the bar.

He took his phone out of his inner jacket pocket and called home.

"I'm on my way," he said.

The bartender dropped a glass on the floor. The floor was made of stone. The man at the bar yelled, "Cheers!" and raised his glass.

"The streetcar is lively, I hear," said Angela.

"Ha ha."

"Be good and come home now," said Angela.

Winter looked around.

"What do you say about a little drink before dinner?" he said.

"It depends on the place," she said.

"It's new and I'm the only one here," he said, watching as the man at the bar climbed off his stool and made some sort of bow toward the bartender and left the bar with the exaggeratedly decisive movements of someone who is half drunk.

"I have to ask Elsa," said Angela.

"Do you have to ask her permission for everything?"

"Ha ha ha."

"I promise not to smoke," said Winter.

"She says it's okay if I come, but she wants to invite herself along to keep an eye on us."

"Södra Larmgatan, right across from Saluhallen."

He hung up and drank his beer. People outside were on their way somewhere. The sun was on its way to the Southern Hemisphere. The sky was colored orange, which meant that the sun would come back tomorrow. The light outside was blue because the hour was blue. A long evening awaited. He thought he would let it take its course; he wouldn't interfere.

The phone rang again. He didn't recognize the number on the screen. He debated letting it ring, but if he did it would be the first time.

There's a first time for everything.

He didn't answer.

He felt a sensation in his body when the ringing stopped.

Something has happened.

He lifted his hand toward the bartender.

This calls for a celebration.

10

Angela came with Elsa, who immediately ordered a drink with bubbles. Angela ordered a dry martini. Winter ordered a Longmorn. Angela had a dark circle under one eye, which was a sign that she was tired. Never more than one circle, and it was never there for more than a few short hours, before a new day. Soon it would be a new day.

"Cheers, and hi," said Elsa.

Winter raised his glass. He looked into Angela's eyes. What kind of habits are we teaching our daughter? How will it be when we're not there keeping an eye on her? What will happen with the bubbles?

"Is it good, Elsa?" asked Angela.

"It tickles my nooose," said Elsa.

Just then, Winter felt a sting in his nose and in the next second he sneezed.

"Bless you!" shrieked Elsa.

"Thanks, sweetie."

"Does your nose tickle too, Papa?"

"Yes. Just like yours."

"But I didn't sneeze!"

"I did it for both of us."

"Ha ha!"

"If you two keep this up, I'll sneeze too," said Angela.

"How can this be explained from a purely medical perspective?" said Winter.

"What?"

"Well, you're a doctor. How do you explain why you have a sneezing reflex when other people talk about sneezing?"

"I don't think the research has come very far in that area," said Angela. "And I really don't know which branch it would be done in."

"Medicine," said Winter. "Ear nose throat."

"No."

"Physiology."

"No."

"Sneeziology."

"No."

"Nosiness," said Elsa.

Her parents looked at her.

I am the father of a genius, thought Winter.

"Where did you get that from, Elsa?" asked Angela.

"You had to say something with 'nose,' right? My day-care teacher told us the story of the nosy boy."

"So you didn't mean that Papa and I were talking about knowing about noses?"

Winter saw that Elsa didn't understand the question, and he relaxed.

"Did your teacher tell you what nosiness means?" he asked.

"I forget."

"What does it actually mean?" asked Angela, looking at him.

"That you take too many liberties," said Winter.

"You're taking too many liberties here," said the man who said that his name was Sigge Lindsten and that he was Anette Lindsten's father. "Even for the police."

Aneta Djanali didn't answer. She still felt dizzy. If there had been anything to take hold of, she would have grabbed it.

"Are you okay?" asked the man.

"Could I have a glass of water?"

The man seemed to make a decision. He no longer looked unsympathetic. Maybe he never had.

"Come in," he said.

She took off her shoes in the hall. She could smell some plant, a scent she recognized but couldn't place.

When she followed the man to the kitchen she remembered that she had smelled the same scent in the apartment that two men were in the process of emptying in front of her. Crazy. Just crazy.

She felt the dizziness again.

"Please sit down," said the man. He filled a glass with water. "Here," he said.

She drank. She saw the wind move in a tree outside, maybe a maple.

The wind had increased the last few days, like a growling promise of autumn. She didn't look forward to it.

She suddenly spun again. Am I becoming seriously ill? she thought.

"Now, what's this about Anette?" said Sigge Lindsten.

That's my question, she thought.

"Is Anette home?" she asked.

"Not at the moment," said the man.

She looked around.

"Is your wife home?"

"She's not home at the moment either," he said.

"Could I see some identification?" asked Aneta.

"I beg your pardon?"

"Identification. I'm sorry, but this is all a bit confusing, and I will explain soon. But first I have to be certain that you're the—"

"Good Lord," interrupted the man, "I'll get my wallet. This should be interesting to hear."

He went out into the hall and came back with his wallet and held it out, and she saw his driver's license in a plastic sleeve. It was in the name of a Sigvard Lindsten, and the relatively recent photograph showed the man who stood before her.

"Thanks," she said.

He closed his wallet.

"Have you heard of Hans Forsblad?" she asked.

"Isn't it my turn to ask some questions?" said Lindsten.

"Just answer this one."

He shrugged his shoulders.

"That piece of shit wouldn't dare come here. If he did, it would be the last thing he did."

"When did Anette move out of the apartment in Kortedala?"

"That's another question."

"I'll explain soon," said Aneta.

Lindsten suddenly seemed to lose interest in the conversation. He turned toward the counter and turned on the faucet and turned it off again.

"When?" repeated Aneta.

"What?"

"When did she move?"

"She hasn't moved," said Lindsten. "Not officially. She has left the apartment but she hasn't given notice yet."

Good God, thought Aneta.

Time to explain.

Lindsten had made himself a cup of coffee. Aneta had declined. She had called dispatch and reported a break-in. She had called the local police.

She had felt like an idiot the whole time.

Would Fredrik have asked for identification first off if he had been her and had come up to Anette's apartment and met a nice but worried dad and a sulky brother? She wasn't sure. She would ask him.

It was an interesting psychological situation. She had wandered right into it. The man who had claimed he was Sigge Lindsten had shown exceptional presence of mind in this situation. Exceptional. She had been under his command. The younger man had been under his command. When she thought back to the hour or so she had spent in the apartment, she realized how skillfully he had handled everything. Almost an hour! They were in the process of emptying an entire apartment and the cops knock on the door and they offer coffee and wave good-bye in the end!

It was comical, but it was also something else.

She had exposed herself.

To the two men.

And to Hans Forsblad. If it had in fact been him.

Was that man also someone else?

"Do you have a picture of Forsblad in the house?"

Lindsten went and got a photograph without a frame. A young woman and a young man, trying to outdo each other's smiles. It was possible that several years had gone by since, but she recognized Forsblad from the meeting in that damn apartment.

It struck her that this was the first time she'd seen Anette, really seen her. She had come here without having a face in mind. That was unusual for her. The first time. But she had also come here. Something had *brought* her here, and there was also something frightening in that thought.

Suddenly she thought of death. She thought of her own death. She felt the sharp but fleeting sense of dizziness again, as though she had been dragged down into an abyss, a darkness.

Something told her that she ought to run away from these people, these events. Run away from everything, *immediately,* hurry away from this case, this investigation, before everything got bigger, even more incomprehensible, worse. More dangerous.

Anette Lindsten had regular features that tried to make her beautiful but didn't really succeed. Aneta held the picture in her hand. Anette's face was long, and the impression was intensified by her hair, which hung free. She was wearing a dress that was bigger than it needed to be. Anette and Hans were sitting on a bench, and it wasn't possible to determine how tall Anette was. The man was of an average build, well over six feet.

Anette held a Popsicle that was in the process of melting.

The picture was taken on a street with cars parked on it. A store was visible behind the couple, but she couldn't see the name. A child was on the way into the store, maybe on the way to the ice cream counter. There were sharp shadows in the photograph. Somewhere outside the picture was a sharp sun.

"It was taken a few summers ago," said Sigge Lindsten.

Aneta nodded.

"And now it's probably time to go to Kortedala and see the damage," said Lindsten.

"I'll drive you," said Aneta.

In the car, she thought of Anette.

Had he already beaten her then? The man sitting next to her in the photograph, with his big smile?

Was she still hoping?

I'll have to ask her. If I ever meet her.

The Winter-Hoffman family was on the way home over one of the bridges when Winter's phone rang.

"Yes?"

"Hi, Erik, Möllerström here."

"Yes?"

Winter heard Möllerström give a cough. Janne Möllerström was a detective and the department records clerk. Everything went through Möllerström just like it went through Winter. But Möllerström kept everything in his advanced data files. Winter had his thoughts, his theories and hypotheses, in his PowerBook. Möllerström had several computers. And telephones.

"A woman has tried to reach you a few times. Sounded a little desperate."

"What's her name?"

"Osvald. Johanna Osvald."

"Did she leave a phone number?"

Möllerström recited the number. Winter recognized it. She had given it to him.

"What else did she say?"

"Just that you should call when you can."

"Tonight?"

He watched Angela and Elsa, who were five yards ahead of him. Elsa's hand stuck out from the stroller. Angela was walking briskly.

He quickly dialed the number he'd gotten from Janne. He released his breath when he heard the busy signal. The phone rang as soon as he hung up. He recognized the number on the screen.

"She called here again," said Möllerström. "Just now."

"It's after working hours," said Winter.

"That's something new to be coming from you," said Möllerström.

"What is it that's so urgent?" said Winter.

"She just said that she wanted to talk to you."

"Mmhmm."

"I assume the best way to find out is to call."

"Thanks for the advice, Janne, and have a good rest of the night at the department."

"Thank you," Möllerström snickered, and hung up.

Angela was waiting at a red light at Allén.

"The mobile office," she said.

"Well . . ."

"There is an off button."

He didn't answer. He thought she was being unfair. She didn't know that he was trying to *avoid* a conversation. There was still a first time for everything.

"For everyone but you," she said.

"What?"

"A button for everyone but you."

"Please, Angela . . ."

Red turned to green. They walked across the street. He saw that Elsa's head was hanging. He would have had trouble staying awake himself if he was being pushed around in a stroller just after twilight.

"They can send a car for you if it's really important, can't they?"

"As long as I haven't left town," he said.

"Left town! Surely you don't have permission to leave town!"

"By written request three months ahead of time."

"In which case you can be wanted if you're away from the house," she said.

"Like now," he said.

"You know what I mean."

He looked at his watch.

"Officially, I'm still on duty," he said.

"Did that also apply to the hour at the new bar?"

"It's my new office."

His phone rang again.

"You have to answer," said Angela. "You're still on duty."

It was Möllerström again.

"For God's sake, Janne!"

"Sorry, sorry, boss, but she called again and said it's about her father."

"I *know* that it's about her father."

He hung up and looked at Angela. They were standing outside their own door.

"I really did try," he said.

"What is it about?" she said, and opened the door with one hand. Winter was steering the stroller. Elsa was sleeping and snoring quietly. The polyps. She would have to have an operation later, Angela had said. Are you serious? he had said. Unfortunately, she said. It happened to me too, she had said.

"Johanna Osvald's father," he said now. "She's tried to reach me several times; apparently she's shaken up."

"Well, call her, darn it," said Angela, and her face was open, and there was no sarcasm in her voice.

He called from the hall. Angela was fixing supper for Elsa, who had woken up in the elevator. It was impossible to sleep in that elevator. It was antique and dragged itself up with tortured protests, loud sighs.

He heard the rings, two, three, four, five, six. He called again. He didn't get an answer.

In the kitchen, Angela was making a porridge out of yesterday's rice pudding.

"No answer," he said

"Well, that's strange."

"*Very* strange," Elsa said, and giggled.

He smiled.

"Do you want porridge, Papa?"

"Not right now, sweetie."

"Soon it will be *gone,*" she said.

"You'll just have to try again," said Angela, scooping porridge into Elsa's deep dish.

He went into the living room and called from there. Three-four-five-six. He hung up and turned on the CD player, which continued where it had left off late last night, with Miles Davis's and Freddie Hubbard's trumpets in "The Court." The court of law. Or a courtyard, if you looked at it that way. Miles's solo, which was like a sharp shadow from a sharp sun. Of course. A long shadow across a courtyard.

He kept time with his foot, not something for a beginner. He had tried to show Angela once quite a while ago, teach her, but she had given up, laughing. Give me rock 'n' roll! she had cried. Okay, he had said. Something simple and easy to digest for mademoiselle. You don't even know what it is! she had said. Yes I do, he had answered. Say something, then! she had said. Say what? he had said. Say a band! A rock band! He had thought and answered.

Elvis Presley.

She had laughed again, a lot. You are truly up to date, she had hiccuped.

He smiled at the memory. But he was up to date. Tonight he would listen to Pharoah Sanders, *Save Our Children.* Good God, he had just bought *The Complete "In a Silent Way" Sessions.*

He tried to call again an hour later. It would have to be the last time. Angela was in the bath, but that wasn't why; it wasn't why he was taking the opportunity right then. He didn't get an answer this time either.

She came back to the living room as Bill Frisell's guitar was running amok as it had so many times before.

"Heavens," she said. It was one of her expressions, like "darn." She sometimes spoke a sort of lively 1950s Swedish that had become the Hoffman family's language when they came to their new country. The language had encapsulated itself in the Hoffmans, and some of it remained with Angela. He had pointed it out to her. You bet, daddy-o, she had answered.

"Is it supposed to sound like that?" she said, nodding at the CD player with a towel around her head. He could feel her warmth.

"I don't actually know how it's *supposed* to sound," he answered.

"Whoever played like that should get it checked out," she said.

"I didn't know you were so prejudiced."

"Prejudiced? It's called considerate."

Bill Frisell ladled it on, and it was worse than ever, better than ever. Viktor Krauss on bass, Jim Keltner on drums like two tiptoeing caretakers while the crazy person ran into walls with his guitar in overdrive, attack after attack. Winter turned up the volume. "Lookout for Hope."

"Good God," yelled Angela. "Elsa is sleeping, you know."

Winter lowered the volume.

Angela grabbed the album sleeve and read:

Gone, Just Like a Train.

"Good title."

"If the train leaves on time," she said.

He lowered the volume until almost nothing was left.

"Are you naked under that robe?" he said.

She put down the album sleeve and looked at him.

"Come here and sit in my lap," he said.

11

Aneta Djanali was back in the four seasons. Vivaldi was far away from here. These were buildings and streets built for heavy metal. One building on the left was on its way down. They had just demolished half of it. There was still concrete dust in the air. A wrecking ball swung in the air like a clock pendulum. A dull echo of an explosion remained.

This is like driving in a war. She turned left and left again. A war against the northern suburbs.

"Good that they're tearing this shit down," said Sigge Lindsten.

"Is it?"

"Who the hell wants to live here?"

"Your daughter, for one."

She turned her head and looked at him. He didn't look at her. They had to stop at a roadblock. A soldier held up his hand, waving with his Uzi. No. A concrete worker showed them the way around with a spade. There was a rumble in the near distance. There were marks on the finish of a car that was parked behind the worker. The blast mats had been made of wide mesh. Stones fell from the sky.

"It was a mistake," said Lindsten.

"That she moved here?"

"Yes."

"Why did they move here, anyway?"

"Back," said Lindsten.

"Sorry?"

"They moved back. She and . . . Forsblad," said Lindsten, and she heard how much trouble he had saying the name. He spat it out quickly. He rubbed his mouth. "The fact is that we lived here before we moved down to Fredriksdal." He looked at her now. "This is like the home district of the Lindsten family." He let out a laugh, a metallic sort of laugh that sounded heavy and hopeless. Heavy metal, thought Aneta.

"It hasn't always looked like this. It might never have been beautiful, but there was something else here, some vital culture around the factories." He turned his head. "This is also some sort of native district."

She nodded.

"Everything revolved around the factories." He hacked out a laugh again; it scratched like iron filings. "And they revolved around us."

"What do you mean?"

"Well, there wasn't really anyone who thought about escaping."

"You did."

"Yes."

"Is that how you look at it? As an escape?"

"No."

"Why did you move, then?"

"Well, my wife inherited some money and she wanted to live in her own house and she's from down by Mölndal."

So that's how it is, thought Aneta. The listener can fill in the rest.

"When Anette was going to move away from home—it was several years ago—at the same time, an apartment that one of my cousins had been renting became available, and, well, it could be worked out."

"It's quite a ways from home," said Aneta.

"She thought it was exciting. That's what she said, anyway."

"Did she and Forsblad move in together right away?"

"No."

"Were they together?"

"Yes."

"What did you think of them moving in together?"

Lindsten turned to her again.

"Do we have to talk about that damned Forsblad the whole time?"

"Don't you think about him? The whole time?"

Lindsten didn't answer.

"When did you last speak to him?"

"I don't remember."

"Repressed?"

"What?"

"Maybe you've repressed it?" she said.

"Repressed . . . yes . . . repressed. Yes. I have."

She could see that Lindsten had gotten a different expression on his face. He seemed to relax. It was something she'd said. What had she said? That he'd repressed the memory of his daughter's husband?

Later she would need to remember this conversation. Perhaps it would be too late then.

They sped away from the powdery construction smoke and drove up in front of the building, which was made of one enormous section.

Lindsten suddenly picked up the conversation from before. "Huge fucking monsters like this didn't exist then. They were built later, when they thought that they could shove half a million slaves into a ghetto." He looked up, as though he were trying to see the roof of the building. "First they built those piles of shit, and now they're tearing them down. Ha!"

She stopped in front of the door. A marked car was parked there. A colleague stepped out; one remained inside.

"Cleaned out," said the woman who had gotten out. Aneta didn't recognize her.

"Cleaned out as in *cleaned out*?" said Aneta.

"Sure is."

Aneta and Lindsten went up in the elevator, which seemed newer than the rest of the building.

"I have to ask you one more thing," she said. "Has Anette been back here since she decided to move?"

"Now I don't understand."

"When she moved back home with you, did she come here any time after that? To get anything or something like that? To check on the apartment?"

"No."

"You're sure of that?"

"Damn it, of course I'm sure. She didn't dare to come back here, for Christ's sake!"

"No one was going to take over the lease?"

"No."

"A relative or something?"

"No."

"Really?"

"She didn't own it, for Christ's sake. And these days it's even harder to work things like that out than it was before."

During their trip to the apartment she had tried to describe the two men to Lindsten. It hadn't been of any help to her, or him. Could be any old bastard at all, any scoundrel at all. He had made a gesture in the air, as though he were sketching a face.

They stepped out of the elevator and went to the apartment door. Aneta opened it with keys she'd gotten from her colleague. There were two locks.

The apartment was cleaned out.

"Well," said Lindsten.

"Why didn't you move all her things when Anette moved?" she asked.

"We were going to do it next week," said Lindsten. He took a few steps into the hall. "Now that's not necessary."

Detective Lars Bergenhem chased burglars, or the shadows of them. A wave of burglaries was washing over Gothenburg. That's how the chief inspector at CID command had put it: a wave of burglaries.

Homes were emptied, cleared out. Where did all their things go? There must have been space somewhere in the city for everything that was stolen. Not everything could join the camel caravan to the Continent.

It was a search, as though in circles.

Bergenhem was used to driving in circles; that's what he did with the portion of his free time that felt more forced, like a compulsion, than it did free. He drove back and forth.

What's going on? he had thought more than once. What's going on with me? What's going on with my life?

I should be happy, what they call happy, or secure, what they call secure.

He worked overtime. He didn't need to, but he might as well have: He drove around town on the thoroughfares and he was paid for it when he was on duty.

Am I someone else? he sometimes thought. Am I on my way to becoming someone else?

Martina's face had become darker and darker. Concerned, maybe.

Ada's face was still bright; she didn't understand, didn't understand yet. That was possibly the worst part: How could he sit here, out on the streets, when his little daughter was there at home?

They hadn't spoken, he and Martina. She had tried; he had not tried.

He continued to chase burglars. He drove to the sea; they weren't there. He could drive down to Hjuvik and just stand there. It wasn't far from home, but it still seemed like the other side of the water.

He could get out of the car and go down to the beach and try to see his reflection in the water if it was calm.

Who am I?

What is it all about?

Who are *you*?

He saw his face from a strange angle. Maybe it was more real.

In the car on the way home, he tried to think back. He had always carried a restlessness within him, as far back as he could remember. But this was more than restlessness, worse than regular restlessness.

Or maybe it's just that I can't live with anyone.

But it's not just that.

Do I need drugs? If I need drugs like *that* I have to talk to a brain doctor first.

Do I need something else?

When he parked in the carport, he didn't know if he wanted to get out of the car or stay in it.

Is this what they call being burned out? he thought.

He heard sounds against the window. He saw small fingers. He saw Ada.

12

In the morning, Winter called Johanna Osvald's number, but she didn't answer; no one answered. There was no answering machine.

It was Saturday. He had the day off. There had been a suspected case of manslaughter or possibly homicide on Tuesday night, but it wasn't a case for him and hardly for any other detective either. The deceased and the perpetrator had both been identified and linked to each other both figuratively and literally, by matrimony among other things. Till death do us part. Some people certainly take that seriously, a detective had said this past week, and then wanted to bite off his tongue when he saw that Halders was sitting there with the remains of his personal grief. But Halders had just said, It doesn't matter, Birkman, I have been like that myself.

Till death do us part.

It was more than just words.

Winter had proposed to Angela and she had said yes: Are you finally going to make an honest woman out of me?

That had been some time ago. She hadn't said anything more, and neither had he.

Now you have to take responsibility, Winter. You can't just talk about things like that. It's a big responsibility, and you have to take it.

He drove south. The sun was on its way up. It was still early morning, and a transparent haze was in the air.

Go ahead, Angela had said. If it will really help. I really hope it helps.

On Monday they had to settle the deal. Okay. He would settle it, clinch it, get the ball rolling. It was just a piece of land. They wouldn't move there right away. He had promised, or whatever it was called . . . offered his decision, a future, yes indeed, the everlasting future up until. Until.

Decisions like this were heavy as stones. You couldn't release them just any way, at any time.

The sun began to hit just right between the roofs of the houses on the

field outside of Askim. He pushed in the CD. It was Angela's disc and it
was Bruce Springsteen. He had given the guy a few chances and he was
worth it. Springsteen was not John Coltrane, and he didn't pretend to be,
either. But Springsteen's melodies were filled with pain and a melancholy
light that Winter appreciated. There was almost always death there, just
like in his life. Springsteen sang nakedly:

Well now, everything dies, baby, that's a fact.

Fact. Dead. That is my job. Sometimes in that order, most often the
opposite.

But maybe everything that dies someday comes back.

Not always as you'd like. But death comes back in a new cloak. But is
it life, then?

Everything floated up, returned in a new guise. Nothing could be
hidden.

Sooner or later.

Even secrets that lie on the bottom of the sea don't stay. He drove past the
swimming beach. All the parking lots were empty and there were no bikes.
He caught a glimpse of the sea, but it was empty too, rolling in toward the
end of the season. Not even on the bottom of the sea. He dialed Johanna
Osvald's number again. No answer. That didn't ease his worry, not enough to
forget it. He felt that he had betrayed something or someone when he hadn't
answered, hadn't answered the first time. At first it had felt good, but now it
didn't feel good. What had he betrayed? His duty? Himself?

For Christ's sake, you don't need to chase after adventure.

The mystery will come to you when it's become a mystery.

Do you chase after crime? Are you calling because you want affirmation?

What's the next step? Are you going to take out an ad in the paper?

Wanted: crime. Contact the eager inspector.

The obsessed inspector.

Everybody's got a hungry heart.

No, no. Come on.

He turned off the impassioned Springsteen on his way from one relationship to the potential other one. He had arrived. The sea rolled gently and heavily like before. He got out of the car, left it in the stand of trees. The grass was still equally green on both sides of the path he and Angela and Elsa had recently made. They had trampled it down as though it would always be there.

He stood at the edge of the beach. He took off his shoes and walked into the water, which was cold but became warm. He turned around and looked across the field. He closed his eyes and saw the house; it could be standing there within a year, maybe even sooner. Would he be happy there? Here. What would it involve, living a life so close to the sea? Could it involve anything other than something positive?

He turned toward the water again. He thought of the conversation he'd had in his office with Johanna Osvald. She had lived close to the sea, much closer than he would ever get. Her entire family. Not just close to the sea, on the sea. The sea had been their life, was their life. Life and death. Death was real in a different way for fishing families; he thought he understood that much. A working life of hazards, a life of worry for those who stayed home.

It must have been very dangerous before. The war. The mine barriers, the U-boats, the destroyers, the coast guard. The storms, the waves, the collisions, the crush injuries, the pressure from all directions. It must have been a very great pressure. How did they handle it?

The colleagues. What sort of life did they live together?

He had listened to Johanna Osvald and he started to understand what she had really been talking about. Behind her words there was an unease that he had not been able to understand but that he thought of now. A fear that had been passed down from generation to generation to generation.

He sat down in the sand, which was still warm after the summer. He heard two seagulls laughing at some inside joke. He could see them now, on approach to *his* land, soon to be his land. Were they part of the deal? Was that what they were having such a damn good time about? Now they were laughing again, belly-landing elegantly on the path, taking off again, rattling out another laugh in his direction, returning to the winds in the bay and gliding out toward the sea. He followed them with his gaze until they disappeared and he could see only the contours of the islands in the southern archipelago. He got out his phone again and called right across the bay to those islands, but no one answered this time either.

Johanna had been the most beautiful person he had seen up to then. She was dark like no one else, as though she came from a different group of people, which was of course true in a way.

He had met her brother, but he was already on his way out to sea in earnest. His name was Erik, too.

Johanna hadn't mentioned him when she came to see Winter.

He and Erik had drunk a beer down at Brännö pier one time, but they never went up to join the dancing. They had spoken, but Winter didn't remember about what. He remembered that Erik hadn't cursed. He remembered that he'd talked to Johanna about it. No one on the islands cursed, ever. There were no curses there.

Life could be hard, but it wasn't necessary to reinforce that fact with words.

He remembered that the Mission Covenant Church was important for the people on the islands, and it became more important the closer they lived to the open sea. Vrångö farthest out. And Donsö. Donsö in particular, she had said, and laughed a laugh that glimmered like the crests of waves around them where they lay on the cliffs on southern Styrsö, looking out over the more God-fearing island on the other side of the sound.

Then she had sat atop him and started to move, slowly, and then faster and faster. The church may have guided her life as well, but she was still just a person, sinful like him.

In the car on the way home his phone suddenly blared from its place on the dash.

"Yes?"

Möllerström again, always Möllerström.

"She called again. You obviously haven't contacted her."

"I haven't done anything *but*!"

"Okay."

"Are you in the office?" asked Winter.

"Where else?" said Möllerström.

"Can she be reached at this number I got before?"

"Yes."

"Thanks, Janne. And take a vacation now."

Möllerström hung up without saying anything more. Winter called again, a number he now thought he would never forget. She answered after the first ring.

13

He came back with trembling hands.
He prayed.

Jesus!

Outside, a child biked by. He went to the window. There was a wind from the sea. The wind tugged at the child's hair, which was black. There were no blond children here. He had thought about that. No blue eyes, no blond hair. Not like on the other side. Why was it like that? It was the same sky, the same sea.

The other place was only a night and a day away, in navigable weather. Maybe it went even faster now. No minefields.

He could see a ferry now and then, when the hard winds forced the vessels closer to land. They were too far north, sometimes too far south. He didn't know where they were going, and he didn't care.

He was finished with the sea.

He lived next to it, but never on it, or off it, never again.

He had been on board when the trawler went under. He carried what had happened with him. What he himself had done. His guilt. The thing that could never be forgiven. He had *been there.* He knew more than anyone else.

There was no one else left.

Jesus had not been able to forgive him.

But 'tis strange:
And oftentimes, to win us to our harm,
The instruments of darkness tell us truths,
Win us with honest trifles, to betray's
In deepest consequence.

* * *

He felt the sea in his face as he walked across the breakwater. He had salt in his face that would never leave his skin. What hit his face now didn't stick, but it wasn't because he washed it away. The wind took it.

He had sores all over his body.

The eczema from the oilcloth had dried and turned into scars all over his body, like patterns.

Like a map of his life at sea. Yes.

He sometimes rubbed his hand across his shoulders and legs. It was in the dark, as if he were blind and could follow his life on his body with his finger. His memories were scars. The scars were soft and smooth under his fingers, and he could imagine that all these scars were the only soft parts of his body. But there were many. His body was more soft than it was hard, but for the wrong reasons. He had a young man's body, but for the wrong reason.

It shouldn't be him. Not him, living an old man's life.

Jesus, *Jesus*!

He stayed standing there and waited for the sun to go down, and it did as the child biked by again; a boy, he lived in the house by the steps and there were always clothes hanging from the line, and he could see a young woman come out and hang the wash, or take it down, and her hair was black, like the boy's, and there was a transparent pallor to her face, which was the sea's fault. The sea marked these people, shaped their forms. Farther up, all the way up in the north, in Thurso, Wick, people were bent like dwarf birches on a mountain, black, pale, blown to pieces, blown through.

He turned in toward the room at the same time as the sun disappeared over to other continents. The room was exactly as dark as he wanted it. He went to one of the easy chairs and sat down and drank again from the whisky that waited in the glass. It was one of the cheap kinds.

He looked around with the liquor still in his mouth. He swallowed.

No. I won't leave this.

It was the last time.

I will stay here.

Present fears
Are less than horrible imaginings:
My thought, whose murder yet is but fantastical . . .

He ran his hand over his right arm; his finger slid across the smooth skin that had been dead for so many years now. There was no life in most of his skin, only a surface that was silky and at the same time, when he pressed a little harder, completely hard, hard as stone.

He reached for his weapon.

He took care of it.

She had said that his violence hadn't changed. Hadn't lessened.

At the Three Kings the windows bulged from the wind, which was coming in from the northwest now. He felt the draft where he was sitting at the bar. He might have said something to the woman who was standing there as though petrified, but she didn't answer, didn't hear.

Sometimes she heard. He had waited to tell her things. He knew that he would need her later.

The door opened. The woman stirred. He heard a voice. Someone sat down beside him.

"Whisky, please."

"Blended or malt?"

"Just give me whatever—"

He heard the stranger interrupt himself.

"—whatever you fancy."

"Well, I don't fancy whisky."

"Give me a . . . Highland Park," said the stranger, nodding toward the shelves of bottles.

The woman turned around and took down a wide-bottomed bottle and poured it into a glass and put it in front of the stranger. She spoke her dialect, which some people considered to be a miserable gibberish:

"This's from Orkney, do y'know?" she said.

"No."

"I thought y'knew," she said.

The stranger drank. The woman had stiffened again. The stranger took the glass from his mouth and turned to him and lifted it an inch or so. The stranger seemed to gaze out the window. There was nothing outside. Now the stranger moved his gaze. He could see this from the corner of his eye.

Someone was watching him.

He turned his head toward the man who was sitting there. He nodded without saying anything.

The stranger was younger than he was, but he wasn't a young man. There was a peculiar look in his eyes. There were lines on his face. The glass in his hand shook. He set it down and hastily wiped his mouth.

The woman had walked away from the bar.

I will have to stop coming here, he thought. Why do I come here?

I know why.

"Are you from around here?" asked the stranger.

14

Winter made it onto the ferry, the *Silvertärnan,* which left Saltholmen at 10:20. His Mercedes was on the east side of the marina, very obviously illegally parked, with the police sign in the windshield.

Someone had once broken into his Merc and stolen the sign. He had looked for it for a long time.

He bought a cup of tea as they traveled out. The sun was alone in the sky. The cliffs were illuminated in gray, in silver. The path out was covered in cliffs, stone. All over, piles of stone that were islands, all the way to the open sea.

Johanna Osvald was waiting on the quay at Donsö. He recognized her there. Time had passed, but she was standing in a place that could have been the same as it was then.

The community behind her climbed upward. Part of it seemed to be cut out of stone. There were many houses, some large, some built from expensive wood. He knew that the shipping industry was big on the island; it had given rise to wealth. The fishing fleet had been big here, but he didn't see many trawlers in the harbor now. But of course they wouldn't be here; they would be out at sea. He saw a modern trawler with two hangers or whatever they were called, he didn't know, mounts for trawls on the stern. The boat was wide, heavy, big, blue. GG 381 MAGDALENA was painted on the prow. He saw a man who seemed to be looking at him, his hand cupped over his eyes, below his cap.

He saw a cross on the gable of a house. Religiousness had been widespread on Donsö, he remembered that. The church was full. That had hardly changed.

People place their lives in God's hands. His will be done.

Johanna raised her hand in greeting. He stood in the prow of the *Silvertärnan* and lifted his arm. People started to get off the boat in front of him. A small gang of boys waited by their bikes, waiting for nothing as usual. Seagulls circled above the harbor, hunting for fish waste. It smelled like innards, fish, oil, fish oil, gas, seaweed, tar, everything that no sea in the world could wash away the smell of.

She had not smelled like fish oil. He had joked about it once on the cliffs. Do country girls smell like manure? she had asked with the sharp part of her tongue.

"You weren't easy to get hold of," he said on the quay.

"You're one to talk," she answered.

They had made a quick agreement over the phone a bit ago.

They sat on the first bench they saw.

Her father had still not been found.

"I think something has happened to him," she said. "Dad would have called by this time." She looked at him. "He obviously would have by now, right?"

"You know him; I don't. You know best."

"I know it," she said.

"I'll put one out on him," said Winter. "A description, I mean. We'll put out an international description via Interpol."

"Yes."

"I spoke with my colleague in London. The Scottish one, from the Inverness area. He may be able to help."

"How?"

"He knows people up there."

She didn't answer. She seemed to look away across the water.

"Well . . . ," said Winter.

"Well what?"

"There's probably not much more I can—"

"I wanted you to come out here," she said.

"What do you mean?"

"There's something that I don't understand here. That I've never understood. I have to talk about it with you. That's why I wanted you to come over."

"What is it?" said Winter.

"That I don't understand?" She looked up. "It has to do with all of this. With Grandpa's disappearance, first of all, with everything that happ—"

"Well, hello there."

The voice came out of nowhere. Winter looked up, and at first he couldn't see anything against the light.

He remembered the voice. And the dialect. The archipelago dialect: the sharp intonation, the indifference to consonants, to indefinite articles—they were interchangeable and so on, and so on, almost like the rolling sea, like the waves themselves. An international sea-speak that was part of the coastal regions all over the North Sea. This island was a few miles from the city of Gothenburg, but there could have been continents between them.

"'Sben a while," said the voice, which still didn't have a face.

Winter got up. The sun disappeared. The face became visible.

"Well, hi," said Winter.

"'Sben a while," repeated the man, who was about his age. Osvald. Erik Osvald. He was as tall as Winter. Osvald offered a hand. He was wearing a black cap and work clothes. Winter recognized him as the man who seemed to be studying him from the trawler as the *Silvertärnan* came into the harbor.

Johanna had also gotten up.

"This'n't good, all this," said Osvald. Winter could sense a distance in the man's dialect, as though he wanted to emphasize something. His sister didn't speak so . . . artfully. No. Not that. She spoke as though she lived on land. Her brother lived at sea.

Winter nodded, as though he completely understood what Osvald meant.

"We ha'n't heard nothing," said Osvald.

"I know," said Winter.

"This'n't like'm," said Osvald.

"Sorry?"

"This isn't like him," translated his sister. Winter might have seen a weak smile in the corner of her mouth. "Dad, he means. Not like him. Not to call. But I've told you that."

"'N't like'm," repeated Osvald, and now Winter realized that he was laying it on thick, extra thick. He just didn't understand why. The guy was as far from a village yokel as he could be.

Johanna nodded past Winter, toward the blue trawler fifty yards away. Winter could see the name again, MAGDALENA.

"Erik has coffee ready in the mess," she said.

Osvald seemed to laugh suddenly, and he turned around and walked toward the boat.

"Did the thing about the coffee come as a surprise to him?" said Winter to Johanna.

"Grandpa was a farmer's son from Hisingen," said Osvald, pouring the coffee. They were sitting in the mess, which was as modern as could be, wooden floors, woodwork on the walls. They left their shoes above deck, in the little hall inside the bridge. Osvald's pronunciation was different now, as though he had wanted to show something, or prove something, earlier.

He had been out of coffee, but he returned from the store with more after five minutes. He no longer looked surprised.

"They were fishermen, too," said Osvald. "They caught sprat and horse mackerel, which they sold to the people on Donsö for longline fishing, which was a tradition here."

"Hooks?" said Winter.

"Exactly," said Osvald, with surprise in his voice. "You know this stuff."

"No. But I heard about longline fishing when we had the house on Styrsö."

Osvald drank his coffee and Winter noticed how strong it was when he drank too. He could have used a knife and fork for it. He would lose face if he asked for milk.

"Grandpa found a woman here, or a girl, I guess you could say, and it went fast," said Johanna. "He came here to work on a trawler. He'd gotten in contact with a skipper."

"He was quite young," said Winter.

"For what?" said Osvald.

"To get married and have kids," said Winter.

Neither sibling answered. But then it wasn't a question. Maybe there was nothing strange about it. Those who lived here wanted to begin life immediately, and continue it.

And to disappear, thought Winter. Quite young to disappear. He had his young family, a son, and another son on the way.

"He had two brothers," said Johanna. "John had."

"What?" said Winter.

"Two brothers came along," she said. "Bertil and Egon. They were on the same boat."

"The same boat? The same boat that disappeared?"

"One of them came back," said Osvald. "Bertil."

"Explain," said Winter.

The Osvald brothers were a few of the people who dared to cross the sea during the beginning of the war. John Osvald was the youngest. The trawlers that could make it over to England and Scotland and unload— there was a fortune to be had. The fish were there; the harbors were farther west. It was a world at war.

Many "passed on," as Osvald put it, "but they were propelled by the money."

A fixed price was put on fish in the beginning of the war. It turned out that the price was extremely high.

"But the other price was even higher," said Johanna.

Winter nodded. The other price was death.

"The ones who made it became rich," said Osvald. "People here were able to build new houses with all the most modern things you can imagine, and when the workmen left the house, everything was paid for! With taxed money."

"The ones who came back," said Johanna.

"But your grandpa didn't come back," said Winter. "What happened?"

He heard the boat move. It was big, bigger than he'd thought a trawler could be, more modern. It must have been very expensive. It must have weighed several hundred tons, have thousands in horsepower. There were mounts for two trawls in the stern. Osvald had seen his glance, and he'd said that this was a twin rigger. He sounded proud.

"*Marino* was out fishing in the North Sea, and they weren't on their way west just then, but the Germans came up from the south and they decided to get out, and fast," said Osvald.

"*Marino?*"

"That's what the trawler was called."

Marino. Not Marina, not a woman's name, like Magdalena.

"How many people were on board?" asked Winter.

"Eight men, normally," said Osvald. "That was the usual number."

"How many are on this boat?"

"Four."

"They had twice as many? On a trawler that was half as big?"

Osvald nodded.

"How was that?"

"Well, they all lived in the forecastle, and it was damp and wet. There were no personal berths like here." He nodded toward a closed door that led to the sleeping hall. "So they couldn't manage to do what we do now. The weather was a big problem, for example, but it isn't anymore."

"Why not?"

"You're sitting on a boat that can handle any weather at all," said Osvald.

"Can you manage to take care of it yourself?" asked Winter. "Could you be alone on it?"

Osvald nodded without saying anything.

"There weren't eight of them that time," said Johanna. "It wasn't fully manned."

Her brother turned to her.

"Did you forget, Erik? There were five of them."

"Yes, right."

She looked at Winter.

"That was everyone who wanted to come along on the last crossing from Donsö. Everyone who would dare."

"The three brothers and two other men," said Winter.

"Yes."

"Where are they now?"

He knew what had happened to the brothers. Egon had gone under with the boat, along with John. Bertil came back and died on Donsö, in modern times.

"Frans Karlsson disappeared too," said Johanna. "That's what we were told by Arne, Arne Algotsson. He came back with Bertil."

"Arne Algotsson?"

"He lives here on the island. He was along with them."

"Oh?"

"But he is hopelessly senile," said Osvald.

"Is he?"

"He forgets his thoughts before he thinks them," said Osvald with a weak smile. "If he even has any." He rubbed his hand over his chin, and the rasp of two days' stubble was audible. "In that condition, he probably doesn't think at all."

The *Marino* had fled from the German destroyers, through the minefields, to the Scottish coast.

"They came to Aberdeen, and it wasn't the first time, but this time they didn't have very much fish along," said Osvald.

"And they weren't from there," said Johanna.

"It was too dangerous," said her brother.

"So they had to stay there," said Johanna.

"In Aberdeen?"

"At first. Then they went up to Peterhead and it became like their home harbor during that year. They went out sometimes, of course."

"But never very far?"

"Well, they probably went around the point at Fraserburgh sometimes, and a bit to the west into the strait, in toward Inverness, I think."

"Inverness?" said Winter, looking at Johanna.

"Yes. Not all the way in, if Arne could be believed before he completely lost his memory. But into the strait there, Firth something."

Winter nodded.

"And then they went to Iceland a few times," said Osvald. "That was pretty bold."

"They were crazy," said Johanna.

"Up to Iceland?"

"The fishing grounds off of the south coast of Iceland," said Osvald. "Witch flounder. They got a very good price for them down in Scotland."

"But still," said Johanna.

"It was on their way home from one of those trips that it happened," said Osvald.

There was no wind when Winter came up on the bridge. The *Magdalena* wasn't moving.

"Do you want to take a look in the pilothouse?" asked Osvald.

Winter saw screens everywhere, telephones, faxes, technology, lamps, switches.

"Looks more or less like dispatch at the central police building," he said.

"Most of it is to keep an eye on the coast guard," said Osvald, smiling. "Especially the Norwegians."

Winter nodded and smiled back.

"That's the big threat to the fishing industry today," said Osvald. "We have so many borders across the sea today, there are so many lines out in the sea today. You can't cross the zones, but lots of times the fish swim all over the place, crossing borders, and it's frustrating, you know, if you know that there's fish a nautical mile away and people from other countries are sitting there pulling them up while we Swedes are spinning our wheels at the border."

Osvald did something with one of the levers on the dashboard. Winter heard a sound like a winch.

"And then it's tempting to go over to that side, and then you have to turn off the satellite transmitter," said Osvald. He looked at Winter. "You understand?"

Winter nodded.

"You won't say anything to them, right?"

"The Norwegian Coast Guard? I don't have any contacts there," said Winter.

"They're not nice," said Osvald, smiling again. "Three inspectors can suddenly be standing in the pilothouse. Their mother ship, a big coast guard boat, it's seven nautical miles away because they know that all fishing boats have a range of six nautical miles on their radar, and they've driven a little dinghy up from the back at thirty knots, and they've snuck up alongside and snuck up on the deck and rushed into the pilothouse. It's happened to us twice!"

"Not nice," said Winter.

"And in addition, he wanted fillet of cod for dinner," said Osvald.

"What did you do?" asked Winter.

"We gave him pork tenderloin," said Osvald. "Who can afford to serve fish these days?"

Erik Osvald was proud of his twin rigger. He shared ownership of it with two other fishermen from Donsö. Three hundred and twenty tons gross weight; 1,300 horsepower.

They had left the pilothouse. Osvald had told him about the wireless sensors on the trawls, which could monitor everything down there: the currents, the bottom, things that were in the way. He described the automatic controls, the regulators, how the winches were operated. The hydraulics.

They stood on the quarterdeck, the work deck. It was dry, dry under the September sun. Osvald said something that Winter would remember and return to when so much more had happened. When he knew more.

"It's always a competition," said Osvald. "At sea. And here."

"What do you mean?"

"When my grandfather came here and started fishing, when he and his brothers tried to buy their own boat—and they did it quickly—it wasn't accepted. They didn't accept it. Not here on the island. They weren't supposed to be boat owners. They were supposed to be the serving class. We, our family, were supposed to continue as the serving class." Osvald looked at Winter. "My grandfather changed all that."

"And you're still competing," said Winter.

"Always," said Osvald. "It's always a competition out there, between boats, across zones, and it's always been a competition here on the island. Between people."

"Mmhmm."

Winter could see the entrance to the harbor, and the bridge over to Styrsö. A ferry traveled out, on its way south to Vrångö, the last island. He hadn't been there in years. After Vrångö there was only the sea.

"For my part, I'm also competing with the shipowners here," said Osvald. "The shipping industry. It's immense here on Donsö. It turns over a billion per year. Donsö is the home harbor for over fifteen percent of the Swedish merchant fleet. Did you know that?"

"No."

"They're my old friends," said Osvald, "the shipowners and officers of those vessels are my age."

"I understand," said Winter.

Erik Osvald changed when he discussed the competition. The Osvald family had come from nothing and become something. Winter understood that. It meant a lot to Osvald. How much? Winter could see that Osvald's thoughts were lingering on the rivalry, the competition. Maybe money. Maybe great risks to attain success, riches.

What risks had Erik Osvald been prepared to take to attain his position, here on the island and out at sea? Winter wondered. Beyond the risk of being out on the great sea. To expose oneself to solitude—or whatever happened out there. It was a lonely life, an abnormal life. People had gone crazy at sea.

"You hav'ta hold your own against that lot and get th' best people for fishin' instead," said Osvald.

15

Aneta Djanali opened two drawers in the kitchen. There was nothing there. She saw herself sitting at the kitchen table that wasn't there now, on a chair that existed somewhere, but not there. Drinking coffee made by a stranger. Good God.

"What happens now?" said Sigge Lindsten.

"Report of theft," she said.

He let out a gruff laugh.

"How will you find the people who did it?"

"I remember their faces," she said.

"And their names," said Lindsten, and she heard a few bars of the gruff laugh again.

"You seem to think this is funnier than I do," she said.

"Well, there *is* something comical about it."

"Does Anette think so too?"

"We don't know, because we haven't asked her, have we?" Lindsten remained standing in the doorway. "She doesn't know that it's happened, does she?"

"I don't think she'll laugh when she finds out."

"Don't say that, don't say that."

Aneta looked at him.

"New start," he said. "This way there are no reminders of him."

"Him? Forsblad?"

"Who else?"

"That might be where they are," she said.

"Sorry?"

"At Forsblad's house. That might be where the stolen goods are. The furniture. Her things."

"The question is just where that devil is himself," said Lindsten. "Do you have an address for him?"

Aneta shook her head.

"Lots of unknowns here," said Lindsten.

"What kind of work do you do, Mr. Lindsten?"

"Excuse me?"

"What is your job?"

"Does it matter?"

"Don't you want to answer the question?"

"Answer . . . of course I can answer." He stepped into the kitchen, the naked kitchen. Their voices were loud in that particular way of rooms without furniture, carpets, lamps, pictures, decorations, household things, knickknacks, food, fruit bowls, radios, TVs, appliances, clothes, shoes, pets.

Everything was naked.

It is extra naked here, she thought. I have been inside a lot of empty places, but never one like this, never this way.

"Traveling," said Lindsten.

After a few seconds she got it.

"What does that involve?"

"Traveling? That you travel and sell things." His words echoed in the kitchen, which had ugly marks on the walls from things that had hung there.

Marks like bullet holes. She had been inside homes where she'd known what kind of holes they were. Others had been there, on their way in or out. Some of them alive, some not. Family affairs. Most often they were family affairs. There was no refuge among the near and dear. She must never forget that. All police knew it. Always start with the nearest, the innermost circle. Often that was enough. Unfortunately, that was enough. It was good for preliminary investigations, but it wasn't good if you looked at it in a different way.

You shouldn't do that. How could you work if you did?

Sigge Lindsten traveled and sold things. She would ask him what he sold, but not right now.

"Forsblad must have a job, anyway," she said.

"Yes. He has a job, but no address. That's pretty unusual, isn't it?"

Aneta stopped Hans Forsblad in the hall. He was carrying three binders. He had company.

"Do you have a minute?"

He looked at his watch as though he were starting a countdown. He looked at his companion, a woman.

"It's already been ten seconds," he said. The woman beside him smiled but looked uncertain. She looked at Aneta. Aneta had the urge to knock the binders out of Forsblad's hands.

"Is there somewhere we can go?" she asked calmly.

He seemed to consider this; he looked at his companion again and then gestured toward one of the doors far along the left side of the hall.

They walked over the marble tiles.

"I don't have much more than this one minute," he said.

He showed her into a conference room that didn't have windows. That must be so the decisions are made quickly, she thought. No one can stand being in a room without windows.

He showed her to a chair, but she preferred to stand.

"When did you last speak with Anette?" she asked.

"No idea."

"What does that mean?"

"That I don't remember."

"Try to think back."

He looked like he was thinking back. The binders were on the table now. There was nothing written on their spines.

"A while ago," he said, taking a step closer; she recoiled, an automatic movement.

"God, take it easy," he said.

"What did you talk about, then?"

"Oh, the usual."

"And that was . . . ?"

"Oh, that it wasn't working out."

He looked at his binders as he spoke and reached for one of them. There's something that works, she thought. Papers in binders always work. This is a courthouse, and binders are useful here. This man is some sort of lawyer, and he is about to depart.

"She has things that are mine, and I need them," he said. "As a matter of fact." He picked up his binders. "Not even you can keep me from them."

I'll explain and then we'll see what happens, thought Aneta.

"There's someone else who has kept you from them," she said.

"Uh, what? What do you mean?"

She told him about the empty apartment. She hadn't said anything about the theft when they were standing in the empty rooms. She didn't tell him that she had met the people who cleaned it out.

"Oh, my," said Forsblad.

"We're grateful for any help," said Aneta.

"Of course. But what can I do?"

"You can start by telling me where you live now."

"What does that have to do with anything?"

She didn't answer. He had put down the binders again. *Maybe I should look inside them. He might have an inventory of everything that was taken from Anette's apartment.*

"Oh, come on! Would I have stolen my own furniture?" He smiled, that peculiar smile that made her feel afraid. "Come on!"

"I asked for your address," she said.

"I don't have an address," he said.

"Are you sleeping under bridges?" She looked at his suit. If he'd slept in it, it must have been in a pants press. The wrinkles were gone. No stones were that smooth.

He smiled again.

"I don't need to give you my address," he said.

"You just said you don't have one."

"And that's why I can't give you one."

"This is a preliminary investigation," she said. "You know very well that the general public is obligated to cooperate with the police. You of all people should know that."

"Preliminary investigation of what?" he asked.

"If you play dumb one more time, we'll have to continue this conversation in a different room," she said.

"That was a threat."

Aneta sighed, barely audibly, and took her phone out of the inner pocket of her light jacket.

"Okay, okay, I'm living with a girl." He licked his lips. She saw that his lower lip had split at one corner. "At the moment, I mean. But it has—"

"The address," she said.

"There's no one there now."

He smiled again, the frightening smile.

Give me strength, she thought. One of the gods from home.

Hans Forsblad was still smiling, or maybe it was her imagination.

"For the last time," she said.

"There was no one there," she said. "But the doorknob was still warm."

Fredrik Halders laughed out loud.

"I think it's your sense of humor I appreciate the most," he said.

"And aside from that? What do you like about me aside from that?"

He looked around.

"The children can hear," he said.

"They're at your house, Fredrik. It's on the other side of the city."

He removed his feet from the edge of the sofa and heaved himself up. He drank some beer from his glass. He looked at her over the edge of the glass.

"We could be sitting there now," he said.

"But then the children would have heard, right, Fredrik?"

"I would have watched what I said in that case," he said.

"Mmhmm."

"What does that mean, *Mmhmm*? What is that supposed to mean?"

"I was just imagining the combination of Fredrik Halders and watching what you say," she said, smiling.

He was quiet and took another drink, as though he were thinking about what words he would choose.

"You know what I mean, Aneta."

"Fredrik."

"You know what I want. What I think."

"I know," she said gently.

He shook the beer can. He got up.

"Do you want more wine?"

She shook her head.

"I'm going to get another beer."

"All joking aside," said Halders, "you have to drop it."

She didn't answer. She couldn't see anything under the blanket, but she could hear his voice from the other side. The voice from the other side. She giggled, to some extent because of the wine; she'd had another glass.

"It could be dangerous," he said. She felt him pull the blanket off her head. "Are you listening, Aneta? Are you listening?"

She felt the light from the lamp on the nightstand in her eyes; she blinked. She saw his face, which was black against the light, black like a black African's. Someone who didn't know him might think he was dangerous. Some who did know him still thought he was. That hadn't always been good.

"You don't exactly have anything to work with, and a guy like Forsblad can be trouble in that case."

"What do you mean?"

She pulled down the blanket and wrapped herself in it. She heard the music Fredrik was putting on, James Carr, which he'd brought with him. "The Dark End of the Street," forty-year-old soul from the South, at the dark end of the street, that's where we always meet.

"The way you describe him, he sounds like a psychopath. If he gets it into his head that you're after him for no reason, it could get nasty."

"Sure, for him."

"For you, Aneta."

"It doesn't matter, does it? If he's a psychopath, he'll get it into his head that I'm after him whether he sees a reason or not, won't he?"

Halders didn't answer.

"Won't he?" said Aneta.

"Don't be so fucking smart, now," he said. He ruffled her hair. "Listen to what I'm saying, even if I'm putting it more awkwardly than you can accept."

She sat up straighter. The blanket fell. She put her arms around her shoulders and across her breasts, as though she were freezing.

"There's something dangerous about him," she said. "I can feel it. I can see it."

"Yes, that's what I'm saying."

"But don't you understand? He's dangerous to *her*. He's going to go after her again."

"You don't know that."

"Oh, yes I do."

Halders got up and went over to the CD player, which had become silent. She heard him searching through the discs, ungraceful as always.

She heard the rhythm and recognized it, of course, and the singer's voice. It was her CD, after all. Gabin Dabiré. *Afriki Djamana: Music from Burkina Faso. Afriki Djamana* reminded him of her.

The music moved like a caravan through the desert, swaying, stepping and sinking. The song was called "Sénégal," and it was about longing, maybe longing for the sea to the west.

"He's not going to leave her alone," said Aneta.

"What? Who?"

"Forsblad, of course. He can't accept that she doesn't want him."

"But he's already living with someone else."

"Yeah, so he says."

"Let him say so, then. Even if it's not true, maybe it will help him."

"How so?"

"I'm not a psychopath," said Halders. "I don't know how he thinks, but I can imagine—"

"It's just more lies," interrupted Aneta.

"I'm not a psychologist either, but if he's creating a world for himself where he thinks that he's with a new woman, maybe it's a good thing."

"A new woman he can beat?"

Halders didn't answer.

"The guy is dangerous," said Aneta. "We do happen to agree on that, you know."

"Leave it," said Halders. "Leave him and her and that entire family, whether it exists or not."

She didn't say anything.

"And the furniture." Halders smiled.

"I haven't even met Anette, not really," mumbled Aneta, but Halders heard. "She hasn't ever reported any assault herself," she said, and she heard him sigh. "But the neighbors called. Several times. And the woman in the same stairwell saw injuries on her face."

"Aneta. She doesn't live there anymore. *He* doesn't live there anymore. She lives at home, safe with her parents. He might be living with a new woman. Maybe he's going after her, too, and in that case we'll nab him right away. But now ca—"

"Do you know how many of these conversations you and I have had while there are new violent crimes happening?" she said. "Assault? While we, who are supposed to prevent crime, arrive at the conclusion that there's no danger and hardly any reason to prevent this particular threat or crime, it happens. It happens again."

"Do you want anything else to drink?"

"Are you listening to what I'm saying?"

"I'm listening."

"Well, answer then, Fredrik."

"I just don't know what we can do in a situation like this," he said, turning to her and reaching for her arm. "We actually can't bring him in, not now."

"We could keep him under surveillance."

"Who would do that?" said Halders.

"Me."

"Come off it. You'd be the last one."

"Someone else, then. This isn't personal, if that's what you think."

"Really?"

"Not personal in that way."

"You know just as well as I do that Winter would never put people on something like this," said Halders.

"It's preventative. Erik is all for prevention."

"He's also for realism."

"What is more realistic than a battered woman?"

"What do you want me to say to that, Aneta?"

"I don't know, Fredrik."

"And even if Winter gave the okay, Birgersson would say no."

"Birgersson? Is he still around? I haven't seen him in years."

"That's how he wants it," said Halders.

Aneta got up and walked across the room.

"I'm going to take a shower," she said.

Halders had made grilled sandwiches. She was still warm from the hot shower, relaxed, a bit comfortably numb after all of her thoughts earlier today. "I couldn't find pineapple," he said, "there was cheese and ham and mustard, but no pineapple."

"You aren't *required* to have pineapple on a warm sandwich, Fredrik."

"Oh, really? Great. I was feeling like a failure there for a minute."

"You've done well, Fredrik."

"A cup of tea?" He held out the pot like the servant of a countess

"You changed the disc," she said, meaning the music.

"I will never cease to be amazed at all the guitars you collect," he said, and she listened and understood what he meant when the guitar solo in "Comfortably Numb" arrived.

"I think he knows the people who stole that whole apartment," she said.

"Oh, Aneta, please."

"Who else would get the idea to do it? How did they get in?"

"Now drink your tea and relax for a minute."

"Answer me. They just went in."

"And then out."

"Exactly."

"I don't think he wants that crap," said Halders.

"I think the exact opposite," said Aneta. "If he can't own her, he can at least own everything that is hers."

Halders didn't answer.

"You're not answering."

"I didn't realize it was a question."

"Come *on,* Fredrik!"

"That analysis seems, well, a little too homemade, if you want an honest opinion. And there's another snag."

"What?"

"Well, even if that crazy Forsblad guy is batshit insane, that doesn't necessarily mean that the rest of the world is, does it? He had to convince those two characters you met that the apartment had to be emptied."

"Like they needed a reason? Are you kidding? Do you mean that today, in this country, it's difficult to get two criminal henchmen to empty an apartment? There are always people for sale who will do anything you need."

"Can people really be so awful?" said Halders.

"Don't joke away your naïveté, Fredrik."

"Do you know what, Aneta," said Halders, reaching for the teapot again. "There is no man born of a woman who can beat you in a debate."

"Debate? Are we having a debate?"

*   *   *

Bergenhem walked across Sveaplan with a strong wind at his back. A sheet of newspaper flew in front of the neighborhood store.

The houses around the square looked black in the twilight. A streetcar passed to the right, a cold yellow light. Two magpies flapped up in front of him when he pushed the button next to the nameplate. He heard a distant answer.

It was just like last time.

But this time he wasn't here on duty.

He didn't know why he was standing here.

"I'm looking for Krister Peters. It's Lars Bergenhem."

"Who?"

"Lars Bergenhem. I was here last year, from the county CID."

He didn't get an answer, but the door buzzed and he opened it.

He went up the stairs. He rang the bell. The door was opened after the second ring. The man was Bergenhem's age.

His dark hair hung down on his forehead just as it had last time. It looked as deliberate now as it had then. His face was unshaven now, as it had been then. Peters was wearing a white undershirt now, as he had then; it shone against his tanned and muscular body.

"Hi," said Peters. "You came back."

"I can have that whisky now," said Bergenhem.

Bergenhem had worked on the investigation of a series of assaults. A friend of Krister Peters's, Jens Book, had been attacked and seriously injured near Peters's home.

Bergenhem had visited Peters and questioned him. Peters was innocent. Peters had offered him malt whisky. Bergenhem had declined.

"I'll pass this time," Bergenhem had said. "I have the car and I have to go right home when I'm done."

"You're missing a good Springbank," Peters had said.

"Maybe there will be another time," Bergenhem had said.

"Maybe," Peters had said.

Peters turned his back to Bergenhem and went into the apartment. Bergenhem followed Peters, who sat down on his dark gray sofa. Magazines lay on a low glass table. Three glasses and a bottle stood to the right of the magazines. Bergenhem sat in an easy chair that had the same covering as the sofa.

"How are things?" said Peters.

"Not so good," said Bergenhem.

"Do you feel like you need someone to talk to?"

"Yes."

"Then you've come to the right place," said Peters.

"Everything is so confusing," said Bergenhem.

16

It was still daylight on Donsö. Winter stood on the *Magdalena*'s quarterdeck. The sun was starting to burn low over the sea. It would soon disappear. Does the sun go out when it goes down in the water? Elsa had asked last summer, when they had been swimming down in Vallda Sandö and lingered there for a long time. It was a good question.

"There must be a lot of sunsets like that out at sea," Winter said to Erik Osvald, standing beside him.

"Well, we don't exactly sit there applauding a sunset," answered Osvald.

"But you must see the beauty in it."

"Yes . . . ," answered Osvald, and Winter understood that the weather and sun and rain and hours of the day and nature's beauty were something different for Osvald than they were for him, for everyone who lived on land.

Osvald watched the sun, which was in the process of sinking.

"Soon it will be a season when you can miss the light," he said in the twilight. "Soon we'll have to have lights on from three in the afternoon to ten in the morning." He looked at Winter. "And in the summer we complain that the sun stings our eyes at four in the morning."

Winter nodded. Everything must be so much sharper out there.

"But there's really no day at sea, and no night."

Winter waited for him to continue. The sun was gone.

"There's no day, there's no night," repeated Osvald.

It sounded like poetry. Maybe it was poetry. Work and everyday life make up poetry because everything unessential has been scrubbed away.

Osvald looked at him again, back in the reality of his job.

"We never really have any morning or any night like this out there, you know. Days and nights go on; every five or six hours the trawl has to come up."

"No matter the weather?" asked Winter.

Osvald squinted at him. He had fine lines all over his face; none were longer or wider than the others. He had a tan that would never disappear when it was dark between three and ten. The slits of his eyes were blue. At that moment, Winter wondered what Osvald thought about when he was out on the lonely sea. What did he think in a storm?

"The weather isn't a big problem for us these days," said Osvald, nodding as though to emphasize his words. "Before, boats went under in storms." He looked out across the sea again. "Or were blown up by mines . . . ," he said, as though to himself. He gave Winter a quick glance again. "Last fall we had very bad weather, but there were only two nights we didn't fish because of a storm. If the wind is over forty-five miles per hour we don't put out the trawl." He gave Winter a smile. "At least not if the bottom is bad. It's not so good if it gets caught when it's forty-five miles an hour."

He turned around to see if his sister was standing there. But Johanna had excused herself for a second and climbed down the ladder off the boat and gone in among the houses, which came almost up to the quay.

"We're a little split on the weather, of course," said Osvald. "If it's bad weather it's good pay. There might not be any others who will risk going out. And there's no fisherman yet who lost by betting on a storm! Prices go up after a storm. And the storm stirs up the stew on the bottom, too. Storms are good for the sea."

The storm stirs up the stew, thought Winter. That's true. Everything is moved around, comes up, is turned over, stones are turned over, everything old is new, everything new is old, round, round, up and down.

That's how it was with his work. That's how he wanted it to be. The past didn't exist as a past; it was no more than an abstraction. It was always there in reality, present in the same manner as the present, a parallel state that no one could sail away from.

He looked at Osvald. This man was at home here, in his own harbor, or rather he was at home out at sea, but the sea was nearby.

"What's the best part out there?" asked Winter. "Out at sea?"

Osvald seemed not to hear. Winter repeated his question. Osvald kept looking out across the water, as though he were waiting for company, as though a ship would become visible on the horizon, like a replacement for the sun that had gone down there. A pillar of smoke. A distant ship's smoke on the horizon.

"Man is king," said Osvald suddenly. He let out a laugh. "If you stand up on the bridge and look around you're higher than everything. As far as you can see, you're higher. In a lot of ways, spiritually, too."

Winter understood what he meant. Osvald was a man of faith.

But he also wanted to be king, a worldly king. To keep being a king at sea. Winter wondered to himself what Osvald was prepared to do to be able to keep his kingdom, and the big trawler that was his throne. Winter considered the risks again. How far would Osvald go? Was there anything that could stop him?

"Think of the contrast with the forest," continued Osvald. "My brother-in-law has a clearing way down in the forest, inland, and when you're there, far under the trees, you're the *smallest* of everything there."

"Yes," said Winter, "it makes one humble somehow, I suppose."

"Humble . . . mmhmm . . . yes, humble. Don't get me wrong, twenty-five years on the North Sea make you humble, it leaves its mark. All year round, all day long . . . you are cocky about some things, but you're not cocky about everything. You are very humble about some things."

Winter nodded. Osvald was serious. It was suddenly as though Winter weren't standing there in front of him. Osvald was speaking to the sea. Winter understood that this was a man who seldom spoke this much, but who sometimes longed to be able to do so, like now. But Osvald spoke in his own way and followed his own logic.

If I keep going with this, the disappearance is a logic that I will also have to follow. Winter felt the wind pick up in his face. This logic, these thoughts, they come from a different world than the one on land. Life in this world is what means something here. And things that are larger than life. That's what Osvald is talking about.

"There's a higher power," said Osvald, as though he had read Winter's thoughts. "Besides the coast guard," he said with a laugh, but he was immediately serious again. "If there isn't a higher power, everything is meaningless."

Winter turned around and saw the community, the big houses, the smaller ones, the narrow roads, the flatbed mopeds, which were the vehicles of the southern archipelago. He saw the crosses. The mission hall. He remembered now that the Osvald family were members of the Mission Covenant Church.

"You said that you were higher than everything out there," said Winter. "Is that like saying that you live near the heavens?"

"Well, which heaven are you talking about?"

"The one you were just talking about."

"The higher one?" Osvald seemed to smile at his words, as though he were joking. The high heaven, the higher one above. "No. Religion has nothing to do with fishing."

"It doesn't?"

Osvald shook his head.

"But don't they have to go together?" said Winter.

"What do you mean?"

"Well, the church is so important here. It's everywhere."

"Mmhmm."

Winter didn't know if Osvald would say anything more. But he knew that this was important. Religion was an important subject here.

"No one from here thinks that it's strange to go to church if you go into a foreign harbor in a storm, for instance," said Osvald after a bit. "No fisherman from the west coast would hesitate to."

Winter nodded.

"All fishermen from the west coast believe in God," said Osvald.

"Does that mean there's a God-fearing atmosphere on board?" asked Winter.

"All of us fear God," said Osvald.

"And no one does anything evil on board?" said Winter.

Osvald didn't answer.

"No one swears on board a fishing boat," said Johanna Osvald as they sat in her house. Her brother nodded. It had grown dark. Winter was going to take the *Skarven* back to Saltholmen at 7:02.

"Not even when they slam their fingers in something?" said Winter.

"Not even then," said Erik Osvald. "I have to say that you really react if you hear someone swear on the radio or something. If it happens, it must be fishermen from the east coast or Denmark."

"Do you have a lot to do with Denmark?"

"We bring our fish on land in Denmark," said Osvald. "In Hanstholm in Jutland. It's on the west side of Jammer Bay. Across from Hirtshals."

"West of Blokhus?" asked Winter.

"Exactly. Blokhus is farther into the bay."

Blokhus was familiar to Winter. Several years ago he'd found some of the answers in a case he'd worked on there. A murdered woman couldn't be identified, and the old clues had led him to Denmark and Jammer Bay. There the past had cast its long shadows into the future, which was the present.

"The *Magdalena* is never here in the Donsö harbor," said Osvald.

"No?"

"No, no, she's just here for an overhaul now. Usually we change off in Hanstholm."

Osvald explained. The routine went like this: The *Magdalena* was out for six days fishing for cod and haddock and went into Hanstholm on the seventh day at five in the morning with the fish cleaned, "gutted," as he said, weighed and sorted and packaged in six different sizes for the cod and four for the haddock. Fifteen to twenty tons of fish. The fish auction took place at seven, the same time all along the North Sea and North Atlantic. During the morning, the four of them worked on maintenance and taking supplies on board. The four relief shift workers came at noon and went right out with the *Magdalena*. The four who had been relieved got into the relief shift's car and drove across Jutland to the ferry in Frederikshavn.

"What happens to the fish?" asked Winter.

"Fish and chips in Scotland," said Osvald.

"Really?"

"The haddock should be just over minimum size, as it's called. So the meat isn't tough. And small cod can also become fish and chips. And it goes by truck on a ferry to Scotland. It's a little strange, isn't it? We sit off Scotland and catch fish that eventually go by truck to Scotland. There's a ferry that goes directly from Hanstholm to Thurso, by the way."

"I didn't know that," said Winter.

"It's not much to know," said Osvald.

Winter wasn't sure he was right. There was something in what Osvald had said that Winter listened for. Something Winter didn't understand then.

Later, when the wind started to become audible out there against the mess, Winter asked, "What's the worst part about being out?"

"Well . . . ," said Osvald, looking at his sister. She hadn't said much for the last half hour. But Winter knew that he would speak with her more.

"Well, the storms have never been able to break us, of course," continued Osvald. "And not wrecks, injuries . . . nothing like that, ever. You just have to grit your teeth and you'll get past it."

"The silence," said Johanna suddenly.

Her brother gave a start. Then he nodded.

"What silence?" asked Winter.

"The silence among the crew," said Johanna. "Or what do you think, Erik?"

He nodded again but didn't say anything. Suddenly it was as though he had become a part of the silence Johanna was talking about. As though he had suddenly become an example. He looked up.

"That can break you," he said now. "Or, it does break you. Discord on board, a bad atmosphere. It breaks you fast."

Winter nodded.

"Then you can easily end up alone as a skipper."

"Sorry?"

"Then you can easily end up alone," repeated Osvald.

"As a skipper?"

"As a skipper, yes."

Winter thought about that. Erik Osvald was a skipper.

His young grandfather, John Osvald—had he also been a skipper?

"Was John Osvald the skipper on the *Marino*?" he asked.

Osvald looked again at his sister, who didn't look back.

"Not at first," he said.

"Not at first? What do you mean by that?"

"Something happened one time . . . it was right before . . . I don't know . . . but Grandpa was skipper when they sailed for Scotland."

"Happened? What was it that happened?"

"No idea," said Osvald.

"The ones who came home after the accident in Scotland. Didn't they say what had happened?"

"We didn't hear anything," said Osvald.

"Did anyone ask?" said Winter.

"Yes," answered Osvald, but Winter didn't think it sounded convincing.

"But no answer?"

Osvald shrugged his shoulders slightly.

"It sounds almost like mutiny to my ears," said Winter.

* * *

"We actually don't know," said Johanna as she followed him to the *Skar-ven,* which was on its way in from Vrångö. "Is it significant?"

"I don't know," said Winter. And significant in what way, he thought.

"Your father left the industry," he said.

"But he was ready to retire anyway, as he put it. He was ready to be put in the Maritime Museum."

"Which section?"

She smiled.

"But he can't leave the sea entirely," she said.

"How so?"

"He worries all the time. About those who are out at sea. About Erik and his crew. He listens to all the Danish weather too, and he starts at six in the morning and ends with the last report at quarter to eleven at night. But he never calls out to the boat."

Winter noticed that she was speaking of her father in the present tense, as though he were sitting next to a radio right now and listening attentively to a monotonous voice repeating numbers, vital numbers.

"Where do they usually fish?" asked Winter.

"Oh, west of Stavanger, maybe, sixty or seventy nautical miles west. They sometimes come near the derricks, which are about fifty nautical miles east of Scotland."

The *Skarven* docked at the Donsö pier with a soft thud. It would leave again in four minutes.

"Do you worry when Erik is out?" asked Winter.

"Naturally."

Winter started to walk toward the boat.

"But now I'm worried about Dad," she said.

"I will do what I can. We will."

"Something has happened," she said. "Something dangerous."

"It would be good if you try to remember everything he said before he left. What he did. Who he talked to. If he wrote anything down and left it. If anyone called. If another letter came. Everything."

"He prayed to God," she said, looking at him. "My father always prays to God." She nodded at the boat. "You should get on now."

She gave him a quick hug.

She kept standing there as the *Skarven* rushed across to Styrsö Skäret. Winter thought of all the women who had stood there throughout the centuries, looking out over the sea and waiting with anxious hearts. That's how it was with Johanna now; once again it was so. He remembered that she had talked about it, briefly, when they were young. Her mother's anxiousness, her own. Her brother's. Winter looked over toward the *Magdalena,* which had two spotlights lit above the quarterdeck. He saw figures in oilcloth moving around the deck. He saw a face outside the pilothouse, which was highest up, the highest one in the harbor. He saw that Erik Osvald was watching him. He felt a cold wind and went in from the deck.

A glow came from the sheltered houses in Långedrag. Winter swung off into the familiar Hagen crossing and continued north among even more sheltered houses. He parked in front of one of them. He knew the house, knew it well. He had spent a great deal of his childhood and all of his teenage years here.

His older sister had stayed here, in this house, first with her husband and children and then, since a long, long time ago, alone with her girls, Bim and Kristina.

But Bim and Kristina were big now. Bim didn't even live at home. Kristina was on her way out. Lotta Winter had watched all of this happen, and she tried to deal with it in a rational way, but it wasn't something that could be dealt with rationally. You'll see for yourself, she had said. See what? See how fucking easy it is. The separation? The separation, *yes;* come back when Elsa says bye-bye. You make it sound so final, Lotta. Well, isn't it? she had said. You know what I mean, he had said. Yeah, yeah, she had said. Forgive me. But it's . . . the quiet. Suddenly it's so quiet. Quiet.

He rang the doorbell. The ring was the same. The same ring for thirty years. She should change it, change it now. Something new and happy and lively, energetic. Zip-a-dee-doo-dah.

She opened the door after four rings.

"Well, well."

"I came by," he said.

"I see that."

"Aren't you going to ask me in?"

She backed into the hall.

He hung up his coat. He always hung his things on *his* hook.

"Well, it's calm and peaceful and quiet here," she said.

"That's nice," he said.

"Like hell it is," she said.

"You've started to curse more in your old age," he said.

"Thanks a fucking lot. For that last bit."

"Why?"

"Why? Why do I have such rough and salty language? I think it's because of the salty and rough winds from the sea that's only five minutes from here by Mercedes."

"They never swear there."

"Sorry?"

"There are no salty fishermen from the west coast who curse."

"How do you know?"

He told her.

They were sitting in the living room. The view was the same. He could see the playhouse where he used to hide sometimes.

"Actually, I salt my language because the children can't hear me anymore," she said. "It's my way of going back to the way I was."

"Mmhmm."

"What does Angela say about you being gone on a Saturday night?"

He looked at the clock.

"I didn't mean for it to be so late."

"So you come here and surprise me in the middle of my loneliness on this Saturday night." She nodded toward the half-full wineglass that stood on the table. "And catch me in the act of drinking."

"Please, Lotta."

"Maybe I'm like Mom? Maybe I have an alcoholic inside? Who's just been waiting for the right moment."

"That's true," he said.

"You see."

"Joking aside, Lotta. Maybe you need someone. A new husband."

"Get remarried? Hahahahahahahahaha."

"Well . . ."

"*You* get married. Do it and then come here and lecture me about it."

"How much have you actually had to drink?"

"Only four bottles of wine and a barrel of rum."

"Where's Kristina?"

"Taken into custody by the authorities."

"I chose the wrong time for a visit," he said.

"You picked the wrong time to come."

Winter placed one leg over the other. He was used to bantering with his sister, but this was a little worse, a little bigger.

"Do you know who that is? Who I was quoting?"

"What?"

"Picked the wrong time—it's Dylan. It's what you're listening to right now. It's this song, actually. 'Highlands.' Can you hear?"

He heard Dylan mumble, "Well my heart's in the Highlands . . . blue-bells blazing where the Aberdeen waters flow."

Well. That was a little odd. Aberdeen. A remarkable sign, and he knew better than to look at it as something that just happened, that didn't mean anything. There were coincidences everywhere, and the important thing was to accept them. To sometimes let yourself be guided by the coincidences.

Everything has a purpose. Yes.

There is a higher power.

Dylan mumbled, on the way to his destruction in a city that was made of ruins and empty of life.

"Music to make you happy," said Winter.

She laughed, actually laughed.

"When did *you* go over to the happy genre?" she said. "Feel-good music?"

"Do you still have a phone?" he asked. "Or have the authorities disconnected it?"

"Why?"

"If we're having a party, Angela and Elsa can come."

"I'm glad you came, Erik," said Lotta.

He nodded. He had called. Angela and Elsa weren't going to come. Elsa was sleeping. Angela was wondering. I'm not a bitch, she had said. But one begins to wonder. Is it strange if I'm wondering?

He was going to go home in a few minutes.

"I don't know what it is," said his sister. "I have to pull myself together. It's suddenly as though nothing means anything anymore."

She looked tired in the ugly hall lighting, tired and sad.

"You know that it does," said Winter. "You have a lot of things that mean something." He could hear how empty that sounded.

"But that's not what it feels like. Not now."

"Come to my house."

"Now? What, I don't know . . ."

"Come to my house tonight. Kristina is already in custody, right?"

She smiled.

"She's out in the islands, actually, at a friend's house. On Brännö."

"Aha."

"Well . . ."

"Come along. You don't even need to finish your drink. I have lots of bottles at home, wine and enough rum for fifteen men."

17

Lotta made Winter call home first. A nice surprise, Angela had said. Of course she should come. Absolutely.

"If only we had something special to offer you," she said when they came.

"Erik promised me fifteen barrels of rum," said Lotta.

She went home when it was almost dawn.

"What we can't do during the day we do at night," said Angela, who was standing at the window watching the taxi disappear into Allén.

"There is no day, there is no night," said Winter.

"No?"

"That's how it is."

"I don't know if what you're saying is positive or negative," said Angela.

"It's a state of being. At sea."

"I don't think I want to hear more about the sea right now, Erik."

"Soon you'll be living a stone's throw from it."

She didn't say anything; she kept standing at the window. There was a faint glow in the east. The sun was coming up but it wasn't above the sea.

"I don't know," she said.

He waited, but she didn't say anything more.

"I really don't know," she said after that.

"What don't you know?"

"About the sea. The land. The house." She turned around suddenly. "I might just end up alone. Elsa and me. It might be isolated. Far from everything."

"The idea isn't that you and Elsa are going to live there on your own," he said.

She didn't answer.

"Did you hear what I said?"

She walked over to the sofa where he was sitting.

"We should probably think it over one more time," she said.

"It's still a good piece of land," he said. "We should probably still buy the land, right?"

On Sunday afternoon they took a walk in the Garden Society. Elsa ate an ice cream and then fell asleep. Winter felt a bit tired. It must have been that last barrel of rum at dawn.

They sat on the grass. A couple paddled by on the canal in a kayak. They heard a laugh from them; it floated on the water.

Angela had a dark circle under one eye.

She was on at five in the afternoon. It would be a long night, but there was no night, she thought now, there is no day in health care, and no night. Everything is governed by the frailty of the body, by the regular rhythm of the nurses handing out medicine. And suddenly the rhythm could be broken by an alarm, by the nasty sound of ambulances outside the emergency entrance.

Everyone to his station.

"You have become very interested in fish all of a sudden," she said.

"Angela . . ."

"Yes, I know that we weren't going to talk about it, but I'm doing it anyway."

"I thought I owed it to her."

"You carry a lot of debts, Erik. Constantly."

"What's that supposed to mean?"

"How many calls do you get every day when people's loved ones are missing or they want to report a stolen bike or they've fallen down the stairs or been punched in the face?"

He didn't answer.

"All those people you're all duty-bound to meet personally, to listen more thoroughly to their problems. God, it has to be hundreds a week. And none of you have time. That must make you feel so guilty."

Winter saw Elsa move on the blanket. Angela had raised her voice, but only slightly.

"Can we talk about this later, Angela?"

"Later? Later when? I go to work at four thirty, darn it."

"She's been trying to reach me for a long time, and it does concern a missing person, after all,"

"Really? How long has this person been missing? A grown man. Is there a bulletin out? Have you contacted Interpol?"

"Yes."

"Yes, you have now, but not when you went out to Donsö."

"It was when I went there that I understood that it was time to go farther."

"And none of that could happen over the phone?"

He heard the sound of paddling again, a laugh again, water. He looked at her.

"I think it was good that I went there and talked to them. Unfortunately."

"Unfortunately? What do you mean?"

"I don't know. It's a hunch. And it doesn't feel good."

Aneta Djanali had decided to let Anette Lindsten go; let her go to an independence without a husband and without violence. Anette would find her own way via her detour to her childhood home.

Aneta had started to feel a bit sorry for Sigge Lindsten. The traveler. She smiled as she sat in the car on the way to the police station. He had never explained what it was he sold. Maybe reference books. About English football. That went like hotcakes among old ladies out in the woods. She smiled again. She was also a traveler. How many of her working hours did she spend in her car? An awful lot.

Fredrik honked behind her. She stopped and he took the last parking spot. She would get her revenge. She had to drive around. More time in the car.

They went in through the glass doors. It was Monday morning. Inside, the usual number of unfortunate souls waited to speak to someone. She could see the usual lawyers wander back and forth with the usual facial expressions. The usual binders. She thought of Forsblad. He didn't work in the court, not in that way.

The unfortunate souls in the waiting room hung their heads. Someone sneezed, someone screamed, someone cried, someone laughed, someone cursed, someone made gestures that could only be made here. Some poor person in a coat with a torn collar stared at the messages on the bulletin boards: Investigators needed in Uddevalla. Yes, thank you. Substitutes on the city squad, temporary positions. Thank you, good sir. I wasn't planning on staying forever anyway.

Police went in and out through the doors to the stairs and the elevators. Someone waved. Someone dropped something solid on the floor. Someone else picked it up.

This was her life, her world. Was it supposed to be like this? Was there any alternative? Was it better somewhere else? Which other paths were there?

She suddenly thought of Gabin Dabiré's music; she played it more and more often, and other music from Burkina Faso; folk music from the Lobi, Gan, Mossi, and Bisa people, and from the surrounding countries. Mali, of course, but also Ghana, Niger. The music was like paths, or like people who walked on the paths with a rhythm that everyone who listened had to follow.

"I'll buy you coffee," said Halders.

"The coffee is free here," she said.

"It's the thought that counts," he said.

The elevator stopped. Möllerström was coming down the hall.

"A man was asking for you," he said. "He just called."

"Who was it?"

"Sigge something," said Möllerström. "I have the number."

"I have it myself," she said, going into the office she was sharing with Halders while they renovated their floor. It would be finished before the new century was over, if everything went well. She dialed the Lindstens' number. The childhood home.

"We're not really rid of him, it seems," said Lindsten in his calm way.

"What happened?"

"He's calling and threatening."

"Threatening? Threatening Anette?"

"Yes, her, and me too if we don't put Anette on the phone. He screamed at my wife."

"May I talk to Anette a little?"

"She's . . . asleep, I think."

"Should I come over right away?"

"Then I heard her cell phone ring," said Lindsten, as though he hadn't heard Aneta.

"Yes?"

"I think it was him."

"She should probably turn it off."

"Yes. I've told her so."

"Forsblad told me he was able to borrow a key from her. To the apartment," said Aneta.

"She told me. It seems he had to get something."

"What was it?"

"I don't know. But he must have been the one who gave it to the people who cleaned out the place," said Lindsten.

"I got it from him. Rather, he threw it at me."

"Keys can be copied," said Lindsten.

"Could you ask Anette to call me when she wakes up?" said Aneta.

"Yes."

"I want her to call."

"So what can you do?"

"I want to talk to her first," said Aneta.

"No one here is making anything up," said Lindsten.

She heard the dog let out a bark in the background.

"I didn't think you were," she said.

Aneta waited for a call that didn't come. She called the Lindstens, but no one answered. She looked up. Halders had entered the room.

"No one is answering at the Lindstens'. I don't like this. Something isn't right."

She told him about the conversation she'd just had with Sigge Lindsten.

"We can go over there, if you want to," said Halders.

"I don't know . . . I've knocked at their door once before. Without an invitation."

"The guy did call you. That's as good as an invitation."

"Okay."

No one opened the door when they rang the doorbell. There was no car in the driveway.

"Flown the coop," said Halders.

A car drove by slowly down the street, behind them. Aneta turned around. The windows were tinted and the sun was at such an angle that the driver was only a silhouette. Halders had also turned around.

"Visitors?" said Halders.

"Can't you go down and check?" she said.

"Scared?"

"I don't like this," she said.

She watched Fredrik walk down to the street. He stood next to the gate, authoritatively, as though he demanded that those in question drive by again, just as slowly.

The car returned. She thought she recognized it. Halders stepped out onto the sidewalk. The car sped up and drove away, to the south. Halders had not raised his hand. He wasn't wearing a uniform. He was in plainclothes, as he had once put it. With emphasis on plain, Winter had retorted. Now she saw him dig out a notebook and write something.

He came back.

"I didn't see a face, but I have the license plate number. Do you want me to call it in?"

"Yes, why not."

"Now?"

Aneta didn't answer.

"Now?" Halders repeated.

"Did you see that curtain move?" she said.

"Where? Nope."

"The window in the gable. The curtain moved."

"Did you ring the bell again?"

"Yes."

"Then the girl has probably woken up," said Halders.

"She should have woken up before," said Aneta.

Halders went over to the window. He had to dodge the tall weeds that were growing under some spruce trees that stood close to the house. It must be very dark in that room, no matter the weather or season. It could be any season at all in there.

"I don't see anything," said Halders with a voice that was audible from where she stood. It was probably audible all the way down to the street.

"There was someone there," she said.

Halders knocked on the window. That must also have been audible from a distance. He knocked again.

He came back.

"We can't break in, you know," he said.

Aneta called the number again from her cell phone. They didn't hear any ringing from inside.

"Maybe it's off the hook," said Halders. "Have you tried her cell?"

"Yes."

"She probably turned it off."

"Something really shady is going on here," said Aneta.

Halders looked at her. He had a new expression on his face now, or a different one.

"Have you met Anette Lindsten?" he asked.

"Barely. Three seconds."

"Do you have a picture of her?"

"No. But I've seen a picture of her. One that was a few years old."

She thought about the younger Anette. The ice pop in her hand. A child in the background was on the way into a store.

"So you don't know what she looks like now?" asked Halders.

"No . . ."

"How will you recognize her, then? When you meet her?"

"It seems as though it's never going to happen anyway."

"If some girl opens this door and introduces herself as Anette, you won't know if it is."

"Quit it, Fredrik. That happened to me once already, and that's enough."

"Yeah, yeah, it just occurred to me."

They heard noises behind them. A car drove onto the property.

Winter was dealing with Axel Osvald's missing person bulletin. He conveyed the information he had received from Johanna Osvald. He had photographs of a man he had never met.

When Winter had met the man's daughter, that one summer, the father was out at sea, maybe halfway to or from Scotland.

He had met Erik Osvald then, but he hadn't seen him as a fisherman. But he was one then, too, a fisherman, a young fisherman.

"Maybe Osvald met someone up in the Highlands and chose to go underground," said Ringmar, who was standing at the window.

"Go underground in the Highlands?" said Winter. "Wouldn't that be easier in the Lowlands?"

"I will never again use a sloppy and careless phrase in this building," said Ringmar. "No linguistic clichés from me ever again."

"Thanks, Bertil."

"But what do you think? That it could have been something he chose to do?"

"I don't think he's the type. And that's not why he went over there."

"Why—exactly—did he go?"

"To search for his father."

"But it wasn't the first time."

"Something new had come up," said Winter.

"The mysterious message."

"Is it mysterious?"

Ringmar went over to the desk. They were in Winter's office. He picked up a copy and read:

THINGS ARE NOT WHAT THEY LOOK LIKE.
JOHN OSVALD IS NOT WHAT HE SEEMS TO BE.

"Well," said Ringmar.

"Is it mysterious?" Winter repeated.

"If nothing else, it's mystifying," said Ringmar.

"Enough to go over there?"

"Well . . ."

"You are clear and direct, Bertil. I like that."

"There's something tautological about this message that bothers me," said Ringmar, looking up. "It says roughly the same thing twice."

Winter nodded and waited.

"Things are not what they look like. That is: John is not what he seems to be. Or is considered to be. Or thought to be." Ringmar looked up. "What is he thought to be? Dead, right? Drowned."

"No one knows. If he drowned, that is."

"Is that what this tells us? That he didn't drown. That he's been dead since the war, but that it didn't happen by drowning?"

"How did it happen, then?" said Winter.

They had hit their stride now, with their inner dialogues turned up to an audible level. Sometimes it led to results. You never knew.

"A crime," said Ringmar.

"He was murdered?"

"Maybe. Or died from negligence. An accident."

"But someone knows?"

"Yes."

"Who wrote a letter?"

"Doesn't have to be the same person who had something to do with his disappearance. His death."

"Things are not what they seem to be," Winter repeated.

"If that's how it should be interpreted," said Ringmar. "Maybe we can't see all the shades of meaning."

"Then we need someone who has English as their native language," said Winter.

"There is someone," said Ringmar. "Your friend Macdonald."

"He's not an Englishman," said Winter, "he's a Scot."

"Even better. The letter came from Scotland."

Winter read the sentences again.

"It doesn't necessarily only have to do with John Osvald," he said. "The first line might have nothing to do with John Osvald."

"Develop that thought."

"It could be about those around him. His history. The people he surrounded himself with, then and now."

"His relatives," said Ringmar. "His children and grandchildren."

"His children or grandchildren aren't what they seem to be?"

Ringmar shrugged his shoulders.

Winter read the sentences for the seventeenth time that day.

"The question is what all of this means," he said.

"What do you mean?"

"The letter itself. Why it was sent. And why now? Why more than sixty years after John Osvald disappeared?"

18

They heard Sigge Lindsten's voice before the car stopped. They heard his steps on the gravel. Aneta Djanali thought she saw the curtain move again. Fredrik had said it was the wind, that the window was drafty.

"Well, no one's here right now," said Lindsten.

That was a strange comment, thought Aneta.

"I thought you all would be here when we came," she said.

"I had to run an errand." He gestured with his hand. "The veterinarian had to look at Zack."

"Anything serious?"

"They didn't know. They admitted the dog, anyway. I guess we'll see."

"Is Anette home?" asked Halders.

"No."

"No?"

"No. She and her mother went to the coast."

"To the coast?"

"We have a little cottage down in Vallda," said Lindsten.

"When did they leave?" asked Halders.

"Does it matter?" Lindsten looked from one officer to the other. "They'd had enough, quite simply. Anette couldn't handle . . . how he was calling."

Running away to yet another place, thought Aneta.

"Does Forsblad know about this cottage?" asked Halders.

"Yes, I suppose he does."

"Is it so smart to go there, then?"

"There's no telephone there. And Anette has the sense to turn off her cell."

"But he doesn't need to call. He can go there himself," said Halders.

"I don't think so," said Lindsten. "I don't think he would dare to."

"What kind of car does Forsblad have?" asked Halders, but at that moment his telephone rang. He answered and listened and hung up.

"The car belongs to a Bengt Marke," he said to Aneta, and looked at Lindsten. "A car drove past here a few times when we got here. A Volvo V Forty, a few years under the hood. Black, but they all are. Bengt Marke. Is that someone you know?"

"Never heard of him."

"We'll have to check him out," said Aneta to Halders.

"I'll call down to . . . Anette and my wife and say that you were here," said Lindsten.

"How can you do that?" asked Halders. "There's no telephone in the cottage."

"I'll leave a message on her voice mail."

"Didn't you just say that she never checks it?"

"I never said that," said Lindsten.

"Okay," said Halders.

"What are you going to do about this?" asked Lindsten.

"We're going to talk with Forsblad," said Halders.

"Can you do that?"

"We can do everything," said Halders.

In the car, Halders wore an expression that Aneta recognized. He was staring straight ahead. Aneta was driving.

"Have you become interested in this too?" she asked.

"Curious," said Halders. "About that Herr Hauptsturmführer Hans Forzblatt. But also about the rest of them."

"Good."

"Not least about the girl who was hiding behind the curtain while we were standing outside that place."

"Are you guessing now, Fredrik?"

"No sir."

"You really saw her?"

"Yes sir."

"How well documented are the events surrounding shipwrecks?" said Ringmar.

"Is it called a shipwreck?" said Winter.

"Answer the question," said Ringmar.

"I don't know," said Winter. "The boat, the *Marino,* sank on their way home from south of Iceland."

"Where did it happen?"

"I don't know."

"But two men survived?"

"Apparently. John Osvald's brother and another crew member."

"Were they on board at the time?"

"I don't know."

"Or were they in harbor?"

"I don't know."

"Has anything been recovered from the wreck? Wreckage?"

"I don't know."

"It must have gotten some attention at the time. Something, at least. In the paper over there."

"I don't know."

"Were there any dives for the wreckage?"

"I don't know."

"What *do* you know, Erik?"

"I really don't know, Bertil."

Hans Forsblad lived as a "boarder" with someone on the northern riverside; that was his expression. It means that he has to go over a bridge from Hisingen to get to Anette, thought Aneta. Always something.

"Look at that," said Halders as they studied the nameplates at the door. "Someone else from the Marke family resides here."

Aneta read: Susanne Marke. Fourth floor. She looked up. Could be that balcony. Or that one. Must be a nice view over the river. You would see several churches. The sea was so close you could dive. You would probably kill yourself, but you could consider giving it a try.

"Does he live with her?" said Halders.

"I don't know."

Winter was alone in the room. He was playing Haden and Metheny, *Beyond the Missouri Sky,* Haden's bass ambling around the walls, Metheny's guitars layered above it, doo-doo-doo-doo-doo-doo-doo-doo-doo-doo-

doo-doo. Spiritual, beautiful like the dawn in September, like a streak of smoke across the horizon, like his daughter's smile, like the beach grove where their house—

The phone rang, doo-doo-doo-doo-doo-doo-doo-doo; he answered without lowering the volume, heard the Realtor's voice, It's about time for a decision, isn't it? Do you know what you—

I know.

19

No one answered the doorbell. Aneta turned around and saw the churches on the other side of the river, and the Seaman's Wife standing and waiting on the pillar outside of the Maritime Museum, looking out toward the mouth of the harbor. Eyes of stone, a body of stone; it was a sculpture that summarized part of life near the sea in this part of the world. She had always been there.

"Do you ever think about what that sculpture symbolizes?" she asked Halders, who had also turned around.

"Isn't it obvious?" he answered.

"What's obvious?"

"She's waiting for her husband to come home from the sea. She's filled with anxiety. Her name is the Seaman's Wife." He looked at her. "Every Gothenburger knows that."

"Including me," said Aneta.

"The pillar was built in the beginning of the thirties, first the pillar and then the woman," said Halders. "The interwar period. Thirty-three, I think."

"The things you know."

"It interests me."

"What? The sea?"

"Oh, this city's history."

Two tugboats were pulling a container ship farther into the harbor. A ferry passed, on its way to Denmark. She could see passengers duck as they glided under the bridge. There was a pale light over there, above the sea, as though everything was unreliable there, hazardous. She thought she could see the Seaman's Wife's gaze against that opening.

"She's actually looking the wrong way," said Halders, pointing at the sculpture.

"What do you mean?"

"I know this, but maybe you can see it from here . . . Well, she's not looking out at the sea; she's looking straight *here,* actually. Toward the northern riverside." He turned to her and smiled. "She's looking straight at us."

"Is there something symbolic about that, do you think?"

"Something that includes Forsblad, you mean? That he lives in this building and the woman over there is leading us here?"

"It's an interesting theory," said Aneta.

"The sculptor had trouble finding the sea," said Halders. "Maybe it was foggy the day the lady arrived."

Aneta laughed. The Stena Line catamaran passed. She could see passengers on that quarterdeck too. Just like the Seaman's Wife, they were gazing at the northern shore where she was standing. She had the urge to wave. She had done so when she was a child, she'd done so often. There were more ships in the harbor back then. Sometimes you couldn't see the other side of the harbor for all the ships.

"She's really standing there as a memorial," said Halders, "a monument for all the sailors and fishermen who were lost in the First World War, and all the ships that sank."

"Then she's waiting in vain," said Aneta.

Winter biked home for lunch. Angela had three days off in a row. She was going to hang around town. Elsa was going to hang around with her.

But right now she was home. The fish was simple and good, just olive oil and lemon and a little butter, tarragon, and another fresh herb that he couldn't identify at first. He could still feel the sweat on his back from his bike ride.

"Who were you trying to beat home?" she asked.

"Myself, as usual," he said, smiling at Elsa, who was taste-testing the fish with a thoughtful expression.

"Who won?"

"I did."

"That's not a bad arrangement, is it."

"Should we bike down to the lot?" he said. "This weekend?"

"Do you want to, Elsa?" asked Angela. "Bike down to the sea?"

"Yes, yes!"

He helped himself to the mashed potatoes.

"So now it's settled," he said. "*The deal is in the harbor,* to use a Swedish expression."

"That deserves a bike trip," said Angela.

Yes, he thought. Everyone here had been waiting for his decision, including himself. But now it was settled. After all, it was only a plot of land.

No. It was a bigger decision than that.

He looked at his family, who looked at him. Fuck, he didn't want other people to have to wait for him to make up his mind.

For one of his selves to make up its mind.

I'm always sliding a little bit farther away, and I have to get back, work my way back.

I'm trying. The other day I didn't answer the phone.

It didn't help.

What am I doing wrong?

It shouldn't be so hard.

It won't be so hard. It's better than ever, right? I'm *here* more than ever, aren't I? I'm *there* but also here, and I'm starting to find a balance. Yes, balance. It's thanks to her. And her. Both of them.

Does everyone think like I do?

One of them said something.

"Uh . . . ?" said Winter.

"Elsa made dessert," said Angela.

"Mmmm," he said.

"It's chocolate mereeengue puffs," said Elsa.

"My favorite," he said.

"Yes!" said Elsa.

"Effective against weight loss," he said, and looked at Angela.

"Do you ever long for your origins?" he said over espresso.

"Why do you ask?"

"I don't know, do you?"

"Longing . . . what would you call it . . . I guess I just wonder sometimes what would have happened if I had been there. Stayed there. Been born there."

"Yes, that's definitely a point of departure," he said.

"If I had been born in Leipzig, it would have been a bewildering life, at the very least," she said. "So much has happened to the people there."

"It still was a bewildering life for the Hoffman family," said Winter.

"Not for me, not like that. I was born *here*."

"Indirectly bewildering for you."

"Maybe."

They heard Elsa in her room. She built something that she then knocked over, built and knocked over, built and knocked over, and yet she had grown up enough to laugh at it. Build and knock over. Well. That wasn't unusual. Things that were built got knocked down.

"I think I would have become a doctor in Germany, too," she said.

"Günther wouldn't have allowed anything different?"

"He would have. But I would have become one anyway."

"Why?"

"There are so many people who need help and care."

"Like who?"

"You, for example."

"Yes."

She circled her fingers around the cup. The saucer made a noise, like faint music.

"When can they start building, do you think?"

"When we say it's time," he said.

"When is it time, then?"

"When we say so."

"And when will we say so?"

He thought about what he'd just thought. Who was waiting for whom, for whose decision.

"When you want to," he said.

Angela and Elsa followed him down in the elevator, to Vasaplatsen.

He led his bike up to the kiosk. Angela and Elsa were on their way to Kapellplatsen and the bookstore.

"Don't you think we should take a trip soon?" said Winter. "Soon. To celebrate. Celebrate the decision."

"We're going to bike to the sea on Saturday."

"Some other sea. Somewhere else."

"When?"

"Soon."

"Sounds good to me. I've banked time off. Weeks."

"Good."

"But you don't have any, do you?"

"Why do you think I've been working nights and weekends, away from our family?" said Winter.

"Ha ha ha."

"Now it's time for the payoff."

"Marbella?" asked Angela.

"Why not."

"Will you call Siv?"

He waved a "yes" and wobbled off onto Vasagatan in the middle of the intersection, and an angry driver laid on the horn.

The black V40 arrived as Halders and Aneta were walking back to the car. It drove fast and then parked two cars away. A woman got out and slammed the door after her. Aneta recognized her.

"I saw her with Forsblad," she said. "In the court."

"In the court?"

"He works in the district court. She was with him."

"The license number matches," said Halders.

"Excuse me," said Aneta to the woman, who was about to walk by them. She looked at them, but she didn't seem to register that Aneta was talking to her. She was blond, but her hair was darker at the roots; she had sharp and rather small features, which didn't really suit her height. She was tall, wearing a dress that was elegant and simple and maybe expensive, and a coat that seemed light and comfortable, but its color didn't match the dress. Shoes that seemed uncomfortable. She was in a hurry.

"Excuse me for a sec—," repeated Aneta, but Halders had already moved into her path and taken out his ID, and the woman stopped. She looked at him, and at Aneta, but she didn't seem to recognize her.

"Susanne Marke?" asked Halders.

"Sorry?"

"Nothing to apologize for," he said. "Are you Susanne Marke?"

"Uh . . . yes." She looked at Aneta again, as though she still didn't recognize her.

She ought to recognize me. A black woman in the courthouse. Maybe she's color-blind. Her clothes seem to indicate that she is.

"What is this about?" asked Susanne.

"We're looking for Hans Forsblad," said Halders. "Do you know where he is?"

"Hans Fors . . . why would I know that?"

"He lives with you."

"What do you mean, he lives with me?"

"Do you live there?" asked Halders, nodding toward the fancy building behind her. He said the address for the sake of clarity.

"I live here," she said.

"Hans Forsblad has given this as his address," said Aneta.

Susanne didn't answer, but it looked like she was silently cursing him.

"This is not his address," she answered.

"But he could live here anyway, couldn't he?" said Halders.

She didn't answer. She suddenly looked out over the water, as though trying to find different answers. As though she were trying to make eye contact with the Seaman's Wife. A ferry passed again, this time on the way in. There were people on the quarterdeck, little heads that stuck up over the railing. Aneta thought of how Forsblad lived at addresses that weren't his. Was that the point? Was there some idea behind it?

"Do you have problems answering a simple question from the police?" said Halders.

"I want to know what this is about," she said, trying to look more confident than her voice indicated.

Halders sighed so she could hear. He looked at Aneta, who nodded. Seabirds started to cry out nearby. They could hear the sound of a hammer or a sledgehammer striking. Maybe Forsblad has some other woman in there, in the flat, thought Aneta. Here we go again.

"We have received a report that involves Hans Forsblad," said Halders. "We want to speak to him, and I really hope that you will help us. I really hope you will."

Said the broken record, thought Aneta, unable to help herself.

"Re . . . report? What is it about?"

"We would like to discuss it with Hans Forsblad," said Halders. "Listen, do you want to answer the question or not?"

"What was the question?"

Halders sighed again. But he remained calm. Aneta saw that the vein in his forehead was pulsing, but Susanne didn't notice.

We have to stay in character. She does, too. It's a question of who is best at staying in character.

"He stayed with me for a couple of days," she said, looking around to indicate the direction. "But he isn't here anymore."

"When was that?" asked Halders.

"When was wh—"

"WHEN DID HE STAY with you?" asked Halders, smiling as he lowered his voice in the middle of the sentence.

"Uh . . . last week. Over the weekend."

"What were you doing up in Krokslätt an hour and a half ago?" asked Halders.

"I don't know—"

"What-were-you-doing-up-in-Krokslätt-an-hour-and-a-half-ago?" Halders asked again, a clearer question.

"I wasn't there," she said.

We know, we know, thought Aneta. Then you would have seen us, and you couldn't have hidden that if you're not an absolute psychopath, or a terminal Alzheimer's patient.

"Your car was there," said Halders.

"How . . . how do you know that?" she asked, looking surprised, but Aneta could also see that she knew something more.

"We were standing on a street in the peaceful neighborhood of Krokslätt, and your car slowly went by, a few yards from us, back and forth," said Halders, holding out the notebook so she could see her own license plate number. She knows he wouldn't have had time to write it down now, thought Aneta.

"I . . . was taking a drive," she said.

"Careful!" said Halders.

"Uh . . . what . . ."

"Be careful what you say. Just tell it like it was." He looked her in the eyes. "Like it is."

She looked out at the water again. What the hell is this? thought Aneta. What have we landed in? Why is she protecting that jerk? Has he threatened her, too?

She tried to look for injuries to Susanne's face, but she didn't see any. She only saw an expression in her eyes that could have been fear, but mostly of Fredrik, or no, more like of his words, of the truth. She knows that you shouldn't lie to the police; that's never good. It's hard to maintain lies, to keep to them. As hard as it is to keep promises.

"I loaned out the car," she said, with her eyes fastened on one of the churches in Masthugget.

"To whom?"

She looked at Halders as though she were waiting for him to scream "Careful!" before she even opened her mouth.

"Hans needed to borrow the car to run an errand," she said. "May I go in now?" She moved. "I'm actually in a bit of a hurry." She started to look in her purse, as if for a key.

"Of course," said Halders, stepping to the side as though he had been blocking all escape routes until just then. Which of course he had been. "Thanks for your help."

They watched her walk to the building, which looked like a fortress, but a modern, pleasant one. There were boats in its moat.

"I love this job," said Halders, and there was no irony in his voice.

They held the meeting in Ringmar's office for a change of scenery. There was a dead plant in the window. Ringmar didn't know what it was called.

"Time to bury that," said Halders, pointing with his whole hand.

"Done," said Ringmar. "It's in dirt, isn't it?"

"Funny, Bertil, funny."

"So what do you want to do?" said Winter.

"Bring him in for questioning," said Aneta.

"Fredrik?"

Halders ran his hand over his crew cut. He thought he looked younger now. His hair had started to thin out, and there was only one thing to do. He looked more dangerous; the whole department could probably agree on that. It was perfect for Halders. Younger and more dangerous.

"Well, I've never had the pleasure of meeting Franz Flattenführer," he said.

"Does that mean that you would like to?" said Winter.

"I don't know," said Halders. "It certainly seems to be impossible to meet his wife, Agneta, and hear what she says."

"Anette," said Aneta.

"What Anette actually has to say," Halders corrected himself. "I don't know Hans Fritz, but I know the type. If he's the type I know, questioning could make him really dangerous."

"For whom?" asked Ringmar.

"For her, of course."

"Her name is Lindsten," said Aneta. "She never changed her name to any of the ones you give Forsblad."

"Why do you do that, Fredrik?" asked Ringmar. "Why do you always do that?"

"What?"

"The names, like you got them out of a war novel by Sven Hassel."

"Because this is a free job," said Halders. "And I like Svein."

Ringmar looked at Aneta.

"Let it go," he said. "Let it go for a little while."

"No," said Aneta.

"What is your reasoning on this, Aneta?" asked Winter. He looks more curious than surprised, she thought.

"We ought to talk to him. I'm tired of all the damn cases where the men are left alone until it's almost too late. And sometimes it *is* too late."

"I want you to have a conversation with the woman," said Winter. "Anette."

"What do you think I've been trying to do for the last few days?" said Aneta.

"I've tried, too," said Halders.

"Well, apparently she doesn't want to talk to us," said Ringmar.

"Have you tried, too?" said Halders.

"I meant 'us' in the sense of the police," said Ringmar.

"She was inside that house, but she didn't want anything to do with the police," said Halders.

"It could have been the mother," said Winter.

"No," said Halders. "It was a younger woman."

"Okay," said Winter, "if you want to bring him in, be my guest."

"Can't you issue a restraining order while you're at it?" asked Aneta.

"He can't get near her anyway," said Halders. "No one will answer the door."

"What about the cabin by the sea?" said Aneta.

"Question him," said Winter. "After that, maybe we won't have a problem anymore."

Winter went to his office and called Nueva Andalucía. He could see the white stone house before him while he waited for his mother to put down her shaker and pick up the phone. No, that was unfair. She had cut back since Dad died. Either that or the abyss, at the bottom of one last bottle of Lariós's local gin.

He'd been down there when his father died, not in the abyss but at Hospital Costa del Sol, with Sierra Blanca outside, and above, and with his father, who took one last breath a day or two after the last conversation they'd had together in their lives; that last little while, which had been the first in many years.

The hours afterward had been the most difficult of his life up to then; the hardest, the sharpest, the meanest, the heaviest, heavy like blocks of stone.

His father lay in the mountain earth. From there you could see across the sea, all the way to Africa, which was a desert there on the other side.

He had thought that he would lose himself during the flight back home, fall, as though from the plane.

He had no nice memories of his flights to Costa del Sol, neither from the way home nor the way there.

His mother answered at last.

20

I'm melting," said Siv Winter. "It's ninety-three degrees here right now. It was over one hundred last week."

"I know it's trying and difficult," said Erik Winter.

"Eh, I didn't mean it like that, Erik."

He smiled to himself. His mother had many merits, but she didn't understand sarcasm. Maybe that's a good quality, he thought. Too many people go about spreading sarcasm around for others to interpret. Oh, you didn't mean it like that? Oh, no. Okay, I guess I'm not smart. I should have understood that you meant it the other way around.

In his branch, people often meant things the other way around. But they weren't being sarcastic. They were just lying.

He lived in a world filled with lies. That was his world.

His job was to interpret lies. How do you end up, then? When you assume that everyone is lying all the time? With whom do you find secure trust, and truth?

"How do the weather reports look for the future?" he asked his mother.

"Eh, it's probably going to be like this for a few more weeks. Maybe a little cooler in a few weeks."

"No rain on the way?"

"No, unfortunately."

"That's good."

"What do you mean, Erik?"

"We're thinking of coming down for a few days."

"Did you say *we*? *All* of you?"

"Yes."

"That would be so nice. Oh, how nice!"

"We think so, too."

"What does Elsa think?"

"She doesn't know yet. I wanted to check with you first."

"But, Erik, you know very well that you're all always welcome. And you haven't been here since . . . since . . ."

She didn't finish her sentence, and she didn't need to. He had come down the day after Christmas last year, and he had drunk seven bottles of whisky—of course, they were those ridiculous little airplane bottles, but still—and beer on top of that, and it had taken half the ground personnel at the airport in Málaga to get him out and to the car. The police had been there, but only to help. Ringmar had called the police commissioner when Winter had boarded the plane: Here's what you can expect in Málaga. Ringmar had understood, and their Spanish colleague understood.

Muy borracho. Sí. Comprendo.

Winter had not understood, not when he left after the Christmastime events in Gothenburg. Who could have understood? Really understood everything? He wanted to understand, soon. It was possible to understand. Nothing bad happened without a reason. It came from somewhere. From people. That made the bad into something comprehensible, but it became simultaneously more terrible.

Ringmar had had to do the terrible finishing up last Christmas. Bertil had been strong, stronger than him. Bertil had had his own private hell, but he was a great person, a real person. Without Bertil there was nothing, he had thought then, and he thought so sometimes afterward. I am weak but he is strong. I become weaker and he becomes stronger. Will it be like that for me, too? Will it change? Do I want it to? Do I want to become stronger?

"I'll let you know the details," he said to his mother.

"Will it be soon?"

"I hope so."

"I presume you're having bad weather as usual at home."

He looked out at the Indian summer sun, sharp as a knife.

"Yes," he lied.

Aneta Djanali drove south and turned off toward Krokslätt. Everything felt like it was a few decades ago here: the houses, the streets, the signs, the stores; stucco houses where the plaster had fallen and been stuck on again, cafés with two tables and five chairs.

She wasn't alone on the streets. She was tailing a black V40 that was one hundred yards ahead, and she wasn't driving her usual Saab. This was another one of the unmarked cars from the garage under the Police Palace, as it was called, on Ernst Fontells Plats.

Aneta guessed where they were going, but she felt confusion inside of her; not the dizziness from before, but something that reminded her of it.

The V40 was driven by Susanne Marke. Aneta had seen her get into the car on one of the deserted streets in the old part of Nordstan. Aneta had been waiting there. She knew where Susanne would be during the afternoon, because she had asked. She had guessed four o'clock as the end of her workday, and it was a good guess.

But she couldn't guess where Susanne would drive. Now she was driving into Fredriksdal, and into the familiar driveway. Sigge Lindsten's car wasn't there. Aneta drove by and saw Susanne getting out of the car. In the rearview mirror she saw her walk toward the house without looking around. Then the road curved and Aneta could only see other houses that didn't mean anything to her.

She turned around in a narrow intersection five hundred yards to the north. When she came back, Susanne's car was gone.

"Forsblad didn't show up at work this afternoon," said Halders when she called from the car. "And there's no one answering in the love nest in Norra Älvstranden."

"I saw her ten minutes ago," said Aneta.

"Are you over there?"

"No, she went to the Lindstens' house."

"I'll be damned."

"It was just a short visit."

"How do you know?"

She told him.

"You still don't know what Anette Lindsten really looks like these days, right?" said Halders.

"No, what . . . ," she said, and then understood what Fredrik meant.

"You're totally wrong," she said.

"It's important to think outside the box," said Halders.

"Do you really *think* so?" said Aneta, mostly to herself. "No, she can't have changed that much."

"Best to check, isn't it? To be completely certain."

* * *

She sat with the phone in her hand. Susanne Marke was Anette Lind-sten, who was Susanne Marke, who was . . .

No.

But Sigge Lindsten had called. That is, if he *was* Sigge Lindsten. He could have had a fake ID. The house in Fredriksdal was fake, maybe just a set like in a movie studio. This was just a movie. She suddenly thought of the film festival in Ouagadougou. She had been to the movies in Ouagadougou, a drafty bunker where the white light from outside filtered in through ten thousand holes in the curtain. It was a domestic film, which surprisingly enough was about people who lived in a city in the desert. The city seemed to lack gods, or spirits. The movie was in Mossi with French subtitles, and she understood the words but never the true meaning of what the people said. It wasn't just another culture, it was another world.

Maybe the two men she had met in the apartment that might have been Anette Lindsten's really were Anette's father and brother. But the apartment was in her name. Susanne Marke's apartment was in Susanne Marke's name. The car was in Bengt Marke's name. Who was Bengt Marke? Was he also named Hans Forsblad? Or Heintz Fritsfrütz? She almost giggled. Then she felt a chill.

She started the car and drove south, far south.

Winter got hold of Steve Macdonald during lunch.

"Guess what I'm eating," said Macdonald.

"I know where it came from," said Winter.

"The fish or the chips?" said Macdonald.

"I know the fisherman who hauled up the haddock," said Winter.

"That's fantastic," said Macdonald. "Is there a stamp or something here under the breading?"

Winter told him about his visit to Donsö.

"And now his father has gone walkabout in the Highlands."

"He is still missing, at least. Or he hasn't contacted anyone."

"Have you put out a bulletin?"

"Yes."

"Send over all the information and I'll have a chat with the people up in Inverness."

"Thanks, Steve."

"Otherwise?"

"I'm going to build a house. By the sea." Winter paused. "I think."
Macdonald laughed.

"I like your resolve," he said.

"It's a nice plot of land," said Winter. "You can smell the sea."

"Good."

"Do you ever go home?"

"Home? You mean to Scotland?" said Macdonald.

"Yes."

"Not very often. And our farm and our city aren't by the sea."

"No, I think you told me that once."

"Dallas is in its own little world."

"What do you mean by that?"

"You can see for yourself when you come here."

"Why would I go there?"

Half a second after Winter said it, he knew that he would go there. Go there soon. It was a feeling he didn't want to feel, that complicated intuition he didn't want to be without.

He felt a chill. Something was about to set sail; he couldn't see what. He suddenly wanted to go south, far south.

Aneta shivered as the wind came in through the half-open window. It cleared her thoughts. The sun glowed weakly over the fields. Everything was green, but only for another week. Then it would turn gold like everything that lies out in the sun too long.

This was the countryside; there were cows. She met a tractor that was driving in the middle of the road. The driver had a cap and seemed a bit backward. He was chewing on hay. He wouldn't have noticed if he'd smashed into her car.

She drove past a farm where pigs were rooting around in the ground next to the road. It smelled like pig shit, but she didn't close the window. This was the earth and the country they all came from; well, maybe she didn't, but all the other hicks in this frozen land did. Freeze-dried, as Halders had once said. We are freeze-dried, we're dry as fuck, and when we're warmed up and get liquid in us, we swell up times ten. She wasn't sure she understood, but it sounded great, like a lot of what Fredrik said. Crazy, but great. At the very least funny. Except for the black jokes, but those were gone now.

She stopped at a pullout and read her notes. The last time they'd met she had asked Sigge Lindsten where the cabin was. Suddenly a car came from the opposite direction at breakneck speed, and gravel flew up in her face. She didn't have time to see the car. She felt a sting on her forehead. She looked in the rearview mirror after the fleeing car, but she only saw dry dust from the road and then her own forehead, on which there was a drop of red. She wiped away the drop with her left index finger and licked up the blood, which tasted like red iron.

She knew that people drove like fugitive lunatics in the country. It was their country, but they rushed around it as though there were no laws. Wanted. Wanted dead or alive.

She had driven too far. She continued for a few hundred yards and found a turnoff and turned around.

She drove back, and there was still dust from the road in the air. She passed the pullout sign, which was old and almost colorless.

She found the right turnoff. Grass was growing in the middle of the desolate road. She was able to park in a natural pocket under a cliff that stuck out from a slope. She got out, and it smelled like the sea, but she couldn't see it. Seabirds were shrieking on the other side of the slope, which was overgrown with pine trees. She started to climb between the trees. The ground was warm.

21

She felt the wind as she stood at the top of the hill, and she could see the sea, which was large. She knew that it was on its way to the shore, but from here it looked like a congealed rock formation that had stretched as far as it could and become a mountain. The sea was not blue, not green, nothing in between.

Aneta went closer. Below the slope on the other side, pines were growing, same as on the eastern side. Between the pines she could glimpse a house. A car was sitting outside the house. She recognized it.

The car was a silhouette in that image.

A woman was standing on the other side of the car, turned toward the sea. Aneta recognized her, too.

The woman turned around as Aneta carefully made her way down between the trees, but she turned her face toward the sea again as though that were natural, as though it were normal that a detective from the city would come sliding down the slope in the threadbare afternoon.

The woman remained standing with her back to Aneta until it was necessary to turn around.

"I wasn't surprised," said Susanne Marke.

"Is Anette here?" asked Aneta.

"Isn't it peaceful here?" said Susanne, looking out over the petrified sea again.

"Do you come here often?" asked Aneta.

"This is the first time."

"But you found it easily," said Aneta, wondering about this conversation and this situation.

"Hans described the way, so it was no problem," said Susanne.

"Hans? Hans Forsblad?"

Susanne turned around, and Aneta could see the resolve in her face.

"Now listen carefully. There has been a big mistake here, and we're trying to fix it."

Aneta waited without saying anything. It would be a big mistake to say something now. She thought she saw the curtain in the only visible window move. That seemed natural, too; a natural repetition when you were dealing with these people.

"Do you hear me? A big mistake, and it won't help if the co . . . the police are running around interfering."

No. Everyone would be so much happier if the police didn't run all over interfering and instead told people to go away when they called to report thefts, assaults, homicides, murders. A mistake. Call the neighbor.

"It started when Anette's neighbors called," said Aneta. "Several times."

"A mistake," repeated Susanne.

"Anette's face was injured," said Aneta.

"Has she been to the hospital?" asked Susanne. It was a rhetorical question.

"Not that we know of," said Aneta.

"She hasn't," said Susanne.

"Could I see your ID?" asked Aneta.

"What? What?"

"An ID," said Aneta. "Your ID."

"Why?"

Aneta held out her hand. She saw how the expression on the other woman's face changed.

"Surely you don't think that . . ."

Aneta didn't say anything, kept holding out her hand.

Then Susanne smiled. It wasn't a pleasant smile. Suddenly Aneta recognized the smile, the expression, the eyes. *The face.*

It was the same face. The two faces had the same origin.

Susanne rummaged around in her handbag and took out a wallet. She rummaged around in the wallet and pulled out a driver's license and thrust it out with the same smile. The smile had stiffened on her face, which had become cold like the disappearing color in the sea and the sky.

Aneta saw Susanne's face in the photo, and her name. The license was one year old.

"Who is Bengt Marke?" asked Aneta.

"My ex."

"Is Hans Forsblad your brother?"

Susanne kept smiling. Aneta didn't need any other answer. She felt an immediate fear. She felt the weight of her weapon, the weight of safety, unexpected and unnecessary; she wouldn't need it. She realized that it had been a mistake to drive here alone. It was the kind of mistake Fredrik made. Had made. It had once come close to costing him his life. He had been lucky. The ignorant and bold were often lucky. They didn't know better. She wasn't bold, wasn't ignorant. Therefore, this could end badly.

These people weren't to be toyed with.

"He will always be my brother," said Susanne.

Whatever happens, thought Aneta. I believe her. I believe her when it comes to that.

"This is one big mistake," said Susanne.

"Where is the mistake?"

"Hans hasn't done anything."

"No?"

"He wants to put everything right again."

"If he hasn't done anything, there must not be anything to put right."

Maybe it was true. He wanted to make good. It wouldn't happen again. But what had happened hadn't happened. Everything was a mistake, and mistakes were always other people's. Everything was a misunderstanding. The beatings were misunderstandings. Aneta had heard of so many misunderstandings during her career in the brotherhood. No one called it the sisterhood; that would have been absurd. She had heard of how language ceased and violence took over. Blows instead of words. The desperate and languageless hit. Men are hard and women soft. Yes. They own, think they own, another person. Dominance. Complete control. A question of honor. In a twisted way, it was a question of honor. A form of honor. It existed here, too, in this fair-skinned country. It didn't belong only to medieval bastards from Farawayistan who murdered their daughters for the sake of their own honor.

"Other people's mistakes. It's about other people's mistakes," said Susanne.

"Sorry?"

"It's about other people," Susanne repeated. "We were talking about mistakes, right? Aren't you listening?"

"And you're going to help fix all these mistakes?"

Susanne didn't answer. She looked at the house. Aneta had also seen the movement in the window. A shadow, a silhouette.

"I'm just going to explain what Hans is actually like to the people who don't understand," said Susanne.

"Explain to whom? To the woman behind the window there?" said Aneta, nodding at the house and the window.

Susanne nodded.

"Is it Anette?"

Susanne turned to her again.

"I haven't had time to check yet, have I? I haven't had time, have I? You came tumbling down through the trees before I had time to knock, didn't you?"

"Where is Hans right now?" asked Aneta. "We're trying to contact him."

"Look in the trunk!" said Susanne, letting out a laugh that was like a bark that echoed away across the bay.

Aneta didn't believe many of Susanne's words, but she believed the half-wild laugh.

Bertil Ringmar stared through the balcony window at the neighbor's yard, which was entirely too visible behind a hedge that was entirely too low. His neighbor was crazy, an administrator from the hospital world who had gone a bit nuts when he had administrated away everything of value within health care; it all went to pieces, *putz weg,* every little bit, including his own job, and now he worked on various bits of his own yard.

The telephone rang.

"Hope I'm bothering you," said Halders.

"As always," answered Ringmar.

"Do you know what Aneta's up to this afternoon?"

"What kind of question is that?"

"I asked Erik, and he didn't know either," answered Halders as though to himself. Ringmar could hear his concern.

"Call her."

"What do you think I've been doing?"

"What is it about?"

"We're going to bring in the wife beater anyway for a little questioning, and I thought that she wanted to be there. We've found *das Schweinehund.*"

"Isn't it *der Schweinehund?*" said Ringmar.

"Or *die,*" said Halders. "In any case, we ran into a remarkable specimen this morning."

"You are a true people person, Fredrik."

"Yeah, right? I protect people, don't I?"

Ringmar was still standing at the balcony door. He saw the neighbor come out and walk down the path built alongside a number of concrete slabs that looked like Viking graves. Candles were burning; they were like bonnets on top of the graves. The first time Ringmar had seen it when it was completed, which hadn't been more than a few weeks ago, he had giggled in the same peculiar way Inspector Clouseau's boss did in the later Pink Panther films before he lost his wits forever. Ringmar liked those films, especially the inspector's unorthodox methods of doing his job.

"Aneta won't do anything stupid," said Ringmar.

"We all make mistakes," said Halders.

"She's worked with you so much that she's learned," said Ringmar.

"To make mistakes?"

"To avoid them. By seeing what you do and then doing the opposite."

"I don't like this," said Halders. "It feels like she rushed off."

"She'll call," said Ringmar, looking at his watch. "It's after working hours."

He heard Halders grunt an answer that he didn't understand and then hang up.

The neighbor out there lit some more lights. Ringmar cradled the telephone receiver and then laid it down in an exaggeratedly careful manner. Dusk was on its way. The neighbor began his uncompromising war against darkness. Try to look at it that way, Bertil.

"Perhaps you'd like to knock?" said Susanne. She made a motion as though she were inviting Aneta to step in front of her in line.

They were still standing ten or fifteen yards from the house, which was larger than it looked from the hill. It had more than one window that faced the sea. There was a veranda there. It must have been sensational to sit there as the sun went down. But today it wasn't going down, not so one could see.

What awaits us in there? Aneta was thinking. *Someone is there.*

There were no other vehicles on the lot. There was no garage.

Susanne made a sudden movement and Aneta gave a start. She thought she saw something moving out on the water, out of the corner of her eye, but when she looked there was nothing there.

It was as though the water wanted to tell her something.

Or that it meant something, something important that had to do with her, Aneta.

The water was a danger to her.

Don't come here!

Go away!

She saw a dock that must have belonged to the house. She saw a plastic boat. It was tied to the dock. She saw oars sticking up. The boat floated calmly in the water.

Susanne stood at the front door and knocked. Aneta walked over. Susanne knocked again.

The door opened slowly. It was dark inside. Aneta saw the outline of a face.

"Go away!" said the face.

Susanne started to say something, but Aneta was faster and showed her police badge.

"Could you please open up?" she said.

The face seemed to retreat. The door was still open a few inches. Perhaps that meant they could step into the cottage.

Susanne did.

Aneta followed her.

There was no light in the hall, which was narrow and long. The light of dusk could be seen outside of a window that was dimly visible where the hall ended and a room began. Someone moved in the room. Aneta saw a face. It belonged to an older woman.

"Mrs. Lindsten?" she said.

There was no answer.

"Signe, hello," said Susanne.

Aha, she's Signe to her. Am I the one she doesn't want to let in?

"Anette isn't here," they heard from the room.

Why did you come here alone? thought Aneta.

Susanne walked down the hall, and Aneta followed her.

The light in the room came from the sea. On bright days, it must be a very bright room, thought Aneta. Right now I can't really see this woman's face.

"Signe, you have to let Hans talk to Anette," said Susanne.

"Can't you leave her *alone*?" said Signe Lindsten in a voice that was more powerful than Aneta could have imagined.

"He just wants to *talk*," said Susanne.

Did he want something else before? wondered Aneta.

"Do you feel threatened by these people?" asked Aneta. "You can tell me."

"Oh, God," said Susanne.

"You understand that I'm from the police?" said Aneta.

She thought she saw Signe Lindsten nod.

"Where is Anette?" asked Aneta.

Signe Lindsten didn't answer. Aneta realized her mistake. A damn stupid question to ask when Forsblad's loyal sister was standing next to her.

"I'd like to ask you to step out for a minute," she said to Susanne.

Susanne didn't move. Aneta realized that Susanne realized that she had to leave, and that she was trying to say something but couldn't quite figure out what.

Suddenly Susanne turned around, said, "*Mistake*," in a loud voice, and left, stomping down the hall in her low-heeled boots, and before Aneta had time to say anything else to Signe Lindsten she heard the car roar to life and drive away. She hadn't seen the road when she climbed down between the trees, but she hadn't looked for it.

Winter walked across Heden. Middle-aged men were playing soccer with contorted faces. That was as it should be. He heard screams that sounded like a cry for help. He looked around for the meat wagon but didn't see it, nor did he see heart-and-lung machines.

He lit a Corps, his first of the day. He was cutting back, but he could hardly cut back more than this. He refrained from smoking during work. If he was going to refrain after work, he would have to ask himself what the point of that time of day, or any time of day, was.

It was the screwed-up viewpoint of a nicotine addict.

But it made sense. He tried to live a different life after the life that had to do with crime and all its consequences.

No smoking then, but smoking afterward. It made sense.

He had tried to explain it to Angela.

"I might understand," she had said. "While you transition. But later. Elsa might like to have you around when she is, oh, twenty-five. You were not twenty-five years young when we had Elsa. You were forty."

"I was still the youngest chief inspector in the country," Winter had said, lighting up. Angela had smiled.

"Have you ever looked that up? Really looked it up?"

"I trust my mother."

"There are two jobs where it's apparently possible to remain young and promising for any amount of time," Angela had said. "Detective inspector and author."

"I still feel young."

"Keep smoking and we'll see in a few short years."

"They're only cigarillos."

"What can I say?" She made a motion to indicate that she was speaking to deaf ears. "What else can I say?"

"Okay, okay. It's not good for me, and I'm smoking less and less."

"It's not for my sake, no, first and foremost it isn't about me, as a matter of fact. We're talking about your health—about Elsa's dad."

He let the thought go. He saw a soccer ball coming his way and he took the cigarillo out of his mouth and connected perfectly, and the ball flew in a beautiful curve back onto the gravel pitch. That's how it's done. First take the cigarillo out of your mouth and then connect with the ball with an extended ankle. That's how it must have been done when soccer was a game for gentlemen in nineteenth-century England.

His cell phone rang as he crossed Södra Vägen. The walk light was still on, but a man in a black Mercedes honked at him when he was halfway across the crosswalk. Winter answered the phone with a "Yes?" and stared at the man, who was revving the motor. The city was not a safe place. All the frustrated desperadoes racing around in their Mercedeses. He should throw that bastard in jail.

He turned onto Vasagatan and listened:

"You haven't heard anything else?" asked Johanna Osvald.

"If I find anything out, you'll know right away," he answered.

"I worry more and more each day," she said. "Maybe I should go over there?"

Yet another generation of Osvalds takes off to look for the last one, thought Winter. Three generations drifting around in the Scottish Highlands.

"What would you do?" she asked.

I would go, he thought.

"Wait and see for a few days," he said. "We have the missing-person bulletin out, after all. And I've spoken with my colleague."

"What can he do?"

"He knows people."

"You don't think something serious has happened?" she asked. "A crime?"

"It's possible he became ill," said Winter.

"Then he would have called," she said. "Or someone else would have called about him."

"We can help you," said Aneta Djanali.

"We don't need any help," said Signe Lindsten.

It was the answer that Aneta expected, but she still couldn't understand it.

"We want *everyone* to leave us alone," said Signe.

"Is Anette at home?"

Signe looked out through the window, as though that was where her daughter was, somewhere on the stony sea. Or in it, thought Aneta.

The sky had grown dark over the water, and everything had become the same color. Aneta could see the dock down there. She could see the boat. A lawn lay like a thin band that soon transformed into sand thirty yards from the edge of the water.

"Is Anette home, in Gothenburg?" asked Aneta.

The mother continued to look out at the shore and the sea, and Aneta did the same.

"Is that your boat?" she asked.

Signe gave a start.

She looked at Aneta.

"Anette is at home."

"In Gothenburg? At the house in Fredriksdal?"

The mother nodded.

"She didn't open the door when we were there."

"Is that against the rules?"

Technically, it is, thought Aneta.

"Is she very scared of Hans Forsblad?"

Signe gave another start.

"What can you do about it if she is?"

"We can do a lot," said Aneta. "I mean it."

"Like what?"

"Put a restraining order on him," she said, and she could tell how weak that sounded. "We can make a short-term decision on it and then hand it over to the prosecutor. We can bring him in for questioning. We've actually decided to do that."

"Questioning? What does that involve?"

"That we can take him in and question him about his threats."

"And then what? What happens then?"

"I don't—"

"Then you let him go, don't you? You talk to him and then that's it."

"He might not dare to—"

"Dare to visit Anette again? If you can call it that. Is that what you think? What the police think? That it's enough to write up some papers that say he can't see her, and that somehow you'll scare him by talking to him? You don't know him."

She was expressing genuine frustration, there was no doubt about that.

But there was also something else.

In the background there was something else. It wasn't just about the man, about Hans Forsblad. Aneta could feel that, see that.

"That's exactly why," she answered. "To see what he's like."

"I can tell you that here and now," said Signe. "He is dangerous. He doesn't give up. He is obsessed, or whatever you call it. He doesn't want to accept that Anette doesn't want to live with him. Doesn't want to accept it. Do you understand? He can't get it into his head!" She turned out toward the sea again, as though to gather her strength; she made a motion. "It's like he's completely crazy."

"Why haven't you contacted the police?" asked Aneta.

Signe didn't seem to be listening, and Aneta repeated the question.

"I don't know."

She hasn't mentioned that her husband called me, thought Aneta. Maybe she doesn't know. Maybe that's not what this is about.

"Were you afraid to?"

"No."

"Did he threaten you?"

"Yes."

"In what way?"

"I don't want . . . it doesn't matter . . . it could . . ."

Aneta tried to put together the pieces of what Signe Lindsten said. It was her job, a part of it, these broken sentences that people spoke out of fear, panic, sometimes with ulterior motives, sometimes out of sorrow, out of schadenfreude, in the effort to come up with the most believable lie. Splintered words that were barely coherent, and she had to unite those words, make them coherent so that she understood, so that someone understood.

Most of the time it was like this. Ragged words spoken by a frightened person.

22

It was so good at first," said Signe Lindsten.

Something happened to her face when she said it. As though the memory lifted her features, as though happy memories could smooth out faces. First comes the sun and then comes the rain and all that crap. Every cloud has a silver lining. All of that. Aneta couldn't see any of those clouds outside because everything was clouds over the bay and the cliffs and the sand and the shore; no silver linings anywhere, only a flash of light here and there in the middle of the mass of stone.

"He seemed so nice," said Signe.

I hate that word, thought Aneta. It doesn't mean anything. It's a false word. Look what happened here.

"It usually starts like that," said Aneta.

"I have a wedding picture," said Signe. "I don't have it here."

"Does Anette have any siblings?"

"No."

She thought of the man who had claimed to be Anette's brother. One of the thieves. Who was he? And his "dad"? I haven't asked Anette's mom.

She described what they looked like to Signe, who said, "What on earth?"

"Didn't your husband tell you about this?"

"No . . ."

"Doesn't that surprise you?"

"It does, yes, but he probably didn't want to worry me."

"Has he told Anette?"

"How should I know? If he had, I would have known about it too, right?"

Good. She gets it.

"Have you seen any injuries on Anette?"

Signe didn't answer. *This* is going to be really difficult, thought Aneta. It's going to be vague. She can talk about threats in a vague way, but not about the concrete details, not yet. It's almost always like this. It almost doesn't surprise me anymore. The woman's fear is transferred to the family. Suddenly they start to stick together about the fear. Won't let anyone in.

The only one who can be let in is the one who causes the fear. It's a paradox. There's always hope that it will get better and that all the fear will go away, and the only one who can make it stop is him, the one who was so damn nice at first, if only he has this one last chance one more time, and sometimes he gets it, and after that it might all be over.

Death might be the only thing left. She had seen it. I've seen what that last chance can lead to. Sometimes there doesn't even need to be a last chance. She saw Signe Lindsten's tormented face. It told her that this would end but that it would not end well.

Away with that thought. This case will be solved. I'm standing here, right?

"You don't need to be afraid, Mrs. Lindsten."

"You can call me Signe."

"You don't need to be afraid to tell me how it is, Signe, or how it was."

May the Lord bless you and keep you. May the Lord let his face shine over you. May the Lord have mercy on you. Did she need mercy, the woman before her? What kind of mercy? The Lord's mercy? Aneta suddenly thought of her father. The man of many gods, at least sometimes. Had she asked him about the concept of mercy in his world? She would call him and try to talk on the hopeless telephone lines to inner Africa. Soon satellite telephones would be the only solution, the only thing that worked in the interior. Swipe one from the storeroom, Fredrik had said.

Signe Lindsten was just about to say something when they heard a car outside. Aneta saw that the woman recognized the sound. Her face didn't change much. Her expression was the same when they heard a man's voice in the hall.

She didn't light up. His face doesn't shine over her, thought Aneta.

He came into the kitchen.

"Oh, here you are!"

Aneta nodded.

"We must have passed each other," said Sigge Lindsten.

"You called, but you weren't there when I arrived," said Aneta.

"No, that's how it goes," said Lindsten, perhaps by way of apology.

"Did Anette come down with you?" asked Aneta.

"No."

"You said earlier that she was here, but she's not."

"Yes, I did say that, yes. In the end she decided to stay home."

"Home? Home in the house in Gothenburg?"

"That's her home now."

"I would like to talk to her," said Aneta.

"Let her decide for herself," said Lindsten.

"That's why I would at least like to contact her."

"You can try to call," said Lindsten.

Aneta saw that his wife was trying to say something again, but she stopped and began to walk away, out toward the hall. Her husband nodded toward her. Neither of them said anything.

It's some kind of act.

"I don't think we'll have any more problems now," said Lindsten.

"You can file a report," said Aneta.

"It's not necessary."

"We can do a crime-scene investigation," said Aneta.

"Where?"

Preferably not in the house in Fredriksdal, she thought. That would mean that another crime had been committed.

"In the apartment in Kortedala," she said.

"There's not really anything to investigate there. Not anymore."

"I got the impression before that you wanted to cooperate on this," said Aneta.

"I don't think we'll have any more problems now," repeated Sigge Lindsten.

Moa Ringmar dropped one boot in the hall, and then one more. Her father got bread and butter and cheese out of the fridge, smoked sausage, cucumber.

"It's possible to arrange boots nicely," he said.

"Come on, Dad."

"When you hear the sound of one boot fall on the floor, there's no peace until you hear the other one too," he said.

"Well then, you got your peace right away just now," she said.

"I was thinking more of when you're sitting in a hotel room and you can hear the people in the room above," he said.

"And how often does that happen?"

"As yet it hasn't happened," he said.

She laughed and asked if he'd been home for long. She cut a slice of cheese and put it in her mouth.

"I've been home long enough to have time to admire our neighbor's yard art," he said.

"You have to let it go, Dad."

"He's alive, isn't he?"

She sat down.

"I may have found an apartment."

"Hallelujah."

"I knew you'd be sad."

"Yes. But I'm thinking of your happiness."

"It's serious when kids live at home when they're twenty-five," said Moa.

"It's only been temporary," said Ringmar. "We actually wrote you off four years ago."

"Good thing Mom can't hear this."

"You're not bugged?" said Ringmar.

"Do you do that at work?"

"No," Ringmar lied. "It's illegal."

"Are you telling the truth?"

"Yes," Ringmar lied. He spooned the tea leaves into the filter of the teapot and poured in the water and placed the pot on the table. "What apartment?"

"Two and a half rooms. Really nice but maybe not the best location."

"What is the best location?"

"I would say . . . Vasastan."

"Vasastan? That's where the worst and loudest crowds are on the weekends. And all summer. Hell, no."

"Erik lives there. Has he complained about loud crowds outside?"

"Only every day."

"I don't believe it."

"Erik Winter lives so high up among the clouds that he isn't bothered by the damage below," said Ringmar.

"That's what I'm talking about," said Moa. "Up in the clouds, the seventh floor."

"Where is this apartment, then?"

"Kortedala."

"Kortedala!"

"Better than Vasastan, isn't it?"

"I'm speechless," said Ringmar.

"You don't have to say more than hallelujah," said Moa.

"Kortedala," repeated Ringmar, shaking his head.

"I'm not moving to the South Bronx or anything."

"Martin was on his way to the Bronx," said Ringmar.

"But he went with the Lower East Side."

Ringmar nodded.

"Which used to be the worst neighborhood in Manhattan," said Moa.

"Used to be, sure. Now only designers live there."

"Like his neighbor?"

"I could sponsor a move for him," said Ringmar.

"Maybe you could sponsor mine," said Moa.

"Are you serious about this Kortedala thing, Moa?"

"Do you know how hard it is to find an apartment in Gothenburg? Do you know how long I've tried?"

"The answer to both questions is yes."

"Then you've also answered your own."

"Where is this nest? Kortedala is pretty big."

She told him the address. It didn't mean anything to him.

"How did you get wind of it?" asked Ringmar.

"Some girl in my class knew someone. I guess there was a guest lecturer who talked about how there might be something free and I got a phone number from this classmate and called, and, well, I might be able to rent it."

"Secondhand?"

"I don't actually know. Maybe at first. It was a little vague, I think. He sounded a little surprised when I called. They hadn't taken out an ad or anything. Like I said, a little vague."

"Doesn't sound too promising."

"Come on. It was a nice old guy who answered. His daughter's the one who moved out of there. At least for now."

"Why?"

"I didn't actually ask."

"What was the nice old man's name, then? Would he give it out, or was that a little vague too?"

"Do you always have to be so suspicious, Dad? Either you seem to hate people or else you're suspicious of them."

She took out a little red notebook.

"Yes, unfortunately. I don't want to say it's an occupational hazard, but . . . ," said Ringmar.

"Sigge Lindsten," she said, reading from the notebook. "The nice old man's name is Sigge Lindsten."

The name didn't mean anything to Ringmar.

Aneta Djanali was given concise directions, and she walked around the hill to the car. Sigge Lindsten had offered to drive her there, but it was only a few hundred yards. Climbing back up the way she came was not something she wanted to do. It was dusk now. She didn't want to get a twig through her eye.

She drove back on the narrow road. It was simpler with the powerful headlights. She didn't meet anyone. She went by the pullout sign, which wasn't any color at all now. She could hear the sea to her right.

Sigge Lindsten hadn't revealed anything more. There's something I don't understand here. But it's my job. You don't understand and when everything is over you understand even less. No. It's possible to understand. The problem is that it just gets worse then.

She had colleagues who refused to understand in order to avoid being neurotic. Neurosis was a concept that lived on within the force. Time could stand still in the force. Old values.

That wasn't always wrong.

When she reached the paved route north, it was with the sense of returning to civilization. At the moment she welcomed it.

She turned after the stop sign and switched on her cell phone. She had wanted it to be turned off when she spoke to Sigge Lindsten. Something had told her that she would learn something important from that conversation. That something had been wrong. Or else she hadn't understood.

Her voice mail beeped in irritation. She listened to the three messages, all of which were from Fredrik, and she saw that he'd also sent a text.

"It's nice to call before you go off into the blue," he had written by way of summary in his message to her.

And that was completely true. What if something had happened? Fredrik knew, and he had never practiced what he preached, and that had become dangerous.

But this is how she had wanted it to be this time.

She called.

"What the hell," said Halders in greeting, since he had seen her number on his screen.

"Same to you," she said.

"You've never done this before," said Halders.

"Has something happened?" she asked.

"That's what I should ask you."

"I went down to the Lindstens' beach house. Or cottage, rather."

"For God's sake, Aneta."

"She wasn't there. Anette."

"You couldn't know that. *He* could have been there."

"He's probably at his sister's house now."

"He has a sister?"

"Susanne Marke."

"The Volvo broad?"

"She is a fanatic supporter of Hans Forsblad," said Aneta.

"Then we should go there and get him," said Halders.

"I'll be at headquarters in twenty minutes."

"I'm the only one here."

"Who's with the kids?"

"My permanent babysitter," said Halders.

"I'm going by Fredriksdal," said Aneta.

"I am too," said Halders. "We can at least see if the lights are on inside."

Everything shone cozily and warmly as they drove through the southern neighborhoods. Someone had lit yard torches. Aneta stopped for a group that seemed to be on the way to a party. It wasn't Friday or Saturday, but this was a big city. Had become one. For some, it was Saturday every day. The group up ahead took their time crossing the street. Another car came from the opposite direction. It looked like the happy group was starting to play charades in the middle of the street. This was their neighborhood. The driver on the other side leaned on his horn. She caught a glimpse of the driver's face. Fredrik.

"As discreet as always," she said when they had parked down the street from the Lindstens' house and walked up the gravel drive.

"They should be glad I didn't run them over," said Halders. "I couldn't see anything as I was driving up. Did you see any reflections?"

Aneta didn't answer.

"Do you see any lights?" said Halders.

"We'll have to walk around," said Aneta.

They walked between the dense bushes and the southern wall of the house. The window where Halders had seen a figure was a dark rectangle against the lighter wall. Aneta felt a branch against her face. Halders cursed quietly when it hit him. She heard voices a ways away. It still sounded like charades.

"There are lights on, anyway," said Halders.

In the back, the veranda was lit up by light from the inside. The light cast a circle across the lawn. When her eyes had adjusted to the brightness, she saw a floor lamp inside the window. The window was broken.

"Well," said Halders, walking quickly up the low stairs to the veranda, but he stayed outside the railing. Aneta searched the room with her gaze, standing next to the small covered lamp, which cast a lot of light. She had her SIG Sauer in hand, and Fredrik had his God-knows-what in his hand. Fredrik would get nailed for that one fine day, or one fine evening like this one; he would hurt someone and the investigation would show what he'd shot with, and it would be the end of this professional team. She had often wondered if everyone actually knew. They ought to know. Did Erik know? Would he forbid it if he knew? Halders kicked down sharp shards that stuck out like icicles. He pulled on a glove and opened the veranda door from the inside. He pushed it open.

It was quiet in there. There was another light on farther in the house.

"I'm calling for backup," said Aneta.

"No reason to," said Halders.

"It could—"

"*Hello, this is the police,*" yelled Halders. She jumped and the hearing in that ear was gone.

"*It's the police,*" yelled Halders again, and he ran through the room out into the hall, and she heard his steps going up the stairs as she came into the kitchen, which also faced the back, and the light over the stove was lit but no one was sitting at the table or standing at the sink. She heard Fredrik up there, marching from room to room. It sounded like three rooms. She heard his steps on the stairs again.

"Empty," he said.

Aneta pulled on her gloves and went out into the hall again and tested the front door, which was locked.

"Came and went through the veranda door," she said.

"Through is right," said Halders.

Said the broken record, thought Aneta; she couldn't help it.

Halders went to the room that faced south. He turned on the ceiling light. Aneta stepped in. They saw an unmade bed and a desk, which was empty. The desk was white. There was a wooden chair in front of it; it was white. A white leather chair stood in one corner, with a little white coffee table in front of it. A white curtain valance hung in the window. The blinds were white. The wallpaper was a shade of white. Two photographs in white frames hung over the bed. The pictures were black as coal in the room. The sheets were white, and they were rumpled. Aneta expected to catch sight of a red stain in that bed, but there was nothing there.

A white rug lay on the floor, which looked like white-stained pine.

"If it weren't for those photos I would be snow-blind by now," said Halders. He turned to Aneta. "Do you think this looks nice?"

"No."

"White is the color of innocence, at least."

"What do you mean by that?"

"Maybe nothing has happened here."

"Someone broke a window and came in."

"Maybe just went out," said Halders. "Maybe she couldn't get out any other way."

"Was she a prisoner in her own home? Anette?"

"Well, maybe she went crazy in this room. Who wouldn't?"

"In any case, she's not here now," said Aneta. "So where is she?"

Halders shrugged. What is with him? she thought. Has he lost interest? Does he just feel silly? I got over that years ago, worked my way past it via lots of failures.

Aneta went back to the living room. Everything seemed to be in its place. Almost nothing was white in here.

She leaned over to the broken window and studied the floor, which wasn't lit by the lamp just there. She didn't want to move it, touch it. The floor was parquet, and it was a yellowish shade. She heard Fredrik behind her.

"Do you have a flashlight?"

"In the car."

"Can you get it?"

Halders went without asking. She heard him walking on the other side of the wall, and she heard when he opened the car door farther down the wall and closed it again and came back and cursed suddenly between the bushes and the trees. He stomped across the veranda and handed over the flashlight.

"What are those spots?" she said.

"Do you want an answer right away?" said Halders.

"It could be blood," she said.

"It could be anything."

She shone light on the broken window right above her. She didn't see anything.

"Give me the flashlight," said Halders.

He shone the light from the outside, a little higher up. There was something there.

"Someone cut themselves," said Aneta.

There will be a crime-scene investigation after all, she thought. But not where I'd thought.

Halders straightened his back.

"We have a message," he said, nodding at something behind her.

A telephone they hadn't seen before on one of the bookshelves had suddenly started to blink. They hadn't heard it ring.

23

The first time they went into Aberdeen, he rubbed his face, passed his hand across his eyes. It felt like being color-blind. It was different than at sea. He knew the color of the sea. But here he was met by a city that was built out of a single granite block.

The Granite City.

They lived on the boat.

Frans tried to stay in Brentwood for a night, but it didn't work.

They sat at the Schooner, which opened at seven in the morning. He remembered a slogan that had been by the door: "Where life begins at 7 o'clock."

Life.

It began and it ended.

They had met the men. Arne had met them, and it did something to him. He changed quickly. Let's stay away for now, he had said.

No one had gone along with that.

Frans had . . . had . . .

Jesus. Jesus.

He got up and walked over to the car, which he had learned to drive faster than he had expected. His body was still agile. He had discovered this when he leaned over and turned the key. He drove back to the east. The roads had improved. When he had come there the first time, freight was pulled by horses. Soldiers marched. Everyone stared at the sky. And the sea.

That was then.

He stopped at an inn and locked the car and went in and asked if he could use the toilet.

He washed off the worst. He looked at himself in the mirror, and he still recognized his own face. He turned his eyes away and dried himself with a paper towel, which was rough, and then he went out and kept driving.

After half an hour in the car he saw the sea far below.

He thought about the first time.

He had wandered along Albert Quay, wandered and waited. Gone down Clyde Street, loitered outside Caley Fisheries, passed Seaward Marine Engineering Co., Hudson Fish, North Star Shipping. Grampian Fuels, day after day he walked there and he could remember the names, and everything that went on there, any time he wanted.

They had been docked next to the *Cave Sand,* which had wintered here but came from Grimsby. It brought up slag and had gotten work south of the harbor. The men were black as Negroes all day long, and that was their life. Like Negroes!

He saw lots of soldiers, but never Negro soldiers, not even when the Americans came.

The cranes in the harbor were yellow and blue. That's not something you forget either. Yellow and blue everywhere.

He wondered whether they had been repainted in the same colors.

He stopped for a cup of coffee. He didn't remember passing this city as they drove west. He had been given some kind of directions, but he didn't remember them now. It didn't matter anymore.

Should I drive straight out into the sea?

At the right speed you could reach it. First you would fly, before you reached the sea.

Aberdeen. He had walked up Union Street and past Virginia and out to the beach where the city opened itself to the sea. The beach was wide; the sea was big here, and visibility was good on certain days. There was always haze and wind.

I was so young.

I didn't have a different name yet.

There had been ice cream trucks on the field that was the amusement park. It was always dark at night there. He could stand and watch the carousels that whirled in the darkness, and the people who whirled in the carousels. The only light came from the sea. Everything that whirled in darkness, an amusement park in darkness. It didn't fit. An amusement park should be a field of light.

*   *   *

They had continued up to Peterhead.

Now it was Europe's biggest whitefish harbor. Had it been the biggest one in the world back then?

Peterhead Congregational Church.

Royal National Mission to Deep Sea Fishermen

Fishermen's Mission.

Everything was fishermen and harbor and fishing industry and trawlers and the smell of the sea and of everything that came from the sea.

And God. Everything was also God.

24

Aneta Djanali called down to the shore in Vallda. Sigge Lindsten answered after the second ring. His voice was calm.

"Is Anette down there?" asked Aneta.

"We're expecting her tonight again," he said.

"There's been a break-in at your home."

"Another break-in?"

"In the house," she said.

"Is Anette there?" asked Lindsten.

"No."

"I'll call her on her cell."

"Give me the number," said Aneta.

"I'll call her now," said Lindsten, and he hung up.

Aneta looked at Halders.

She dialed the number again and heard a busy signal.

"I'll call forensics," said Halders.

He went back into the hall with his phone. She heard him talking. She dialed the number to the Lindstens' beach cottage again. Lindsten picked up.

"She's not answering," he said.

"Where could she be?"

"What actually happened?" asked Lindsten.

"We don't know."

"Was anything stolen?"

"We don't know that either," said Aneta. "I swung by here on my way home from Vallda and saw that the glass from the veranda door was broken."

"And Anette wasn't home then?"

What kind of question is that? thought Aneta. Would I have called and said what I said if she were?

"Is there any evidence?" asked Lindsten.

Evidence of blood. But I won't tell you that. And not before I know what it is. And not before I know what you were doing this afternoon.

"Did you leave a message for your daughter?" she asked.

"Of course."

"What did you say?"

"Oh, not much. I said she should call as soon as possible. That we were worried."

"We want to speak with her too. As soon as possible," said Aneta.

"We're coming home right away," said Lindsten.

"Good."

She hung up and Halders came back.

"A guy is on his way. Reluctantly."

"Doesn't matter how he gets himself here."

Halders let out a short laugh.

"Did you tell him that we're talking about a disappearance here that might involve violence?"

"Yes," he said, "but maybe I didn't sound so convincing."

"I have a bad feeling about this," she said.

"I guess I do too," said Halders after a bit.

"Have you called Susanne Marke?"

"Yes. No reply."

"Try again."

Halders took a deep breath.

"Well, we have to wait to hear what forensics says anyway."

"We should go there now."

"One of us can go," said Halders. "No, wait. There have been enough solo trips." He seemed to be listening for the sound of a motor from the road. "We can ask for a car there. In the meantime."

"I'll call dispatch," said Aneta.

They drove across the bridge. The river was lit up as though by torches on both sides all the way to the sea to the west and up through the land to the east. Ferries came and went.

"They say that Gothenburg is a dead harbor, but that's hard to believe when you're looking down from here," said Halders.

"Doesn't it have to do with the shipbuilding industry?" said Aneta. "It must."

"The hammers have become silent," answered Halders.

"You sound sad about it."

"There's always a reason to be sad," he said. "Who doesn't light up to the sound of hammering?"

"They're lighting up here, anyway," she said as they parked in the new residential area. The attractive houses glistened and seemed to preen in the light from the torches.

"Can't be cheap to live here," said Halders.

"Obviously not."

"How can Marke afford it? What was it she does?"

"Clerk at the district court."

"Financial crime?"

"No," said Aneta.

"Then I don't get it," said Halders.

"Her ex probably has money. We'll have to check."

"If we need to," said Halders.

Aneta took three steps to the left.

"Her car is home," she said.

Susanne Marke opened the door after the first ring, as though she had been waiting just inside.

She doesn't look as cocky anymore. Aneta could see an uncertain expression on her face, or maybe it was a puzzled one.

Susanne invited them in with a gesture. She told them to keep their shoes on.

The living room window had room for all the lights on the other side of the river. Halders could see the illuminated Seaman's Wife. She looked him in the eye.

A woman was sitting in one of the two white leather easy chairs. She had a bandage on her left hand. Aneta recognized her face.

"What really happened?" she asked straight out.

"When?" said Anette Lindsten.

"At your . . . at your parents' house."

"What do you mean?"

"The glass in the veranda door is broken."

"Oh, that. I ran into it."

She held up her hand. The bandage was starting to fall off. It was only a few loops of cheap gauze.

"I was trying to open it—it sticks—and suddenly the glass broke and I . . . I cut myself."

"Down by the doorstep?" said Halders.

"That's where it . . . stuck," she said, darting a look at Susanne.

Is this a lesson she's reciting and checking with Susanne? thought Aneta. Is this a threat, too? But then why did she come here?

"Why did you come here?" asked Halders.

"She can go where she wants, can't she?" said Susanne.

"Shut up!" said Halders.

"I got—"

"We've tried to contact you, Anette." Halders interrupted Susanne, but without taking his eyes from Anette. "Why have you been avoiding us?"

"I haven . . . haven't been avoiding you."

"According to several reports from your neighbors in Kortedala, you have been subjected to violence," said Halders. "Violence and threats. We would like to talk to you about that. We don't like violence and threats in general, and especially not against women."

"What do you call your coming in here and harassing me?" said Susanne.

Her uncertainty seemed to be gone. Aneta tried to read something in her face. Had Anette come here? Just come here, just shown up? Or had Susanne asked her to come?

"Why did you come here, Anette?" Aneta asked gently.

Anette didn't answer. Was she trying to catch the eye of the Seaman's Wife? Or was she studying the shining church steeple all the way up to hea—

"I have nothing more to say," she said. "You mu . . . must leave me alone."

"And I must ask you both to *leave*," said Susanne.

"We can give you a ride wherever you'd like to go," said Aneta.

How did she get here? Did she get a ride here? A taxi?

"I'll drive Anette when she wants to go," said Susanne.

"Do you want to go home?" asked Aneta.

Anette shook her head.

"We can drive you down to your parents' in Vallda," said Aneta.

"They're on their way he . . . on their way home," said Anette.

"Have you spoken with them?"

She nodded.

Halders looked at Aneta.

"We can go somewhere and talk for a bit," he said.

Anette shook her head.

I feel helpless, thought Aneta. Something is very wrong here, but there's nothing we can do about it right now. We can't take her with us. We can't force her to tell us what's happened to her, no more than we can ask her to write everything down and sign it while we stand here tapping our feet on this damn parquet floor.

"Where is your brother?" said Aneta, turning to Susanne.

"I don't actually know," she said.

Aneta tried to look at Anette's face. It was averted.

"Isn't he staying here anymore?"

"No."

"We need to have a rather long conversation with him," said Halders, looking at Anette, who was still sitting with her face averted.

"We can actually bring him in for questioning," said Halders to the averted face. "We have that right whether Hans Forsblad likes it or not. Anette? Can you hear me? Just so you know."

"He isn't here," said Susanne.

"And we're going to do it," continued Halders.

"Where did he move to this time?" asked Aneta.

"He didn't actually say."

The darkness of Indian summer was outside. Aneta could smell lingering scents from the summer gone by. It must be sixty degrees. She heard voices from a sidewalk café on the other side of the building. A laugh bounced across the river.

"Pure continental," said Halders.

"Aren't you furious?" she said.

"I was about to become really angry at Forsblad's sister," said Halders.

"That would have been perfect," she said. "On top of everything you said."

"Hmm."

"She might report it."

"Good. Then at least someone will."

They got into Halders's car. Aneta's car was still outside the Lindstens' house.

"They're probably home by now," she said. "The Lindstens."

"She is fucking freaked out," said Halders.

"Yes, but why isn't she saying anything? To anyone else?"

"How do you know she hasn't said anything to anyone else?"

"Yes, that's true . . ."

"To the gal in there, for example."

"Susanne? Do you mean that she's protecting her?"

Halders turned to her with a crooked smile.

"Not a thought you really want to think, is it. She's not worth it, is she."

Aneta didn't answer. They were on their way over the bridge again. The city's lights were like a dome all the way from the flatlands in the north to the forests in the south. A sign for the ships out there to the right. For everyone who could see. Could see. Could . . .

"There's something here that we haven't seen," she said.

"Isn't it always—"

"Something obvious," she interrupted. "Something totally, completely obvious that we haven't seen. What it *is*. What happened."

"Do we know what's going to happen, too?" asked Halders.

The Lindstens' house was unlit and quiet. Halders looked at Aneta's questioning face: Shouldn't the Lindstens be here?

"It's almost like I don't care anymore," said Halders.

Their colleagues from forensics had left shortly after Halders and Aneta had arrived. There had been two of them. We needed to come out anyway, as one of them had put it, and the other cracked up and they went on their way.

No one was laughing now. There was no car in the driveway. Aneta called, but Sigge Lindsten didn't answer, nor did his wife.

"Are you up for another drive?" said Aneta.

"Aren't we going home? You said you'd come home with me."

Halders looked at his watch. He had called the babysitter. Hannes and Magda were watching a quiz show that he had okayed. After that, straight to bed. He had said good night to the children just in case. But he had thought he would make it back. He and Aneta.

Aneta looked at him without answering.

He understood.

"No, Aneta. Not that. Not tonight."

"Why not?"

"It's late. We're tired. Anyway, we can't set up a . . . "

"Good interrogation? Who says it's Hans Forsblad we'll find there?"

She left the car at home in Kommendantsängen. "Governor's field." It was an interesting name for a concrete jungle. A beautiful concrete jungle. They heard drunken roars from Gyllene Prag over on the corner. Everyone was enjoying the reprise of summer. Two cafés had moved their furniture out again. The people of the city were out on the streets. It smelled like grilled meat and rapidly warmed wind from the south. They heard ambulance sirens out on Övre Husargatan.

"Someone else is in trouble," said Halders. "In the dark I hear a siren . . . Someone else is in trouble. I am not the only one." He started the car again. "Eric Burdon and the Animals."

They drove through Allén.

"I'm glad you came along, Fredrik."

"Well, of course I'm curious. Too."

The world of the seasons was unlit, and the contrast to downtown was great. Smoke rose from the large factories, or maybe it was fog that was rising in the sudden warmth.

The houses towered up like transatlantic ships in dry dock, but with their cabins lit up.

There were no people on the street. Shadows, but no people. Cars drove by at great intervals, but they seemed driverless. There were no sidewalk cafés.

"Cozy," said Halders.

"It's the in place to live now," said Aneta.

"I know. Why else would we be here?"

"We've arrived," she said, nodding toward the building.

"My God," said Halders. "Does this monster of a house end anywhere?"

*   *   *

Graffiti had been written over the top of graffiti in the elevator. Some people called it street art. Halders stared at that shit with a hateful look. Not so long ago, Swedish Television had called the CID and asked for a policeman who could participate in a debate program during prime time about graffiti versus street art, art versus damage. Some joker at the switchboard must have sent it up to Möllerström, and Möllerström proved that he had a sense of humor when he transferred the call to Halders, and Halders said yes.

Birgersson had managed to put a stop to the whole thing at the last second. It's for your own sake, he had said to Halders. Someone has to find out the truth, Halders had said. Soon, Birgersson had said, soon. The police commissioner had sent someone from a department no one had heard of, and Halders hadn't watched the piece of shit.

"When did you last see a mirror in an elevator in a building like this one?" he said, turning to Aneta, who was trying to prepare herself for their arrival on the floor above.

"It was before your time, anyway," continued Halders, and let out some sort of laugh. "There were mirrors everywhere. Jesus, it's almost like you can admire how naïve they were back then!"

"It was a belief in the future," said Aneta. "Don't be so cynical. They believed in the residents."

"Cynical? Me?"

"There are still mirrors in elevators," she said.

"In hotels downtown, yes. And in Winter's building!"

"Are you ready?" she asked.

Halders followed the numbers above the elevator door and nodded.

The elevator stopped.

The doors opened automatically.

All the doors in the stairwell were closed.

The light went out above them as they walked up to the door.

There was a light coming from inside.

25

Aneta Djanali rang the doorbell. They couldn't kick in the door. It wasn't ringing in there. Aneta didn't remember the doorbell being broken. She heard steps inside; it sounded like steps. Was it the thieves? The ones who said they were father and son? The criminal always returns to the scene of the crime.

"Don't stand right in front of the door," said Halders.

He knocked, or banged.

The shuffling inside stopped. Halders banged on the door again.

They heard steps again.

"Who is it?"

Aneta recognized the voice.

"Police," said Halders.

They heard the voice again, but no distinguishable words.

The door opened.

"So we meet again," said Aneta.

"What are you doing here?" asked Halders.

"I thought Anette was here," said Sigge Lindsten.

"She said that she had spoken with you tonight."

"Have you spoken to Anette?"

"Just now," said Aneta, "at Forsblad's sister's house."

"I was already on my way here then," said Lindsten.

"Why would she come here?" asked Halders.

"If she wasn't at home or with us down in Vallda, well, where else could she be? This was the only place I could think of."

"What about Susanne Marke's?"

"No," said Lindsten.

"No, what?"

"I didn't think she'd be there."

"Why not?"

"Not after . . . what happened."

"Where could Forsblad be now?" said Aneta.

"Not at his sister's, then?" said Lindsten.

"No."

"He could have been here," said Halders.

"He doesn't have a key," said Lindsten.

Is he that naïve? thought Aneta. Forsblad could have made any number of keys he wanted to.

"I was just about to go," said Lindsten.

"What is that smell?" said Halders.

"I don't smell anything here."

Halders pushed past Lindsten before he had time to say anything more. Aneta saw Halders turn into the kitchen on the left side of the hall.

She heard Halders's voice: "Coffee. Brewed pretty recently."

Aneta looked at Sigge Lindsten.

"I felt like a cup."

"Food in the fridge," Halders's voice said.

"Were you hungry too?" asked Aneta.

Lindsten threw a glance over toward the hall and the kitchen.

"It's for Anette's sake," said Lindsten.

"Sorry?"

"If she has to come here. Suddenly. If something else happened."

"Isn't this the last place she would choose?"

Lindsten didn't answer.

Halders came out into the hall again and walked into the bedroom on the other side and came back.

"Are the air mattress and sleeping bag in there for her sake too?"

"Yes."

"Apparently you think of everything," said Halders.

"It's still my apartment," said Lindsten. "I can do what I want here."

"When is Anette coming home again?" asked Aneta. "Home to the house in Fredriksdal?"

"Tonight, I assume."

"Is your wife there now?"

"Yes."

"I would like the two of you to check whether anything has been stolen from your house," said Aneta.

"Been stolen? But Anette told me that she happened to trip and break
the window. Didn't she tell you that too?"

They didn't answer.

"Didn't she tell you?" repeated Lindsten.

"She did," said Aneta.

"Someone could have come in after that," said Halders.

"Am I supposed to believe that?"

Halders looked around.

"What will happen to this apartment now?"

"Nothing," said Lindsten.

Bergenhem drove north. He passed Olskroken, Gamlestaden. He was
driving aimlessly. He stopped for streetcars. They seemed to be running
empty. They had had a problem with a streetcar driver last Christmas.
"Problem" was not the word. It wasn't even the first syllable. Where
would it end? Your wall's too high, sang John Kay inside the car. I can't
see, can't seem to reach you, can't set you free.

There was a rumbling out there somewhere. Could be thunder, could
be cannons, could be fireworks. He passed the SKF factory. The façade
looked threatening, like a black memory. People have good memories from
there, he thought. All the Italians who came here in the sixties and built
welfare for the Swedes. The record years. Now there are no more records
left to break except this one: most trips around the city in one week, one
month, one year. John Kay sang "Born to Be Wild." No choppers passed
him. Otherwise, he was in Chopperland. There were different laws here,
chopper laws. Biker laws. *That* was the rumbling; he heard it again. Har-
leys in the courtyards among buildings that had been blown into the air,
or would be. The sound of motors would remain, cylinders, wheels, gears.
Though SKF wouldn't remain, not here. They would be relocated to South
America, maybe southern Italy. The residents of Kortedala would have to
move to Calabria and produce new welfare for others. New record years.

Born to be wiiiiiiiild. Bergenhem sang along; he had to do something. He passed giant buildings. Something strange had happened
to Aneta in one of those. Brazen scoundrels who had pretended to be
someone else, right in the face of the law. Stole a whole apartment right

in the face of a detective. Gothenburg's Finest. It could have been him. It could have been here. He drove more slowly, read the street signs, saw the building that grew up out of the darkness and covered the whole sky, saw the lighting of the stairwell, the numbers. It *was* here. Sure as shit, it was here.

He backed up and read the street sign again.

Number five. He remembered number five. It was such a special story that he remembered the number. He drove forward again, a little bit. Number five. A car was parked where cars were not allowed to be. He thought he recognized the car. He stopped. It could be Halders's unmarked police car.

He stood still twenty-five yards away. Steppenwolf was no longer singing. He could hear the streetcar passing far behind him; he saw its lights as a flash.

He saw another flash; a cigarette being lit in the front seat of a car that was parked ten yards behind Halders's car, if it was in fact his.

Bergenhem took his binoculars out of the glove box. Yes. It was Halders's car. He moved the binoculars. A man was sitting in the car behind it and the cigarette glowed as he took a drag. Now he was picking up a cell phone. Now he was putting it down. Now he was smoking again. Completely normal behavior. Now he was smoking again. He looked straight ahead, at door number five.

He's waiting for someone, thought Bergenhem. Or he's trying to decide whether to go in.

Or he's waiting for someone to come out.

So he can go in.

Shit, I'm worse than Winter. Never letting it go. Seeing what might be happening when things aren't as they should be. When they aren't good. When there's a reason to be suspicious.

Assume that everyone is a suspect. Act accordingly.

Assume that everyone is lying. Act accordingly.

Winter's Law. And Halders's Law, to be sure.

Now he was smoking in the car again.

Bergenhem got out his phone and called.

Halders's breast pocket was ringing. They were on their way to the elevator. The door to the Lindstens' apartment was closed behind them.

Lindsten was just going to drink up the coffee, as he said. Café ooh la la, said Halders when they'd left.

Halders took out his phone, which sounded loud in the bare, graffitied brick hall that shone with silver and gold. Halders read the screen. Blocked number.

"Yes?"

"Bergenhem here. Where are you?"

"What the . . . I'm in a cozy little villa in Kortedala. Some season address, I don't have the exact—"

"I'm standing outside."

"Repeat," said Halders, looking at Aneta and rolling his eyes.

"Listen up, Fredrik. I don't know what it's worth but I was driving by and remembered yours and Aneta's gig and I stopped. I recognized your car. It's right outside the door. There's—"

"What are you getting at, Lars?" interrupted Halders.

The elevator came up. Bergenhem heard it, recognized the noise.

"*Listen,* for fuck's sake, Fredrik. Wait a second when you come out of the elevator down there, and think. I'm sitting out here, and I'm sitting behind some character who might be keeping tabs on your car. Maybe he's waiting for someone else. Maybe he's been thrown out. I don't know. I just had a hunch."

"What kind of car is it?" asked Halders.

"A Volvo. V Forty. Might be black, but all cars are black in this light. Or dark."

Bergenhem could hear Halders whistling, or maybe it was the elevator whistling itself down. Apparently it was possible to talk on a cell phone in the elevator. Or maybe it was a satellite. Aneta had said something about a satellite phone.

"Is he alone?" said Halders.

"Yes. If no one is lying on the floor in the backseat."

"He's watching us," said Halders. "It's Hanzi Fanzi."

"Who?"

"Forsblad. Hans Forsb . . . oh, fuck it, is he still there?"

"He's just lighting another cigarette. He's sitting behind the wheel."

Bergenhem heard the elevator doors glide open.

"This is what we'll do," said Halders.

* * *

When Halders and Aneta came hurtling out of number five, Bergenhem was standing behind the Volvo and he rushed up and yanked open the door before the driver had time to start the car.

Life is full of surprises, thought Bergenhem as he was driving back in the night. The city suddenly looked different. There was a different light over Gamlestaden, then Bagaregården, Redbergsplatsen, Olskroken. No local police here anymore. The territory went back to the enemy. The chopper gangs. Get your motor running.

He felt a freedom in his body, almost a happiness.

They got a room after waiting for fifteen minutes. They walked through corridors that looked about like the stairwell in the colossus in Kortedala, minus the graffiti. It's only a matter of time, thought Halders. Soon those devils will be in here too. Maybe they're already here among us.

"I've never seen the like," said Hans Forsblad suddenly. "This is going to cost you."

In the car he had been quiet. Aneta had thought she heard a giggle. Must have been a sob.

When they came up to his car he had sat without moving. Naturally, he had looked surprised.

And yet he hadn't.

He had come along without Fredrik having to knock him out.

Forsblad knew. He knew the law, at least on paper.

26

Forsblad knew that they could hold him for six hours plus six hours. He wanted to get out before then. He squirmed on the chair in the interrogation room. He wasn't comfortable there. It wasn't pleasant.

"What is your occupation, Hans?" asked Halders.

"What does that have to do with it?"

"Just answer the question, please."

Forsblad was silent.

"Is it a secret? Your job?"

"What is this? What do you mean?"

"Clearly you don't want to tell us."

"I'm a lawyer at the district court."

"What kind of law?"

"Sorry?"

"Do you work with civil rights or with—"

"I thought all policemen knew our lawyers," said Forsblad.

"Do you know us, Hans?" asked Halders.

"Uh, no."

"We asked around about you a little, and you're as unfamiliar to the other lawyers as you are to us. As a lawyer, that is. Are you with me, Hans?"

"Uh . . . it . . . I don't understand."

"You're an archivist, aren't you? Nothing wrong with that. But you don't need a law degree for that job."

"I'm a lawyer," said Forsblad. "I have the degree."

Aneta could tell by looking at him that he was telling the truth, but a truth that belonged only to him.

"Your job is to be an archivist," said Halders. "But you have expressed a wish to attend courtroom proceedings. That's unusual."

"I've noticed how the job could be done better," said Forsblad. "I'm the one who's slaved away retrieving the documents, aren't I? I'm the one who's done the work I've read all the documents. I've made thousands of copies of them."

Have you read all the copies, too? wondered Halders.

"What have I gotten for it?" said Forsblad. Aneta noticed that a little bubble of saliva had formed at one corner of his mouth. Suddenly Forsblad noticed that she had noticed. He gave her a look that said he realized she had noticed. It was a dark look. It said that he didn't forgive her. For seeing him as a shady guy. For despising him just like everyone else despised him. He hated her. She was the enemy, one of the many in the army that marched against him.

Is that how it is? Am I reading all of that into that look? In any case, it's nasty. He's looking at me again. There's a message.

Forsblad licked the corner of his mouth.

"You don't like your job?" asked Halders.

Forsblad snorted, twice.

"Are they nasty to you at your job?" asked Halders.

Forsblad snorted again.

"Are there more people who have been nasty to you?" asked Halders.

Forsblad looked away, at the wall, which was painted a gaudy shade of green. We do not look our best in this room, and that's the point, thought Aneta. Fredrik looks like a death camp commander.

"Was Anette nasty to you?" said Halders.

"Don't bring her into this," said Forsblad.

"Oh?"

Forsblad looked at the recorder, which was small and like a part of the table. There was no video camera this time. Maybe next time.

"Don't bring her into it," Forsblad repeated.

"Are you at all aware of why we're having this conversation?" said Halders.

"No," Forsblad said, and smiled.

Halders looked at Aneta. No, Fredrik. You can't hit him for answering like that. You gave yourself away.

"We have spoken to Anette," said Halders.

"I have, too," said Forsblad.

Halders chose to ignore that comment.

"We told her that we want to help."

"Help with what?"

Halders looked at him. Forsblad looked back. He doesn't really seem to be following the conversation, thought Aneta. He's drifting in and out of it.

"Protect her," said Halders.

"Protect her? Protect her from what?"

"From you," said Halders.

Forsblad said something they didn't hear.

"Sorry?" said Halders.

"I'm not the one," said Forsblad. "It's not me."

"Is there someone else who's threatening Anette?"

Forsblad nodded twice, up and down. Like a child. He acts like a child, thought Aneta. This is like interrogating a child.

Forsblad nodded again. She could see that Fredrik saw what she saw. She saw what Fredrik was thinking: Hanzi shouldn't be sitting here, he should be in the madhouse.

But there were no madhouses anymore.

The lunatics were sitting here instead.

Willkommen. Bienvenu. Welcome.

"Who is threatening Anette?" asked Halders.

Forsblad didn't look at him; he was looking at Aneta, who was sitting behind and to the left of Halders.

Suddenly he stretched out his hand and pointed at her.

Halders abruptly turned around.

"My colleague? What do you mean, Forsblad?"

"She's threatening her with all these questions. Running about and sniffing around. Everywhere. Doesn't understand. She doesn't understand."

"What doesn't she understand?" said Halders.

Forsblad gave a sudden laugh. It was an ugly laugh.

"What don't *I* understand?" said Halders.

"That would be quite a bit," said Forsblad.

"Anette has been subjected to assault. We have witnesses. Who is it that has subjected her to this assault?"

"A physical assault?" asked Forsblad.

Every answer is an adventure, thought Aneta. We don't know from question to question and answer to answer where we'll end up. But maybe we'll end up somewhere. Maybe Forsblad isn't lying. Maybe it's worse.

"There isn't anything known as solely physical assault," said Halders. "It's all connected."

"Interesting," said Forsblad. "Interesting that you should say that."

Aneta could see the pulse pounding in Fredrik's neck. Take it easy, now. Easy.

"We're not done talking to Anette," said Halders.

"Me neither," said Forsblad.

The pulse was visible in Fredrik's neck.

"Starting now, we will know where you are," said Halders. "Where you go."

"Is that a threat?" said Forsblad, and smiled.

Halders's pulse hammered. His hand jerked.

"Fredrik!" said Aneta, and Halders jerked his hand back and looked at it as though he had seen it for the first time. He seemed, for one second, not to be there.

"I suggest we take a break," said Aneta.

"He's trying to mess with me, that bastard," said Halders. They were sitting in the break room. Halders was trying to drink a scalding-hot cup of coffee. Once it cooled, it was undrinkable.

"He's afraid," said Aneta.

"Afraid of me?"

"Afraid of everything."

"You'll have to explain that."

Halders tried to drink again, and he grimaced.

"Afraid at his work, afraid of other people, afraid of . . . I don't know," said Aneta.

"Someone else who's threatening him?"

"I don't know."

"Is he protecting someone else?"

"It's as though there's someone else here, too."

"The dad? The Lindsten guy?"

"Maybe."

"He's definitely fucking shady."

"I was thinking about that break-in, or whatever it was, the theft from the apartment out in Kortedala. Could Forsblad have known about it?"

"Yes, why not?"

"Or the dad. Sigge Lindsten."

"Why not both?" said Halders.

"Would he steal from himself?" asked Aneta. "Lindsten?"

"He didn't steal from himself," said Halders. "He stole from his daughter."

Aneta thought of Halders's words. She watched him drink. Drink coffee and survive.

"What are we really trying to figure out, Fredrik?" she said after a little while.

"Well, not the theft, anyway. Not in my case."

"You don't think it has to do with this?"

"If by 'this' you mean the assault, then I don't think so."

"And what is 'this' for you?"

Halders pushed his paper cup away with yet another grimace.

He scratched his chin, which had nearly a day's stubble.

He was blue under the eyes. The unforgiving light in the break room shone through his crew cut and revealed his scalp. He had called home once to make sure that the babysitter had everything she needed to stay overnight tonight. He scratched his chin again.

"I've almost gotten to be like you were about this, Aneta." He looked at her with tired eyes. "But I'm not sure that Forsblad is really a wife beater. Or that we're protecting his wife by clamping down on him." Halders grew quiet. He looked as though he were listening intensively to the hissing air up by the intake behind them. It wasn't a pleasant sound. He ran his hand over the back of his close-cropped head. "There's something damn suspicious about all of this. About all of them. Every-one involved."

Aneta nodded.

"Something more than we know," said Halders. "Much more."

"Forsblad?"

"I'm not sure."

"Lindsten?"

"The dad? Yes, it's possible."

"Anette?"

Halders didn't answer; he seemed to be listening to the rush of the ventilation system again, the tittle-tattle in the corner. He looked at Aneta again.

"We don't know anything about Anette, do we?"

Forsblad looked like he'd been sleeping when their colleague from the jail brought him into the room again. He still had his jacket on, and his tie, the white shirt, the odd pants, which weren't particularly wrinkly, the shoes, which were no longer shiny. Forsblad's thick hair looked recently combed, but in a way that suggested he had just run his hand through his hair and it was done.

"Why were you sitting in your sister's car outside the house in Kort-edala?" asked Halders.

"That's my right as a citizen," said Forsblad.

"Why there in particular?"

"I recognized the place."

Halders looked at the recorder to make sure it was turning. He looked like he wanted to reassure himself that it was working so he could listen to the answer later and analyze it.

"Why then, in particular?"

Forsblad shrugged.

"Was it because my colleague and I were in there?"

"How should I have known that you were there?"

"Where are you living now, Hans?"

"With my sister."

"She says that you aren't."

"I see."

"Do you have any permanent residence?"

"I'm working on it," he said.

"Where?"

"It will work out."

"You know that there's a restraining order against you?" said Halders. It was a lie, but not for long. "Our short-term decision has been extended by the prosecutor."

Forsblad looked like he wasn't listening or didn't care. As though all of that had happened a long time ago. He seemed to be listening for other voices inside his head, or to the air conditioning that was hissing in there.

He looked up. He fixed his eyes on Aneta.

"Maybe I can live with you," he said.

Aneta didn't answer. She avoided his gaze. You should never make eye contact. In Africa there were crazy apes that had rabies, and they tried to make eye contact, and when they did it was dangerous; it was very, very dangerous.

"You've been clinging to me this whole time, after all," said Forsblad. "I'm starting to wonder what it is you actually want."

He was released after midnight. To go home, but in this case that was just an expression. Or else he had a home, or a bed, a sofa, an air mattress.

"In an hour we ought to break down the door in Kortedala and wake him from his beauty sleep," said Halders.

They were on the way home to Aneta's place. Halders was driving fast but avoiding the few boozers who stumbled out into the road, on their way home from that evening's entertainment.

"If we hit someone we'll pretend it's a badger," he said.

"If he's sleeping in that apartment, then Anette's dad is in on it," said Aneta. "We can't tromp in there again."

"Of course we can," said Halders. "But not tonight."

Aneta looked around when they parked. She couldn't see the glow of any cigarettes in any front seats, no silhouettes.

"Do you think he was serious?" she said.

"About sleeping at your place?"

"Did you think it was funny?"

"Oh, Aneta, it was just another way to provoke us."

"You didn't see his eyes."

"I did, too."

"He was trying to make eye contact with me," she said.

Halders opened the front door.

"He wouldn't dare come here," he said.

"How do you know?"

"Because I told him I'd kill him if he did. It was when you were inside and I was outside waving good-bye."

The morning was light and warm. There were people smiling on Vasagatan. The sun was round and kind. The sky was blue. Birds were singing.

Winter was walking to the Palace. He saw the temperature on the gauge over Heden: sixty degrees. Already. No one was playing soccer on the fields at Heden. A mistake on a morning like this. The air was easy to breathe in and breathe out. He yearned to sacrifice an ankle.

The sun shone in. Ringmar stuck in his head after Winter had sat down and started to go over the cases: thefts, assault, homicide, robberies, threats, more thefts, criminal damage, another homicide, two more robberies. Reports, testimonies, statements. Papers, cassette tapes, videotapes. Many cases, all at once. A suspected murder. A confessed murderer. A drunk dispute in a neighborhood in Gamlestaden. Almost all homicides and almost all murders looked like that. Case open and closed within twenty-four hours.

"Do you have a minute?" said Ringmar.

"No, I have two," said Winter, putting down a sheet of paper.

Ringmar sat down. His face was sharply lined. He was twelve years older than Winter, which meant that he had some hard years behind him that Winter had in front of him. Maybe the hardest. And Ringmar had twelve years more of duty as ombudsman and protector to the public in front of him. How would the lines in his face look then? And Winter had twenty-four years left, t-w-e-n-t-y-f-o-u-r years in front of him, in the same role. Dear God. A third of a *life* the same way as this. Lift me up, take me away.

At the same time, this *was* his life. He knew this life. He was good. He had knowledge and aggression, maybe not as much aggression as Halders, but more knowledge. He had patience. He could work hard. He could think. That was *that*. One could think here; it was still possible to take time for thoughts. And thinking could lead to results. A person who didn't think well didn't get results. Not the big results, the ones you got from thinking outside the routine. Thinking outside the beautiful melodies. Winter listened to Coltrane when Coltrane was in his most discordant period, and it was a similar atonal platform that he, Winter, started out from. It never worked to think in a straight line. It was possible to follow logic, but it was logic that couldn't be followed by anyone else. It was his logic, the same way it was Coltrane's logic, Pharoah Sanders's logic, or Miles Davis's logic. He had sent off for a book from Bokus .com and he'd received it yesterday: *Kind of Blue: The Making of the Miles Davis Masterpiece,* by Ashley Kahn, and he was going to try to start reading it tonight if he had time to listen first, which he was starting to do now. The Panasonic was on the floor. He was playing *Kind of Blue* for the thousandth time.

"'So What,'" said Ringmar.

The first song. Ringmar knew *Kind of Blue.* It was simply part of a general education to know that album. Winter didn't really understand people who didn't understand it. There was nothing to understand, incidentally. You just had to listen.

"The woman from Donsö called half an hour ago," said Ringmar. "Möllerström transferred it to me."

"Good."

"It was this Johanna, in other words."

"I understand that, Bertil. What did she want?"

"Just to ask if we'd heard anything."

"Have we?"

"No."

"Has Möllerström checked with the national control center?"

"I assume so."

"How did she sound?" said Winter.

"Calm, I think. But of course he's been gone a few weeks now, her father."

"Yes. Something has happened."

"Must have," said Ringmar.

The music continued, "Freddie Freeloader." Winter thought of Johanna Osvald, of her brother, her father, her grandfather. He thought of Scotland, of Steve Macdonald.

Ringmar rubbed his hand over the lines in his face.

"How's it going, Bertil?"

"Not bad. Moa has a new apartment on the way. Good for her, I suppose. But for my part, she could have lived at home for a while longer."

Winter looked at him.

"You'll understand in twenty years," said Ringmar.

"Okay, we'll discuss it then." Winter fingered for his pack of Corps, but no. He wanted to be strong. There were many years left.

"Where is she moving to?" he asked.

"Kortedala," said Ringmar.

27

The news came via Interpol before the morning was over. Or maybe it came directly from Inverness to Möllerström. He was the one who came in to Winter with the printout and directed him to the department's intranet.

"Just tell me," said Winter.

"He's dead," said Möllerström.

Winter tried to call but couldn't get through. He tried again five minutes later.

The chief inspector's name was Jamie Craig, from the Northern Constabulary, Inverness Area Command. He didn't sound like a Scot but like an Englishman like anyone else, a dry accent, clinical, technical.

"He seems to have been wandering around town for a little while," said Craig.

"You mean Inverness?"

"No. Fort Augustus. It's on the southern tip of the lake. Just a village, really."

"The lake? What lake?"

"Loch Ness, of course."

Of course. The world-famous waterway southwest of Inverness. Nessie. The lake monster. Winter had not visited Loch Ness, hadn't seen Nessie.

"But they found him a bit up east, in the hills, by a minor road, and by a small artificial lake called Loch Tarff. At least I think it's artificial."

"And the car?"

"No car."

"Where is his rental?" asked Winter.

"We don't know. He didn't have a car when we found him, and he didn't have any clothes on."

"Come again, please?"

"This looks strange, sure. He seemed confused when he wandered around the town but he was fully dressed and he paid his way in a pub. Bought a pint and a ploughman's, I think."

Craig described what he knew.

A man of about sixty had shown up in Fort Augustus and walked around as though he hadn't been completely right in the head. People in the city were used to eccentrics from all corners of the world coming there to discover the lake monster again, become famous too, but this man hadn't been crazy that way. He had moved strangely, spoken incoherently to people he ran into. He had gone into the pub next to the gas station and drunk a Scotch ale and left his ploughman's lunch: bread, cheese, relish.

Someone had seen him wandering off to the east. Then the bulletin about Axel Osvald was released, and this someone called Craig at Longman Road.

After that it was only a question of a little time. They had driven on the old road, B862, east of the lake, back toward Inverness, and had people comb the countryside, and they hadn't had to climb around in the hills and the rocks for more than half a day, and hardly that.

"He was on the other side of that little lake," said Craig, "hidden from the road."

"Without clothes?"

"Not even socks," said Craig, and Winter wondered to himself if that was an English expression for someone who was truly naked.

"But you think it's our man, Axel Osvald? Why?"

"This is where it gets even stranger," said Craig. "Of course I can't be one hundred percent sure that it's him, not yet, but the fact is that his clothes are spread out on the ground almost from down by the southern tip of the lake and up to where we found him. It's a distance of a few miles. You can get the precise distance if you want, naturally."

Naturally. Pronounced with dry self-certainty. Winter wasn't sure that Steve Macdonald knew this man, not personally. They seemed to have made opposite journeys. Craig might have been from London, and he was a chief inspector in Inverness. Steve was from Inverness and a chief inspector in London.

"So we find a naked man and in the area we find a whole set of clothes, including shoes and outerwear, and we think, aha, there might be a connection here," said Craig. "We gather up the clothes. We find a wallet with a driver's license in this Osvald guy's name, and the photograph looks like the dead man."

"How did he die?" asked Winter. "Your preliminary assessment, I mean. The Interpol message mentioned possible natural causes."

"His heart," said Craig. "That's as preliminary as I can be. Of course, they're not done in pathology but there's no outward sign of violence on the body, no wounds or anything. The doctor has bet two pints on a heart attack. It was cold up there. An older man up in the mountains at night, without clothing, possibly confused—well, it probably couldn't have ended any other way."

"Heart attack," repeated Winter.

"I don't actually think I could survive a night up there naked," said Craig. "At least not if I was alone," he repeated in the same expressionless voice.

"When can you have a complete report ready?" asked Winter.

"About what?"

Still the same voice, clinical and analytical.

"I was thinking first and foremost of the cause of death."

"This afternoon, I think."

"Thanks."

"Everything else will be in the reports tomorrow, I hope. Everything we know, that is. It's not so much. But the case, if we can call it that, sure seems to be clear."

Winter had expected Craig to say "open and shut" about the case, but he didn't say it. For that matter, it wouldn't have been consistent with his image.

"But the rental car is still missing, then?"

"Yes. We spoke with the people at Budget; it was rented for two weeks, and it so happens that the time wasn't up until yesterday. They filed a report of a possible theft with us, and that meant that we, well, took a little extra notice about this . . . the disappearance, the missing-person bulletin. Along with the witnesses from Fort Augustus, of course."

Winter could hear a change of nuance in Craig's voice, as though he might feel that he needed to justify his actions. That it had taken longer than it should have to start the search for Osvald. But Winter had no such views. He was aware of the assumptions and the reality. It couldn't have been the first time a stranger had wandered around Loch Ness.

"Shouldn't the rental car be somewhere nearby?" said Winter. "In the city there, Fort Augustus."

"It should," said Craig. "That bothers me. But if it had been in the same place for a few days, it was probably stolen. There are lots of cars and lots of car thieves around Loch Ness."

"I understand," said Winter.

"We have a bulletin out on the car, of course," said Craig. "It will probably be found somewhere in the area, cannibalized, as usual." He paused. "Naked, as we say."

"The dead man," said Winter. "How long had he been lying there?"

"The doctor said forty-eight hours the last time I spoke with him, within six hours either way."

"Could he have been moved to where he was found?" asked Winter. "Could he have died somewhere else?"

"No," said Craig. "We're quite certain that he got to the place where he died on his own."

"Then the question is why," said Winter.

"Isn't it always?" said Craig.

"Yes. The big question."

"Steve told me that we would end up there sooner or later if I talked to you," said Craig.

"Steve? Steve Macdonald? You know him?"

"Yes. We worked together for a while in Croydon. He put in a good word for me when I was trying to get the position as chief inspector up here." Craig paused. Winter heard something that could have been a short laugh, dry as sand. "I don't know if I should thank him or not."

There was a drop of warmth in Craig's voice. Winter couldn't help but smile. He had gotten a lesson in Englishness. Craig wasn't the one who'd started this conversation with talk about their mutual friends. It was also a question of being professional, of course.

"What do the witnesses say?" asked Winter.

"Well, what I said before, more or less. He had acted confused, as though he didn't really know where he was. He had said things . . . it seemed like he was asking questions; that was the impression one person had gotten from him. And the pub owner. He had repeated something that sounded like the same thing, if I can say so. But it wasn't possible to hear what it was."

"Why not?"

"Why not? It wasn't in English, or Scottish. I assume he was speaking Swedish, but that's not our everyday language in Fort Augustus." Craig paused again, briefly. "Of course this is old Viking land, but I don't think people remember the Nordic language."

Old Norse, thought Winter. There are many Nordic words in Scotland, words for places, other things.

"So he walked around speaking to people in Swedish," said Winter. "He wasn't just talking to himself? You said yourself that he seemed to be confused."

"Well, we haven't really asked in detail, but the witnesses have said that he spoke to them as though he were asking something."

"Mmhmm."

"I can't help you there. I can certainly press them a little more about how he spoke to them and whether he might have been asking questions, but I can hardly get farther than that, can I?"

"No."

"If worse comes to worst you'll have to come here and test Swedish words on people," said Craig. "I've heard that there aren't so many."

28

W ill you tell the next of kin?" Craig had said, and Winter had said yes. That was part of his job, a much too large part. There was no practice for it in the police training, and entirely too much experience of it later.

He called Johanna Osvald's cell but only got her voice mail in his ear. This wasn't something you could tell someone on voice mail.

He looked at the clock and looked up the timetable for the southern archipelago. He looked at the clock again. He would make the 10:20 *Skarven* if he drove too fast on Oscarsleden.

Winter stood on the deck with the wind in his hair. Someone was fishing on the cliffs just behind the harbor. He had gotten a bite, or was about to: the gulls were wheeling in their own circles, screaming encouragingly to the man, who was wearing a wide cap for protection against the bird shit that sometimes fell like snow from the sky.

The *Skarven* moved out. No café on board. Few passengers were going out to the islands at this time of day, and at this time of year. Two months earlier there wouldn't have been room for him on board; the archipelago boats swerved out like overloaded passenger junks in the Yellow River, brown limbs everywhere, children, strollers. Last summer he and Elsa and Angela had planned to go to Vrångö but fled the boat when they got to Brännö Rödsten. Too many people, like a sun-and-sea-and-salt-and-sand madness that seized the people of the city when the sun was at its warmest.

Madness. Winter tried to brush his hair out of his eyes and thought of something Erik Osvald had said when they met out on Donsö.

"There's nothing wrong with mad cow disease," he had said. He saw everything from the professional perspective of a fisherman: "We like to see one of those crazy cows on TV at regular intervals!"

Skarven went directly to Köpstadsö. There had been a strong wind out on the open sea during the journey over, as though the weather had changed. Winter could see black clouds in the west now, on their way up from the other side of the earth.

On the water down there, Erik Osvald and his three crew members were engaged in the eternal, anxious search for fish, the attempt to bring up the maximum legal amount.

There is a higher power, Erik Osvald had said, besides the Norwegian Coast Guard! It was a joke, but there was gravity to it. A higher power. If there isn't, everything is so meaningless, he had said.

This life changes you, twenty-five years on the North Sea, all year round, all day long. It's freedom. It's loneliness.

It's an old-fashioned way to live.

But we Swedish fishermen are still out one week and then home one week. The Swedes are almost the only ones who use that system, and it means that we earn less than the Danes and the Scots and the Norwegians.

And the past. He had spoken about the past: My dad went out Monday morning and came home on Saturday morning.

A life at sea until he became tired and stayed on land and listened to the weather reports when his son was out there.

Axel Osvald, if it was Axel Osvald that Craig's men had found; if it was him, his death had been strange and tragic, strangely tragic, alone and naked next to a pitiful little lake next to another, larger lake in a mountainous inland, miles from the sea.

What had he been doing there? How had he ended up there? How had his thoughts wandered while he himself wandered up slopes and rough terrain? Winter had not been to Fort Augustus, but he could imagine what it looked like.

The sea was calm between Styrsö Skäret and Donsö. Winter couldn't see Osvald's modern trawler, the blue *Magdalena*. They were out for a new week, west of Stavanger and east of Aberdeen, hunting for whitefish. In six days they would put in at Hanstholm and go home in the afternoon with invoices in hand. But Erik Osvald would come home before that, and he, Winter, was the one who was coming with the information that would make the fisherman return home. Or how would it happen? Would a helicopter pick him up? Or would he set course for Scotland and Moray Firth and the harbor entrance to Inverness right away? Go through the canal in the city, the river Ness, and down into Loch Ness and down to Fort Augustus? No, not with that monster of a trawler. And no, because his father was lying and waiting in a refrigerated room in Inverness. His son could anchor in the harbor.

Skarven lay still, and Winter went ashore. The time was as the time-table had predicted: 10:55. The quay was empty. There were a few older trawlers out along the edge, and Winter wondered whether any of them had belonged to Axel Osvald. Or maybe had even existed in John Os-vald's time.

John Osvald both existed and didn't exist. He had the unique phan-tom quality that people get when they disappear and are never found; their souls get no peace, and those who survive them don't either.

But if he were alive? If John Osvald were alive? Those who still ex-isted, those who were here . . . could you call them the surviving relatives, then? Was Johanna Osvald a surviving relative?

Winter asked a woman outside the store for directions to the school. She answered and pointed, a crooked movement.

He walked along a narrow street without sidewalks and could smell the sea, and he listened to the peculiar silence that is created by lots of space in every direction. The wind had disappeared in here, as though it didn't exist. The clouds had disappeared; the sky was completely blue. He felt warmth on his face.

There were many children on the playground, more than he'd expected. He heard shouts but no words. A soccer ball rolled his way and he sent it back. It flew over the goal and the fence behind it and disappeared into the crevice of a cliff.

"Aaah-oh," said a boy who looked like a short fisherman.

The other children looked at Winter and then at the cliffs. He un-derstood. He went out again and around the playground and he climbed down into the crevice. The ball wasn't there. He dug around through grass and other strange plants, maybe seaweed. To the right was a hole, like a cave. He peeked in but didn't see anything. He started to crawl. He felt the ball before he saw it, and he wiggled himself backward and his suit stretched at the seams, protesting. Winter got up with the ball in his hands, a triumphant gesture. All the children were standing in a line up there, and they applauded. Winter threw the ball up and the little

fisherman took it. He and all the others turned around when they heard
a female voice.

"And *what* are you all doing here? The bell rang, didn't you hear it?"

Winter saw her come up to the edge of the cliffs and look down.

"Oh . . . hi."

"Hi," said Johanna Osvald, giggling.

Winter couldn't help but smile. He didn't want to, not with the message he had brought.

"Is it really him?" she asked. They were sitting in a little workroom that
was Johanna's. A large Mac stood on the desk, an older version, gray.
There were papers all over, and binders. More paper than in Winter's office in the Palace. Through the window he could see the cliffs where he'd
dug up the ball. She must have seen him, too, or the children who had
lined up to study the fool from the mainland down there. An interrup-
tion in archipelago life.

Children's drawings hung on the walls on both sides of the window.
For a split second he thought of what it must be like to spend all your
days with children but not have any of your own. Maybe it was a relief to
come home; a silence to keep and to tend to.

Winter had told her as soon as there was a fitting opportunity. He had
chosen his words carefully.

"It could be a mistake," she said now.

He nodded but said nothing.

"You believe it too?"

"I don't know anything, Johanna, no more than I've told you. But my
colleague in Inverness also found a photograph . . ."

"Yes, I heard that, but how easy is it to recognize people in photographs? To compare a photo with . . . with a . . . a dead person . . . ," she
said, and hid her face in her hands.

Winter looked at his own hands. What should I do with them?
Should I hold her?

He leaned forward and touched her arm, which was bare. She shivered and he got up, took a cardigan that was hanging on the desk chair,
and placed it over her shoulders.

Photographs. Dead people. He had seen enough of both for a lifetime.
She was absolutely right. There were no similarities between the living

and the dead. Eyes that could see; eyes that couldn't see. A superficial likeness, yes, but no *likeness*. Everything he had seen, a living face, a young girl, a young boy, a smile from a shelf in a home that was suddenly shattered by an incident that could never be described. The silence that would be there forever. A shallow silence. Nothing to keep and to tend. The same face, but without life. I can't stand it, he thought every time he stood there. This is the last time.

There was always another last time.

It was for a lifetime; he had seen enough. An eternity. No. Life didn't belong to eternity, it was death that was eternity; life was the pause between the quiet eternities. For many, it was a short pause; he knew because he had been there, just after eternity had taken over.

And the photographs of the dead. There were always photographs of the dead on his desk. What a fucking job, photographs of dead people on your desk, broken cheekbones, empty eye holes, mouths like mine shafts. Choke marks like tattoos across the throat.

And the pictures of those who were completely still, untouched. They looked like they had fallen asleep. Pictures like that were often the worst.

He placed them all under other pictures, of houses, roads, vehicles, cliff crevices, whatever the fuck else, or under papers filled with words, because words were not as gruesome at a distance, not from a yard away.

Now he could hear children's voices, shouts, laughter. He saw several children through the window. Recess again. Forty-five minutes go by quickly.

Johanna Osvald looked up.

"I have to go there, of course," she said. "There's only one way to make sure that it's . . . Dad."

Winter nodded.

"They're probably waiting for me to come," she said.

"Do you have anyone who can go with you?"

She looked at him. Did she mean . . . no, he didn't think so. This was for her, her family. There was no murder, no marks. No blunt objects.

But there was still a why. That had been with him on the way here, on the archipelago boat, in the car before that, in his conversation with Craig, in his conversation with Johanna. Why.

"Where is Erik now?" he asked.

"I don't know, exactly. I'll have to call out there to him."

Winter nodded again.

"He can do what he wants," she said. "But I'm going to try to fly over there as soon as I can. Today, if possible."

"I can help you," said Winter, and made a call from the telephone that stood on the desk between them.

She would be able to make it. The next boat was the *Skarven* back at 11:40, but that would be too late to make the plane from Landvetter to Heathrow. She would connect there.

"It's things like this that make it a disadvantage to live on an island," she had said after two phone calls.

Right now there was no one available who could drive over to Saltholmen.

But there was another way to get to the mainland.

Winter had called dispatch, who transferred him to the marine police at Nya Varvet.

"We have a patrol boat down by Vargö," his colleague had said. "They're not doing anything anyway."

"Are you sure you want to go right away?" Winter had asked Johanna, with his hand on the receiver.

She had nodded in her rush to go home and throw her things in her overnight bag.

On the way over he asked about Axel Osvald. The boat went fast, faster than Winter had thought was possible in the interior waterways. No sirens, but apparent speed and apparent right-of-way.

"It wasn't the first time he went to Scotland to look for his father . . . your grandfather," said Winter.

"No, as I believe I said before."

"What did he tell you about those previous trips?"

"Not so much. Almost nothing."

"Why not?"

"My dad was a man who didn't talk very much," she said.

Winter noticed that she spoke of her father in the past tense. She didn't seem aware of it herself. He had seen it many times. A sort of mental preparation for the worst. To know before you know for sure. To start the task of mourning right away.

He had done it himself, on a plane to Marbella a few years ago. His father was sick and Winter knew, knew without knowing.

"What did he tell you when he did talk about it, then? You must have asked, right?"

She saw islands and rocks and skerries swish by. She turned around, as though she wanted to make sure that that really was Brännö, Asperö. This was her world. Winter looked around too. Everything was familiar to her, everything near the water. Downtown Gothenburg was not on the sea. *This* was what was on the sea, even *in* the sea.

"There were only two trips," she said. "I mean, before this one."

He waited. They were on their way in; he could see the buildings at Nya Varvet, the Nordic School of Public Health in the old flotilla barracks that had gotten new clothing. Everything had gotten new clothing there. Everything in the entrance to the harbor was familiar to him, even the transformed façades. He had biked through Nya Varvet ten thousand times in his youth, and many times after that as well. He walked there sometimes with Angela and Elsa. In the summer, the restaurant Reveille had nice outdoor seating that few people knew about, and that was good too. A beer, twenty yards from the water, a few grilled fish dishes, a skewered turkey dish that turned up on the menu year after year.

"When was he there the last time?" asked Winter.

"It was a long time ago, at least ten years ago."

"Why did he go this time?"

Johanna Osvald looked at Winter.

"I don't actually know."

A marked car was waiting on the quay. This was quicker than if they had gone in via Saltholmen and Winter had then had to drive on the narrow, slow road through Långedrag.

"Will I make it?" she said as she got into the car.

"You'll make it now," said Winter, nodding at Detective Inspector Morelius, who was the driver. An old friend from a different time.

"Are we allowed to do this?"

"What?"

"Go by police boat and a police car to make a plane?"

"Yes."

Morelius started the car.

"Call me when you get there," said Winter. "When you've . . . made the identification."

It sounded awkward, but what was he supposed to say? When you've seen your dead father?

She nodded.

"My colleague in Inverness, Craig, he'll meet you at the airport or send a car."

She nodded again, and Morelius went up toward Kungssten and the highway past Frölunda, to the east. Winter looked at his watch again. She would make it. They had gotten a move on. She could have waited a day, but he wanted to know too. He didn't know and he wanted to know. He felt the pull . . . he couldn't stop thinking about Axel Osvald. Or about John Osvald. There was something here, something he wanted to know, or search for.

There was a mystery.

"We're going out again," said the skipper of the police boat. "We can let you off at Saltholmen."

He stood on deck during the short trip back to the marina.

He continued to think in his car on the way into the city.

Mystery. There's a mystery. Something happened once that led to what's happening now. There are no coincidences. There's a reason Axel Osvald was found where he was found. Or for why he died. Someone or something led him to his death. I don't think it was a higher power. Or was it? Some sort of higher power?

They were eating dinner. Halders had made farina at the request of first Magda and then Hannes.

"I've never eaten farina," said Aneta.

Everything on her plate was white: the farina, the milk, the sugar. The plate was white. If she hadn't heard Magda's request she might have suspected Fredrik of yet another kind of joke.

"Sure you have!" said Magda.

"No, it's true."

"You just did! I saw you take a spoonful!"

"Well, now I have. But I never had before."

"What kind of porridge did you eat at home when you were little?" asked Magda. Her big brother looked embarrassed. That's none of your business, he seemed to be thinking. He's becoming more and more like Fredrik, thought Aneta. Big gestures, a look that doesn't let you go. But he's more calm. Let it stay that way. He doesn't say more than he needs to. He keeps to himself in his room. He thinks about his mom. Fredrik is worried about him.

"Oatmeal," said Aneta.

"Millet pudding," said Halders.

"What's that?" asked Magda.

"A kind of grain that's common in Africa," said Aneta. "It's actually a grass."

"But you haven't been to Africa, have you?" asked Magda.

"Stop it, Magda," said Halders.

"I've been there," said Aneta, "but I was born here, as you know."

"Did you have millet pudding?" asked Halders.

"My mom hated millet," said Aneta.

Halders scooped more of the white goo onto her plate.

"That's actually the reason my mom and dad left Africa," said Aneta.

"Really?" asked Hannes.

"No," answered Aneta, smiling at the boy. "I was just kidding."

"Why did they move, then?" asked Magda.

"They would probably have ended up in prison otherwise."

"Why?" asked Magda. "Did they do something wrong?"

"No."

Halders got out the teakettle again. They were sitting in the living room, which looked different since Halders had moved in after the death of his ex-wife. Not a huge transformation, but different.

The children were playing Pass the Pig in Hannes's room. They could hear the howls when one of them got a double razorback.

"So you got to talk about Burkina Faso's difficult past," said Halders.

"Is that a problem for you?"

"Quite the opposite."

The Everly Brothers were crying themselves out of the record player, track by track. Crying in the rain. It started over, feelings betrayed on repeat. Bye bye love, bye bye happiness, hello loneliness, I think I'm gonna cry.

"That song is the same age as I am," said Halders. "Nineteen fifty-seven."

"Good lyrics," said Aneta.

"Yes, aren't they?"

"A bit final, maybe."

"Mmhmm."

"It's almost worse than Roy Orbison," said Aneta, "in terms of how depressed they are."

"Roy Orbison isn't depressed," said Halders.

"Then we have different views on the concept of being depressed," said Aneta. "Or is it called distressed?"

Halders didn't answer; he drank his tea. He listened again. All I have to do is dream.

"If you want to, you can read anything at all into song lyrics," he said.

"In the case of these guys, there aren't really all that many alternatives," said Aneta. "It's about love that has disappeared, right?"

"So sad to watch good love go bad," said Halders.

"Yeah . . . about like that."

"It's one of the Everlys' best songs," said Halders.

"There you go. Then it's a good example."

She drove home late. Fredrik had asked her to stay but she wanted to wake up in her own home. It was like that sometimes.

Fredrik had been disappointed, really disappointed. He hadn't wanted to show it, but she could tell. He hadn't been able to go out and cry in the rain, because it wasn't raining.

"It's Hannes," he'd said. "Fuck knows what's going to happen."

But of course it wasn't just Hannes, or Magda, or just Fredrik. It was what everyone knew, that nothing would ever be the same again. No mom, no grandma later on, when they were adults themselves and had families. Only Grandpa Fredrik. Maybe. It would never be as it had been, but it could be better than now. It could be as good as it could get.

Fredrik hadn't said anything, nothing really dead serious like that. But they both knew. She needed to think. It was as though she never had time to think about it, or could think about it. There was time to think of everything but that.

I have to think.

Of going with Fredrik to his beloved Ouagadougou. Only that. Good God. A week in Burkina Faso and we'll see how tough you are, Detective Inspector Halders.

She laughed out loud there in the car, quickly and impulsively.

She drove off of Allén and onto Sprängkullsgatan. People were taking shelter from the rain outside the Capitol Theater after the last show. It was no later than that. Everyone was blue in the face, blackish blue from neon and night. Like a gang of black people from Ouagadougou, on their way out of the movie theater, one of many. At least we have that. What am I thinking? "We."

She parked on Sveagaten.

Do I miss it? Is that what's starting to happen? Will I eventually be drawn back to the Africa I was never born in? My Africa. Because it always has to be that way? My rhythm is there.

When she unlocked the front door facing the street, she saw something behind her that shouldn't be there.

She turned around quickly and a car flashed its lights and took off to the north with a roaring start. She didn't have time to see the license number, and it wasn't a model she recognized.

She saw a figure disappear quickly to the south, a man or a woman. A hasty departure. Bye bye love.

But she wasn't smiling when she closed the door behind her.

29

Winter called in from the car. Möllerström put him through to Ringmar, who was working on a homicide in Kärra. Open and shut. All that loathsome, never-ending paperwork for an event that took no time at all, but no secrets, no mystery. A drunk who beat another drunk to death because of some reason the killer had forgotten when he woke up. He didn't remember any beating, any killing.

"What do you say to a drink out on the town," said Winter. "I don't have the strength to go back to my office today."

"I never saw you clock out," said Ringmar.

"See you at Eckerberg's in twenty minutes," said Winter.

"Do they still have those shrimp sandwiches there?" said Ringmar. "I love those shrimp sandwiches."

"If they don't, they'll have to make one," said Winter.

There was only one shrimp sandwich left when Winter arrived, but they were happy to make one more. "Make it twice as big as that one right there," he said, nodding at the refrigerated counter. "I'll pay the difference."

"Yours is bigger," said Ringmar when they sat down at the table.

"I didn't get any lunch," said Winter.

"Fucking weird," said Ringmar, who was still comparing sizes. "Does the deli girl have faulty perspective?" He rotated his plate, as though to see whether his sandwich was bigger on the other side. "This is ridiculous. There's half a pound more shrimp on yours. And the diameter of yours exceeds mine by—"

"I wouldn't accept that if I were you," said Winter. "After all, you're the one who paid for it." Winter chewed on yet another shrimp. "It's unfair."

It had been Ringmar's turn to pay.

Ringmar raised his hand discreetly in order to get the waitress's attention, and then Winter had to tell him what was up.

* * *

"When is she going to call?" Ringmar asked when their plates were empty and Winter had told him what had happened that morning. "Will she make it there tonight, or is she staying overnight in London?"

"She should be there at six o'clock local time if she makes her connection at Heathrow," Winter said, and looked at his watch. "That's seven o'clock here."

"Have you spoken with Macdonald?"

"No. Should I?"

"Well, before he goes to too many of his old—"

"I think that Craig guy has already informed him. He said he would give Steve a call."

"Hmm."

"Sorry?"

"Hmm," Ringmar repeated.

"What is it, Bertil?"

"This is a strange tale, you know. I don't know, I think I smell crime." Ringmar held his glass in his hand and drank the last of his sparkling water and put down the glass. "There was actually some kind of message about the father, this John Osvald. Someone in Scotland, maybe in Inverness or somewhere around there, someone is interested in shaking up his family in Sweden." Ringmar ran his finger around the edge of the glass and looked up. "Axel Osvald leaves immediately after he sees the message. Takes off right away. So the question is whether he saw something in it that we didn't see. Something he recognized."

"Or if something else arrived that we don't know about," said Winter. "Other messages. At the same time."

"Yes."

"He'd been there before," said Winter.

"Perhaps he knew who'd written that thing about how nothing was how it appeared to be," said Ringmar.

"Or he guessed."

"But his earlier trips hadn't gotten results," said Ringmar.

"We don't know that," said Winter.

"And apparently no one else knows either," said Ringmar.

"Yes they do," said Winter.

"Who?"

"He does. Axel Osvald himself."

"Yes. Maybe."

Ringmar decided to have another cup of coffee and got up and went over to the lovely little wooden table where the coffeepot stood on the warmer. He had seen the newly brewed batch arrive a minute ago.

Winter followed him with his eyes. No one else drank as much coffee as Bertil, and no one else could stand all the peculiar witches' brews that went along with the job. Coffee was offered in every context. It was worse than being a mail carrier out in the country. The contents of some cups had to be eaten with a spoon. And Ringmar would still ask for a refill.

He came back and sat down.

"It sure seems like Axel Osvald went insane," he said.

Winter shrugged.

"Doesn't it?" said Ringmar.

"If we assume that he was the one who took off his own clothes, item by item, as he climbed up the hills," said Winter.

"Well, he had been acting confused in that town or city or whatever it is."

"Who actually said that?" said Winter.

"Weren't there several witnesses?" said Ringmar.

"When did you start trusting witnesses, Bertil?"

"Hope no one heard that," Ringmar said, looking around.

"Maybe they thought he was confused, but that could be because of the language, couldn't it? A person who no one understands might seem strange."

"Yes," said Ringmar, "now that you mention it. And especially in the case of Brits. Isn't anyone who doesn't speak English as their native language considered confused? Isn't that the English point of view?"

Winter smiled.

"But these are Scots," he said.

"So?"

"They're probably closer to us Scandinavians."

"That didn't help Axel Osvald in his attempts to communicate," said Ringmar.

"No. You're right about that."

"But of course, it's possible he was trying to say something that wasn't crazy," said Ringmar.

"He *could* have been confused," said Winter.

"By what?"

"Too much alcohol?" said Winter.

"Did you ask his granddaughter about his use of alcohol?"

"No."

"Do you think he was drunk?" said Ringmar.

"Not according to Craig, and not according to his witnesses," said Winter. "I asked him, actually." Winter leaned forward. "The autopsy will show the blood alcohol content, of course."

"Was he poisoned?" said Ringmar.

"By what?"

"Some kind of drug. Some poison."

"By 'poisoned,' do you mean secretly poisoned?" said Winter.

"Yes. Someone could have snuck something into a beer or into his food or . . . well . . ."

"Should we ask the Scottish pathologist to look for something? If he hasn't already."

"I don't know, Erik. Maybe we're letting this conversation get too far off track."

"Isn't that our method?" said Winter.

"It is."

"So where are we? We've talked about alcohol and drugs. More?"

"Fear," said Ringmar.

"Fear of what?"

"Of something he saw."

"Of something he heard?" said Winter.

"No. Saw."

"What did he see?"

"His father."

"Would he be afraid of that?"

"It depends."

"Depends on what?"

"Who his father was," said Ringmar.

"Who he was? Not *how* he was?"

"Who he was. Who he had become."

"Yes."

"Or who he had always been."

"Hmm."

"It has to do with the past," said Ringmar.

"Doesn't it always?"

"Here more than ever," said Ringmar.

"How so?"

"Whatever happened with the dad has to do with what happened on that monster of a sea."

"How so?" Winter repeated.

"He found out," said Ringmar. "He finally found out what happened."

"And it led to his death?"

"Somehow," said Ringmar.

"He had no memory of his father," said Winter. "He was only a baby when he saw John for the last time."

"Does that matter?"

"I don't know, Bertil."

"And there are other people who have memories of him," said Ringmar. "Of John Osvald."

"Yes and no," said Winter.

"What do you mean by that?"

"The only survivor from the war years—the only *known* survivor from those years, I should say—his name is Arne Algotsson, but he's got complete dementia."

"Have you met Algotsson?" asked Ringmar.

"No."

Ringmar looked at him.

"There hasn't really been a reason to, Bertil." Winter looked at Ringmar. "And the question is whether there is one now."

"Who told you that Algotsson is demented or totally senile or whatever he is?"

"Johanna Osvald. And her brother." Winter looked at Ringmar again. "Are you saying they could have lied?"

"I'm not saying anything. I'm just wondering whether they've made the correct diagnosis. Has anyone made the correct diagnosis?"

"Arne Algotsson is pretending to have dementia, you're saying?"

"I'm still not saying anything," said Ringmar. "But maybe it couldn't hurt to have a few words with the old fisherman. Or try to have a few words with him."

Winter nodded.

"If there actually is a reason to, as you just said yourself," said Ringmar.

"Just the fact that we're sitting here working our way through our method as though this was a case makes it into some kind of case," said Winter.

"So how do we move forward?" Ringmar said.

"By trying to talk to Algotsson," said Winter.

"The salty old survivor," said Ringmar.

"Mmhmm."

"And then?"

"Then we'll see how much of a mystery we think this is."

"And the granddaughter will call tonight," said Ringmar. "That will guide what we do in the future."

"I think I know what she's going to say," said Winter.

Halders and Aneta were on the afternoon shift together. Halders rubbed his eyes as they stood in the elevator.

"Are you tired, Fredrik?"

"I stayed up after you left," he said.

She didn't answer, just nodded at his image in the mirror.

They were on their way down. Something in the elevator stank.

"The jail was allowed to use this elevator," said Halders, who saw Aneta's expression. "Theirs is striking."

"I can understand why it would," she said, wrinkling her nose.

"Are there elevators in Africa?" asked Halders as they walked through the reception area.

"Only at the hotel."

30

Halders and Aneta drove over Fattighusån. The water was black. It seemed to stand still, unable to decide which way it should flow. They passed SKF. There was a dull shine to the factory façades. Halders stared at the large windows. He could have been in there now, wandering in and out day in and day out. Maybe he was actually made for a different life, that life. He could have been a renowned union chairman, or a notorious one. He could have been the director of the whole thing. He could have been all of that, but he couldn't be a chief inspector. Why?

Why, Aneta had once asked when he was complaining, and she had meant why in the sense of why do you want to strive for that? It's not that much more money. There's not more independence, or whatever you call it. You wouldn't actually have more power. Yes, I would, he had said. Power to use how? she had said. He didn't know, he couldn't answer that.

There was also a dull sheen to Fastlagsgatan. Aneta guessed there were places on the street that were never touched by the sun.

A pickup from Statoil stood outside the fifth entrance. They could make out furniture under the cover but they couldn't see people to carry it.

"Coming or going?" said Halders.

A man of about twenty-five came out through the front door and hopped up into the pickup and pulled some sort of wicker chair to the edge and hopped down again and carried it in.

"Coming," said Halders.

The guy came back quickly and took another piece of furniture and carried it in again.

"He's filling the elevator," said Halders.

"Which apartment in that stairwell is empty, do you think?"

"The same one you're thinking," said Halders, opening the car door.

"There's nothing we can do," said Aneta. "Take it easy."

"We're just UN observers," said Halders.

* * *

In the stairwell, the elevator doors were closed and the elevator was on its way up. Aneta hesitated.

"Should we stomp in there and tell them that this apartment they're moving into has recently been the scene of several crimes?" said Aneta.

"It's not as though someone has been murdered," said Halders.

"Could have been," said Aneta.

The elevator rumbled down again. They waited. The door opened and a young, dark-haired woman stepped out. The elevator was empty. She propped the door open with a chair. She nodded hastily and continued out through the door, which was fastened open. She ducked into the pickup.

She came back with a box that seemed heavy. They were still standing there.

"If you're not doing anything else, maybe you can carry things," she said.

Halders laughed. That was his style. Aneta didn't laugh. She saw the woman smile and shove the box into the elevator. She had seen this woman before. A few times in a car that stopped outside the Palace to pick up a tired chief inspector. She knew his name, and she knew her name.

"What are you doing here, Moa?"

Ringmar and Winter were standing in the stern when the *Vipan* set out at 2:35. Winter was smoking a Corps, his first of the day. He told this to Ringmar, who congratulated him.

They had made two phone calls after they'd made their decision. Now here they stood, with a sudden sun over all the mountains that stuck up above the surface of the water. But that was only a small part of it, a tenth of a percent. Everything was below the surface. The iceberg effect. These weren't icebergs, but the effect was the same. That's how it was with good books. Ringmar pondered that concept. The simple words were only the topmost layer. Everything was underneath. Books, but also the work in their world. Their world was words, words, words. Spoken, written. Bawled out. Complete, half complete, broken into pieces, broken off. Forced out. Dissolved sentences. Lies and truths, but often those didn't matter since most of it was still below the surface. They only saw the tops of the truth or the lies.

"A person should probably live out here," said Winter. "It's always cloudy in the city but when you come out here, it clears up. It's always like that."

"Well, you're going to build by the sea."

Winter didn't answer.

"Right?" Ringmar observed him. "You did buy the land."

"Mmhmm."

"Mmhmm? Aren't you sure? Didn't you both decide?"

"Yeah, I guess we did."

"It's great to hear young, enthusiastic people talking about their future."

Winter squinted at the sky.

"You have a family, and you and I both know what Angela wants. And imagine how Elsa will love life by the sea."

Vipan sped up toward Asperö East. They saw the bathing beach, the bay, and the houses on the right, which were visible behind the passage, Asperö North, Brännö Rödsten. Life by the sea. It had its different sides, dark and light.

But this was life on the islands, all around him; it was different from life by a beach on the mainland.

"Get started building now, Erik. I can help out with the administration of your topping-out party." He shivered suddenly in the gusty wind. "What do you say to a cup of coffee?"

They asked their way to Arne Algotsson's house. It was on one of the sheltered streets. The colors of the houses hadn't been transformed by the wind and the sun and the salt, not like on the other houses they'd passed. The front of the house lay in shadow. Maybe that was the reason.

Ringmar knocked on the heavy door, which seemed to be sunk into the ground. If they were allowed in they would have to duck. The woman who'd answered when Ringmar called had sounded dismissive but accepting, at least then. Her name was Ella Algotsson and she was Arne Algotsson's sister; she had always lived on Donsö and had never been married. She was over eighty years old and she took care of her brother now. Arne lived his life in there. According to Johanna Osvald, he never went out.

Ringmar knocked again, and they heard sounds, as though iron bolts were being lifted away on the other side.

The door opened and the woman nodded warily. She was short and thin. Winter could see the skin on her arms; it was like pale leather. Her face had more wrinkles than Ringmar would ever get. They ran in all directions. She looked at Ringmar, who was the shorter of the two inspectors. Her eyes were transparently blue, a washed-out shade, whitewashed, and Winter thought for a moment that she was blind.

"What is't this time?" she said.

"Sorry?" said Ringmar.

"What you sayin' sorry fer?" she said.

Ringmar looked at Winter, who was smiling a little. These were literal people.

"I'm the one who called," said Ringmar.

"What?"

"I'm the one who called. I spoke to a woman who answered here and the—"

"That was the assistant," answered Ella Algotsson as though she were the CEO of Västtrafik public transport, which had taken over the archipelago lines. "She isn't here now, so you can go again."

"But you're the one we want to talk to, Mrs. Algotsson. She—"

"Miss."

"Miss Algotsson," said Ringmar. "She said that it would be okay for us to talk to you and your brother for a little bit." Ringmar took out his wallet, showed her his ID. "My name is Bertil Ringmar and I'm a detective in Gothenburg, and this young man is Erik Winter and he's *my* assistant."

Winter showed his ID. Ella Algotsson looked at it, then looked suspiciously to Winter and then to Ringmar.

"Can'e really mek food?"

"Make food?" Ringmar gestured toward Winter. "That's what he's best at."

"Arne's sleepin'," she said.

"Can we wait?" said Ringmar.

"He's tired, Arne is."

"We can leave for a bit and come back," said Ringmar.

She didn't answer.

"Has anyone else been here asking about Arne?" asked Ringmar.

"What's that?" she said.

"When we came, you wondered what it was this time."

"Axel was here," she said.

Ringmar looked at Winter.

"Axel?" asked Ringmar, who got to be in charge of questioning. His assistant had the sense to know his place and keep quiet. Winter had backed up a few steps. "Axel Osvald?" Ringmar leaned a bit closer. She didn't seem to hear. "Was Axel Osvald here recently to talk to Arne?"

"A few weeks ago," she said, without hesitation. "They sat in the parlor. I wasn't there."

"What did they talk about?"

"The' talked abou' before o'course," she said. "That's all Arne can talk about. Ev'rythin' else he's forgot. But before he ca' remember some'a."

He can remember the past, Winter translated to himself.

"His Erik were here too," she said. Ringmar hadn't asked anything further. But he had earned her trust. She hadn't asked what brought the inspector here, why he wanted to speak to her elderly brother. It didn't seem to be of concern to her. Did she know something? Something more than that John Osvald had disappeared once upon a time? Winter tried to see her face behind the wrinkles that *were* her face, and there were her eyes with that strange, glimmering blue color that was almost a source of light in the dim hallway where she stood, and those eyes were directed at Ringmar the entire time. Did she know something that her brother Arne had once known but had forgotten long ago? Had some secret ended up within her? She had said that Axel and Erik Osvald had been looking for her brother, but maybe they'd also spoken with her.

They hadn't asked about that.

"Erik?" said Ringmar. "Erik Osvald?"

"Yes."

"Was he here along with his father? With Axel?"

"No. It was after."

Moa Ringmar released her grip on the box and straightened up. She looked first at Aneta and then at Halders. Now she recognizes me, thought Aneta. It's not some local darkie standing here.

"Didn't Dad tell you? Isn't he the one who sent you here?" asked Moa, whose eyes had become sharper.

"Moa!" said Halders. "Now the gears are starting to turn. You're Moa Ringmar!"

"Bertil didn't send us, Moa," said Aneta. "We're here on duty. And he has no idea what we're doing here."

"The state can't afford to let us work as moving men too," said Halders.

"And moving women," said Moa.

"Yes," said Aneta.

"I meant that he meant that you were to keep an eye on me in general."

"Why would we do that?" asked Aneta.

"Because this is dangerous and unfamiliar territory for someone from idyllic Kungsladugård," said Moa.

Never trust idylls, thought Aneta. They are even worse.

"Which apartment are you moving into?" asked Halders.

She told them, and they asked who she was renting it from.

"His name is Lindsten."

"Is it a sublet?"

"Yes, for now. It's a rental, of course. It could be—"

She stopped talking and looked from one detective to the other.

"Have I done something illegal here?" she asked. "It wasn't a problem for the landlord."

"I'm going to tell you something, Moa," said Halders.

Ringmar took a deep breath, in and out, up on a cliff behind the houses. They could see the open sea and the coastline past Näset, to Askim, Hovås, Billdal, Särö, and down to Vallda. A fog was floating above the water, but it didn't ruin the view. Ringmar threw out his arms.

"All of this can be yours, Erik."

Winter had an unlit Corps in his mouth. He tried to see the little bay south of Billdal. It was impossible.

"The message has been received, Bertil."

"Do you think the old man will be more conscious this afternoon?" said Ringmar.

"We can talk to the sister," said Winter. "Maybe she knows everything."

"Yes."

"Should I continue to play your kitchen aide all afternoon?" asked

Winter. "Or maybe it's called a home health aide within the health-care field."

"It can only be good for you," said Ringmar.

"Are you done breathing?" said Winter.

"You should do it, too," said Ringmar as Winter lit his cigarillo. "Breathe in the sea."

"I prefer to eat it," said Winter.

"I've tried," said Ringmar, "but oysters are not my thing."

"Too bad for you, Bertil."

Ella Algotsson opened up after three knocks.

"I thought ya'd gone back," she said.

"There's a boat at four thirty," said Ringmar.

"Is Arne awake?" asked Winter.

She didn't answer.

"Is Arne awake?" asked Ringmar.

"That he is," she answered.

"May we come in for a bit?"

Arne Algotsson looked like a larger version of his sister. There was no doubt that they were siblings, as though their advanced age had enhanced their common features. Arne Algotsson was sitting on a red chair in the kitchen, and he turned around as they came in. His face was illuminated by the light from the horizon, which was visible though the window. There was a different light on the back side of the house; a different space. You could see the strip of mainland.

Arne Algotsson nodded. His eyes were blue in the same way as his sister's, as though the sea wind had scrubbed everything clean out there, even eyes. Everyone who lived there for a long time ended up with the same worn blue haze in their eyes. But the man's eyes lacked his sister's lucidity and focus. He seemed to look through the visitors without holding on to anything.

Winter let Ringmar off at the Margreteberg roundabout and drove home via Linnéplatsen, Övre Husargatan, Vasagatan.

The parking garage smelled like leaking oil.

The elevator smelled like cigars.

He heard children's laughter in the stairwell. It was about time in this building. Everyone was twice as old as he and Angela were.

He loved this building.

It had always been there. It was larger than life, was there before he came, would be there when he was gone.

They could sublease it, for the time being. When the house was finished down on the beach. Bertil's Moa needed a place. If she hadn't settled into Kortedala too much. This would be suitable for her. A little big for one, but she could share.

He unlocked the door and Elsa came running through the hall.

They made toast and brewed tea. Winter fried a few slices of haloumi for its saltiness. There were olives on the table.

"Let's have a glass of white wine too," he said.

The phone rang as he uncorked the bottle.

"I'll get it," said Angela.

"No, me, *me!*" yelled Elsa.

She answered, a confident *hello?*

They saw her listening intently. Suddenly she giggled and said, "*Yes, suw.*"

"Steve," said Winter to Angela.

"*Ya prata svinska,*" said Macdonald when Winter took the phone.

"And Elsa speaks English," said Winter.

"Yes, sir." Macdonald excused himself for a second and said something to someone and came back. "I just got home."

Steve Macdonald lived with his wife and their fourteen-year-old twin girls in a house, a cottage as he said, down in Kent, just over an hour's drive south of Croydon. Croydon was part of London, but it was also one of England's ten biggest cities. It wasn't exactly idyllic, Croydon.

"Same here," said Winter. "I just opened the wine."

"Jamie called in the car," said Macdonald.

"I spoke with him," said Winter, "if you mean Craig."

"Yes. The daughter has arrived."

"And?"

"She's identified the body as her father. There's no doubt."

"When did this happen?"

"Just now. Half an hour ago."

"Then she'll call me soon," said Winter.

"Was he prone to depression? Or had he been mentally ill in some way?" asked Macdonald, direct questions.

"I don't know, Steve. Not according to the daughter, anyway. Nothing that was treated."

"They haven't found the car," said Macdonald.

"Craig figured it had been stolen. It's common."

"It should have turned up by now."

"What does Craig say?"

"He agrees with me." Winter heard Macdonald mumble something to someone again and then returned. "Sorry. We're just going over to a neighbor's soon to celebrate because his loutish son is moving out." Macdonald coughed out a short laugh. "Okay. Just for your information. We did have time to put out a bulletin about this Osvald before we found him, and a number of tips and . . . observations have come in."

"What did those tips say?"

"They say that people have apparently seen him about up here during the last few weeks. In fact, it seems he's been seen all over Moray and even down by Aberdeenshire."

"What does that imply? The area, I mean?"

"I don't know if this will mean anything to you, but it's all the way down along the coast over to Fraserburgh and then down to Peterhead. We've even gotten a report from Aberdeen. It's rather a long way to Aberdeen. And someone says they saw the man inland as well."

"Does that matter, Steve?"

"I don't know, my friend."

"Something happened to him," said Winter.

"Yes," said Macdonald.

"Is it connected to his travels?"

"Why else would he have made them? Roaming around in our god-forsaken district?" said Macdonald. "He sure wasn't there on holiday."

Speaking of holidays, thought Winter.

"One more thing," said Macdonald. "He wasn't alone."

"I'm listening."

"If it's our man the witnesses saw, one of them saw him with company."

"Has the witness described this company?"

"It was an older man."

"An older man," Winter echoed. He could feel the hair on the back of his neck, as though it suddenly moved. He saw that Angela noticed.

"I know what you're thinking," said Macdonald.

"Is there more?" said Winter.

"Well, I don't know. It's up to Craig in Inverness. It seems that more will probably come in."

"Craig is an efficient man."

"Yes, you can say that about him. An efficient asshole."

"I thought he was a friend. I thought you recommended him for the job up there."

"Why do you think I did that?"

Winter laughed. Elsa laughed when he laughed. She liked English. Angela looked at him with a wrinkle between her eyes.

"The farthest commissioner's office in all of Great Britain. Why do you think I recommended Craig for that?"

"Okay, okay."

"He doesn't like it," said Macdonald.

"No, I can understand that."

"I don't mean the job or the place. I'm talking about this case," said Macdonald. "Craig is an angry bastard, but that's also to his advantage. In his career. He says that things aren't what they look like."

"What did you say he said?"

"Things are not what they look like," repeated Macdonald. "That's what he said."

Winter felt the hair on the back of his neck again. Angela saw how serious he was.

"They're doing another autopsy," said Macdonald.

"Has Johanna accepted that? The daughter, that is."

"Yes. According to Craig. But he didn't think they would find anything there."

"Where will they find something then?"

"Don't ask me, Erik."

"And what will they find?" said Winter.

"You sound quite involved in this," said Macdonald.

"I have actually thought about it quite a bit," said Winter. "Worked on it a little."

"It sounds like it."

And suddenly Winter saw what he would be doing in the near future. What he *wanted* to do. He saw an opportunity to see Steve again, an obvious opportunity. Some would call it obvious.

Angela was playing backgammon with Elsa now. She had made a meaningful gesture toward the wine bottle. He had nodded, and she had poured half a glass for herself and brought one to him. In three days they were supposed to go to Marbella for a week.

There would be other opportunities.

"It's . . . interesting," said Winter.

"Now you've started to get me interested," said Macdonald. "You and Craig."

"If it hadn't been for the information I just received," said Winter.

"You've thought about it before," said Macdonald.

"What?"

"Don't even try," said Macdonald.

Winter didn't answer; he took a drink of the wine, which was cold and dry. He thought, thought. He felt the old feeling, the old, wonderful, damn feeling. He thought of Marbella, of Angela, Mother . . . it could work out. Elsa might think it was nice. He could ask Siv . . .

"What do you say?" said Winter. They hadn't needed to say out loud what they were discussing. It was the so-called iceberg effect. "Is it possible for you?"

"As a matter of fact," said Macdonald, "I've been planning to take a trip home soon. I've actually been putting it off for too long."

"Can you get away on short notice?"

"How short?" asked Macdonald.

"Three days."

"Yes. It might work."

"I might not come alone," Winter said, looking at Angela, who had stiffened during the last minute of conversation.

"Me neither," said Macdonald. "Sarah is ready for a trip. We have even arranged for a babysitter. If you can say that about taking care of girls who are almost fifteen."

"I'll call you later tonight," Winter said, and hung up.

"What was that?" Angela said.

"Oh . . , ," Winter said, blinking quickly and making a motion with his head toward Elsa, who was concentrating on her pieces, "Steve wanted to talk a little."

Elsa was sleeping like a little rock. Winter snuck out into the hall and into the kitchen. Angela was playing a round of solitaire that appeared to be coming to an end.

"Well?" she said.

"What do you say we go to Scotland for a few days?" he said.

31

It was late when Moa Ringmar came home. Her father was on the phone. It was afternoon in New York. Bertil paused and put his hand over the mouthpiece:

"Martin got that loft on Third Avenue," he said.

"How nice for him."

"What is it?"

"We'll talk about it later, when he's done talking."

"He wants to have a few words with you."

"Tell him I'll call."

"Okay, okay." Ringmar resumed his conversation with his son. "She'll call you later. Okay. Yes. Yes. Right. Yes. Talk to you soon. Bye."

He hung up.

"So what is it, Moa?"

"That apartment is hot, Dad."

"Sorry?"

"You don't have to apologize. You can't know everything that's going on in the department."

"I need some background," said Ringmar. "I'm not really following you."

"That apartment I was going to rent is involved in a restraining order, and there was an assault there and it's been completely cleaned out by crafty thieves and the guy I was renting it from has been acting strange and suspicious toward two of the country's sharpest detective inspectors."

"Halders and Djanali," said Ringmar.

"You knew!"

"When you said the two sharpest. No, joking aside, I know they've been working on a case that involves an apartment in Kort . . . exactly, in Kortedala!" He quickly got up and took a step closer. "Surely you don't mean it's—"

"That's exactly what I mean."

"Well, what do you know."

"It's a small world, isn't it?"

"How did you find out?" Ringmar asked.

"They showed up as Dickie and I were moving in my things. Fredrik and Aneta."

"What were they doing there?"

"A routine check, I suppose. They're keeping an eye on this woman's ex. It's not looking good."

"They're not supposed to tell you that."

"It was Halders," said Moa. "He offered me photos to put up at the student union."

"He's always been a discreet investigator," said Ringmar.

"Dickie has my things in his garage for now."

"You moved out again?"

"What do you *think*, Dad? Am I supposed to lie there sleeping and get woken up by some crazy person putting a key in the lock and crashing in?"

"No, no."

"This is the first time I've moved in and moved out on the same day," said Moa.

"I'll have a chat with that Lindsten," said Ringmar.

"I haven't paid yet."

"I'm still going to have a chat with him."

"Has he done anything illegal?"

"I don't know," Ringmar answered. "I don't know yet."

Johanna Osvald called as Winter was making a double espresso in order to have the energy to think. It was better and cheaper than amphetamines. Coltrane was blowing "Compassion" in the living room, along with another great tenor saxophonist, Pharoah Sanders. It was music for wild thoughts, asymmetrical, tones for his own head. Coltrane's instrument wandered like a lost spirit, on its way through black and white dreams, through sparse halls. Elsa had gotten used to falling asleep to extremely free-form jazz. Winter wondered what that might lead to.

What drew him to jazz first and foremost was the individual expressions of the music. The best thing about jazz was that it gave the jazz musician the chance to be himself. To be his own self. It was music that first of all stood for expression, for immediate reflection, not interpretation. It was all about improvisation, but not in an irresponsible way. Quite the opposite. In improvising, the musician took on a responsibility, and the result depended on talent and his own resources, and experience. Emotional experience. It was music for emotions, from emotions.

Angela had gone out to think as well, a round trip to Avenyn.

"It's him," said Johanna into the phone. "It's my dad."

"I'm sorry," said Winter.

"They've taken good care of me," she said formally. It was a slightly strange comment. Perhaps she was in shock. There was a sharp edge to her voice. "This policeman Craig has helped with everything."

"There's nothing you need?" Winter asked.

"Noth . . . nothing you can help with," she said, and he thought she started to cry. It sounded like it, but it could have been the line.

I'm not sure, thought Winter. Maybe we can help. Maybe when it comes to answers.

"Have you spoken with a doctor about your father?"

"Yes."

He waited for her to continue, but she didn't say anything.

"What did he say?"

"That it was a heart attack that . . . that killed him. He had extreme hypothermia." Winter heard her breathing. "It's cold up here. I went out for a minute to think, and it was cold and raw."

"Are they going to do more tests?" asked Winter. He didn't want to say the word "autopsy." She knew what he meant anyway.

"If they need to," she said. "If there's something they need to do to come up with a . . . cause, they can do as many tests as they . . ." She stopped talking. "What is that horrible noise in the background?" she said.

"Where?" said Winter.

"On your end. What is that racket?"

"Just a second," Winter said, walking into the living room and turning the music off in the middle of "Consequences." "It was a record," he said into the phone when he came back.

She didn't comment.

"So, what are you going to do now?" he asked.

"I'm . . . I'm going back to this medical center tomorrow and then there's some paperwork and I hope to be able to fly home with Dad as soon as I can."

"Yes."

"He has to come home," she said.

"Of course."

There was a sudden whistle on the phone, like a wind through the line, which must have run across the North Sea, from Inverness to Aberdeen to Gothenburg. Aberdeen and Gothenburg were at exactly the same latitude on the map. Or maybe it was Donsö and Aberdeen.

"I just spoke with Erik," she said.

"Where is he?" asked Winter.

"Out at sea," she said. "They're on the way down to Hanstholm with their catch." He heard her blow her nose. "He's coming right home after that. He'll be there when I . . . we . . . arrive."

"Good," said Winter.

"I think something happened up here," she said, suddenly and quickly. "Something that caused this. Something . . . awful."

"I think so too," said Winter.

"Something that has to do with Grandpa."

"Yes. I think so too."

He didn't tell her about his visit to the elderly Algotsson siblings.

Angela came back with redder cheeks and damp hair. She smelled like blue autumn evening and salty wind and black mud and gasoline fumes, which together made up this city's perfume. It was a blue evening. Vasaplatsen was a blue address. Kind of blue.

"I've thought about it," she said, pulling off her long scarf.

"What do you say, then?"

"Well . . ."

"Is that a summary?"

"I don't know if we can work things out with Elsa. If she wants to. If it will work."

They had talked about letting Lotta have Elsa for a few days. His sister had nagged and nagged. Bim and Kristina had nagged. Maybe it could be worked out. He and Angela had done things without Elsa during these four years, and at those times Elsa had stayed with Lotta. It had worked. There were no grandparents in Gothenburg for Elsa, but Aunt Lotta was there, and her cousins Bim and Kristina.

"We've never gone abroad alone," said Angela. "Without Elsa."

"We can take different planes."

"Is this something to joke about?"

I might not be joking, he thought.

"And of course Siv is expecting us."

"Nueva Andalucía will always be there, and she will too," said Winter.

"Don't be too sure of that."

"She can always move home," said Winter.

"That's not what I meant," said Angela. Her voice seemed to change.

"Do you know something I don't?" He pushed the chair back a few inches. "I'm talking to you as Dr. Hoffman now."

"Nothing serious, from what I understand," said Angela.

"Do you two keep secrets from me?"

"She's a little tired, Erik. I'm sure that's all."

"Tired? Tired of what?"

"She's not exactly young anymore," said Angela.

"I don't think it's good to be in one-hundred-degree weather half the year," he said.

"That's mostly a question of drinking," said Angela, "of getting liquids."

"And there's the next risk factor," he said.

"I was talking about water," Angela said, raising an eyebrow and smiling slightly.

"I was talking about gin," he said.

"Gin and tonic," said Angela, "don't forget that water. But seriously, Erik, you know that she hardly drinks at all since Bengt passed away."

"And her consumption before that?"

"It's probably not a problem," Angela said.

"Maybe we should ask her to come home for a while," said Winter.

"Maybe now," said Angela.

"You mean *now*, if we go over to Scotland?"

"Yes. But we have to talk to Lotta first. And Siv might not think it's a good idea. And we have to talk to Elsa."

* * *

Angela came back from the bathroom. Winter was staring straight up at the ceiling from the bed. He had undressed only halfway.

"You've never met Steve's wife," he said.

"So does she think this is a good idea?"

"I don't know," said Winter. "Why wouldn't she?"

"For the same reason you just gave me, only the other way around."

"Hmm."

"I suspect that we'll be left on our own quite a bit. And we don't know each other. If you and Steve are going to investigate this strange story."

"Just a few days, max," said Winter. "Maybe not at all."

"Where are we going to stay, then? On Steve's farm?"

"Hell, no. There are nice hotels in Inverness. I have Steve's word on that."

"I want to see a few of the options."

"Of course." Winter lay on his side, facing her. "Steve's sister works in Inverness too, you know, as a lawyer."

"I'm sure she'll be really happy to take care of us. Welcome to my world."

"Exactly."

"Erik. This can't be solely on your terms."

"Is it? I'm just trying to look on the plus side here. We'll do things together and Steve and I might go off for a bit to . . . well, I don't know. But suddenly I felt like we could see each other again and that we could do it all together. That everything was sort of falling into place."

"Have you met his wife? Sarah?"

"No."

"How old is she?"

"Exactly forty," said Winter. "Like you."

"Is this a vision of the future?" said the thirty-five-year-old Angela, tossing a pillow.

"We're living in the future," he said. "We're on our *way*," he said, slinging a pillow in her direction; it intercepted her throw.

"I thought this whole story was about the *past*," she said, throwing the pillow back again, and Winter ducked and the pillow knocked over the alarm clock, which thudded onto the varnished pine floor.

"Now you've ruined the *floor*," Winter said, firing off his last pillow.

Angela seemed preoccupied by something, and she took it right in the face. Winter turned around to see what she was looking at.

"What are you *doing*?" asked Elsa, who was standing in the door with the clock in her hands.

"I have to talk to her first," Angela said as they were lying in bed. It was dim and quiet. "Steve's wife. It's important. I imagine she thinks so too."

"Of course."

"And then there's Lotta and Siv and the—"

"I know. This is assuming that all the ifs disappear."

"In which case, it's not a bad idea," she said.

"Thanks," he said.

Light was coming in from the hall, where there was a nightlight under the table that the telephone was on. He could hear a soft whirring from the fridge.

"I have one more question," she said.

"Yes?"

"This thing you're trying to get some clarity about, what you're going to do . . ." He saw her silhouette come closer. "It isn't dangerous at all, right, Erik?"

32

The espresso was doubly useful. Winter could not sleep, and he could think. At three o'clock he slid out of bed and walked through the hall and looked in on Elsa, who was sleeping on her back with her eyes half open. He could tell because he was holding his face four inches from hers. He could barely hear her breathing, so he listened for a long time. At that moment Elsa let out a snore, only one, and turned onto her side, and Winter tiptoed out.

He sat down in the living room, in the dark, which would last for another several hours. The usual blue light came in through the window. The streetcars hadn't yet begun to rumble by down there. He could hear the sound of a lost car on the way to some blue address. Suddenly he heard a cry from up by the kiosk at Vasaplatsen, which had a functionalist-style neon sign that glowed just as it had during the record years.

All of these sounds and lights would be inconceivable and just plain threatening in the house by the sea. Silence could be heard from the sea. Was that what he was afraid of? Was he even afraid?

Had Arne Algotsson been afraid? Or his sister? Or both of them?

Winter got up from the easy chair and walked over to the balcony door and opened it enough so that he could go out. He had stepped into his slippers, which were always next to the door. There was no wind out there, but there was a faint chill that smelled like autumn. A different moisture in the air, an acid scent that actually meant everything he could see growing down there was dying for now, but he seldom thought that way. He thought of the acid, and of the salt that you could sometimes smell when the wind came from the northwest. A pinch of salt.

Arne Algotsson had looked as though he had rubbed his face with salt; there was a gray film on it, like a crust of old salt that had solidified and formed a mask that had started to crack a long time ago. His eyes were deep set. There was a light in them, but Winter couldn't see where it came from, not then, not as he was sitting across from the old man and trying to ask his questions along with Ringmar.

His sister's name, Ella, had been mentioned early on. Ella. She had been sitting next to her brother.

"Yes, tha's right, I have a sester called Ella," he had said, turning to Ella Algotsson. "D'ya know her?"

She had looked at Winter and Ringmar as though to say, See, my brother is as demented as a trawl door. Or a broken trawl. Everything just falls right through. You just have to look at him, and listen to him.

"Did you know John Osvald?" Winter had asked.

"John's a fisherman," Algotsson had said from inside his world. "He was the skipper later."

"What do you mean? You said he was 'the skipper later'?"

"Shall we eat?" Algotsson had said.

Winter had looked at Ella Algotsson.

"We just ate," she had said, leaning forward and laying her hand on his arm, and he had started. She had seen that they noticed his sudden movement.

"It's his old injuries," she had said.

"Sorry?" Ringmar had said.

"His old fishing injuries. Thay always got eczema out on the boats before. Thay always had the rabber clothes on. Thay got complaitly scraped up. Arne still has the marks on his arms. Thay never go away, the marks."

"Rabber clothes," her brother had echoed.

They, that is to say Ringmar, had had a necessary conversation with Ella Algotsson before this. Her brother had looked at Ringmar and Winter as they came in, but then he seemed to forget. He had stared through the window, into the cliffs that floated like soft waves behind the house. There were no sharp edges there.

"You can't get anything sensible out of him about that time now," she had said.

"But then?" Ringmar had asked.

"Then? When?"

"When he came home from Scotland. The last time. What did he have to say then?"

"Not much." She had cast a glance at her brother, who was sitting with his face illuminated by the daylight outside. A pillar of salt.

"He did talk about the accident, of course, but there wasn't so much thay knew."

"What did they know, then?"

"You know too, don't you? It was that thay had come down from Iceland and the boat sank."

"It wasn't so far from land, from what I understand," Ringmar had said.

"The boat couldn't be seen from land, in any case," she had said.

"Where was Arne, then?" Ringmar had asked.

"On land," she had said.

"Yes, but where?"

"In one of those towns where they stayed. I dunno. I don't remember what thay're called."

"Aberdeen?" Ringmar had asked.

"No. That's where thay were first. It wasn't there."

Ringmar had looked to Winter for help.

"Was it Peterhead?" Winter had asked.

She hadn't answered and hadn't looked at him.

"Peterhead?" Ringmar had repeated.

"FISHERMEN'S MISSION TO FISHERMEN'S VISION TO DEEP SEA NATIONAL MISSION," Arne Algotsson had suddenly uttered from the armchair next to the window, in a loud, wooden old man's voice. He hadn't moved his head, but he must have been listening.

"He repeats that sometimes," Ella Algotsson had said.

"What is it?" Ringmar had said.

"Didn't you hear?"

"I didn't understand it."

"Me neither." A sad smile had come to the old face, which was thin but strong. "He's said it sometimes recently, now."

"Recently?"

"Yes. In recent . . . years."

"Since he became ill?"

"Yes."

Ringmar had looked once more at Arne Algotsson, who had been looking at the waves of stone outside.

"Peterhead," Winter had said in a loud voice.

"FISHERMEN'S MISSION TO FISHERMEN'S VISION TO DEEP SEA NATIONAL MISSION," Algotsson had chanted.

"Other than that he never speaks English," Ella Algotsson had said. "He's forgot that. Too."

"We said PETERHEAD," Ringmar had said.

"FISHERMEN'S MISSION . . ." Algotsson repeated it, like a parrot. It had an uncanny effect, but a funny one at the same time, inappropriately funny. Winter had felt ashamed somehow, as though they were using the old man and his sister.

"Well, it's clearly a name that means something to him," Ringmar had said.

Ella Algotsson had looked like she was thinking about something else.

"But he was in another city when it happened," she had said. "I remember it."

"Fraserburgh," Winter had said, looking at Arne Algotsson at the same time. But he hadn't said anything, hadn't moved.

Then Ella Algotsson had looked at Winter.

"What was that?"

"Fraserburgh," Winter had said. "Was the city called Fraserburgh?"

"Fras . . . yes, I think so."

"Did Arne come right home afterward?"

"No. He wasn't there the whole war but he was there for a little longer."

"How long?"

"A year, I think. He came home with a fishing boat. Thay were brothers from Öckerö who dared to come home again. Thay were crazy."

"From Öckerö?" Ringmar had asked.

"Thay're dead," she had said.

Winter had thought he had seen Arne Algotsson nod, slightly, as though he concurred with what his sister said.

"Who else sailed home with Arne?" Ringmar had asked.

"Bertil," she had answered. "John's brother. But he's dead, him too." Ringmar had nodded.

"Another brother disappeared in the accident too, right?" Ringmar had said.

"Egon," she had said. Nothing more.

"Was anyone else from here on the boat when it went under?" Ringmar had asked.

She hadn't answered, not directly. She had sent a quick look at her brother, to see if he was listening. Or maybe it was something else.

To make sure he didn't answer?

"There was one more," she said after a moment that seemed long. Her eyes had changed, as though they had clouded over. They couldn't see.

"Another person from here?" Ringmar had asked.

She had nodded.

"What was his name?"

"Frans." She had looked up again, with the strange fog in her eyes. "Frans Karlsson. My Frans."

Winter saw that face before him again when he came back into the room.

She had looked so infinitely sad when she said that. My Frans. She had told them in very few words that Frans Karlsson was hers, that they were betrothed and that he never came home and she had waited, and she was still waiting. Like the seaman's wife she never became. Like a living memorial to the men of the sea who didn't return. He thought of the Seaman's Wife down by the Maritime Museum. But she was made of stone. Ella Algotsson was not made of stone.

She hadn't said more, but he knew through Johanna Osvald that Ella Algotsson had never married.

Her fate was connected to John Osvald and his family; their fates were linked to one another; the chain continued through the years from the past to the present. Binding the nations on both sides of the North Sea.

"He lies down there too," she had said after a little while. "Thay never found the boat. The *Marino*. And nothin' else neither."

Ringmar had looked like he was preparing himself.

"Did you know that Axel Osvald went over to Scotland a few weeks ago, Miss Algotsson?" he had asked.

She had nodded.

"Do you know why?"

"No."

"Erik Osvald didn't say anything about it when he was here?"

She had repeated a "no" but suddenly it was as though she no longer had the strength. Her face had fallen. The clouds in her eyes were gone, but her eyes had a new kind of faintness. She seemed tired now, dead tired. Winter had again felt ashamed, as though they were using these people without really knowing why. As though nothing good could come of this.

As though this would only make everything worse. What was it Erik Osvald had said one time? Storms are good for the sea? That they stir up the stew on the bottom. That no fisherman yet has lost by betting on a storm.

What was it they were tearing up with their questions? He thought about that now, in the dark of his flat, where he'd spent the better portion of his adult life.

Would this investigation be good for anything?

He saw Ella Algotsson's face again. He blinked and it remained. He saw Arne Algotsson nodding again, as though he were concurring with something again.

They had concluded their conversation with Ella; they had tried to speak with Arne. They had moved their chairs up to the window.

They had asked questions, but all his responses had been nonsensical. It was both comic and tragic.

Arne had no more to say about "Skipper Osvald."

Winter had wanted to know more. John Osvald hadn't been the skipper when they set out. He became skipper. Why?

Why weren't Arne Algotsson and Bertil Osvald along on that last trip?

What relationship did the young men have with one another on the little island that had been their home?

How had they functioned together out at sea?

Winter had thought about Erik Osvald's words again, about the silence on board, the relationships on board.

Had something happened on board?

How had they functioned together in their involuntary exile?

He thought about it again now, sitting in the middle of the city he'd always lived in. He wanted to know. He wanted to look for answers to all of those questions, and to several others that couldn't be answered here, only there. Possibly. Over there in Scotland.

It was a fascinating story. There were many parts. Spread across more than fifty years, across the sea.

There was a great sadness here, but there was also something else.

He wanted to know.

There were those who knew more than he did but didn't want to say anything.

Yes.

Axel Osvald found something in Scotland that he'd been searching for his entire life, and it ended his life. Did such a truth exist, such a reality?

Maybe.

It was connected to the sea. The fishing. The trawlers. The cities. The islands. The villages. The winds. And so on.

Winter got up to go into the bedroom and try to get a few hours of sleep.

It was as they were going to leave the house on Donsö, as they were about to say good-bye to Arne Algotsson. Ringmar had said something about Scotland, Winter didn't remember exactly what, something about Scotland in general. Ringmar had said "Scotland" several times in a row.

But he remembered what Algotsson had suddenly answered, or said, more like said straight out to no one in particular, more like said straight out the same way he had chanted about his mission earlier:

"The buckle boys are back in town" was what it sounded like.

"What did you say?" Ringmar had asked, but of course Algotsson wasn't rational like that; he didn't repeat himself on command.

"The buckle boys are back in town," Ringmar had repeated, because it was easy to say; it flowed nicely.

"The buckle boys are back in town," Algotsson repeated, as mechanically as before.

"You said SCOTLAND before," Winter had said to Ringmar, but also to Algotsson. "Scotland."

"Cullen skink," Algotsson had said, and then he had been completely silent.

The words were still there in Winter's head. He still hadn't made it to bed; he was standing halfway in the hall. Cullen skink. Those were damn strange words. It sounded Scottish, it did, but what did it mean? Or maybe he'd said something else? Collie skink? Collie sink. Had he said "sink?"

Just as Winter had that thought, the faucet in the kitchen dripped, a sound only heard at night. An irritating sound that would stop if only he would change the washer. Drip down in the sink. That sinking feeling.

He walked back to the living room. The clock on the wall was no longer on three; it was four thirty. He could hear the first streetcars. The sound of a delivery truck getting bread down in the bakery, or leaving flour. Suddenly *Göteborgs-Posten* dropped down through the mail slot in the hall behind him. He still wasn't tired. He walked over to one of the bookcases and selected one of the atlases, taking out the one he thought was the best.

Scotland.

The buckle boys.

Cullen sink.

He turned on the floor lamp and remained standing.

He searched for map 6, northern Scotland. He found Inverness in the innermost part of the bay called Moray Firth. He saw Thurso and John O'Groats way up there, but they didn't mean anything to him. He read the names of towns and cities from Inverness to Aberdeen. It was far, but not that far. He started inland, from west to east. He came across Dallas, a little dot, but still there. Proto-Dallas. Maybe Steve's father had started the milking there now, along with Steve's brother. Mom was making oatmeal like mad, Scotland's delicious national dish.

Winter came to Aberdeen with his finger, and now he let it run north. He came to Peterhead. He came to Fraserburgh at the northeastern tip. He continued straight west, back toward Inverness, along the coastline now, village after village: Rosehearty, Pennan, Macduff, Banff, Portsoy, Cullen.

Cullen. Cullen as in Cullen sink or skink. Sink from Cullen. A kitchen sink from Cullen, Scottish kitchen sink realism.

So there was a Cullen between Portsoy and Portnockie. Something had told him it was a place.

He continued west along the coast, but only to the next city.

Buckie.

The Buckie boys are back in town.

33

He was home again. This was the only place he called home now. He was walking on the beach. The protruding rock formation in front of him, to the west, was called the Three Kings. Everyone here had always called the rocks that. It had to do with the sea. Ruling the sea, being the master out there.

In a different time this had been a city of *life,* a royal burgh for the future. No more.

No trawlers went out for herring, none came back. Haddock wasn't smoked here anymore; there was no haddock and therefore no smoke that stung your nose. Once there had been three smokehouses. Now the smoke smelled like garbage when it came up out of the houses where the poor souls tried to get warm. The smoke hit the sky and it too was petrified.

He turned around. It was a blue day. He could see. The sky was cracked as though from some cursed strikes of a hammer, and it had collapsed at the edges and was wide open, and he could see across Seatown and the viaducts and the city above and the hills above the city and the blue sky above the hills. That was what he wanted to see. It was why he had walked here, wandered down Castle Terrace and climbed over the Burn. He could still climb. He could do a lot, still.

Jesus!

He closed his eyes and saw the water and the quarterdeck and the storm that still hadn't come, not *the* storm, and the faces and the eyes and the movements and . . . and . . . Frans's eyes. Just afterward. When *he* knew. The hand that Frans tried to reach out.

Egon's scream.

Jesus. *Save me,* Jesus!

He stumbled and nearly lost his balance. There was a sharp pain in his hip.

Why couldn't he forget?

Where are they? Gone? Let this pernicious hour
Stand aye accursed in the calendar!

Some became old and forgot everything. They managed to get sick. There was nothing left for them; it was washed away like the offal on a deck, all that crap was gone, overboard with that, the deck lay shining in the sun, or the moon, washed clean. No memories left. No traces. They could move on, free from memories, go to Jesus with consciences washed clean.

He limped as he went back across the sand. A dead whiting lay at the edge of the beach. The fish came willingly in to land to die when no one here went out after them. He heard the waves strike against the kings behind him. He covered his ears for a brief moment. Someone screamed inside him. He kept the scream inside with his hands over his ears, and then he let it out.

A man he recognized was sitting there when he stepped into the Three Kings. Another one. He debated turning around, but the man hadn't reacted when he stepped in. He had only looked from stranger to stranger with a cold gaze and then looked out at North Castle Street, where the shadows were sharp under the viaduct. The houses on the other side had a thorny pattern, as though they were covered in graffiti. In an hour the sun would have moved so much that the shadows would be gone, replaced by the smooth stone. There was no graffiti here. The young people who would have made it fled west and east as soon as they could fly, to Inverness, Aberdeen. This was exactly in between them; presumably they fled farther than that, to Edinburgh, Glasgow. Some all the way down to London.

He ordered his pint and his whisky. A woman he didn't recognize was standing behind the bar. She wasn't young and not old either, on her way from nothing to nowhere. She spilled foam on the bar and sighed and got a rag. He could smell the rag. His ale smelled the same as he drank. He washed it down with whisky. He who wanted to hold his liquor must follow that order. Beer on whisky, mighty risky. Whisky on beer, never fear.

He took another sip of ale. The man over by the window got up and walked toward the door. Suddenly he turned around and said, "Good-bye," and he nodded in answer. The woman behind the bar nodded too, but he had felt that the farewell was meant for him. He didn't like it. He drank quickly and took the whisky glass and stepped off his stool. There was a sudden pain in his hip again. He saw the man closing the door of a car across the street, and the car started and drove out onto Bayview Road and disappeared. He didn't know the man, had never seen him. Why had the man said good-bye to him? He finished his whisky and placed it on the table where the stranger's beer glass was still standing.

He walked south on North Castle, took a left onto Grant Street, and came to the square. An empty bus stood on the square. The passengers and the driver were presumably eating lunch in the Seafield Hotel, on their way to Aberdeen since that was the name on the sign on the front of the bus.

The Seafield was not for him, not now and not ever.

He hadn't even gone to a place like that in Aberdeen.

But they'd been at the Saltoun Arms Hotel in Fraserburgh.

They had washed up in a restroom that had been shining clean like the sun on the sea on a day without clouds.

That was two nights before.

Was there anyone who knew? Who had guided them there? Only two days before . . .

They'd eaten dinner in a room where there were big green plants, and everything had smelled nice. The food had been warm and tasted good. They had eaten a pudding afterward; it had been sweet and red. It had quivered like the belly of a deep-sea fish.

He hadn't been there since.

People came out of the hotel. They got onto the bus. It drove toward Aberdeen.

They had docked out at Abercromby Jetty and then in Tidal Harbour. He had walked ten thousand steps on Albert Quay.

Across Victoria Bridge. Down to Timber Yards.

Up again to Commercial Quay.

He had sat at the Schooner and seen the dusk over Guild Street.

They wouldn't let him get away.

He had known that. He had thought.

They waited. Someone waited.

Outside, he had climbed up the steep steps to Crown Street. Would he be able to get up there today? Maybe. Well, not today with that hip, but another day.

He had walked north on Crown and then along Union. The war was all around, in the shop windows, in people's everyday clothes, in the soldiers' uniforms. Everything was as dark as it could be, blacked out. The dark ages. Those were the dark ages.

He had written letters. He had written to his family.

He remembered the light in the mess, how it flickered in the wind as he wrote.

He asked about Axel.

He had thought of the letters in his loneliness all these years.

He had never wanted to see any of the letters again. It was someone else who had written them.

He walked south on Seafield Street, away from the sea, past the hotel, town hall, the police station where no one cared about him; he didn't think any of the younger ones knew who he was, or that he existed, and all the older ones were gone, everyone was gone.

He continued eastward, across Albert Terrace, Victoria Place, back toward the cemetery, where he didn't know where he would lie. No one knew.

There was a darkness over the sea when he returned, walking down the stairs to Seatown. He met someone on the stairs, but he was invisible again. He could move in and out of it. He could reach out a hand, no one would see him.

The children's clothes on the line next to the nearest house moved in the evening breeze. The black windows, covered by shutters.

The red paint of the telephone booth glowed. It was as though it were fluorescent. He had stood in there, he had been forced to use it. He never would have believed it. At first he hadn't understood what to do, but he could read. His hands had shaken so hard that he had to try several times before it worked. Then he had asked her.

As he walked past it rang!

He gave another start and felt his hip. He kept walking and didn't look around. It rang and rang.

At home he lit the fireplace. The humidity had increased while he was away. He kept his coat on as he readied the fire. It flamed up from the newspaper and then began to lick at the sticks in the middle. He warmed his hands.

He looked into the blaze, which was growing now, pulled up by the air, which was a spiral through the flue. The fire was like iron that burned and turned to glowing rust. Rust. Yes. Everything was stone and rust around here now. There wasn't anyone with hammers anymore.

They had gone into the old capital, the one for the fishing fleet. Back then it had been like a teeming square next to an open harbor.

He had gone there, and he had felt the message that burned in his coat pocket. It was like sharp flames inside him. He had driven by the ship-yard and two rusty ships lay as though frozen in the red sludge. There was only silence, no blows.

He had seen the monument again. He remembered; he had been there.

He had sent his message over the sea. He knew that Hanstholm was a second home harbor now for boats from his old harbor. The auction. The bunkering.

The few boats from home.

Before the war there had been forty fishing boats on the island.

They had gone twenty hours west, two hundred nautical miles. Mondays.

They set the trawl. They fastened well. To pipe was an art. It was gone now.

They dragged the trawl. It ran one hundred fathoms deep.

He had missed that. He had always missed it.

They pulled up the trawl by hand. He missed that too. In rough seas it could wash over. Missed it. Speed set at three knots. The last pull, the last time they lifted the trawl for the night. They cast the anchor and were still. Lit the stern lights.

On Fridays they went to the fishing harbor with the boxes. Two hundred boxes. He knew how to shovel ice.

Bertil had stood in the cabin. Egon had run the machinery. Arne had taken care of the tools.

He and Frans had done all the other scut work. They were the youngest. They had rushed back and forth across the deck, slipping, hauling, lifting, undoing knots, and watching the fish run down into the bin. They had cleaned. Their hands had been red and cold.

They had had to prepare food. The youngest prepared the food on board.

They had gone to sleep too late and been woken too early.

Trawl haul!

Their work continued.

Later he would be at the helm himself.

They fished in the dark.

They fished all night.

They continued westward.

God!

He had sung in the Mission congregation.

Almost half the people on the island had been members of the congregation.

There was always a Bible on board.

It had been good to have someone to turn to out there.

His own father had said that no matter what happens, good things will come to a man who loves God.

34

Angela had made a decision in her sleep. If it worked out with Elsa. If it wasn't for too many days.

"But I can always come home early," she said. "Different plans and all that stuff we talked about."

"I'll call Lotta," said Winter.

"Don't forget Siv."

Wonder of wonders. Siv Winter decided within half a minute to come home and stay in Gothenburg while they were gone. She would stay with Lotta, who would take a "time-out" from the hospital.

"Everyone else is taking a time-out all of a sudden, so why not me?"

Steve Macdonald was also taking a time-out. Winter called him during the morning.

"My dad isn't feeling well, so I have to take a trip up there anyway."

"I'm sorry to hear that."

"He'll be okay."

"Angela is coming along. But she wants to speak with Sarah a little bit first."

"Sarah said the same thing."

"I met a survivor yesterday," Winter said, and described the conversation, or whatever it was, with Arne Algotsson.

"He said something that I think was Cullen sink. Cullen is a city or a village, according to the map," said Winter. "Cullen sink or something like that."

"Cullen *skink*," Macdonald said, letting out a laugh. "I don't believe this!"

"What is it?"

"Cullen skink is a local specialty, a soup made of smoked haddock, potatoes, onion, I think, and milk."

"I see."

"So this senile old man was sitting there talking about that soup," said Macdonald.

"It must have made a strong impression on him," said Winter.

"Smoked haddock tends to have that effect," said Macdonald.

"A strange combination of ingredients in that soup," said Winter.

"You ain't seen nothing yet," said Macdonald.

"So he had a connection to Cullen," said Winter.

"Or the soup," said Macdonald. "They have it all over Scotland."

"Okay."

"Unfortunately," said Macdonald. Winter heard his smile across the line from south London. "Just like the smell of smoked or fried haddock. Why do you think I fled to London?"

"But London's called the Smoke, isn't it?"

"It's a different smell," said Macdonald, without clarifying further.

"Algotsson also talked about a coastal city that might be Buckie," said Winter. "Do you know it?"

"We're practically talking about my hometown, here," said Macdonald. "Buckie? It's a classic fishing harbor. The biggest one up there during the war, I think, and for a while after."

"He mentioned Buckie," said Winter, "or at least it sounded like it."

"Didn't the chief inspector record the conversation?" said Macdonald.

"You weren't there," said Winter. "And I wasn't a chief inspector at the moment."

"Buckie," said Macdonald. "The Cluny Hotel is something special; the Victorians would be proud. There's a particular hotel in Cullen, too. It's well known up there, but I don't remember what it's called."

Bergenhem was hunting for stolen goods. It was a large operation, with people from all over the city. He crossed the no-man's-land north of Brantingsmotet. Ångpannegatan, Turbingatan. There weren't many tips, but some of them seemed worth checking out. It was always a calculation. No one did anything for the sake of mankind. There was always a reason. Sometimes it had to do with revenge, sometimes jealousy, sometimes calculated favors and return favors, sometimes disappointment, sometimes arrogance, sometimes pure mistakes. It was like in other parts of this so-called society. The underworld wasn't different from the regular world. Everything had a price.

A gasoline barrel was burning in a deserted roundabout. Some distance away, a few old men were hunching over their lunches, liquor. Bergenhem was playing Led Zep and looking for the address. Robert Plant was howling at heaven about the stairway up there. Bergenhem turned up the volume during the break. He could see Plant's corkscrew curls. He had seen Zep in Copenhagen, that hair all over the stage. Jimmy Page seemed to be using his guitar as a crutch. He had been high as the sky. They could *play*. Bonham would die soon, but he beat his drums to pieces and got new ones onto the stage. Jeez.

Bergenhem found his way in another roundabout and drove up to the warehouse and turned off the motor. He looked around and dialed the number to operation command, which was in Kvillebäcken for some reason. Maybe it was the McDonald's at Backaplan that attracted them there.

"I'm outside now," he said.

"Where's your colleague?" crackled the communication radio.

"There's no colleague here. Where is he supposed to be?"

"He was supposed to wait."

"Then he probably got tired," said Bergenhem, and he saw a small truck drive up to one of the loading docks and stop and stand with its motor running.

"A vehicle," he said into the microphone, "a truck with a canvas cover. Looks like it's privately owned."

"What are they doing?"

"I don't see anyone. It's idling. In front of dock D."

"Do they see you?"

"If the driver turns his head one hundred eighty degrees, yes."

"Your colleague is supposed to be standing there," scratched the voice. "Right there."

"Good thing he wasn't, then," said Bergenhem. He saw the cloud of smoke from the tailpipe before the truck shot off. "Now it's taking off!"

"Fuck."

"Should I stay here or follow it?"

It crackled again, suddenly *loud,* like rusty metal against a rough stone.

"He's disappearing," said Bergenhem.

"Tail him."

Bergenhem rolled out of the area where the warehouse stood in an angular semicircle, trying to surround rusty containers that were piled on one another like building blocks.

"There could be people in there, in the warehouse," he said into the microphone.

"We're on our way," said the voice.

Aneta Djanali was having a few words with Ringmar.

"Is it true?" Aneta cried.

"Nothing has time to cool down in there," said Ringmar. "Old Lindsten is working hard."

"I'll talk to him."

"Wait a little. Wait and see for a day or two."

Aneta thought of the Lindsten family. The apartment that was the daughter's was really the father's. Hans Forsblad didn't appear, not inside and not outside. Anette was living at home, but maybe not. Sister Susanne had a permanent address. She was the only one who seemed to have one apart from Mr. and Mrs. Lindsten, but they seemed to be in eternal orbit between the beach cottage in Vallda and the house in Fredriksdal.

Where was Anette right now?

"Okay," Aneta said to Ringmar. "There are other things to do."

Bergenhem tailed the truck toward Frihamnen. He didn't think that the driver of the truck up there had seen him. My car wasn't visible. Something else caused him to leave. Maybe my colleague popped up from inside and I didn't see it.

The warehouse was suspected of being full of stolen goods, or almost: It was being filled.

The truck up there, a Scania, could be full of stolen goods. Or maybe they were supposed to fill up in the warehouse and then ship to fences. There were lots of fences in Gothenburg.

He thought they were on their way to Ringön, but the truck lurched onto the viaduct and steered toward the bridge.

Aneta called Anette Lindsten's number, and after two rings she got an answer she couldn't understand.

"Is this Anette?"

Another mumble, and loud traffic noises.

And silence as the connection was broken.

She dialed the cell number again.

Busy. Dee-dee-dee-dee-dee-dee.

She waited, walked through the brick hallway, which was dry and cool and smelled like absolutely nothing. Möllerström went by with a box of printouts in his arms, and he moved his head in some sort of greeting. Möllerström produced tons of printouts and then carried them around, here and there. He moved in mysterious ways. She watched him go.

Should they trace the route of Anette's phone? No. No one would agree to do it if she didn't have stronger grounds.

Her phone rang.

She answered and heard the loud traffic noises again; an indistinct mumbling. Then a voice:

"Is this Aneta?"

It was Bergenhem. She could hear his voice now, but just barely. The traffic roared and it sounded like a large bell was ringing in the background.

"Yes, sir."

"Where's Möllerström?"

"Lugging a box. What did you expect?"

"Can you check a license plate for me?"

Bergenhem followed the truck around Polhemsplatsen. The *Göteborgs-Posten* building bulged out above the traffic. The driver of the truck seemed to hesitate again but veered off toward Odinsgatan at the last second and ran a yellow light just as it turned red, and the maneuver caused a car in the next lane over to slam on the brakes and swerve to the right.

It was an illegal maneuver, but Bergenhem only had time to move around and past and keep an eye on the now-familiar vehicle up there; its cover was painted blue and white, the colors of the city; a rope or something fluttered like a tail from the covered bed of the truck.

But I'm the tail, thought Bergenhem.

They rolled through Odinsplatsen and continued east up Friggagatan and turned into Olskroksmotet and the truck lurched again, as though the driver had been interrupted. He's talking on the phone, thought Bergenhem. Maybe he's getting directions.

They continued across Redbergsplatsen, past Bagaregården, and up onto Gamlestadsvägen.

Bergenhem's phone jangled.

"Yes?"

"The plates belong to a Berner Lindström," said Aneta.

"Gothenburg?" Bergenhem asked.

"The interesting thing is that they're stolen," said Aneta. "Because you said it was a truck, right?"

"Yes. But repeat that first part, please."

"Berner Lindström owns a ninety-one Opel Kadett Caravan, and two weeks ago his license plates were stolen in Falkenberg, down in Halland. He reported it to the police right away, of course."

"We've found his plates," Bergenhem said, and he swung right onto Artillerigatan but had to wait for another truck that came rushing by as though it had been shot out of a cannon. He tried to see past some cars in front of him but couldn't see any blue or any white. What the fu—

"Where are you?" asked Aneta.

"I can't see him," said Bergenhem. He made a fist and thumped the wheel. He was going forty-five; he looked to the left just before the roundabout and caught sight of a splash of blue and white.

"Lars?" he heard Aneta's voice.

"I see him!" shouted Bergenhem, mostly to himself.

"Where is he?" said Aneta. "Where are you?"

Bergenhem spun through yet another roundabout.

"Kortedalavägen," he said.

"What?"

"On the way north through Kviberg."

"All roads apparently lead to Kortedala," Aneta said.

"Now I'm turning in to Kortedala Torg," said Bergenhem.

"Oh God."

"Now we're passing the police station. Our truck just did the same."

"They haven't seen you, you think?"

"No."

"Are you sure?"

"No. But it seems like the driver has other things to think about. I think he's following directions. A stranger."

"From Halland."

Bergenhem laughed.

"From Falkenberg," he said.

"Where are you now?" Aneta asked.

"Guess," said Bergenhem.

"You're just about to turn right at the Uno-X station," said Aneta.

"That's one right," said Bergenhem.

"Will I get the next one right, too?"

He could hear excitement in her voice.

"We'll see . . . they're turning right . . . they're driving up to the yard or whatever you call it, the front of the house . . . driving up to one of the entrances . . . yes, that's it . . . I'm driving by now . . . looking in my rearview . . . it's number five, where we caught that guy Forssomething, now I see someone coming out of the truck . . . now I have to turn left here, Aneta."

"I'm coming," she said, and was already on her way.

35

Winter called Donsö. Erik Osvald answered. He had come home late at night. The catamaran from Frederikshavn had been delayed considerably by wind and rough seas.

"You feel a little powerless," said Osvald, and Winter wasn't sure what he was referring to.

But Osvald had spoken of lack of control, his own control.

He mentioned the latest trip, spontaneously, without Winter having asked. The news from Johanna that had come at an "exciting" time at sea.

He talked and Winter listened. It was like a need Osvald had, in order to channel his sadness.

"In the best case you find a type of fish that there's no quota for. And preferably one of the biggest fishes. And it seems like we've succeeded in doing that now."

"What is it?" asked Winter.

"Anglers and crawfish," said Osvald. "We've found a hiding spot. We searched and then we found an area where they were moving in the same . . . well, area; no one has been in that exact spot before because it's a really rough bottom. And we got an awful lot of anglers."

"That's an expensive fish," said Winter.

"We brought up several million anglers," said Osvald.

"Good."

"But we ripped up a lot of trawls. That fish stays pretty stuck to the bottom; it's really easy to just scrape their backs. But we managed to dig up quite a few."

"All right."

"It's listed as a 'miscellaneous' species in Norwegian waters," Osvald said, and Winter thought he heard a note of wonder in his voice.

"Can I come out there for an hour?" asked Winter.

"Why?"

"There are a few things I'd like to ask you."

"Can't you do it over the phone?"

"I'd prefer not to."

"Uh . . . when?"

"I can be on Donsö in just over an hour."

"There's no boat that goes then, is there?"

"I've arranged one," said Winter.

"Oh, I see. You were sure I'd be here?"

"No," said Winter. "Have you found the letters?"

When they'd last met, they had decided that Osvald and Johanna would try to find John Osvald's letters home to his family. If it was possible.

"There are a few," Osvald said. "They were among Dad's things." He paused. "I've actually never seen them." He paused again. "I haven't read them yet."

"I'll be there in an hour," said Winter.

"So that's what this is about?" asked Osvald.

Osvald met him on the dock. He was pale. His trawler wasn't at the quay where it had been before. It was like there was a hole where the boat had been. Winter knew it was on its way back out into the North Sea with the replacement crew on the hunt for anglers, crawfish, cod, haddock. Smoked haddock. No. Danish trawlers, Swedish ones, Scottish ones, on the hunt for whitefish that would be smoked and fried and steamed. The cod fillets would end up on tables in Brussels. Winter thought about what Osvald had said about mad cow disease. It was a complicated world.

Out there they were their own people, a sort of royalty. They were spared the Norwegians, who only had their sights on the Barents Sea. And the Dutch fished only for flatfish; they were no competition.

Winter heaved himself onto the quay from the police boat with Osvald's help. Some young boys on bikes stared from their group. Osvald made a signal and the group scattered. He smiled. One of the boys bucked his bike like a horse.

"My boy," said Osvald.

"Will he be a fisherman too?"

"He'll have the opportunity," said Osvald. "By the time he's twenty he'll have to know what he wants to do." He took off his cap and scratched his hair, which had started to thin. His forehead was red, chapped by sun and salt and wind. "After that it's too late."

"Is it difficult to find a crew?" Winter asked.

"No."

"Are there many boats from here out at sea?"

"No."

"Really?"

"There was a generation shift here on Donsö that went wrong." Osvald had started to walk toward the houses, and Winter followed. "The men were very angry, the ones who were my father's age, maybe a little older." Osvald was speaking straight out; he didn't look at Winter. Screeching gulls circled above them. There was a gull sitting on a section of rock. "They never budged, those men, just kept their crews. And they *were* really good, but they didn't let any of the younger ones in." He looked at Winter. "And then up came the possibility for an uneducated fisherman to be a sailor on the Stena Line, and everyone jumped at the chance." He gestured with his arm, like a jump from a considerable height. "But of course they couldn't come back to fishing, not then and not now."

"Why not?"

"It takes too much money today to get established. You've seen my boat. Well, it's not cheap, three hundred twenty gross tons, thirteen hundred horsepower." He turned around as though the boat would be there and he could point to it. "If we stopped now we would get a lot of money for it."

"Would you want to?" asked Winter.

"Stop? Never. The EU wants us to. But I don't want to."

Osvald lived in one of the older houses. Both men had to duck as they went in but the ceiling was high inside, an arch of wood above the large room. There was a tall, wide window that let in light and cliffs and sea and horizon. It was a perfect room.

Winter heard a sound from somewhere else in the house, and he turned his head.

"The cat," said Osvald. "You're not allergic, are you?"

"I don't actually know," said Winter. "I've never had a cat."

"You've petted one, right?"

"No."

"No?"

"I actually never have," said Winter. It was the first time he'd considered this, and it was really pretty ridiculous. A man over forty who'd never petted a cat in his entire life. He needed a place in the country.

"Now's your chance," said Osvald, bending down and grabbing a small, thin, coal-black shorthaired cat under its stomach and holding it out to Winter, who tickled its chin and stroked its head, and that was that. Osvald put the cat down, which took a lithe leap over the doorstep.

"We had that one's ancestor when, oh, that summer when you and Johanna had a little something going on," said Osvald.

"I was never here then," said Winter.

It was true. He could have stood in that room more than twenty years ago and seen the same sea then as he did now, the same angular boulders. This house had been the Osvald siblings' parents' home. Erik had taken over, and his father had moved to the annex, and Johanna had her own little house farther up, closer to the school.

"Have you spoken with Johanna?" asked Osvald.

"Yes. Have you?"

"Of course I've spoken with her. What do you mean?"

"I mean since you came back. If you've heard anything more about the trip home."

"We chatted this morning," said Osvald. "The doctor there, the pathologist I guess he's called, is supposed to analyze something. But I'm sure you know that."

It depends, thought Winter. I haven't heard anything today.

"Do you know what it's about?" Osvald repeated.

"I haven't heard anything this morning," said Winter.

"That's not what I meant." Osvald looked at him with those pale eyes that reminded him of a blue sky in January, with a faint light around the pupils. They were like everyone's eyes here. They were exposed to the open light, and no fisherman could wear dark glasses and still retain his honor. Only tourists wore sunglasses on the islands in the southern archipelago. "I mean, the reason he died."

It was the first time they'd mentioned Axel Osvald.

"I only know what they said before," said Winter. "That it was a heart attack."

"Do you believe that?"

"I did then."

"That's not what I asked," said Osvald.

"What's the alternative?" said Winter.

"That's a question for you, isn't it?" said Osvald. "You're the detective."

"But if I were to ask *you* to think about it."

"I haven't gotten that far yet," said Osvald. "I'm not sure that I will get there, either." He began to walk to the door, stopped. "What is the point of it?"

"I don't actually know," said Winter.

"But you don't seem to have completely accepted that explanation," said Osvald.

"Did something happen one time when your father traveled to Scotland? When he was looking for clues, or information about what happened to John?"

"He wasn't looking for clues," said Osvald.

"No?"

"Not that kind of clues. We had all accepted that Grandpa went down with that ship. With the *Marino*. He was trying to find information about *how* it happened. He wasn't looking for Grandpa, or anything."

"Did he tell you all of this?"

"Is that so much?"

"Did he tell you what you just said?" Winter asked again.

"More or less," said Osvald. "That's what he was thinking, anyway."

"Then it must have been an enormous shock when that letter came."

"I don't know," said Osvald.

"Weren't you at home?"

"Yes and no. But I think he, Dad, I think he still believed that nothing new had really happened. That it was more, well, the circumstances."

"Which are pretty unclear," said Winter.

"You could say so."

"How much did he find out about that, then?"

"What people knew in general. The boat goes out and doesn't come home."

That was probably the fastest way that the event could be summarized, thought Winter.

"But not all of the old crew was along on that last trip," said Winter.

"No, which was lucky for them."

"But why not?"

"There are different explanations depending on who you ask," said Osvald. "And now there's no one to ask anymore." He took another step. "I'll go get those letters now."

36

Bergenhem kept the truck under surveillance. The two men who had gotten out and were standing next to it seemed to be doing the same, or waiting for something or someone.

One of them, the older one, looked at his watch.

Bergenhem had parked on the cross street on the other side of Fastlagsgatan, among a row of cars that were all past their prime. His own unmarked service car would actually have stood out if it weren't so dirty.

He was communicating via a secure radio with the operative commander, who had changed location. It sounded like he was chewing when he answered. Hamburger. There was an echo, feedback.

"We're inside the premises," said command, "the warehouse."

"I ended up in Kortedala," said Bergenhem.

"Where's the truck?"

"It's parked fifty yards in front of me."

"Good. It probably contains stolen goods."

"I think it's empty. I think they're picking something up." He saw one of the men, the younger one, light a cigarette. "What should I do?"

"Keep them under surveillance for the time being."

"How does it look in there?" asked Bergenhem.

"We've found half of Gothenburg's household goods," said the commander, whose name was Meijner. "It's practically IKEA in here."

Bergenhem smiled.

"The guys found the same thing up in Tagene," said Meijner.

"So Hisingen finally has an IKEA," said Bergenhem.

"Looks like it."

Bergenhem watched the men move around their truck, if it was in fact theirs, and converse as though they were trying to make a decision.

"Is the stuff definitely stolen?" he said.

"We've already identified a lot of things here," said Meijner.

"Okay."

A car drove up behind the hangar of apartments and parked behind the truck. An older man got out. Bergenhem wrote down the license number.

The three men seemed to be carrying on a discussion about something that lacked a solution. The man who had just arrived pointed up and then in a different direction. One of the truck men, the younger one, shrugged his shoulders. His older friend started to climb into the truck. The newcomer made some sort of circular motion with his hand.

Everything seemed to be a misunderstanding.

The newcomer looked around and then went through the front door.

The truck started, spewed clouds of diesel fumes, the worst kind. Bergenhem was forced to make a decision. He started the car as the truck passed. The younger man was driving. The older one was talking on a cell phone.

Bergenhem swung out and followed them south. Three hundred yards and he met Aneta Djanali. He saw that she saw him. He even had time to see her start punching in the numbers. His phone rang.

"Obviously I missed something," she said.

"Here we go again," said Bergenhem.

"What happened?"

"Nothing. They never went in."

"No?"

"Another guy showed up."

"Explain."

They passed the police station again. It seemed deserted. There were no cars outside and no one was going in or coming out, or being led in or out. Bergenhem pondered whether this one had also closed for good, like the one down in Redbergslid.

"Well, another guy showed up, an older guy, and he went into the building and the others left." Bergenhem turned left. "It was the same entrance as before."

"Is he there now?" Aneta asked.

"I assume so. That was five minutes ago. He parked the car outside. I wrote down the number. Do you need it?"

"I'll get it later," she said. "Bye."

"Aneta!" Bergenhem shouted before she hung up. "Don't say anything about the truck."

"Of course not."

"I'll call later."

Bergenhem kept going, now to the south, on the same roads as before. Round-trip to Kortedala, he thought as he passed Olskroken and continued into the city on Friggagatan. At Odinsplatsen he saw the blue and white truck turn left, and he followed it over the river and through a green light and up onto Skånegatan and past the police station. The driver seemed to like passing police stations.

Aneta parked behind Sigge Lindsten's car.

The elevator was up. She called it down and waited and listened to the wind that was whistling around like a spiral through the stairwell, up, down. It hissed like a voice.

In the elevator she looked straight ahead at the wall where the mirror had been. She was staring into black circles made with paint that never went away, around and around, and she thought more had appeared since last time.

The door to the apartment was open. She knocked, twice.

Sigge Lindsten came out into the hall from the kitchen. He didn't look surprised.

"What is it now?" was all he said.

"It's still empty in here," said Aneta.

"Yes."

"No one has moved in after Anette?"

"No."

"Why not?" Aneta asked.

"What does it matter?" said Lindsten. "And if someone had, can't I do what I want? It's mine, isn't it?"

"How is Anette?"

"Fine, I think."

"Where is she?"

"At home. But please leave her alone now."

"Forsblad hasn't contacted her?"

"No."

"'And his sister?"

"She hasn't either."

"What do you think about his sister?"

"Nothing. And perhaps now I could be allowed to continue what I'm doing?"

"Why did you come here?" asked Aneta.

Lindsten didn't answer. He took a step backward and disappeared into the kitchen again. Aneta took a few steps into the hall and saw him standing in front of one of the cabinets. He quickly turned around when he saw her. There was something in his eyes that caused her to back up immediately and walk out into the stairwell and run down three flights, five flights, six, until she was down in the entryway. She felt surprised as she walked to the car. She felt cold. What had happened?

Winter read the letters, one after another. They were short, written in stumpy handwriting from a young John Osvald to his young wife. They weren't dated. But in the second one there was a reference to something that had been mentioned in the first one. Winter read it again. He looked up.

"Did your dad tell you about these letters?"

"No."

"Has he read them?"

"They were in his bedroom. He must have taken them out to . . . well, there was a box there and it was on the shelf and it was still open, and I think he kept them in there."

"Are there more?"

"We haven't found any. And like I said, he never said anything."

"Why not?"

"Why not? It was probably hard for him. I don't know. You can see there's a greeting for him in that second letter, and . . ."

Osvald didn't finish his sentence.

"The second letter seems to have been written from a different location," said Winter.

"Yes, maybe."

Winter quoted: *"We hope that we will have a better time here."*

He looked up again.

"They had moved."

Osvald nodded.

"It was probably up to Peterhead," Osvald said.

"Did they have a 'better time' there, as he writes?"

"I don't know, Erik. As far as I know, there's no one who knows."

"Listen to this," Winter said, reading out loud again: "*That thing you heard about before isn't what you think. You must believe me.*" He looked at Osvald. "He's referring to something he'd written about earlier, apparently. Or to something she'd heard about."

"Maybe," said Osvald.

"Your grandmother . . . didn't she ever talk about it?"

"Not that I remember. We were little when she died."

Like your mother, thought Winter. Both of the women in the Osvald family had left children and husbands behind. Now the children only had each other; everyone else was gone. Two brothers disappeared in the sea off Scotland, almost within sight. Now the children's father had died there, too.

Erik Osvald had his own family, his wife and son. Johanna Osvald had her brother. He thought about what she must be thinking about up there in Inverness. He wasn't sure that she'd still be there when he arrived.

Osvald sat motionless, as though he were meditating, with his eyes on the cliffs outside the window. Did he sit like this every week when he was home? A week out there, a week in here.

"I'm flying up tomorrow," said Winter.

"What?"

"I'm flying to Inverness tomorrow."

"What are you saying?" Osvald said, and he appeared to give a start. He took his eyes from the window.

"Are you surprised?" Winter said.

Osvald scratched the thin hair above his forehead, an unconscious movement.

Winter waited. A flatbed moped drove by outside; the noise swung around the house and bounced across the cliffs.

"Is it Johanna?" Osvald said with his hand still on his head.

"Sorry?"

"Is there still something between you and Johanna?"

"Do you mean that would be the reason I'm going there?"

"What other reason is there?" said Osvald.

That caused Winter to become silent for a second.

"Did you go mute?" said Osvald.

The moped drove by again, from the other direction. Some seabirds cried out again. Winter thought he could hear the bellowing of a boat from the archipelago lines.

"There are two reasons," said Winter, "and they're probably connected."

Bergenhem followed the truck. It was easier than ever. Skånegatan was wide and straight. The radio crackled. He answered and yielded at Korsvägen. The truck continued onto Södra Vägen toward Mölndalsvägen.

"The plates on that vehicle are stolen," he said to Meijner.

"Oh, fuck."

"Why did they drive to the warehouse only to turn around?" said Bergenhem.

"They probably got a call and were rerouted," said Meijner.

"That could be."

"Should we send some cars and bring them in?" said Meijner.

"Don't we want to know where they're going?"

"Yes," said Meijner.

"This is probably a big operation you're in charge of, right?"

"Very big," said Meijner. "Very, very big."

"Then we might mess something up if we crack down on these rascals now," said Bergenhem.

"Your assessment of this whole thing is quite correct," said Meijner. "Continue surveillance according to orders but do nothing, and stand by for further orders."

Bergenhem shook his head and smiled to himself.

"And give me the number on those plates, Bergies."

"Talk to Aneta Djanali at CID," Bergenhem said, and hung up.

They were on Mölndalsvägen now, passing the south entrance to the Liseberg amusement park. The road was still wide and straight. At Sörgården it changed names to Göteborgsvägen. The truck passed the Krokslätt factories. Bergenhem tried to keep four cars between him and the truck.

They continued up onto Kungsbackaleden. Bergenhem checked the gas. All cars that were taken out were supposed to have full tanks. This one didn't; it must have been somewhere else just before he got it. But it would last another sixty miles, maybe seventy.

They drove through Kållered. At the southern exit the truck swung to the right, and Bergenhem had time to follow; he watched it turn right again and drive around the parking lot and park outside IKEA.

Bergenhem parked. The men had gone in, two people among hundreds.

Bergenhem opened the car door and sat there. It smelled like gas in the parking lot. It smelled like grilled hot dogs.

He had grilled hot dogs with Krister over the weekend. On Stora Amundö, not so far from here. Well, pretty far.

They had talked about everything.

Martina thought he was working. He didn't think she would call and check. Sometimes he had the feeling she didn't care anymore.

She looked away. She always looked away.

This isn't working, he had thought as he drove to Linnéplatsen to pick up Krister.

He had said it out there, on the cliffs. The sea around them was full of sails.

This isn't working anymore.

Don't you want friends? Krister had said.

I don't want to sneak around with them, he had said.

You don't need to sneak around, Krister had said.

But I do. Martina. I'm sneaking around. I'm lying about periods of time.

Tell her.

What should I say?

You would know best, Krister had said.

The hell I would, he had thought.

He had seen Krister four times.

Nothing had happened.

Everything was confusion.

Maybe it was him and Martina. Maybe that was the problem. Their so-called relationship. Maybe they should go talk to someone. Maybe it was that simple and that complicated.

He had missed Ada out there. It was a wonderful day. The sky was wonderfully blue. He had suddenly missed Martina.

This is fucking nuts, he had thought. I'm here and they're there.

I'm sneaking around.

I'm lying.

We won't see each other for a long time, he had said to Krister in the car on the way back.

Okay, Krister had said.

They had shaken hands at Sveaplan.

Winter had told him about Macdonald. But that was just the small reason. He tried to explain the other one, the big one. It wasn't easy.

"I'm not usually wrong," he said.

Osvald looked out through the window again. It looked like dusk was coming, but it wasn't time for that. A cloud must have come in over the island.

"If there's anything more to know, then of course it's good if someone investigates," said Osvald.

Winter nodded.

"So there is?"

"I don't know. That's why I'm going."

"I understand," said Osvald.

"Someone got your father to go over," said Winter.

"What do you mean?"

"He got a letter, didn't he?"

"Yes, yes, right."

Winter looked at the two old sheets of paper that lay on the glass coffee table. He could see the rather jerky handwriting from here, but he couldn't read it.

"I would like to borrow those two letters for a while."

"Why?"

"So we can take a closer look at them."

"Fingerprints?"

"Why would you think that?" asked Winter.

"Well, I don't know, it's just what I thought of."

Winter didn't say anything. He heard the moped for the third time out there, brutt-brutt-brutt-bruuuuuuut as it passed, brutt-brutt-brutt. He suddenly thought of an old movie in which a motorcycle regularly, or rather irregularly, showed up in the middle of groups of people, in a city, suddenly it was there and then it was gone. *Amarcord*. Fellini.

There was also another movie . . . it was the same thing, a character on a motorcycle, and it was an obvious wink at Fellini's film. What was the other one called? He saw a village and a sea . . . it was called *Local Hero*. And as he recalled it was filmed somewhere in Scotland, a small community by the sea where everyone was suspicious of new-comers.

"Isn't it to look for fingerprints?" said Osvald.

"Maybe," said Winter.

He thought of the letter that had come a month earlier and that had caused Axel Osvald to journey away toward his death. He looked at his son and saw that he was thinking about that too.

"Are you going to *compare*?" said Osvald.

"Maybe," said Winter.

"But surely you don't think that . . ."

Winter didn't answer. The moped went by for the fourth time. It must be different mopeds, but in that case they sounded completely identical. He saw that film from Scotland pass by in his mind for a few seconds. The houses were close together. There was an inn. An artsy type ran it. He and an American had discussed selling a beach.

"That's completely idiotic," said Osvald. "That would mean Grandpa was still alive." He got up from his chair. "Do you really think he is?"

"What do you think?"

"No, no."

"What did your father think?"

"Not that. Not that it's . . . like that."

"Are you sure?"

"Maybe he hoped it was. At one time. But that's another story."

Belief. Or hope. Was it different? In Winter's world, in the world where he had thus far spent most of his time, in his adult life, belief and hope sometimes slid into each other.

"I want to ask you about one more thing, Erik," said Winter.

"What is it, Erik?" said Osvald.

"Do you have any photographs at home of your grandfather when he was young?"

Osvald moved his hand up to his forehead again. He rubbed his hair. He was standing in the middle of the floor.

"Anything other than that probably doesn't exist," he said. "We only remember him as young, you know."

"Is there a picture?" asked Winter.

"Yes," Osvald said, and left the room.

Bergenhem was standing four rows away from the truck, which seemed to sway in the wind when the cover moved. He could see that it was stretched over a van, which was peculiar. He looked at his watch. He had been sitting there for half an hour. He got out and approached the truck. He looked toward the entrance, where hundreds of people were going in and out and pushing carts full of flat packages. IKEA's business idea was flat packs, and they sailed around the world. All over the world people bought the packages and assembled their homes, their worlds. Bergenhem still had a scar on his knuckles from trying to assemble a TV stand in which the predrilled holes in the hard-as-stone glued sheets of beech didn't match the hardware. He had sworn and bled. But it had been cheap. In the end he had pounded in the screws with a hammer.

He looked at his watch again, at the truck again. He walked toward the entrance.

Half an hour later the parking lot began to empty.

The truck was still there.

Bergenhem began to realize what had happened.

Fifteen minutes later the truck was alone in its row. Bergenhem understood perfectly now. He called Meijner.

37

Harbour Office. It looked the way it always had, mostly like a wall against the sea. He had parked outside the shipyard and walked back along the quays. There was no wind.

It fit in. It was quiet here, a quiet no one wanted to have. Peterhead had taken over everything now, or almost everything. The shipyard behind his back was empty and quiet. A hammer strike coming from there would have caused passersby to jump. But there were no strikes.

He himself had held a hammer in there, in the red dust.

Suddenly he turned around, right in front of the fish market, which was partially built on poles above the water. People streamed out on their way to the buses that waited in the parking lot. He heard American voices, like sheep bleating their way up to the buses. Brae-brae-brae-brae.

In one of the docks there were still boats with meaningful existence, trawlers from here and from the horn: the *Three Sisters, Priestman, Avoca, Jolair, Sustain*. A familiar name: *Monadhliath*.

That couldn't be right.

A man came up onto the quarterdeck. He walked by as fast as he could, with his eyes on the Marine Accident Investigation Branch on the other side.

He shifted his gaze. He didn't need any reminders.

Absolutely nothing had happened to the houses behind the shipyard. The stone walls were like the bottom of the sea; it would take millions of years to get them to change, to wear away. He walked up and down Richmond. It took four minutes; the street wasn't even a hundred yards long. He had lived in number four. The windows were black. The door was new, of a type of wood he didn't recognize. It could be from a ship. It ought to be. The wind from the sea that swept through Richmond Street *was* the sea, as damp as the sea. Anyone who walked here became wet and cold. Not right now, the wind was from the south, but often otherwise.

The street was one of ten identical ones. Without the names no one would be able to find their way home. The shipyard workers had been too drunk to remember which street was theirs. Even though most of them could read, at least the names of their streets, their birth certificates; the family had been able to read the death certificates. It was a hard life; it was cold. He hadn't been here during the terrible years, and yet he had been so close. He had burned away most of the memories. It hurt to return. He knew how it would feel.

At the Marine Hotel, a single room cost twenty-five pounds. Back then, that had been his livelihood for a month.

He walked around the building. The bar had been moved. There was a notice about the "Cunard Suite" by the entrance. It had been there then, too.

He stood in the cramped hallway to the reception area.

It was the same smell.

Jesus.

"Can I help you, sir?"

She wasn't from that time. Her hair was blond. Her skirt was long; that was unusual on a young person. She didn't look at him, really. It was surprising that she had seen him at all.

"I just wanted to . . . ," he said, and that was all, and he turned and went out again, and up past Forsyths and Moray Seafoods, up the hill to the square.

The old hotel looked untouched. No bombs had fallen on it. He had to sit down on one of the benches in front of the city hall. It wasn't a city hall anymore, he could see that much. Old folks were going in and out; some seemed to be fifty years older than him. An old person was sitting on the bench across from him, sitting and sleeping in the pale autumn sun.

It was here. It was *here*. He had panicked and never returned. This was where it started.

It was all the people, thousands, tens of thousands.

The war was over. What was it, the twentieth anniversary of the monument? Yes. Maybe. They had celebrated peace, and that monument, which was twenty years old. It had been so crowded that he thought it might become hard to breathe.

* * *

He looked at the monument; naturally, it was still there, in front of the city hall in the old part of the square. You could touch it.

The War Memorial.

The memorial for the dead of the first great war.

In Proud and Grateful Remembrance.

Their Name Liveth For Ever.

That's what it looked like. But that's not how it was.

He got up with his memories and crossed the street. He had stood here, among all the others. Then he had turned around. There was a sound. A clicking sound.

They had stocked up a few times in Buckie. Maybe it was only twice. Arne had wanted to stay. Not this time, they had said. We'll come back. That was the last time. The Buckie boys are back in town, Arne had said when they docked. He repeated it as they drank beer at the Marine.

They had gone out at the same time as the *Monadhliath*. It was the next day.

The *Monadhliath* had run into drifting mines. That was another day later. He might have heard the explosion. He had seen a light in the night.

Two hours later the *Marino* had gone under.

He had convinced Bertil not to come along. No. He had forced him not to! That was in Fraserburgh. They had received their final instructions.

Arne wasn't coming along anyway. He had a meeting in the mountains. He traveled hidden under a tarp in the bed of a truck. More weapons. Always more weapons.

Arne didn't know German. Others knew German.

Egon came along out to sea. He couldn't force him to stay on land. He tried. Egon forced himself along on the last trip.

He didn't speak to Frans. They weren't speaking to each other anymore. Only when necessary. Only if the worst happened.

"John, you are lost," Frans had said.

"We're all lost," he had said.

Frans had talked about Ella. Crazy talk, insane. Frans had accused him. Don't try to take her, he had said. Ella is *mine.* It was insane. It was lies. Frans drank. Frans talked like a madman. Frans was careless with the weapons. Frans was afraid.

Egon looked afraid. Egon stayed away. Egon kept to himself in the mess. Egon was afraid.

He stood in the cabin. He drank. He froze. He listened to the wind. He was afraid. He had a premonition. He hadn't been able to explain it to Egon.

A gale was blowing when they went out, sheltered by the cliffs of Clubbie Craig.

The meeting was outside of Troup Head. He couldn't see the village in there under the cliffs. Everything was dark. Suddenly they could see the signal above Cullykhan Bay. The other boat came out.

They went north. They unloaded and loaded up again. They kept going. They unloaded. They kept going. The wind increased. They couldn't go home yet. They went into the storm.

He wasn't afraid now. Egon was afraid.

Frans wasn't afraid. Frans came into the cabin. Frans was waving a German army pistol.

"Should we shoot the haddock?" he screamed.

He didn't answer. There was a strong gust. Frans reeled.

"We have lots of these!" screamed Frans, waving the pistol. "And bigger ones too!" He waved it again. "We can shoot whales!"

Frans had stolen weapons. How much had he stolen?

It was punishable by death. It didn't matter how little you kept. Or how much.

Almost everything was punishable by death.

"Put that down," he yelled.

"Should we set the trawl?" Frans screamed. "Ha ha ha!"

"Go belowdecks," he yelled.

Frans lost his balance in the rough sea. The *Marino* fell, fell twenty yards, thirty. The sea was crazy. The water was a wall. The water was hard as stone. The water was a stone wall. The water was death.

Frans dropped the pistol, then picked it up. Frans lost his balance. Then Frans was on his way out, a yard from the door. He reeled suddenly.

Egon was on his way in. The storm threw him in.

A shot went off. Another shot.

Egon exploded. Egon's head split. Egon's body fell.

Frans was still holding the pistol in his hand. He dropped it. He ran out through the cabin door.

Egon was motionless on the wet floor. The water rushed in through the doorway.

He turned the rudder. He dragged the body to shelter. He looked for Frans. He called his name through the storm. Frans didn't answer. He knew that he was still on board. He found him. Frans tried to say something. He didn't listen. Frans looked at him. He closed his eyes.

Jesus!

38

They landed at Inverness Airport at eleven thirty. The sun was out, but it was low and weak. In the taxi to the city Winter saw an open landscape and a glimpse of water to the north and the silhouettes of the big mountains south of the city. It was the Highlands.

"They're higher than I thought," said Angela. "It's beautiful."

Inverness was built of old and new. Loathsome concrete roundabouts spun their way in toward a medieval downtown. They could see the castle high above. The taxi slowly made its way through town and crept along the river Ness. They passed a bridge and continued on Ness Bank along the river for five hundred yards and stopped outside the little Glenmoriston Hotel, which Winter had booked on Macdonald's recommendation. Cozy and well kept and expensive, as Macdonald had said.

The room was large and it was on the second floor, and they had a panorama view over the river and the park beyond it, as well as the three-hundred-year-old granite houses on either side of the cathedral. Winter opened the window. The wind was still warm. He could see people on park benches on the other side. It wasn't far. Gulls circled over the benches. Pigeons hopped around them. People were eating their lunches on the benches, spread-out papers of fish and chips. Haddock that had been pulled up by Erik Osvald. Potatoes that had been delivered by Steve Macdonald's dad. Vinegar from whatever distillery was available.

Winter could see two bridges over the river. It was still early October, but the sky above the river was very low and had a color like stone; the sun was gone now.

The sky brushed the bridges.

Angela stood beside him.

"The ceiling's a little low here," she said, looking out at the sky.

"I've never seen anything like it," said Winter.

"Haven't you been here before?"

"That was in the summer. The sky was blue, if I remember correctly."

"Don't you always remember correctly?"

She smiled kindly.

"Not anymore," said Winter, thinking of Arne Algotsson. No one knew what was in store, at least if you didn't analyze your DNA. He didn't intend to do that.

Angela hung up some clothes. He let his bag lie unopened. She sat on the bed, which was large and yet looked small in the room.

"I like this room," she said.

Winter looked in the bathroom, which was tiled in a warm shade. It was the same color as the low sky outside.

"Nice hotel," he heard Angela say behind him.

It was. The lobby was small but not too small. To the right there was an inviting bar with leather chairs and a counter and shelves well stocked with bottles. To the left was the restaurant.

"I'm going to call home," said Angela.

He washed his hands and heard her voice and walked out into the room. She held out the phone: "Elsa."

He took it and heard his daughter, who had already started telling him what had happened during the day. No day care while they were gone. Elsa was totally the center of attention, with Grandma Siv, Aunt Lotta, and her cousins Bim and Kristina in a circle around her. Total spoiling. But that was nothing new. He believed in spoiling young children. All the laws and rules and decrees and prohibitions would still be there, soon enough. Most people didn't escape adult life, and there was no one to spoil you there. You were alone there. Out there you're on your own, he thought.

"We're making Christmas candy!" said Elsa.

Why not. There were only three months left until Christmas.

Or maybe his mother had lost her sense of the seasons after almost fifteen years under an eternal sun.

"Have you spoken English, Papa?" she asked in the impatient, half-stumbling way of children.

"Sure have. With the taxi driver and people here at the hotel," he answered.

"Not with Mama?" she said, giggling.

"Not yet," he said, laughing too.

"Is it a nice hotel?" said Elsa.

"Very nice," he said.

"I want to stay at a hotel too," she said, but he didn't hear any disappointment in her voice. It was only a statement.

"You'll get to stay at lots of hotels, sweetie."

"Promise!" she yelled.

Of course he promised. Up to a certain age, you could promise things, and perhaps sometimes later too, but at some point she would have to keep her own promises. Out there. On her own.

He knew that it would go quickly; he had the proof around him. Look at Bertil and his Moa. Winter had started working with Ringmar when Moa was about the same age as Elsa was now, a little older. It went quickly, the days rushed by like wild horses across the hills. Winter had had a word with Ringmar about the circus in Kortedala before he left. Bergenhem had told some story about IKEA. The truck was still there in the morning. Smart guys. They must have seen Bergenhem. Or else someone had called them in the truck. Aneta had had her suspicions about who.

Their room phone rang. Winter had just ended his conversation with Elsa.

"Call for Mr. Winter," the receptionist said.

He heard Macdonald's voice. "The trip went well?"

"Excellent."

"Is the hotel okay?"

"It's excellent, too. Where are you?"

"We got into town just a little while ago. Have you eaten lunch?"

"No."

"May I treat you then? Right now? I suggest the Royal Highland Hotel. It's right next to the train station. Go straight into the lobby and we'll be sitting on the right in the bar. Sarah's hair is black as sin and I'm wearing a kilt in the Macdonald clan tartan."

"How am I supposed to recognize that?" said Winter.

He heard Macdonald's laugh.

"Red and black," said Macdonald.

"Will we have time, then?" said Winter.

"We're meeting Craig in two hours," said Macdonald. "He's out on some job now."

"Have you spoken to the daughter?" asked Winter.

"Today, you mean?"

"Yes."

"Yes. She's going to be there too."

"Any news about the autopsy?"

"Yes. There's no poison in the body. And preparations have been under way so she can fly home with her father as soon as tonight."

"So soon?"

"No reason for the body to stay here. And there's a late-afternoon plane from London to Gothenburg this evening."

"Okay. Is the Royal Highland up the main street, as in the one that goes right at the bridge?" asked Winter.

"Yes. You remember, I see."

"Wasn't it called the Station Hotel before?"

"That's exactly right, too. Go up Bridge Street a few hundred yards and then take a left on Inglis and then you'll see the station. How is Angela, by the way?"

"She's excellent too. And Sarah?"

"She thinks it will be fun to meet Angela. I've told her so much about her."

"You have?"

Macdonald laughed again and hung up.

The lobby of the Royal Highland was large and grand, which wasn't surprising since the hotel had opened in 1854. The place had obviously been renovated recently, but everything still seemed to be a hundred fifty years old, from a century that had apparently been as showy as everything they could see in there. Angela let out a whistle, and Winter felt the same.

Macdonald got up from a table in the open cocktail bar to the right. He wasn't wearing a kilt, but Winter recognized him anyway. He hadn't changed that Winter could see. The same villainous, swarthy looks, the same long, bony body that seemed as strong as hemp. Macdonald raised his hand and said something to the woman who had also stood up, and then Winter saw that Macdonald's ponytail was gone.

* * *

It was a pleasant lunch. Macdonald had suggested fish and chips in all seriousness, because it was the bar's famous specialty, with tartar sauce.

"I've never eaten fish and chips," said Angela.

"Jeez, then it's about time," said Macdonald.

"Some things are worth not trying," Sarah Macdonald said, placing her hand on Angela's arm, "and this may be one of them."

Angela laughed. She thought she would get along well with Sarah Macdonald. Steve's wife was taller than average and thin, but in a strong way like her husband. She looked like Steve, including her face, almost as though they were siblings. The two had met when he started working as a green constable in Inverness.

"I s'pose this is the time and place for my first fish and chips," said Angela, in response to Sarah.

"One should try everything once, except incest and folk dancing," Macdonald said, and he looked around and called the waiter and ordered food and drinks. Winter had declined a glass of malt whisky—later, later—but said yes to a pint of Scotch ale whose name he didn't recognize.

The food was good. To be sure, it was only fish and chips, but this was the place.

It was a good reunion. Winter had missed Macdonald, and maybe Macdonald had felt the same. Angela had met him when he came over to Gothenburg during the resolution of a painful case he and Winter had worked on together, in Gothenburg and London. They had become close. They had supported each other emotionally, because it was a matter of keeping one's head during the almost unmentionable incidents that they had not only been forced to witness, but also to be involved in. That was the worst part of their respective jobs on either side of the water: to be forced to witness and to be forced to be involved.

"What do you say?" he heard Sarah ask.

"Suits me fine," Angela said, and turned to Winter: "Sarah has offered to show me the city."

"Then perhaps I may treat you to dinner this evening?" asked Winter.

"You may," said Macdonald.

"May I suggest the Italian restaurant in the Glenmoriston?" asked Winter.

"You may do that too," said Macdonald, and Sarah nodded.

*   *   *

The sun was out again as they stood outside the hotel, but the sky was still veiled by low clouds. Angela and Sarah went to the left and Macdonald showed Winter toward the station building.

"We can walk through it and out the other side, to the car rental place," he said.

They walked through the departure hall, which was smaller than Winter remembered. He had sat here for an hour or two, waiting for his departure for Edinburgh via Perth. The train had gone straight over the Highlands, with a certain amount of effort, and he still remembered the odd landscape. It had been like an ocean floor a thousand meters above the sea. And it had suddenly become very cold in the train car. He still remembered some of the towns up there, not so far from here, Aviemore, Kingussie, Newtonmore, and Dalwhinnie at the northern point of Loch Ericht, Lake Eric you could say. There was a decent malt whisky from the distillery in Dalwhinnie, but he wasn't sure that Macdonald would agree with him.

They walked past the tracks and out on Strothers Lane and directly onto Railway Terrace. Winter could see the Budget sign and the shining rental cars in the parking lot behind the office.

"Not a trace," said the man behind the counter, who said his name was Frank Cameron, and he got up and followed them out. "It's damn strange." He had been the one who helped Axel Osvald.

"Customers must have their cars stolen sometimes, right?" asked Macdonald. Winter thought that Macdonald's Scots accent became stronger when he spoke with this man, whose accent was quite strongly pronounced.

"Yes, yes, but the car is just gone now. In other cases we always find them. Or the cop. . . . police find them sooner or later. Often sooner." He looked around and pointed at a metallic green three-door Toyota Corolla, which a younger man was in the process of washing in the courtyard. "It was the twin of that one, this year's model, same color."

"Do you remember the customer?" Winter asked.

"No," said Cameron. "I didn't remember him when your colleague asked me last week and I didn't remember him the week before either, when we reported the car missing, and I don't remember this Swede now."

"Are there that many Swedes?" asked Macdonald.

"Some," said Cameron. He gave Macdonald a sharp look. Cameron had a prominent hawk nose. He seemed irritated that he didn't remember. "What about it? We probably had a lot to do that day. I don't remember him, okay? I have some weak memory of a slightly older fellow but that's all."

"That's good," said Macdonald.

"If that was him, he didn't say anything," said Cameron, "if he's the one I . . . well, hardly remember, he was quiet as an Orkneyman and that doesn't do much for the memory."

"Maybe that's why you remember him," said Macdonald.

"But I don't remember him, I've said."

Macdonald nodded as if to say "What's that got to do with it?" and asked for copies of the contract.

"Your friend from the police has them."

"Craig?"

"Yes, maybe that's his name. A stuck-up Englishman."

"That's Craig," said Macdonald. "I'm sure he's told you to sound the alarm if the car shows up."

"How would that happen?" said Cameron. "The fellow who rented it is dead, right? He can't drive it here. Is whoever stole it supposed to drive it here?"

"Someone might find it," said Macdonald.

"It would probably be the police, in that case," said Cameron. "But I doubt it." He let out a laugh that was mostly a snort.

"Well, that's all for now," said Macdonald. He turned to Winter. "Wasn't your wife going to rent a car this afternoon?"

"Yes, right," said Winter.

Cameron's face changed. His eyes became soft and merry.

"You know the place, lads!"

They said good-bye and continued along Railway Terrace toward the police station, which was only a few hundred yards away.

"Cameron!" said Macdonald, and it mostly sounded like a snort.

"What?" said Winter.

"Cameron is a strange clan," said Macdonald. "They're from up in northern Argyll, in the isolated central Highlands, and that's where they belong."

Winter smiled. Macdonald stopped and turned to him.

"You saw that character, right? He was a perfect example of a Cameron, perfect. Did you see his nose? Do you know what the name Cameron means? In Gaelic it's *Cam-shron* and it means 'hawk nose.'"

"Are you racist, Steve?"

"Ha ha."

"Do you know a lot about different clans?" asked Winter.

"Mostly about my own," said Macdonald.

"You'll have to tell me sometime. It's interesting."

"It's mostly very sad stories," said Macdonald.

39

An abandoned stroller lay upside down in the concrete stairway in the viaduct. It was yellow and blue. It immediately reminded Winter of an earlier case, still painfully in his memory. Macdonald turned it over without saying anything.

The wind on the bridge was harsh. Winter had a view over the city and the river and the mountains to the south. There was a closed-down bakery to the left down there. They walked a hundred yards along Longman Road and turned off at the police station, which looked relatively newly built, and for that reason stood out among the buildings around it.

They walked in under the bilingual sign: Inverness Command Area. Sgìre Comannd Inbhirnis. The office reminded Winter of the Police Palace at home, the same worn charm, the international brotherhood's surly reception of a public in need. Some of them were sitting in there with the same expression as everywhere else. A mixture of helplessness and fear, of solitude in a world that wasn't kind. A woman was standing at the counter and carrying on a conversation in something that must have been Gaelic; her voice was high and hollow like a cracked muffler, and the words seemed to rasp through the room. There was a notice on the other side of the wall: *Dèiligeadh leis a h-uile tachartas de ghiùlan mìshòisealta gu h-èifeachdach.* There was what Winter presumed was a translation next to it: *To effectively tackle all incidents of antisocial behavior.*

A proud task for the international brotherhood, his and Steve's. Put quote marks around "effectively." But we try. At the same time, the damned society doesn't want to stand still so we can get some order in the middle of everything that is antisocial, or has become antisocial.

Another poster was hanging on the wall in yellow and black: Going to the Hills? Let Us Know *Before* You Go.

Axel Osvald hadn't followed this request. But he hadn't climbed that high.

Jamie Craig came out from a door to the right of the glassed-in reception area. He looked like he sounded. Brutal. His cheeks were red and chapped, which might have been due to whisky or the Highland air or both. He greeted Macdonald with a professional handshake that lacked enthusiasm, and he pressed Winter's hand quickly and firmly.

"Let's go," he said.

They walked through underground corridors. The lighting was weak and it cast shadows that might have been anything at all from the last hundred years. Winter thought of the gas works, which he'd seen from the bridge. Maybe there was a running hundred-year agreement between the police and the gas company.

When they came up, the light was blinding and electric. Johanna Osvald was waiting in a room.

Winter gave her a hug. She greeted Macdonald. They stood in the middle of the room.

"I'm . . . we're leaving in a few hours," she said.

"I know," said Winter.

"You wanted to see him?"

"Yes."

"Why?"

"I don't know," said Winter, but he knew; he knew something he couldn't explain, even to himself.

"But it was a natural death," said Johanna with doubt in her voice: I do not accept death as natural. Not this one.

Axel Osvald looked like he was sleeping. Winter sat at his head for two minutes and then got up. Osvald's hair was brushed back, and there was a weak shadow of stubble on his cheeks. Winter couldn't tell whether he'd been unshaven or recently shaven when he died. The beard continued to grow on dead men, and the nails too. It was natural.

Macdonald and Johanna and Craig waited in the bare room.

"Let's go," said Craig.

They returned through the same corridor. Johanna's hair looked like gold. Winter thought he smelled gas. It was cold down there, colder since he'd seen the body. He felt goose bumps on his upper arms. These passages must have existed when the buildings above had been different, in another time. They had been saved as a reminder.

They came up into a new light that blinded their eyes. Craig showed them into his office, which was a glass cage in the middle of an office landscape. He could see all of his subordinates, but they could also see him. Winter couldn't have stood being there for ten minutes, but Craig moved about as though he could see out but no one could see in, the way it was in rooms they had used before for witness lineups. But the other way around.

Craig showed them to three chairs that had been put there for this purpose. He sat behind his desk, which was clear of papers, pens, stands, baskets, ashtrays, everything. The top of the desk gleamed, as though Craig devoted all his time to polishing it. Winter met Macdonald's glance. One of *those*. The telephone stood on a little side table. Behind Craig people were working to effectively tackle all incidents of antisocial behavior. Winter could see this through the glass. Men and women in and out of uniform were moving back and forth, telephones were picked up and put down, computer screens flickered at random. Winter saw two officers come in wearing bulletproof vests and helmets, with machine guns strapped on. A man who looked southern European and dismal was sitting next to one of the desks closest to Craig's glass wall, and he seemed to be staring at the back of Craig's neck.

"I believe we've done all we can here," Craig said, scratching that neck.

"We appreciate it," said Winter.

Johanna Osvald nodded. She had been very quiet during the hike through the corridors, as though she were already sitting on the plane with her father in a coffin among all the Samsonite suitcases in the belly of the plane.

"There's still that car," said Craig.

"We met the rental guy," said Winter. "Cameron."

"Nice fellow," Craig said with a thin smile.

"Stolen cars usually turn up right quick," Macdonald said.

Craig seemed to stiffen, just barely.

"That's why I'm bringing it up," he said, and he got up and walked to a filing cabinet and opened it.

He came back with a piece of paper and sat down and put on a pair of reading glasses.

"Between April and July this year we had one hundred twelve auto thefts in the greater city and all but one of the cars showed up," he said. "We also caught forty-six car thieves in the act." He looked up. "It was peak season."

"Admirable," said Macdonald.

"Which part is admirable?"

Craig smiled; perhaps there was an ironic wrinkle in one corner of his mouth.

"Your statistics."

"We're the best in all of Scotland," he said.

"This car," said Winter, "that it didn't come back. That indicates a crime, of course. Maybe a violent crime."

"Yes," said Craig, "that's exactly why I'm bringing it up. But of course it's not necessarily connected to the death." He looked at Johanna, who was looking at something else through the window walls. "He could have gotten rid of the car somewhere else."

"Is that likely?" said Winter.

"No."

"Someone could have given him a ride in a different car to Fort Augustus," said Macdonald.

"In that case we're really talking about a crime here," said Craig.

"But remember, no marks on the body," Winter said with a glance at Johanna, who didn't seem to be there. As though she didn't want to hear this.

"It was a heart attack," said Craig. "His heart packed it in. The question is why."

"You don't have more information about his acting confused in town?" asked Macdonald.

"It wasn't that conspicuous," said Craig. "He walked around a little and maybe asked a few questions that no one understood and talked to maybe three or four people."

"Do you know who might have been the last one?" asked Winter.

"Who *might* have been, yes. But the times are a bit unclear, of course." He scratched his neck again. "One of the most irritating parts of this job is people's fuzzy perception of time." Craig suddenly heaved himself forward. "Isn't it? We can know with one hundred percent certainty that different witnesses met someone, say around lunchtime, and one of those witnesses will swear that it was at midnight and the other at dawn!"

"What kind of time span are we looking at in the case of Axel Osvald?" asked Winter.

"A few hours," said Craig. "Early afternoon."

Winter nodded.

Craig looked at Johanna's profile.

"He died the same night."

"He got very excited," Johanna said suddenly, catching everyone off guard.

"I beg your pardon, Miss Osvald?" said Craig.

"I've thought a lot about it." She turned to them. "When that letter came, he didn't seem very . . . astounded or whatever you'd call it, not as agitated as you might expect. But then, after a few days he suddenly became . . . well, agitated, and he called about a ticket up here and left that same afternoon, I think . . . no, it was the morning after." She looked out at the office landscape again. "It was like something more had happened. Something different."

"Did he get another letter?"

"Not that I saw."

"But he could have?"

"Yes; I wasn't home those two days. I was at school." She looked at Winter. "I had the morning off when that first one . . . no, what am I saying, when that letter came, I saw it."

"Was anyone else home then, Johanna?" asked Winter. "Anyone besides your dad?"

"Erik was home," she said. "It was his week at home."

"But he hasn't said anything about another letter?"

"No."

"No telephone call?"

"No."

Winter didn't say anything more. It was quiet in Craig's cage of an office. He heard voices from the outside but couldn't make out words. It could be Scots English or Gaelic, or Swedish.

"What do you think about your father acting confused?" Macdonald asked, straight to the point.

She just shook her head.

"Does it sound unlikely?" Macdonald continued.

"Yes," she answered.

"But you said he was agitated . . ."

"Not that way," said Johanna, "never that way. He has never had problems like that, I can tell you that for sure. He had both feet on the ground, as they say."

On deck, thought Winter. Had both feet on deck. Maybe that was even safer. At the same time, he trusted in God above the earth.

"Something must have happened to him," said Johanna. "Something awful must have happened."

They drove over Ness Bridge in the car that Craig had loaned them, and they turned right onto Kenneth Street and then onto Ross Avenue, which was one of a hundred little streets lined with row houses of stone. They drove slowly and stopped in front of one of the houses. A sign was hanging on the wall between the door and the window: Glen Islay Bed and Breakfast.

"Glen Islay," said Winter. "Sounds like a brand of whisky."

"Bed and breakfast and whisky," said Macdonald.

Winter looked around as they got out of the car.

"I've been here," he said.

"Here? On this street?"

"Yes. I stayed at a B and B on this street."

"Maybe this one," Macdonald said.

Maybe, thought Winter as they stood in the cramped hallway, which also served as the lobby. Stairs led upward. It smelled like eggs and bacon and dampness, maybe mold. Burned bread. A rattle came from the pipes that ran on strange courses along the wallpaper, which could have been put up during Edwardian times. Everything was as it should be.

A telephone stood on a rickety table. An older woman stood next to it, one of those little old ladies who ran their guesthouses through the centuries.

"So Mr. Osvald drove away in a car, Mrs. McCann?" Macdonald asked.

"I'm absolutely cerrrrtain," said Mrs. McCann. She looked quite positive. "And I'ave told the otherrr policemen exactly that."

"Did he have visitors while he was staying here?"

"No."

"Was he alone when he checked out?" Macdonald asked.

"Yes, of course. What do you mean, Officer?"

"No one was sitting in the car out there?"

"I couldn't see. I didn't go outside when he left." She waved her hand toward the outer door, which had two windows that were covered by some sort of lace.

Winter could see their car out there, but not whether anyone was sitting in it. He nodded toward Mrs. McCann.

"Could we see his room?" asked Macdonald. "If it's empty."

"At the moment it's empty," she answered.

"Have any other police visited it?" asked Winter.

"No."

Winter looked at Macdonald, who shrugged. Craig wasn't investigating a murder, after all.

"May we see the room?" Macdonald repeated.

She took a step away from the telephone.

"Did Mr. Osvald get any phone calls while he was here?" asked Winter.

"I've already answered that," said Mrs. McCann.

"We usually ask several times," Macdonald said, smiling.

"Why don't you write it down right away?" asked Mrs. McCann.

"We try," said Macdonald.

"I told the other officer that there were three calls and I took them and it was a woman every time," said Mrs. McCann.

"Was it the same woman?"

"Yes . . ."

"She said who it was?"

"She said it was Miss Osvald."

"Okay," said Macdonald. "The room . . ."

"Has anyone else stayed there since Mr. Osvald did?" asked Winter.

"No, it's not the high season anymore. At the moment I don't have any guests, unfortunately." She seemed to consider something. She looked up. "But I have cleaned the room."

"We completely understand, Mrs. McCann," Macdonald said.

"He hadn't forgotten anything," she said. "If you're looking for something."

"We only want to see the room," said Macdonald.

"It's on the second floor," she said, and walked straight across the hall and took a key out of a cabinet on the wall.

It was a room that evoked Winter's memories of all small guesthouse rooms like this one. It had two windows, facing different directions. The room was filled with a thousand small odds and ends, to make it cozy. There was even a hot water bottle at the foot of the bed. A cheap picture hung on the wall to the right of the bed; it depicted a monster with a long neck swimming in a lake. The picture had a frame shot through with orange. It was a special picture, a special frame.

Good God.

I have slept in this room.

Winter looked at Mrs. McCann. What could she be? Maybe sixty-five. He remembered a matron from back then. A woman just over forty. Like he was now. He didn't remember what she looked like. But he wanted to know, know for sure.

"Mrs. McCann, how long have you run this place?"

"For exactly thirty years," she answered with a resolute expression.

"Good. Have you perhaps saved the check-in registers that go back in time?"

"Naturally." She looked at Macdonald. "There's a law about it now. But I did it before, too, I did. And my mother did, too."

"Sorry?"

"My mother. She ran Glen Islay before me."

"How long have you actually been letting rooms?" asked Macdonald.

"Since thirty-nine," she answered. "The war had started and there were lots of soldiers up here and Mother said now we have to help these poor boys to have a good roof over their head and a nice room to stay in."

"Could we look at the registers?" asked Winter.

"Weren't you going to look at the room?" she asked.

"I can do that," said Macdonald, after exchanging a glance with Winter.

It smelled like dry dust in the part of the cellar where the books stood in piles of red imitation leather. There seemed to be hundreds. He didn't feel any moisture in the room, which meant that the books would be well preserved.

"What is it you want to look for?" asked Mrs. McCann.

Winter told her about his visit during the early eighties. It had been in March.

"Then I ought to remember you," said Mrs. McCann.

"I had a beard," Winter said.

"We had several Scandinavian youngsters," Mrs. McCann said.

Winter nodded. He walked between the piles, which were numerous and relatively short. Winter could see that there were scraps of paper with dates attached to the walls behind them. She picked through one pile and came back with a register.

"This is the spring," she said, browsing through. Winter stood next to her and saw the wide columns with illegible signatures and printed names and addresses. Mrs. McCann lifted a few pages from March. There were surprisingly many guests. She held her finger to an entry from March 14. Winter read his address in Hagen, his parents' home in Gothenburg; he saw his signature as it was then, much neater than it was now, uncertain and neat at the same time, sprawling.

"Well, that must be you," she said. "Isn't it strange?"

"Yes," he answered.

"And there are so many B and Bs in this part of town," she said. "This is where most of them are."

He nodded.

"Did someone put you on to it?" she asked.

"I walked here from the station after asking there," said Winter. "I assume most people do that."

"Yes. They call from the room information at the station when people come here by train. Or sometimes from the airport."

"How was it with Mr. Osvald?" asked Winter.

She thought for several seconds.

"He called," she said.

"He called? Himself?"

"Yes."

"He called here himself and reserved a room?" Winter asked.

"Yes, that's what I just said."

"Could you hear where he was calling from, at all?"

"Yes . . . it wasn't from the city, anyway. There was some crackling and buzzing and so forth, so I took for granted that it was from abroad. If someone calls from abroad that's what it sounds like."

Winter thought.

"It's not possible that Mr. Axel Osvald had been a guest here before?" he asked.

"When would that have been?" she asked. "No, I don't remember him. And not his name either. I would remember." She nodded toward the piles of red books. "But it's easy to check."

"You didn't remember me," said Winter.

"That's different," she said. "You were young then. And had a beard."

Winter told Macdonald. They stood in the Room of One Thousand Things. Macdonald smiled at Mrs. McCann's words.

"'When I Was Young,'" he said. "Eric Burdon and the Animals."

Mrs. McCann had left them alone for fifteen minutes.

"Axel Osvald must have been told about this place," said Winter. "Or else he had been here before."

"Sometime during the last forty years," said Macdonald. "We just have to start browsing."

"No thank you," said Winter.

"If we'd had a murder here, Craig would have given us a team," said Macdonald. "But not now."

"I can see myself browsing," said Winter. "But not for Axel Osvald's name."

Macdonald had followed him down into the cellar again, along with Mrs. McCann. She was very cooperative. Macdonald commended her on the well-kept guesthouse. Winter promised to recommend this excellent place to half of Gothenburg. They had taken informational brochures and business cards. There was no Internet address, no www.glenislay .com, and there would hardly be one soon.

"I just started a new one after this one," she said, lifting up the top register in the rightmost pile.

Winter had asked for all the registered guests during the days Axel Osvald had stayed there, and the days immediately before and after.

He and Macdonald read through the pages together. There weren't very many names. They saw Osvald's signature. Mrs. McCann had noted when he checked out. There was a note for everyone who checked out. Everything was very tidy.

The day before Axel Osvald checked in, an Os Johnson checked out.

Winter read the slightly shaky signature. It was relatively large, but it seemed to lack force.

Os Johnson.

Winter had had John Osvald's name in his head for so long now that he connected it immediately when he saw "Os Johnson" written in an uneven and weak hand. Os Johnson. Osvald Johnson. John Osvald.

Something had led Winter to these books. His idea. He couldn't blink now. Something had led him to Glen Islay again.

"Do you remember this Os Johnson?" he asked, placing his index finger on the signature.

She leaned forward and then looked up.

"Do you think I'm senile, Officer?" She shook her head. "It was only a month ago." She looked at Macdonald. "Mr. Johnson was so sweet. A truly honorable man, like they were back then."

"Back then?" Winter asked.

"Mr. Johnson was a little over eighty years old," she said. "But he managed on his own. All on his own."

Winter and Macdonald looked at each other.

"Was he from here?" Macdonald asked. "From Scotland, I mean? Or perhaps England?"

"He didn't say much," she answered. "But I think he probably was. It sounded like it. He didn't talk much, like I said. But I helped him mail a letter."

"Sorry?"

"He wanted to mail a letter and I offer that service, too. I have stationery and envelopes and stamps and everything, and then I can take it to the mailbox if my guests want help with that. Some are in a bit of a hurry and are going to leave, and then it's nice to be—"

"Excuse me for interrupting, Mrs. McCann," said Macdonald, "but did you see to whom this letter was addressed?"

"Absolutely not. It would never occur to me to steal a glance at something like that."

"Had Mr. Johnson put on the stamps himself?" asked Macdonald.

"Yes . . . ," she said.

"Aren't you sure?"

"Yes . . . but there was something . . . I don't remember now . . . the envelope wasn't from here. I mean that it wasn't one of the envelopes I offer. And there were more stamps than normal on it. *That* I remember, because I saw it when I put it in the box along with the others. It was a small pile."

Winter opened his shoulder bag and took the original envelope out of the plastic sleeve. He could see the Inverness postmark on the edge, on top of the three stamps.

"Was this the envelope?" he asked.

She looked for a long time. She really wanted to help. Sometimes you have to be very critical of the extra helpful. Some mean so well, they want to help put together the puzzle. Like in a strange country where everyone points a different way when you ask for directions. To be helpful.

But Mrs. McCann held back any misdirected helpfulness.

She looked up.

"I can't say. But I don't think so."

Winter took yet another ace from his bag, the last one.

He showed her the photograph he had gotten from Erik Osvald.

John Osvald was about half his grandson's age in that photograph.

He was smiling from the quarterdeck. Nets were hanging around him. The sky was open above the young man and the boat. He held ropes in his hands. He was wearing a brimmed cap that shaded his eyes. Most of what remained was a smile.

"Who is this?" she asked.

"Os Johnson," said Winter.

"Really?" she said. "Well, everyone was young once."

"It could be him," said Winter.

"Well, I don't recognize him," she said. "It can't be." She looked up. "Why, it's completely impossible."

Winter nodded and put the photograph away and took out a different one. John Osvald in profile this time, shortly before he sailed away, never to return.

"No," said Mrs. McCann.

Winter closed his bag.

"May we come back if we want to ask anything else?" Macdonald asked.

She nodded.

"Is there anything in particular you remember about Mr. Johnson?" Macdonald asked.

"What might that be?"

"Anything. What he said. Did. Some gesture. Whether he called. Anything about his appearance. Whether he had guests. Everything. Anything at all."

"That was a lot," she said.

"Think about it," said Macdonald, "and call me if you think of anything, Mrs. McCann. Anything at all, like I said."

They could see that she hesitated.

"Yes?" said Macdonald.

"That letter . . . ," Mrs. McCann said, avoiding their eyes. "That I sent."

"Yes?" repeated Macdonald.

"I happened to see a bit of the address when I put it in the box."

"That's completely natural," said Macdonald.

"It would be strange if you hadn't," said Winter.

"I only saw which country," Mrs. McCann said, looking up at Macdonald, "which country it was being sent to."

"Which country was it?"

"Denmark."

"Denmark?" Winter said, and looked at Macdonald. "It wasn't Sweden, Mrs. McCann?"

"No. It said Denmark on the envelope."

They rounded the corner out onto Kenneth again. Macdonald stopped for pedestrians and then turned right onto Tomnahurich Street.

"Maybe Axel Osvald didn't have visitors," said Winter. "We asked about visitors, but maybe the person he was meeting was already there."

"And called for him," said Macdonald.

"Yes."

Macdonald gave Winter a quick look.

"Are you beginning to enjoy this?"

"No."

"You know what I mean."

"In that case, yes."

They passed a large chip shop. Winter could smell the fried fat right across the busy street.

"The air in there is so greasy that a human body leaves an impression," Macdonald said, nodding toward the door. "You can see the outlines of bodies in the air. It's like in Siberia, where seventy-below temperatures have the same effect on the air."

"I believe you," said Winter.

"We even fry black pudding," said Macdonald.

"That might be necessary," said Winter.

They stopped at a red light. In front of them the A82 continued to Loch Ness. They kept going and passed a cemetery and the sports center and the Aquadome and a sign for an all-weather football pitch.

"Is there more than one kind of weather up here?" Winter asked, pointing at the sign.

"No, and it's just like Gothenburg, from what I hear," said Macdonald.

Winter looked at the clock and took out his phone and dialed a number from his notebook.

Johanna Osvald answered on the third ring.

"Hi," he said. "How is it going?"

"Good. They've been extremely helpful. I . . . we are at the airport now. The plane leaves in forty-five minutes."

"Sorry we couldn't help you," he said.

"We've already discussed that, Erik. It's better that you and Macd . . . Steve are doing what you're doing."

"I have a question," he said, shifting his weight on the seat as Macdonald took a hard right onto the narrow main road. "How many times did you call your dad at the bed and breakfast place here in Inverness? Glen Islay?"

"Uh, two, I think. Two."

"Try to remember."

"Does it matter?"

"Yes."

"Why?"

"First think of how many times," said Winter.

"Two."

"Are you sure?"

"Yes." A second of silence. "Completely sure."

"Axel got three calls," said Winter. "At least according to the woman who runs the place. Three calls and it was a woman every time."

40

These streets. The first time he was here. The bus from the sea had been late and he had walked south from the station and it was night, one of the warm ones.

He had turned around several times but no one had been following him.

He was someone else.

The street looked like it had then. It smelled like it had then, a smell that had been heavy not long ago.

Was it the same room? It was the same view. Guest rooms changed places. People came and went. Wars came and went. There was a picture of Jesus on the wall, and there had been that time too, the first time. He had fallen to his knees and tried to say something to Jesus. He hadn't gotten an answer. He knew why.

Jesus!

The woman had looked at him, studied him. He had handed over his letter.

It was time.

Jesus had answered. No. It was someone else.

He wandered back and forth across the bridges. Waited. He tried to listen, to wait again. At a pub in a nice hotel he had looked at his hands when the bartender looked at them.

He had looked as though he knew. His hands around the rope.

Around the neck.

He received his ale and watched it clear up.

The sea had been crazy that night, it had been c-r-a-z-y. They had all been crazy. Crazy.

It wasn't just the money. Or the women.
Or God.

On the last night he took the bus to the southern point of the sea.
He wandered up in the mountains.
He found a place that could be a peaceful place. If the wind were right. If the light would just disappear.

In the evening he waited. Someone had lit a bonfire on the beach. He saw the faces like flecks. Someone was banging on a guitar, a ragged sound that floated out on the water. He thought he saw a movement out there.

At night he cried. He tried to write a new letter, in the old language. He tried to sort his memories into different piles, far away from one another. Before it became day, he planned to take out some of those damn piles and throw them on the fire and let them burn up. He heard his thoughts, the strong words he'd never articulated but was thinking now.
Words were nothing compared to actions. Words could hurt, but not like *that,* never like *that.*

There was one memory he kept at bay.
He had said that it didn't concern him: This doesn't have to do with you.
It was a good day.
Stay on land, he had said. Stay here.
I don't want to. Why should I do that?
Stay.
No.
Stay.
But . . .
You're not going on board. *You're not going on board. You're not coming along.*
It hadn't ended up that way.

The car was green like the algae he'd held in his hand three days earlier.
Jesus! Take me away from here!

41

Winter saw the lake for the first time at Lochend. It looked like a fjord; the mountains were high on the other side of the water, which was black and white, in layers.

"How's it going with the monster?" Winter asked. He thought he saw a movement on the surface of the water, a waving movement. He pointed.

"Nessie?" Macdonald followed his gaze. "She stays away."

"Does she exist?"

"Naturally," said Macdonald.

"You have to say that," said Winter. "The tourist industry here rises and falls on the monster." He saw road signs that announced the Loch Ness Monster Exhibition in Drumnadrochit three miles down the road. The water to the left was still black and white.

"It's not that simple," said Macdonald.

"What do you mean by that?"

Macdonald didn't answer. He looked serious.

Winter let out a laugh.

"Come *on,* Steve."

Macdonald looked out across the lake, which was wider here.

"There are places," he said.

"What kind of places? Places where you can *see*?"

Macdonald nodded slightly.

"Do you know something no one else knows?"

"Maybe," Macdonald said.

"But you don't want to reveal it?"

"Certain secrets must remain secret," said Macdonald.

"The first rule of the chief inspector," said Winter.

"Nessie hasn't been accused of anything, as far as I know," said Macdonald.

Winter looked at him, turning around in his seat.

"You like the monster, don't you, Steve. You really believe this."

"She has always existed," Macdonald said with an innocent expression, and Winter couldn't tell what was serious and what was some kind of subtle joke. "Nessie is part of my youth." He turned to Winter. "I'll show you something another time."

"Why not now?" Winter asked.

"Wrong season." He looked out over the water. "Maybe the wrong season."

Winter saw the monster center emerge just before the city limits of Drumnadrochit. No passerby could avoid it. The water was still visible to the left. Far to the south where the lake ended and turned into the river Oich, Axel Osvald had met his death, possibly in a confused state. Most likely. What was it? Was there something evil down there, beyond exhibits and the idiotic tourist industry and legends of monsters and medieval ruins that stood like mangled sand castles around Loch Ness? Did it exist? Had Axel Osvald met it? What had he met, whom? Why here? Why right here?

"I'm thirsty," Macdonald said, turning off and parking outside Hunter's Bar and Restaurant, which was right across from the exhibition.

"Have you seen the exhibit?" asked Winter.

"I don't need to," said Macdonald.

"Now you've hinted so much that soon I will insist that we make a serious attempt to solve the monster mystery," Winter said. He got out of the car. "We'll be world famous."

"I don't want to be famous," Macdonald said. "I just want to be rich." He got out and locked the car with the remote. "Like you."

"And I just want to be famous," said Winter.

They went into the bar. A movie poster was hanging on the wall, an ad for a ten-year-old Hollywood production about the monster myth, with Ted Danson in the lead role. Winter didn't feel disappointed that he hadn't seen it.

Macdonald ordered two pints of Scotch ale.

Winter took out his pack of Corps and lit one of the cigarillos.

"So you haven't given up that crap yet," said Macdonald. "I thought you'd quit."

"Soon," Winter said, pulling in the pleasant smoke and letting it out again as discreetly as he could.

* * *

Fort Augustus was two rows of houses in a U-turn, gas stations, pubs. It smelled like fried fat and gas and maybe rotting seaweed in the parking lot in front of Morag's Lodge.

Macdonald read from a piece of paper. They walked down the street to Poacher's and went in. The air was thick with smoke from the late-afternoon drinkers. The volume was loud.

The manager showed them to a room behind the bar. His face was gray from way too many years in the poisoned air. Perhaps he had never been closer to the sea than this.

"Funny geezer," said the man, an Englishman whose name was Ball. "Didn't seem to know what he was doing, or why."

"Apparently he was asking questions," Macdonald said.

"Apparently," said Ball. "But in any case I couldn't answer them, because I didn't understand what he said."

"No words at all you remember?"

"Nix."

"Was he agitated?"

"No, he was . . . confused, but on the other hand that's nothing strange in here," Ball said, smiling, "and people become agitated rather often when they've drunk their wallet empty and aren't allowed more credit."

"How would you care to describe him, then?" Winter asked.

Ball looked at him.

"Are you a Swede too, like him?"

They knew that Ball knew that the dead man was a Swede.

"Yes," said Winter.

"I can barely hear it," said Ball.

"What was he like?" Macdonald repeated.

"Well, since you asked, he seemed . . . spooked. Scared. Wacky somehow, and, well, scared." Ball made a movement with his head. "Like this, you know, it was like he was looking around for someone who was after him. He acted like he was being followed or something."

"Did you see anyone?"

"What, following him?"

"Yes," Macdonald said.

"Nah."

"When he left the pub, then?"

"Nah. I suppose I watched him go, because he seemed strange, but then he shut the door behind him and that was that."

"So he didn't say a single word in English?" Winter asked.

"Nah."

"Did you talk to anyone else who talked to him?" Winter asked.

"Only old Macdonald down at the Old Pier," said Ball. "It seems the Dane was staying there, from what I hear."

"Sorry?" said Macdonald.

"The Dane had a room there, right?"

"The Swede," said Winter.

"Yeah, yeah, what the hell difference is there? Anyway, he definitely had a room there."

"Not that we know of," said Macdonald, looking at Winter.

"Then it must have been a different Swede," Ball said, smiling with teeth that were not Scandinavian. There was a certain degree of difference in the status of teeth in Scandinavia and Great Britain. "Old Man Macdonald talked about a Swede."

"Not to the police," said Steve Macdonald.

"Probably no one asked," said Ball. "Old Man Macdonald doesn't say anything if you don't ask straight out."

Macdonald asked Macdonald straight out. Yes. A Swede in "the older ages" had stayed at the Old Pier for a night. The guesthouse was on the north shore of the lake, north of Fort Augustus. The smell of water and overgrown stones was strong as they walked up the steps. Old Man Macdonald was in the older ages himself. He steadied himself with a cane. A fire was burning in the large room. It snapped like a pistol shot from wood that wasn't completely dry.

"You should have let the police know," said Macdonald.

"I never got around to it," Macdonald said, scratching with his cane like a tic.

"What do you mean when you say he was old in general terms?" Macdonald asked.

"Over eighty for sure, but moved like a fifty-year-old or something," said Old Man Macdonald. He could have been over eighty himself. There were black flecks on his face.

"What was his name?" Winter asked.

"I'll have to look in the register," said Old Man Macdonald.

They followed him to the reception desk.

He flipped back a few pages.

"John Johnson," he said.

Yet another Johnson. Winter saw that Steve noticed.

"When did he stay here?" asked Winter.

John Johnson had rented the room the night before Axel Osvald had shown up in Fort Augustus and then wandered from there up into the mountains.

"When did he leave? Early? Late?"

"Probably morning."

"What time?"

"Well . . . nine, I think."

"What did you talk about?"

"When?"

"Whenever," said Steve.

"He didn't say a word," Old Man Macdonald said.

"How did you know that he was Swedish, then?" Macdonald asked.

"He probably said something then," said the old man.

"What?"

"Don't remember."

"Are you senile?" Macdonald asked.

"Do you want a beating, you damn cocky island fool?" Old Man Macdonald said, raising his cane.

"Calm down," said Steve Macdonald.

The old man lowered his cane. Steve Macdonald smiled. The old man grinned. "Damn Mac," he said.

"So what made you think he was Swedish?" asked Steve Macdonald.

"I knew some Swedes during the war," Old Man Macdonald said. "Fishermen."

"Yes?"

"Well, it was probably just something I thought. That the old man was Swedish. And his name. Johnson."

They continued to ask questions for a little while, but the old man had become tired.

"Get in touch if you remember anything else, and thanks," Steve Macdonald said, and gave the old man his phone numbers.

"If I remember to remember," said the old man.

"You're sharp as a knife," Macdonald said.

They were standing outside again.

"How did he get here and how did he leave?" Winter asked.

"Car," said the old man.

"Did you see it?"

"Green," the old man said, waving his cane again, "about like the shrubs on the beach here in the winter."

"Metallic," said Steve Macdonald.

"Yes, it was some kind of strange glittering," said the old man. "But don't ask me about the model." He spit suddenly. "The damn things all look the same to me nowadays."

"Was it new?" asked Winter.

"The damn things all look new to me nowadays," said Old Man Macdonald.

Steve Macdonald laughed.

"But there was someone else in the front seat when he drove out onto the road over there," the old man said, lifting his cane to the east.

"A relative of yours?" Winter asked as they drove east. It was starting to get dark. The water in Loch Ness was more black than white now.

"Hell no," said Macdonald. "That character probably belongs to Macdonald of Clanranald, up on the north islands."

"What's the difference?" asked Winter.

"Didn't you see?"

"Besides age," said Winter.

"My clan is originally from the western islands," Macdonald said. "Macdonalds from Skye. Proud old clan."

"How did you end up on the mainland?"

"My great-grandfather took the ferry over when he was very young," Macdonald said drily, "and kept going a bit but stopped in Dallas. He really had no other choice but to leave. There was some agreement that went wrong with a MacLeod." Macdonald turned his head. "That's the other big clan on the islands."

"So that's why that old man called you a damn cocky island fool," Winter said.

"Yes. He could scent it out."

"Interesting," said Winter, "considering that he's also an island fool, originally."

"But it's okay that we ended up a bit away from the sea," Macdonald said, "and it might not be forever. The clan's motto is *Per mare per terras.* Do you know what that means?"

"'*Mare*' is 'sea' and '*terra*' is 'land,'" said Winter.

"By sea and by land," said Macdonald. "That's the motto."

"Very majestic," said Winter.

"The name Donald comes from Gaelic *Domhnull,* which means 'water ruler,'" said Macdonald.

"I'm impressed," Winter said, looking out over the lake as they started to go up the narrow road at the southeastern part of the lake.

"Not that water," said Macdonald. "The *sea.* The Atlantic!"

Sheep were grazing on the green slope down to the water. It hadn't changed to metallic yet. The gray coats of the sheep shone like the stones in the grass below.

The landscape around them suddenly changed dramatically. Up on Murligan Hill it was like on the moon. Winter rolled his window down halfway and heard the wind. It had immediately become colder. The road was narrow. In the rapid twilight it looked like something that couldn't be trusted.

There was a feeling of darkness up here that might have belonged to the lake but wasn't necessarily part of it; it might have come from the naked, rough landscape.

The lake turned its back on this landscape. On the western side you could reach the water after a comfortable and short walk; here you would have to jump thirty yards from pointed cliffs.

They parked next to the little man-made lake, Loch Tarff. It stared up at the darkening sky like a blind eye.

They got out. Winter shivered in his coat. He noticed that Steve was shivering.

To lie here without clothes would have meant death for them too. To be naked in this nakedness.

Macdonald studied the sketch that Craig had drawn. Craig had offered to come along, or to send someone who had been along then, but they had declined.

Macdonald pointed to the left of the motionless surface of the water. They stepped through rough grass over a small hill and down on the other side into a hollow that was shallow and wide.

"He was lying here," said Macdonald, crouching down.

"And he *walked* here, in other words," Winter said, looking off across Loch Tarff; he could glimpse the ridiculously narrow road to the left and a bit of the water of Loch Ness, which was now as black as the sky would be soon.

"That hasn't been proven," said Macdonald, who was still crouching. "They found his clothes out in the open below Borlum Hill and up here, but we don't know that he put them there himself, do we?"

"No."

"Now we know that someone else was with him in Fort Augustus."

"Do we?"

"It was Axel Osvald who was sitting beside Johnson in the car. Whoever Johnson is."

"Anyone could have been sitting beside him," Winter said.

And Johnson could be anyone, he thought.

Macdonald grunted and changed position but kept crouching.

"What did you say, Steve?"

"Do you want to believe this, or what?"

"What do you mean?"

"That it's a crime."

"I hope it's not a crime," Winter said.

Macdonald grunted again. Maybe it was in Gaelic. He got up. It was as though the darkness was falling at one hundred miles an hour now. Winter could see Macdonald's teeth and the shape of his head. Steve mumbled something and turned around, toward land, toward the Monadhliath Mountains. Aviemore, the skiing paradise, was on the other side of the chain of mountains. But there was no paradise here, only wind and cold. Winter felt the tip of his own nose become cold. He had no gloves. His fingers started to become cold.

"Why this place?" Macdonald said now, as though to himself. He started to walk away, quickly.

"It *is* a crime," he said as they stood next to the car. "The question is what kind." He opened the car door. "It could be worse than we thought."

"You don't need to think out loud, Steve," Winter said, and climbed in on his side.

Angela came out of the bathroom. Winter was lying crosswise on the bed with his head at an uncomfortable angle.

"Is that an acrobat trick?" she said.

"I have to get the blood back into my head," he said.

She sat down on the edge of the bed.

"Yes, you seemed a little sluggish during dinner."

"I did?"

"You and Steve both did, to be honest."

Winter lifted his head and sat up.

"Like we said, it was a strange feeling to be up there this afternoon, in the mountains."

"Mmhmm."

"I'm sorry if I ruined dinner."

"No, no, it was nice."

Winter climbed up from the bed and walked over to the console table and poured out a little whisky from the bottle he'd bought at the airport. He lifted the bottle but Angela shook her head.

Winter drank the whisky, which was a Benrinnes. He saw his own face in the mirror. It still looked frozen from the wind on Murligan Hill. He rubbed his chin. He saw Angela's amused face in the mirror. He made an ugly face. He thought of Old Man Macdonald. Steve had told Angela and Sarah about him during dinner, and about other strange things having to do with the clans in Scotland. It was, as Steve had said earlier, mostly very sad stories. But many of them were also senseless, comical.

Winter turned around.

"So we get to see Dallas, then," he said.

She nodded.

"But you two will get there first," she said.

He and Steve would leave early in the morning. Angela and Sarah would wait for Steve's sister, Eilidh, and the three women would leave around lunchtime.

"It's funny," said Angela, "when I hear the name Dallas, or read about it, I immediately think of the name Kennedy." She waved a finger. "I think I'll take a whiskey after all, a small one." Winter took a glass from the table. "But of course this is a different Dallas. Proto-Dallas, as Steve said."

Winter nodded and poured out a half inch.

"But Kennedy is also the name of a Scottish clan, isn't it?" she said, and took the glass

42

Halfway to Nairn, Macdonald pointed to a road sign: Cawdor Castle.
"Do you know your Shakespeare?" he asked.

Winter saw the sign.

"Give me a minute."

Cawdor, Cawdor, Cawdor. Thane of Cawdor.

"*Macbeth,*" said Winter.

Macdonald tipped the hat he didn't have.

"Do you believe that story, too?" asked Winter.

"Not about the castle," Macdonald said, "even if it is from the early thirteen-hundreds. But I believe the myth."

"That was a true tale of murder," said Winter.

"You could say that I grew up near two monsters," Macdonald said, "Nessie and Macbeth."

"How has that affected you?" asked Winter.

"I don't know yet."

They drove between fields that breathed sea. Winter looked to the right, across the river Nairn.

They drove through Nairn, which was built of brown granite. The sound of gulls was intense. The sky was blue; there were no clouds. The city was next to the sea.

"This is the best place for sun in Scotland," Macdonald said. "We came here to swim sometimes when I was a child."

They continued on the A96 toward Forres. Winter saw the clouds inland.

How far is't call'd to Forres? What are these
So wither'd and so wild in their attire,
That look not like the inhabitants o' the earth,
And yet are on't?

Macdonald swung through two roundabouts and parked on High Street in front of Chimes Tearoom. They got out of the car.

"This is the street of my youth," said Macdonald. "Forres was the closest I got to a city." He looked around. "It isn't much more than this street."

Fraser Bros. meats on the other side of High Street displayed a sign for "Award Winning Haggis." Winter knew that haggis was the national dish of Scotland, a hash made of sheep stomach and oatmeal. He had refrained from eating it thus far.

"Great chieftain o' the puddin'-race!" said Macdonald, who noticed his gaze.

Winter smiled.

"Robert Burns," said Macdonald. "Ode to a Haggis":

Fair fa' your honest sonsie face,
Great chieftain o' the puddin'-race!
Aboon them a' ye tak your place,
Painch, tripe, or thairm:
Weel are ye wordy of a grace
As lang's my arm.

"I wish we had poetry like that in Sweden," said Winter. "Poetry in honor of hash."

"Then let's have coffee," said Macdonald, and they stepped into Chimes and sat down at one of the tables in the window. A woman their age came up and took the order from Macdonald: two caffe lattes and two slices of Dundee cake. She had short, dark brown hair and an open face. She lingered at the table.

"Isn't that Steve?" she said.

"Yes . . . ," said Macdonald, suddenly getting up. "Lorraine."

She reached up and gave him a hug.

"Long time no see," she said.

"Very long," said Macdonald.

She turned around and saw that the line was beginning to grow at the counter, where her coworker was raising an eyebrow.

"I have to work," she said, throwing a quick glance at Winter.

"A Swedish friend," said Macdonald, turning toward Winter.

Winter got up and extended his hand. They greeted each other. She gave Macdonald another smile.

"Will you be here this afternoon?"

"I'm sorry, Lorraine. We're on our way to Aberdeen."

"Ah."

She turned around and walked quickly to the counter. Macdonald and Winter sat down. Winter saw a note to the right of the counter: "One person needed for washing dishes and pots, Wednesdays and Fridays 11–2."

Macdonald cleared his throat discreetly.

"Old flame," he said.

"Mmhmm," said Winter.

"Like you and Johanna Osvald."

"Did I tell you about that?"

Macdonald didn't answer. He looked around, looked out through the window. People went into Fraser Bros., came out with prize-winning haggis.

"It's been quite a few years since I was here last," said Macdonald.

Winter didn't answer. Macdonald met his gaze.

"I don't know," said Macdonald, "you almost get some sort of feeling of . . . shame when you come back. Like you're guilty of something. Like you're ashamed that you left here once, failed them, maybe. I don't know if you understand this, Erik. If it's even possible to understand."

"I've lived in the same city my whole life, Steve. I haven't experienced what you're experiencing."

Such different lives we've had, really, thought Winter. Macdonald came from a little one-horse town; he had taken his first independent steps on the streets of this small town. Winter was a big-city boy.

Lorraine came with the coffee and the fruitcake, which was heavy with fruit.

"How's it going, Lorraine?" asked Macdonald.

"It's going," she answered.

"I see you need dishwashers," Macdonald said, smiling.

"If you're in town on Wednesdays and Fridays, well . . . ," Lorraine said.

Macdonald smiled again but didn't answer.

"Otherwise it's pretty much like for everyone else here," said Lorraine. "Divorced from a jerk of a guy and two half-grown kids to support."

"Who was the jerk?" asked Macdonald.

"Rob Montgomerie," she answered.

Macdonald raised an eyebrow.

"Yes, I know," she said, smiling a smile that might have been acid, "but you weren't here anymore, Steve, were you?"

Macdonald suddenly looked guilty. Winter noticed that he lowered his eyes. Lorraine walked back to the counter. Macdonald watched her go.

"Now I *really* feel guilty," he said.

"You knew that guy?"

"He *was* a jerk," said Macdonald. "Poor Lorraine." Macdonald turned to Winter. "Sometimes it doesn't matter how grown-up you are, there are people you will dislike your whole life." He looked at Lorraine. "She must have been desperate."

"She's gotten away from it," said Winter.

"I'm not sure," said Macdonald. "Rob was a violent type."

As they left, Macdonald took Lorraine aside for a second. Winter waited outside.

"That bastard has stayed away so far, anyway," Macdonald said when he came out to the sidewalk.

"You look like you're back in high school," said Winter.

Which is true, he thought. When Steve comes back here he becomes the person he was then. That's how time works.

"There are a lot of wife beaters here," said Macdonald.

"Where isn't there?" said Winter.

Aneta Djanali was waiting in the room when they showed Sigge Lindsten in. It was an important distinction: He was *shown* into the room; he wasn't *brought* into it.

Halders cleared his throat and they started, and the tape recorder turned. Lindsten answered everything as though this had all been well rehearsed. But he didn't know anything.

Halders asked about various addresses on the outskirts of Brantingsmotet. Lindsten was the least-aware person in the world.

"I'm going to tell you more than I need to," said Halders. "Stored in those warehouses I just mentioned are stolen goods from burglaries of many houses around Gothenburg."

"I see," said Lindsten.

"Headquarters," said Halders, "on the way out to the fences and buyers."

"It seems things like that are becoming more and more common," said Lindsten.

"Like what?" Halders asked.

"Thefts, and organizations, or whatever they're called."

"That's right," said Halders. "A large organization."

"But what does this have to do with me?"

"Well, I'll tell you one more thing," said Halders. "We followed a truck that was leaving those crammed warehouses on Hisingen, and it drove through the entire city to Fastlagsgatan in Kortedala and stopped outside entrance number five, and guess who arrived shortly thereafter and spoke to the driver?"

"No idea," said Lindsten.

"It was you!" said Halders.

"Why, that's a surprise," said Lindsten.

"And one more thing," said Halders. "The truck had stolen license plates."

"How do you know that?"

"Sorry?"

"Maybe it was the truck that was stolen?" said Lindsten.

"And the plates weren't stolen?" Halders quickly looked to the side, at Aneta. "Is that what you mean?"

"It was just a thought," Lindsten said, shrugging. "Who were they, then?"

"Who?" asked Halders.

"The guys in the truck," said Lindsten.

"Who said there was more than one?" said Halders.

"I was there, wasn't I?" Lindsten smiled a smile that had to be called sly, thought Aneta. "And I *was* there. And I remember that a truck was parked outside the door when I came out, and I told them that they couldn't park there, and then they asked directions to somewhere and then they left." He inhaled through his nose twice. "I don't know if your witness heard what we said, but if he did then he can confirm that."

"They were waiting for you," Halders said.

Lindsten made a gesture that might have expressed resignation to dealing with the feeble-minded person across from him.

"I'm going to tell you one more thing," said Halders.

"Why should I listen to all of this?" said Lindsten.

"In one of the warehouses on Hisingen we found what we believe is the entirety of Anette's belongings from the apartment in Kortedala," said Halders. "We have checked the lists from the record carefully. We have been there. And there are a few framed photos."

"That's good news," said Lindsten. "Is that why I'm here? To identify the things, or whatever it's called?"

"Most of the stuff in that warehouse was all helter-skelter, but Anette's things were placed very neatly on their own behind separate screens. Everything was very neat when it came to your daughter's belongings."

"I'm thankful for that," said Lindsten.

"Why do you think that was?" asked Halders.

"No idea," Lindsten answered. "I'm just glad that her things might have turned up."

Lindsten went on his way to Brantingsmotet in a marked car. Aneta and Halders followed.

Lindsten recognized the things as Anette's.

He signed some papers.

They waved good-bye out on the pavement.

Inside it was like a hangar with odds and ends and furniture and kitchen appliances and the devil and his grandma.

"There's more than I expected," said Aneta.

"There are more warehouses like this one," said Halders.

"My God."

"What is it that I'm not getting here?" said Halders.

"And me," said Aneta.

"Lindsten's daughter is subjected to threats and suspected assault by her husband. The neighbors report it. She doesn't want to file a report, which is all too tragically familiar. She flees to her home. Her apartment is cleaned out under the supervision of Detective Inspector Aneta Djanal—"

"Please," Aneta interrupted.

"—Djanali, and that very apartment is then sublet to Moa Ringmar of all people, and she moves in and moves out quick as fuck when she learns about the history of the place. At the same time, Gothenburg's

Finest are working on a large operation to crack a gigantic theft ring with an IKEA-class warehouse on Hisingen, and a truck leaves from there, maybe on a mission, maybe not, and it drives straight to Anette's apartment but before anyone goes into the building Sigge Lindsten comes out and calls it off."

"What is it he calls off?" said Aneta.

"That's my question, too," said Halders. "One guess is that they were going to clean out the apartment again. But the guys in the truck didn't know it was already empty. Eventually someone tells Lindsten that they're on their way there and he shows up and explains the situation and the thieves take off again."

"He could have just called," said Aneta.

"Maybe he didn't dare."

"Was he already so suspicious? Of us?"

"He's not dumb," said Halders. "And he probably didn't think Bergenhem was tailing the truck."

"So Lindsten rents to people who are then robbed of all they own."

"Yes."

"Why not," said Aneta.

"That is what we were thinking when we brought him in just now, isn't it?"

"And others are doing the same thing?"

"Yes, or they have good contacts among the landlords."

"Mmhmm."

"Then of course there's the question of why, in that case, he stole his own daughter's belongings."

Aneta thought. She thought about her short encounter with Anette Lindsten, about Hans Forsblad, about his sister, who seemed as nuts as her brother. About Sigge Lindsten, about Mrs. Lindsten, about all those people, all of whom seemed extremely dangerous, no, not dangerous, peculiar, evasive, like shadows who got tangled in their lies. They disintegrated, became something else, someone else. She saw Anette's face again. The broken cheekbone that had healed but didn't look like it once had, and never would. Her eyes. A nervous hand up in her hair. A life that in some ways was over.

"A warning," said Aneta.

"He wanted to warn his daughter?" said Halders.

"A warning," said Aneta, nodding to herself. She looked up at Halders. "Or a punishment."

"Punishment? Punishment for what?"

"I don't know if I dare to think about it," said Aneta. She closed her eyes and opened them again. "It has something to do with Forsblad. And his sister." She grabbed the arm of Halders's jacket. "It has to do with them. But not how we think."

Halders had the sense to keep quiet.

"It's not like we think," she repeated. "They're playing some game. Or keeping quiet about something they don't want us to know. Or they're just scared. One of them, or some of them, are scared."

"Like I just said," said Halders. "What is it that I'm not getting here?"

Maybe we shouldn't know, she thought, suddenly and intensely. We shouldn't know! Maybe we should let it go, like a hot coal. Maybe Fredrik was right when he said that a long time ago. Maybe it's dangerous, really dangerous, for us, for me.

For me.

"So she's done something to her father that he has to punish her for?" Halders scraped his hand across the back of his head. "He steals the furniture?" Halders looked at Aneta. "Of course, it could also be as simple as that the warehouse out on Hisingen is a perfect storage facility for her things for the time being. Lindsten had the manpower and the vehicle, and Anette wanted out of the apartment fast, so Dad sent his thieves there to get the whole lot and then they drove to the warehouse and stacked it up nice and neat. Think of how it's arranged all by itself, behind screens. Most of the other stuff is all helter-skelter out there."

"Does Anette know about it, do you think? The warehouse? And the stolen goods? The trafficking?"

"No idea," said Halders. "But surely she wonders where her things are."

"If she knows, maybe it's yet another reason to keep quiet," said Aneta. "She doesn't dare to do anything else."

That evening she ran a hot bath. The sound of the water rushed through the entire apartment. She walked to the bathroom and dropped her clothes behind her. She had always left her clothes everywhere, and her mother had picked them up after her.

Now Fredrik picked them up.

"Jesus Christ," he sometimes said when pieces of clothing were lying from the door to the bathroom.

It was the first time he followed her the whole way.

She had dragged him down into the half-full bathtub before he had had time to take off a damn thing.

That had been good.

She threw her panties into the hamper next to the washing machine and climbed carefully into the hot water and turned off the faucet. She sank very slowly down into the water, one inch, two, three, and so forth.

She lay with her chin underwater. There was foam everywhere. The water started to cool, but she intended to keep lying there. It was quiet in the apartment. No steps up above that was rare. No banging from the elevator door out in the stairwell; that was rare too. No sounds of traffic; it wasn't audible from here. She heard only the familiar sounds of her own home, the refrigerator in the kitchen, the freezer, some other hum; she'd never really figured out what it was but she'd accepted it long ago, the faucet that dripped slooowly behind her neck, some sigh that could have been from the electronics that were scattered here and there in modern homes.

She heard a sound.

She didn't recognize it.

Macdonald led the way north on High Street. They passed many shops and cafés. Here there were neighborhood services for the locals; we crushed those long ago in Sweden, thought Winter. This place might be poorer, but not in that way.

Macdonald stopped at one of the dark stone houses. A sign hung above the door: The *Forres Gazette*—Forres, Elgin, Nairn.

They went in. They were expected.

"Awful long time, no see, Steve," said the man who came up to them. He gave Macdonald a punch on the back.

Macdonald clipped him back and introduced Winter, who quickly extended his hand for safety's sake.

"Duncan Mackay," said the man, who looked older but was the same age as Macdonald, who had told Winter about his classmate in the car.

Mackay's hair was coal black and shoulder length. He had matching circles under his eyes. He guided them in behind a wooden counter.

They sat down on two chairs in front of Mackay's desk, which contrasted almost comically with Chief Inspector Craig's in Inverness. They could barely see the editor on the other side of the piles of paper. Even though he was standing.

"Coffee, beer, whisky?" asked Mackay. "Claret? Marijuana?"

Macdonald looked at Winter.

"No thanks," Winter said, pointing at his pack of Corps, which he had taken out. "I have smokes."

Mackay had a lit cigarette in his mouth.

Macdonald shook his head at Mackay.

"We just saw Lorraine," he said when Mackay had sat down and rolled a bit to the side in his chair.

"Steve the Heartbreaker Macdonald," said Mackay. "It took her some time." He turned to Winter. "To get over it."

"She told us about Robbie."

"Yeah, shit."

"No doubt he's disappeared."

"He'll show up," said Mackay. "Unfortunately."

They sat in silence for a few seconds, as though to reflect upon the fate of humanity. The room lay half in shadow.

Mackay got up and searched through the top of the piles of paper. He held a paper up to the light from the window.

"I asked the local editors to look around, but no one has seen this Osvald guy," said Mackay. "Axel Osvald, right? There was a bulletin that went out, too, and obviously we checked then too—a foreigner who dies in Moray—but nothing about the man."

"Okay," said Macdonald.

"Your colleagues over at the Ramnee haven't seen or heard anything either," said Mackay.

"I know. I called a few days ago."

"Have you been there?"

"Not yet."

Mackay read from his paper again.

"There's just one thing . . ."

"Yes?"

"Billy in the editorial department in Elgin did a thing about the fish market's new dismal numbers, and he interviewed people up in Buckie.

That was before the bulletin." Mackay looked up. "Billy's a little slow, but he's good. But slow. Okay, he was talking to some of the old forgotten guys at the shipyard and he had parked the car on one of the little streets right across from there, and when he came back and he was going to drive home he saw a Corolla parked on the same street. It had been there when he arrived, too. Metallic green."

"Did he get the number?"

"Hell no. Why should he have? He wasn't even thinking about that then. He didn't remember it until after the bulletin came out. No. Not then. It was when I called him yesterday. And actually, not even then. He called this morning and said that he'd seen the car."

"Is he sure?"

"He's pretty good with cars. And of course it appeared to be new, he could see that. A new car in Buckie . . . well, you don't see that every day. At least not on those streets."

43

He had made a journey he hadn't planned on. It was a farewell. If you saw it on a map it looked like a circle, or at least part of a circle.

When had he last walked down Broad Street? Years or days or hours. A red sky. Down toward Onion Street and toward the harbor the sky was always red, always.

Four hundred boats per year!

Biggest whitefish port in Europe.

And out there, there were people he could have been close to. Maybe. No.

The smell. It was the sea, as it has always been, and then something more, which he hadn't smelled then but did now: oil.

This city had changed after the oil. The trawlers were there, still a forest of masts, but people who walked the streets came because of the oil too.

The city had grown. The entrances were different, that was a sure sign of everything that had happened.

He stood on one of the western breakwaters. The trawlers here were largest. There was a blue one twenty yards away. He saw a man moving on the quarterdeck. He read the name on the trawler, which was made of steel.

That was something else, a hull of steel.

He heard a yell from the man down by the mess, a few words.

He lingered outside the Mission.

It was here.

The next-to-last night.

Meals 7:00–2:30, then and now. The Congregational church. Sick bed. Emergency facilities.

A notice that hadn't existed then:

Zaphire went down in October 1997, four lives.

Everyone knew almost everything here. There were exceptions. There was one.

He walked in but turned around in the outer room. He was pushed away by the memories, and by something else: A man looked up from the counter, an expression on his face.

He was on his way out, didn't look around, he wasn't invisible here, he was deaf to the voice behind his back, the shout.

Caley Fisheries was still there. The fish market. There was a new notice at the entrance. Prohibited: smoking, spitting, eating, drinking, breaking of boxes, unclean clothing, unclean footwear. A guide for life, too.

Men in blue rubber garments and yellow boots were loading boxes of flounder or lemon sole. A truck to Aberdeen, and on to the south.

He walked on Crooked Lane; it was as crooked now as it had been then.

He walked toward the summit. The sky opened out. It was windy.

He felt the weapon against his thigh. It was just as cold. He wanted to fire it.

Half an hour later he was on his way, straight across and to the north. A long farewell. He drove through Strichen. He looked in his rearview mirror. Was anyone following him? It was possible, but he didn't think so.

The weapon was under his jacket in the front seat.

He drove along the narrow roads to New Aberdour and through the village and stopped three yards from the formidable edge down to the sea. Three yards. He let the motor race. From where he was sitting he could only see sea and sky. Everything was one. The sea and the wind roared. He opened the car door. He got out. He held the pistol in his hand. He shot at the sky.

There were two roads down Troup Head. Over the slope and down the road to the community that hid itself from the world.

He knew. He had hidden here when the houses were still red like the cliffs, when the smugglers still defined life there. That was why no one had asked any questions.

When the cameras came he ran away.

Like now.

He sat in the car again.

He felt his foot on the pedal, a longing. A *longing*.

Jesus. *Jesus*.

Now he could see only the sky.

44

Spey Bay was still. Buckie Shipyard was empty and silent. Two trawlers from before were rusted in place in the shipyard frame, like a symbol.

It wasn't an entirely unfamiliar sight for Winter. He came from a city with dead shipyards.

They had parked on Richmond Street. This was where the local editor Billy had seen the green Corolla.

"How many people in Buckie own that kind of car in this year's model?" Macdonald asked straight out during the drive north, and he called Craig in Inverness.

Craig had put a guy on it. The answer came while they were still driving through the harbor.

No one.

There were sixteen front doors on Richmond Street, eight on each side. The row houses looked like they were built out of one stone block. Only one car was parked on the street. It was a wreck from the seventies.

"What the heck," Macdonald said, and rang the first doorbell.

People were home at all but one of the addresses; they were all women. They would have been happy to be at work. No one drove a new Corolla and no one had any immediate plans to do so. No one knew exactly what that model looked like. No one had had a visit from anyone in a Corolla.

"Sometimes people who are going to the shipyard park here," said one of the women, older, wearing a dress with a large floral pattern that had survived two world wars.

"What are they going to the shipyard to do?" said Macdonald.

Just then they heard heavy hammering from the other side of the shipyard wall. It was a strange noise. It was suddenly everywhere, like a reminder. Doonk—doonk—doonk.

They said good-bye to the woman and crossed the intersection to the shipyard and found the large gate, which was locked. Next to that, a twenty-foot section of the nine-foot-high fence was missing. They walked in.

The hammering had stopped but started again, doonk . . . doonk . . . with a hollow echo that sounded different in there, where everything was reminiscent of a cemetery. The blows came from inside a building that looked like a partially bombed cathedral. One of the walls was missing. Inside everything was dark. They walked closer and went in. The hammering stopped; someone had seen them first.

"You're trespassing," said an unfriendly voice.

"Police," said Macdonald into the darkness. It smelled like rust and dirty water, iron, burned steel, sulfur, fire, earth, tar, sea. It's a smell from the past, thought Winter. I remember it from when I was a child.

"What tha fockin' is a'matter?" they heard the voice say, and a man stepped forward, and he still held the hammer, a sledgehammer, in his hand. Behind him stood something that looked like a bow door, and he had banged the shit out of one side. Winter suddenly felt a strong urge to grab that sledgehammer and devote himself to attacking the masses of iron, strike them until he collapsed, powerless. That must be good for you.

The man with the sledgehammer didn't look like he was here for therapeutic reasons. He wore a coverall that had been around so long that it had lost all color and looked most of all like the skin of the man's face, which was possibly gray, possibly black and white. A cigarette butt hung from the corner of his mouth. The worker was around sixty, maybe younger, maybe older. In the car, Macdonald had said that it wasn't exactly easy to determine men's ages up here. Thirty-five-year-olds might look sixty-five. It was seldom the other way around.

"We just want to ask a couple o'questions," said Macdonald.

"Aye," said the man, spitting out the butt and hobbling toward them with a severe limp. He moved the sledgehammer from his right to his left hand as though to compensate for his lack of balance.

He was surprisingly tall, almost as tall as Macdonald, who was the tallest Scot Winter had seen yet. Winter had commented on this earlier. I kept away from the haggis, Macdonald had said. It pushes you toward the earth. It's like rice for the Japanese.

Bullshit, Winter had said.

It was a conversation that Winter hardly understood; actually, he didn't at all. The man spoke an awful gibberish, and Winter suspected that Macdonald was guessing at half of it. And suddenly the conversation was over, without ceremony. It was like watching a sport you didn't understand.

They walked back to the car on Richmond. A double sheet of newspaper blew across the main road to Portessie. Winter could see half a headline, like half a message.

"He's unemployed, but he goes there for old times' sake," said Macdonald. "He's not alone in that."

"But he hadn't met any Johnson or Osvald or anything, from what I understand."

"No."

"But our man could have been here," said Winter.

"Which one?"

"Well, that's one of the questions," said Winter.

They drove slowly back through the harbor district: Harbour Office, Marine Accident Investigation Branch, Carlton House, Fisherman's Fish-selling Co. Ltd., JSB Supplies Ltd., Buckie Fish Market. Winter could see trawlers in the small wet dock; he read off the boats' sterns: *Three Sisters, Priestman, Avoca, Jolair, Monadhliath.*

"We might as well ask at the Marine," said Macdonald.

The Marine Hotel looked like it had been taken from a noir film. If walls could talk, Winter thought as they stood in the lobby. The woman behind the desk was a dyed blonde and maybe fifty and had lively eyes. Behind her was a sign for the "Cunard Suite," which must have been the most charming the hotel had to offer.

But even in the lobby there was wall-to-wall carpeting.

Winter noticed that the carpets covered all surfaces. The British had a special relationship with wall-to-wall carpeting, as though the myth of British properness was reflected in these carpets that had to cover all naked floors.

Their colors were reminiscent of the hammer man's coverall.

"I'll get the man'ger fur ya, luv," she said, and lifted the telephone receiver.

They stood on the square, Cluny Square. There was a hotel in front of them that looked like a castle. The Cluny Hotel. It was the lunch hour.

Winter could see a group of little old ladies mince their way in through the hotel's wide entrance. Time for tea.

"So," said Macdonald about the conversation they'd had with "the man'ger."

"Could be the old man making a return visit," said Winter.

"Could be any nostalgic at all," said Macdonald.

"This isn't a nostalgic," said Winter.

"What is he, then?" said Macdonald.

"According to all reports, dead since the war," said Winter.

"Well, then there's probably not much nostalgia left."

"Shall we have a cup of tea?" said Winter, nodding toward the hotel.

Macdonald looked at his watch.

"Okay," he said.

"When were the girls getting to Dallas?" said Winter.

"About the same time as us," Macdonald said, and smiled.

The hotel had been built in 1880, Victorian up to its trusses. It had six rooms and a dining room in all the shades of pink God had given to man. A young woman who looked nice showed them to a table that seemed fragile. The chairs were narrow armchairs.

Macdonald looked like he was sitting in a child's chair. Winter realized that he looked the same himself.

The little old ladies were sitting at a larger table next to one of the windows, ten feet away. They smiled at them, someone giggled; a few whispered.

"Good morning, ladies," Macdonald said, and Winter nodded as well.

A wide, rounded staircase led down from the dining room. Framed black and white photographs hung on the wall all the way down to the reception desk. It was, you could say, a nostalgic display, or a sad one. Most of the pictures showed the former fishing fleet, when it had been proud and great: In the photos from the harbor there didn't seem to be room for all the boats. Masts stretched as far as the eye could see, like tree trunks in a forest. Like mobile trees. Winter thought of Macbeth again as he stood there looking at the forest of masts. Not until the forest moved toward him did Macbeth have to fear anything in his castle.

He had the witches' shrill word on it.

Macbeth shall never vanquish'd be until
Great Birnam wood to high Dunsinane hill
Shall come against him.

And no man born of woman could threaten him.

But Macduff, the man born by Cesarean section, cut down the trees and fastened them to his body and marched.

Winter moved his eyes from the photograph of the masts.

They continued down the stairs, past other pictures, of houses, more boats, of people from other times.

They stood on the street again. The Buckie boys are back in town. Arne Algotsson's demented drivel popped up in Winter's memory. It really must mean something. Was John Osvald a Buckie boy? Or was it just an expression? They had asked, but so far no one had known.

On the square was a war monument for World War I. Winter stood in front of it and thought the impossible thought that he had seen it before. He read on the stone: "Their Name Liveth For Ever."

They were alone in front of the monument. That said something to him too, but he didn't know what. It meant something that they were standing there alone.

On the north side of the little square was a building that looked like a community center. There was a sign, but it was on the wall and they didn't notice it: "Struan House—Where older people find care in housing."

Two old people were sitting on a bench on the opposite side of the square.

"Well," said Macdonald.

They walked to the car, which was parked in front of the Buckie Thistle Social Club.

"The local football gang," said Macdonald. "Buckie Thistle."

"I know Patrick Thistle," said Winter.

"Do you? The Glasgow gang?"

"Yes."

"I'll be damned. They're in division two now, I think, but they're the favorites for all the celebrities."

They got into the car and rounded the hotel. Macdonald pushed a disc into the CD player and a woman from the past started to sing about lost love and bittersweet dreams.

"Patsy Cline," said Macdonald.

Winter suddenly felt sad. They were back on the A96, driving south to Dallas. It was a no-man's-land here, no sea, no mountains. Patsy Cline sang about another life, or rather cried. Sweet dreams of you, every night I go through, why can't I forget you and start my life anew, instead of having sweet dreams about you.

Aneta Djanali felt herself freeze under the water. She grabbed the edge of the bathtub.

She heard one step, two steps.

A harsh sound from the kitchen or the hall.

Another harsh sound.

The bathroom door was half open.

She had a telephone on the wall out there, but it was ten thousand miles away.

Stay calm, stay calm, stay calm, stay calm.

Her heart started to beat like a hammer, donk-donk-donk-donk.

"WHO IS IT?" she yelled.

And now she was already up out of the bathtub and into her robe and she kicked the door hard with her heel and the door flew into the wall without hitting anyone and the hall was empty and untouched, and she couldn't hear any harsh sounds now.

She stood in the doorway and yelled:

"IS SOMEONE THERE?"

Nothing.

She heard sounds from out in the stairwell, could be anything. A car honked on the street below. Life continued outside her apartment, but in here it felt like it was holding its breath, taking a break. Waiting. Waiting for what? She took a step forward and one into the kitchen, but there was no one there.

She could hear the rain on the window now. It had been raining on and off all afternoon. She saw water on the floor. A few pieces of gravel or some kind of dirt. Puddles on the floor, small, but they were there. Her feet suddenly started to freeze, as though her naked feet were standing in that ice water. She looked down, followed a trail that led from the kitchen out into the hall, or vice versa. There was water on the floor of the hall, and it hadn't come from her shoes.

She looked at the knob of her apartment door. Fingerprints? Hardly. She looked at the floor. Footprints. Uh-uh.

She felt her knees weaken. She was about to lose her balance, but she managed to stagger into the bedroom and lie down and dial the number and wait for an answer.

"Are you really sure?" Halders said after she had quickly explained.

"I'm sure," said Aneta. She felt more calm now.

"Well, shit," said Halders.

"It might have been him," she said. "Shit."

She heard Halders breathing.

"We'll look at the lock," he said. "And the doorknob, and the floor."

"Whoever was here must have had a key," she said. "Or a picklock."

"We'll probably find out," said Halders.

"God," she said. "What is this?"

"You're not renting from Sigge Lindsten, are you?" said Halders.

"Is that supposed to be funny?"

"Sorry, Aneta, sorry. I'll ask the guys up at Lorensberg to come by right away."

"Yeah, yeah."

"They can give you a ride home—to here."

"Thanks."

"You live here, starting now."

"Fredrik . . ."

"Doesn't it make sense?"

She couldn't answer.

"At least until we've checked the lock and changed it and installed a deadbolt and dug a moat," said Halders.

For a microsecond she saw Halders sneaking around the apartment while she lay in the bathtub. Fredrik did everything he could to get her to move to his house in Lunden.

But he wouldn't have had time to get back to his house before she called.

God. She needed something strong. She was suddenly tired, dead tired.

45

They took the road through Forres again. On High Street Winter saw a poster he'd missed earlier: Nairn International Jazz Festival. Jane Monheit, David Berkman Quartet, Jim Galloway, Jake Hanna. It had ended two weeks ago.

The police station was next to the south exit, right across from the Ramnee Hotel, which looked like a colonial manor. Everything around here sure is Victorian, thought Winter.

But the police station wasn't Victorian, it was built in the bunker style of the brotherhood. A teenager was playing with a ball on the lawn outside, one-two-three-four-five on his foot. A police van was parked on the graveled area that served as a parking lot. "Crimestoppers" was painted in white on the van's black side. It might as well say "Ghostbusters," thought Winter. At least if Steve and I were driving around in it. We're hunting ghosts.

It wasn't possible to determine whether the windows were tinted or just dirty. Leaves were blowing across the lot. Fall was here.

Winter knew that Macdonald's uncle had been a policeman here and had retired quite recently.

"There was a period in my teens when I was a little wild," Macdonald had said in the car. "Uncle Gordon picked me up discreetly once, in a neighborhood south of High, and that was kind of a turning point."

"What were you doing? Robbing cars?"

"It wasn't anything that ended up in the papers," Macdonald had answered, and that was that. Winter hadn't asked any more questions. Whatever it was, maybe it had caused him to become a policeman, and a good policeman at that, he thought.

Inside, a woman got up from a desk behind the counter, which was partially made of steel. Never seen *that,* thought Winter. Wood and steel. The woman was dressed in a black uniform with white bands. She had to be near retirement. Winter noticed her powerful upper arms. There was an open door behind her.

She didn't recognize Macdonald. He greeted her and introduced himself and asked for someone.

"Oh, it's you!" she said enthusiastically. "Jake has told us about you comin' here."

"Just a wee short stop," said Macdonald.

"Local laddie make good," she said, looking proud. "Hows't down in the Smoke?"

"It's smoky," said Macdonald, and the woman smiled with her Scottish teeth.

"How's things 'ere?" asked Macdonald.

"Pretty quiet since you left town, my lad," she said, smiling again. "From what I've heard."

"I've tried to behave myself since then," said Macdonald.

"That's outside the statute o'limitations," said a loud voice from the doorway. A man came through it with difficulty; he was about as wide as the door and slightly shorter.

"Hello, Jake," said Macdonald.

"Hello, my boy," said Chief Inspector Jake Ross, giving him a handshake and the traditional punch on the shoulder.

Macdonald introduced Winter. Ross showed them into his office. Through the window, Winter could see the kid playing with the ball. Ross noticed that Winter was looking.

"Comes here every day," said Ross. "I don't know if he wants t'tell us somethin'." Ross went on. "I spoke with Craig in Ness."

"Was it the first time?" asked Macdonald.

"Come on, Steve. I might not like that Englishman, but we're all professionals 'ere, right?" Ross looked at Winter. Winter nodded in agreement. Ross took out a bottle of whisky and, with professional skill, poured some into three small glasses.

"Not bad," said Macdonald after a first sip. Winter held up the bottle. Dallas Dhu 1971. He tasted it. Ross studied him.

"Well?" Ross asked.

"It's almost chewy," said Winter.

Ross looked at Macdonald and then back at Winter.

"You've had this b'fore, my lad?" asked Ross.

"No," said Winter. He kept the liquor in his mouth and swallowed. "Isn't there some dark chocolate and a dash of bitter on the palate?"

"There certainly is, there certainly is," said Ross, smiling. "Why don't you start working for me, laddie? We could use professional people up here."

"Professional drinkers," said Macdonald.

"The finish, the finish?" asked Ross, who hadn't heard Macdonald.

The next test. Winter delayed his answer, thinking.

"Smooth, of course. Dry and very long. Kind of oak-sappy. But it also goes with that flowery sweetness that still lingers in the nose."

"*Yes,*" Ross said, raising his glass. "You've got the job."

"The distillery is unfortunately closed," said Macdonald.

"You're drinking history here, my lads," Ross said.

Macdonald told the tragic story as they drove south on the A940. Dallas Dhu Distillery, which was three miles ahead of them, had closed in 1983, on its hundredth anniversary, put out of business by the Distillers Company. Several of the oldest and smallest distilleries in Speyside had disappeared.

There weren't many bottles of Dallas Dhu left. They had, as Ross pointed out, drunk history.

"What does 'Dhu' mean?" Winter asked.

"'Black,'" said Macdonald, "or 'dark,' in this case. It's actually the same Gaelic word as *Dubh* in MacDuhb, MacDuff." He turned onto a smaller road. "And the name Dallas is Gaelic for 'valley and water.'"

They were driving through valleys now. Winter saw water. There were forests, but they were small, like clusters of trees. The trees looked like they might move at any moment.

Winter saw the sign for the distillery.

"The interesting thing is that Historic Scotland rebuilt the place into a gigantic museum," Macdonald said, slowing down. "It's the only one of its kind in Scotland. And the equipment is the original Victorian stuff. There's no electricity there."

Victorian again. Winter saw another time in his mind's eye. Horses, riders, a different and stronger scent in the air.

"No good going down there now," said Macdonald.

Ross had told them that Dallas Dhu Distillery was closed on Tuesdays.

He had said that he could arrange a visit anyway. Macdonald had looked at Winter. Did they have time? They didn't, really. They were on their way to Dallas, and Aberdeen, and maybe other places.

"We'll do it next time, Jake," Macdonald had said.

"Ross has plans to open the place again," Macdonald said, driving through a sharp curve. "He's really far gone, actually."

"Was that what he meant about giving me a job?" Winter said.

"You never know," said Macdonald, letting out a laugh. "Interested?"

"You never know," said Winter.

"Everything is actually in good order down there," said Macdonald. "It would only take four or five weeks to get it up and running again."

"Mmhmm."

"I hope Ross fixes it up. The whisky is really very good." He flung his hand out. "It's the valley and the water, and the wind. The grain in this region is special."

"I would like to buy a few bottles while I'm here," said Winter.

"We'll do it on the way home," said Macdonald.

There would not be any such way home.

Winter saw a cluster of trees again, like a platoon on its way to the castle.

Everything looked peaceful, but this was a violent region, wild. Steve had told him about all the violent men there were and had been per square mile in Moray and Aberdeenshire. Blood flowed under the soil.

They drove in a long arc, past Branchill. Macdonald played Little Milton at a high volume, another of the forgotten black masters. "Let Me Down Easy": I gave you all my love, don't you abuse it, I gave you tender love and care, oh baby don't you misuse it. He had played Joe Simon, O. V. Wright.

They drove past a black church behind a black cemetery on a low hill. Macdonald lowered the volume. Winter saw the sign on the side of the road: Dallas. There were low houses on either side, small cottages with plaster walls that had cracked here and there. The fourth building on the right side was a closed-down gas station with the VALIANT sign with the picture of the prince. The pumps were still there, like something out of a rusty film from the fifties. A wrecked RV was leaning against the gas station, which was missing windows. There was junk everywhere. The image reminded Winter of the shipyard in Buckie.

Diagonally across from that was Dallas Village Shop and Post Office. Macdonald parked the car and they got out. He cast a glance at the ruins of the gas station and then at Winter.

"The first impression is important," he said, nodding across the street.

"I suppose it has looked different," said Winter. "And I like the melancholy."

"It was melancholy even when the pumps worked," said Macdonald.

Winter looked down the street. Dallas was a single straight street, or road, with a single row of houses on each side. That was all. The association was obvious.

"Looks like something out of the Wild West," he said.

"Naturally," said Macdonald.

Winter smelled smoke from a fire in the air. He didn't hear any sounds, but then he heard a dog barking. There were no people out. There were three cars parked a hundred yards farther up the road. Winter thought he heard a cement mixer start up. It was two o'clock in the afternoon, and the sun broke through and it suddenly became warm. Winter could see silhouettes of mountains around the hollow of the valley.

"Might as well show you our *supermercado* too," Macdonald said. "Now that you've seen the gas station." He took a step. "Then you will have seen everything."

The country store/post office was in a little bungalow of red brick, and it was closed. There was a sign in the window that said "Dallas—the Heart of Scotland" and "Open 10–1, 4–6."

"The heart is closed for us," Macdonald said.

Through the window Winter could see a stack of cans, a pile of papers, candy, a small counter, and a small cash register.

They walked back in the sunshine and got into the car. Macdonald drove down the street and it took two minutes. They passed a construction site. The cement mixer Winter had heard was on. The three construction workers turned toward the car. Macdonald stretched his arm through the open car window. One of the men raised his hand.

They were through, and they stopped at an intersection.

This was the end of the world. If Winter had been anywhere that might be the End of the World, this was it. The ironic name; that was part of it. A wild name, here and there. Dallas. Dallas, Texas. Dallas, Moray. Dallas, Scotland. It made him think of the film *Paris, Texas*. The same feeling of tragic irony, a play on associations with names that stood for completely different things. Or not.

Macdonald turned right onto a gravel road and drove up to the house and stopped the car. There were several buildings on the plot of land. Chickens were running around in the yard. Winter saw three hunting dogs in a kennel. The dogs hadn't barked a single time. There were two modern Ferguson tractors with muddy back wheels alongside the wall of a barn.

A golf bag was leaning against one of the tractors.

Winter saw the club handles sprawling against the cow shit on the tires. Maybe not a common sight on a farm in backwoods Sweden. But here. People played golf the way the Swedes took nature walks. Along the roads in Scotland, Winter had seen many golfers, men, women, in tweed, in rags, old, young, healthy, disabled, in wheelchairs, like something out of P. G. Wodehouse's golf stories. And now—golf clubs and manure. A man stepped out of the barn. He had on a cowboy hat.

"This is it," Macdonald said, turning off the ignition, and Little Milton was cut off in the middle of another relationship problem.

Lucinda Williams was cut off in the middle of an attempt at consolation. Blue is the color of night. Halders turned off the CD player when the telephone jangled out a ring that he'd forgotten to turn down.

"The guys are here now," said Aneta.

"Good."

"Something else has happened."

"What?"

"Forsblad's sister just called."

"She has your number?" asked Halders.

"I gave it to her."

"Hmm."

"The important thing is what she said. She said that she wants to talk to me about 'things you don't know.'"

"She probably wants to back her brother up," said Halders.

"She also asked if I had seen Anette in the past few days."

"And?"

"If I knew how she looked," said Aneta.

"What does that mean?"

"That means that I'm going to her place to hear what she has to say," said Aneta.

"Have you looked for her? Anette?"

"No one answered at any of the numbers."

"Ask one of the guys to drive you to Älvstranden," said Halders.

"I will."

"And to wait there for me while you're chatting with the gal."

"I'll ask."

"Who's there?" asked Halders. "Let me have a word with someone."

"Bellner is standing next to me and eavesdropping," said Aneta. "Ask nicely."

"Of course, what do you think?" said Halders, waiting to hear Bellner's voice.

"Listen up, Belly, if it isn't too much fucking trouble," Halders said when Bellner had said hi in his pleasant voice.

Susanne Marke looked jumpy, or maybe it was the light, which never seemed to be natural this close to the river and the city lights on the other side. The light moved across her face like nervous twitches of her skin. In the window behind her, Aneta could see one of the Denmark ferries passing. It looked like it was only ten yards away.

"Anette called me," said Susanne.

Aneta was still standing in the hall. Bellner and Johannisson were going to wait in the stairwell, at least for the first few minutes. The door was standing open.

"Are you alone?" asked Aneta.

"Alone? Of course I'm alone."

"What did she want?"

"Her dad had hit her," said Susanne. "Again."

"Her dad?"

"Yes."

"And . . . again?"

"Didn't you realize that's what's going on?" said Susanne.

"Why didn't you say so before?" asked Aneta, who was still standing in the hall.

"She didn't want to. Anette."

"Why not?"

"I don't know."

"Where's Anette now?"

"Down by the sea," said Susanne.

"Alone?"

"Yes, what the fu . . . what do you think?"

"Where's her dad, then?"

"In town."

"Where in town?"

"I don't know. But he's not down there. That's why she drove there."

"Drove there? How?"

"In my car," said Susanne. "She borrowed my car."

"Where's your brother?"

"I don't know."

"He wasn't along in the car?"

"No, no."

"It's important that you tell the truth, Susanne."

"The truth? The truth? What do you know about the truth?"

"I don't understand," said Aneta.

"You think that Hans was pursuing Anette, but you don't know anything."

"Tell me the truth, then."

"Hans may have his different sides, maybe he can seem stra . . . seem wei . . ."

Aneta watched the light come and go on the woman's face.

Why has Anette herself been so quiet?

There's something else. Something more. A different silence.

"I called down there. She didn't answer," said Aneta.

"She's there," said Susanne.

46

After their overnight visit with Macdonald's uncle, they drove into Aberdeen before lunch. The city gleamed in its light granite, which became darker as you got closer.

They drove directly to the train station. Sarah and Angela's train to Edinburgh would be leaving in twenty-five minutes. It had been Sarah's suggestion.

"Angela really has to see Edinburgh and you two are about to go in the other direction."

"It's wild and beautiful on the north coast," Macdonald had said.

"Maybe we can meet up again there," Angela had said. "And I'm happy to go with Sarah down to Edinburgh."

"Civilization," Sarah Macdonald had said.

"Let's say two days max," her husband had said. "Maybe we can meet up again in Kingussie." He had explained to Winter and Angela: "Good place up at the top of the Highlands. There's a train from Edinburgh via Perth up to there. Doesn't even take two hours."

Winter and Macdonald drove directly to force headquarters on the other side of Union Street. It was right across from the Aberdeen Arts Centre and was flanked by two churches.

Police Inspector Marion McGoldrick received them on the seventh floor. She was thin, very small, and she had a determined chin, dark eyes, and a sharply tailored uniform. She was another old acquaintance of Steve Macdonald's.

"Now's the time to use them," he had said the day before.

Marion McGoldrick was around thirty-five. There was a little pile of documents on her desk; she had done what she could. Macdonald suspected that she had done it on her own time. In Aberdeen there was no time for the police to mess around with favors during normal working hours.

"I hope I didn't take up your free time, Mar," said Macdonald.

"You did. But I don't have anything else to do."

"That's too bad."

"On the contrary, Steve. On the contrary." She gave a quick toss of her thick black hair and smiled thinly.

"What have you found?" Macdonald asked, straight out.

"The accident," she said, "but of course that's no surprise."

"And nothing new has popped up?" asked Macdonald.

"No," said Mar. "The trawler was on its way in with its course set for the lighthouse at Kinnaird Head, I assume, and something happened somewhere, some unknown number of nautical miles northwest, and it went down. With everything." She looked down at the paper. "*Marino*. Funny name. Usually boats have women's names. Like Marina. Now there's a classic name for a boat."

"The crew had stayed here in Aberdeen before then," said Winter.

"Yes. Lived on the boat in the harbor, mostly down in Albert Basin."

"All of them?" asked Macdonald.

"Yes; apparently they were a gang who didn't go around telling every Tom, Dick, and Harry that they were here. But the authorities registered them, of course, once they had ended up here on the other side of the minefield. I have the names here."

She held out a piece of paper. Winter took it.

He read the names on the copy of an official document, written in neat handwriting: Bertil Osvald, Egon Osvald, John Osvald, Arne Algotsson, Frans Karlsson.

There were five of them, thought Winter. He knew that. But why weren't there eight? A fishing boat in those days had a crew of eight.

"There were three of them along on the final journey, of course," said Mar.

Winter nodded. Egon Osvald, Frans Karlsson, John Osvald.

Now Bertil Osvald was dead and Arne Algotsson was in his own world.

"But it wasn't just those three who went out, was it?" asked Macdonald.

Mar made a little movement with both hands.

"There's no information to indicate that any other fisherman hired the *Marino,*" she said. "A thorough investigation was done after the boat disappeared, of course, but no one else seems to have been along. And no next of kin made contact after the accident." She put down the paper she was holding in her hands. "That says a lot right there."

"And the boat was never found?" asked Macdonald. "I mean the wreckage."

"No."

"Maybe it isn't a wreck," Winter said, taking a step forward. None of them had considered sitting down in the little room. "Maybe you just uttered a Freudian slip, Steve."

"Please explain, Chief Inspector," said Mar.

"Maybe the *Marino* never went down," said Winter. "Maybe they just disappeared. For some reason. Crime, revenge, I don't know. Sailed in a different direction."

"Rio de Janeiro," said Macdonald.

"Haven't you had that thought, Steve?" said Winter.

"They wouldn't get away," said Mar.

"No?" said Winter.

"Absolutely not. You have to understand that it simply wasn't possible to hide a boat on the coast at that time, least of all a fishing boat, a trawler. There was a war. You can say what you want about the coast guard today, but at that time they took their duty seriously. It was just a fact that there were German U-boats in the water around here, and destroyers, and God knows what out in the North Sea, and we took it seriously."

"But the smuggling did continue during the war," said Macdonald.

"Not with the Germans," said Mar.

"But it did continue." Macdonald sat down suddenly but immediately got up again. "There were harbors. Secret harbors, or at least as secret as they could be for their purposes."

"No one smuggled secretly back then," said Mar.

"I call that a contradiction," said Macdonald.

"The authorities knew everything," said Mar. "Believe me, Steve. I know something about it because my grandfather was one of the worst. Or the best, if you look at it that way."

"Best worst what? Coast guard or smuggler?"

"Smuggler," she said, smiling. "Up in Sandhaven."

"This sounds like *The Godfather*," said Macdonald.

"He made good money at it," she said. "That's what it's all about, right? He didn't exactly smuggle for idealistic reasons, did he? Or because it was fun or something." She tapped the thin bunch of papers as though to emphasize her words. "It's always a question of money."

"Mmhmm," said Macdonald.

"You're not convinced?" asked Mar.

"Who witnessed the accident?" said Macdonald. "There must have been some ship out there, right? Someone must have received a signal, right?"

"No," she answered. "No to both questions."

"A ghost ship," said Macdonald.

"Was there anyone who checked the harbors right after the accident?" asked Winter. "To see if the trawler ended up somewhere?"

"The harbors were checked all the time," she answered.

"So no one was looking for the *Marino* in particular? Or what if it changed names?"

"Not that I know of."

"Which are the most notorious smuggling harbors along this coast?" asked Winter.

"It's a secret," she said, smiling, possibly ironically. "Otherwise they couldn't do business, could they?"

"Okay, okay, Mar, I have faith in you and your grandfather and the authorities. Erik here does too. But answer his question."

"Most notorious? Well, Sandhaven, like I said. The Bay of Lochielair. Pennan probably has the longest history."

"Pennan?" Macdonald looked like he was remembering something. "Pennan . . ."

"It's always been a special village," said Mar. "The cliffs there are red, of course, and people painted their houses red and the road was already red, so the village was invisible from the sea. And then of course it's under a giant outcropping, so it's invisible from land as well."

"Pennan . . . ," repeated Macdonald.

"Is it far from here?" asked Winter.

"Oh, fifteen or so miles west of Fraserburgh," answered Mar. "The coastal road toward Macduff. But like I said, you might miss the village."

"*Local Hero!*" Macdonald shouted.

Winter jumped. Macdonald had solved his problem.

"Have you seen the film *Local Hero,* Erik?" he asked, turning to Winter.

"Uh, yes. Wasn't it in the eighties?"

"It was filmed in Pennan," said Macdonald. "Bill Forsyth wanted to have a really creepy place, and he chose Pennan!"

"When you say it like that . . . ," said Mar McGoldrick.

"We'll do it on the way back," said Macdonald.

Mar held the paper in her right hand again.

"You might as well take this. There's a little more about what happened, what they did. They sailed up to Peterhead and stayed there for a while, and then they went on to Fraserburgh. And then it was over."

"What happened with those two who survived, or whatever you call it?" asked Winter.

"They stayed here for a while and then they were just gone," she said.

"How did that happen?" asked Winter.

"It was probably like when they came here," said Mar. "Daredevils from Scandinavia who went through the minefields for the money. Presumably another gang like them came in and sold the load off quickly and sneaked out again, and then these two Swedes were probably along on board. We don't know, no one knows. Suddenly they were gone."

They parked at the church north of Broad Street, which ran down to the fishing harbor. There was a tight forest of masts there.

"No problem for a boat to hide," said Macdonald, nodding toward the harbor.

They walked down the street and passed the Fishermen's Mission. The building looked relatively modern, but it was an optical illusion.

The hall smelled like smoke and damp clothes.

They knew now that the Osvald brothers and the two other fishermen from Donsö had gotten some help from the Royal National Mission to Deep Sea Fishermen, which had been here in Peterhead since 1922.

A large photograph in a frame was hanging in the lobby. It was black and white and depicted a fishing boat that seemed to have guns mounted on it. There was a caption:

TRAWLERS AT WAR.

A man looked up from behind something that resembled a pulpit. They hadn't seen him back there.

"Can I help you?" he said, and he got up slowly. They saw that he was an old man. He looked as though he'd been sitting here since the war. He must have been the one who put up the photo of the war trawler, Winter thought.

"Can I help you?" the old man repeated.

They walked up to the pulpit and explained who they were. The man introduced himself as former assistant superintendent Archibald Farquharson.

"I sneak over here and sit sometimes, for old times' sake," he said.

"You must have seen many people come and go," said Macdonald.

"Indeed I have," said Farquharson.

"We're looking for information about some Swedish fishermen who might have been here during the war," said Macdonald.

"I was here," said Farquharson. "Well, not here exactly, but at the Mission."

"We're looking for information about a John Osvald," said Winter.

"I remember John," said Farquharson.

"Sorry?"

"We were the same age. I remember him more than his brothers. He had two brothers, right?" Farquharson quickly rubbed his hand over his old-man's cheeks. "Terrible about the accident."

They asked him about the accident. He didn't know any more than anyone else. Nothing about reasons, wreckage, deaths.

"I've thought about it on occasion. About John." Farquharson suddenly looked past them toward the door. "It's a little odd; a few times during the years I've been sitting here and looked over at that door and it was as if . . . as if John Osvald were about to walk in. Strange, isn't it? It probably has to do with that mysterious catastrophe. That no one knew. Like a ghost ship, right?" He looked at the two policemen. "And then, a few weeks ago or so, I see him walk in through that door!"

47

Winter and Macdonald turned around at Farquharson's words, as though John Osvald would be standing there to prove them right. But no one was standing in the door, which was closed and painted a kind of sea blue. There were remnants of yellow on the door frame. Yellow and blue are Scotland's colors just as much as white and blue, Winter thought.

He turned around again and tried to read Farquharson's face. The old man wasn't confused. He seemed certain, but without emphasis. It was merely a statement.

"I think he saw me," said Farquharson.

"We should probably start at the beginning," said Macdonald.

"It's as though time doesn't change anything," said Farquharson. "It's more like it sharpens things. Like appearances, for example. People's facial features." The man's eyes flashed. "Only the essentials are left."

Winter took out the photograph of Osvald, the one where he was half in profile. When he looked at the photograph he felt the same frustration as before, as though he were holding something there in his hands that he should be able to make use of. Something he had seen and yet not seen.

"Mmhmm," said Farquharson. "That's him, all right." Farquharson looked up. "That's the Swede."

"And you mean to say that the same man walked in here a little while ago?" Macdonald asked.

"A few weeks ago," said Farquharson.

"You're sure, Mr. Farquharson?"

"Yes. It was him."

"Can you say exactly when it happened? The date?"

"Well, if I can think a bit."

"What happened?" Winter asked. "When he came in here?"

"He turned around in the doorway," said Farquharson. "I think he saw me."

"What do you mean?" Macdonald asked. "Did he recognize you?"

"Yes. I think so."

"In the same way you recognized him?"

"Yes."

"What did you do then?"

"Nothing. I guess I didn't realize until after a bit that it might be the Swede, and then I went out on the street, but he wasn't there, of course."

"Why did he come here?" Winter asked. "After so many years."

"Couldn't he have been here before?" said Farquharson.

"But you haven't seen him?"

"No. But he could still have been here."

"But he's been declared dead," said Macdonald.

"I know."

"You seem calm, Mr. Farquharson. It didn't occur to you that you saw a ghost?"

"I don't believe in ghosts."

"But the ship disappeared with Osvald," Winter said.

"That's what they say," said Farquharson.

"You don't believe it?"

"I don't believe anything. I don't know anything."

They heard someone coming through the door behind them and they turned around. It was two younger men in thick sweaters and knitted caps. They nodded to Farquharson but didn't seem to notice Macdonald and Winter. The men walked through the hall and in through another door.

"Norwegian fishermen," said Farquharson. "We have some Norwegians, and Icelanders. Not many Swedes."

"Do you have any Swedes right now?" Winter asked.

"We don't have many rooms," said Farquharson. "This is no hotel. It's more so that they can have a change of scenery for a little while, a night or so, if something's going on with the boat and such."

"No Swedes?" Winter repeated.

"Not this week. Last week I think there were some."

"Do you have a register?" Winter asked. Macdonald looked at him. "Where they sign in—do they give the name of the boat then?"

"Yes, those are the rules."

Farquharson had only to reach for a black binder, which was thick. It was already open. He flipped back three pages.

"The Swedes," he said to himself. "I wasn't here then." He looked up. "A little operation on my hip." He looked down. "The trawler was called the *Mariana*. The only name I have next to the trawler's name is Erikson." Farquharson looked up again. "I assume it's the skipper. It's enough for him to sign in."

"Do they have to write down their home harbor?" asked Winter.

"Yes," said Farquharson, "but I can't read it." He turned the binder around. Winter read on one line:

MARIANA. STYRSÖ. ERIKSON.

And a date.

It was two and a half weeks ago.

Winter knew that there was a trawler from Donsö called the *Magdalena* and the skipper was named Erik.

Was there a trawler from Styrsö named the *Mariana*?

Why wouldn't there be?

He would call Ringmar and ask him to check.

Farquharson offered them a quick cup of tea. There were pictures of trawlers hanging everywhere. Winter heard a laugh from somewhere, but there was a seriousness in the walls and the pictures and the memories here.

Farquharson gave a short explanation.

"The Royal National Mission to Deep Sea Fishermen was founded in 1881 after Mr. Ebenezer J. Mather visited fishing fleets at sea and really saw the crews' inferior and dangerous working conditions."

Macdonald and Winter nodded.

"It has improved, of course," said Farquharson, "and we hope we've contributed to that. But it's such a special occupation. Fishermen are so strangely cut off from the usual human influences by their work." He looked at Winter. "There's not much left of the usual human community out there at sea."

"You must have seen many people be influenced by that," said Winter.

"Naturally."

"Can it make people . . . inhuman?"

"What do you mean?"

"I don't know," said Winter. "That it makes a person someone else. Into someone . . . worse."

"I believe it does," said Farquharson.

"What about with John Osvald?"

"That was a long time ago," said Farquharson.

"You have a good memory."

Farquharson drank his tea and his gaze became hazy, very hazy. He had been a fisherman himself, before the war. He had gone ashore a long time ago.

"They were nervous," he said after the pause. "Nervous."

"How so?" asked Winter.

"There was something . . . something they had done, I think. People came asking after one of them. Well, I assumed it had to do with smuggling. Money. I don't know."

"Smuggling? Why smuggling?"

"Why not?" Farquharson said, smiling. "It wasn't an unknown phenomenon up here."

"So the Swedes were involved in smuggling?" Macdonald asked.

"I don't know," said Farquharson. "I didn't ask. But something was going on."

"Smuggling of what?"

"Anything at all. There was a war."

"But didn't they fish all the time? With their trawler. The *Marino*."

"Did they?" Farquharson said with a sort of lightness in his voice, perhaps a bit of mocking.

"What role did John Osvald play?" asked Macdonald.

"In what?"

"In the group."

"He was the leader. He was young, but he made the decisions." Farquharson put down the heavy earthenware mug he'd been holding in his hand. "Well, I wasn't well acquainted with the Swedish fishermen that came to harbor here. These are really more like observations I made."

"And then they left," said Winter.

"Yes. I didn't know where to, but since then I've heard that they were up in Fraserburgh for a while."

*   *   *

The Saltoun Arms Hotel in Fraserburgh was on Saltoun Square in the middle of town; the hotel was Victorian, and so was the restaurant: palms in the windows, and on the floor, attractive wall-to-wall carpeting; flowery wallpaper on the ceiling; colonial fans that moved at an old-time speed; a glass case with cakes and cookies. A wisp of a melody that might have been Glenn Miller, or rather a British big band from the past. The staff seemed to come from a different era. The other guests in the half-full room were dressed as though they came from the past. A small child screamed a few times and the young couple at the east window did what they could to make the baby happy.

Winter and Macdonald sat with an ale each and waited for their food.

Macdonald looked around discreetly. A waitress passed with a steaming soup tureen.

"I assume that this is what they call larger than life," he said.

"Mmhmm."

"This was here before we came, and it will be here when we're gone. Larger than life."

Three pictures with country motifs hung on the north wall, like a dream of something other than the sea and the steep cliffs to the west. A farmer was walking behind a horse with the plow. It was the very symbol of work.

Another waitress served their lunch: breaded haddock, chips, green peas. It was a large plate. Winter blew on the hot haddock fillet, which had been fried very lightly. He tasted it.

"Not bad at all."

It was a classic meal. The waitress, a motherly woman, came back and asked how it tasted.

"The best I've ever had!" said Winter.

"I hope it's not the first," she said.

"No, no, no."

Macdonald helped himself to the tartar sauce. He held up a piece of fish and nodded. He looked proud. Winter didn't have the heart to say that the fish had most likely been hauled up by Scandinavian fishermen in international waters and shipped here in trucks from the fish auction in Hanstholm.

After lunch Winter bought a *Press and Journal* from a news shop on Broad Street. There was a full-page article on the front page: A fisherman on a trawler from Fraserburgh had been washed overboard off the Norwegian coast.

The Grampian Police had their headquarters on Finlayson Street, North Aberdeenshire Sub-Division. The street was in the northern outskirts, where strong winds blew in all directions. The sky was blue and the houses gray. There was a chill in the air. The house directly across from the police station was called Thule Villa. Winter thought of Prince Valiant on the crooked sign above the closed-down gas station in Dallas.

They were met by Sergeant Steve Nicoll, a skinny young detective with a determined expression. He didn't know Macdonald but he knew of him. Macdonald had called the week before. Nicoll had done what he could.

"There's not much about those blokes," he said. "They kept to themselves."

"What happened after the trawler disappeared?" Macdonald asked. "With the two Swedes who stayed behind?"

"They were here during the investigation of the shipwreck, at first, and then they just disappeared."

Winter nodded.

"They showed up in Sweden, I assume."

Winter nodded again.

"There are suspicions that they were involved in smuggling," said Macdonald.

"Are there?"

"Yes."

"Well, it's not impossible."

"What kind of goods could it have been?" asked Winter.

"Hmm . . . I guess everything was worth smuggling during the war."

"What was the hardest?" Winter asked. What was worth disappearing for, he thought. Committing serious crimes for. Possibly dying for. "Was there anything that was taboo?" he asked.

"Possibly weapons," said Nicoll. "Depending on where they came from and who they went to."

"The resistance movement?" asked Winter.

"There were several," answered Macdonald.

Nicoll nodded.

"There were those who hated the English more than they hated the Germans," said Macdonald.

They were standing out on the stairs. The wind tore at the leaves above the open field between the row houses. There were two marked cars outside the station. There was a notice in the stairwell behind them: WE WILL DO OUR BEST.

"How many of you are there here?" asked Macdonald.

"Thirty men," said Nicoll. "The CID is in Aberdeen."

"How many detectives?"

"Twelve. The chief inspector is in Peterhead." Nicoll waved a greeting to two young policewomen who passed them going up the stairs. Both had blond hair. They each cast a glance at Macdonald and Winter. Nicoll smiled. "Both of those gals are unmarried," he said.

"Unlike us," said Macdonald.

"So?"

"What's the biggest thing you work with here?" asked Winter. "The biggest problem?"

"The usual old stuff in new forms," Nicoll said. "Smuggling. Now it's heroin."

"Really?"

"Yes. Unknown ten years ago, familiar now."

"It's like at home in Gothenburg," said Winter.

"It's like everywhere," said Nicoll. There was clear resignation in his voice. It was something you only showed to your colleagues, and seldom even then.

Macdonald scratched his head.

"Where would you have hidden if you wanted to disappear for good during the war?" he asked.

Sergeant Nicoll squinted at the sun, which hung above Thule Villa and felt surprisingly strong. Winter felt for his sunglasses in his jacket pocket.

"There are several places along the coast," said Nicoll. "Fishing villages, smuggling villages where everyone learned to mind their own business and not ask questions. And sometimes to tolerate strangers."

"Name a place," said Macdonald.

Winter put on his black sunglasses. Nicoll and Macdonald got darker skin.

"Pennan," Nicoll said, jerking his head to the left. "I would have chosen Pennan."

Winter and Macdonald drove via the B9031, which was smaller and close to the sea, through Sandhaven and Rosehearty, strongholds of smuggling with medieval skylines.

The road down to the villages was marked with a barely visible sign. Here there were open spaces and steep slopes down to the sea. The road curved with a thirty-five-degree grade. It was like driving on a roller-coaster.

Pennan was a row of small, white-plastered stone houses next to the quay, two hundred yards long at most. The harbor was small and protected by broad breakwaters. The wind was strong over Pennan Bay. The water was tossed up toward the houses, which lay in shadow under the red cliffs that hung like half a threat. The beach was full of stones. A black log of driftwood sat halfway up the beach.

They had parked outside a house with a dolphin on the wall: Dolphin Cottage, number ten.

"Do you remember the film?" asked Macdonald.

"Yes," said Winter, "and I actually thought of it not so long ago."

"Do you recognize the village, then?"

"I think so . . ."

"The houses are still here," said Macdonald. "But the film is an illusion. Or a bluff, if you prefer. A good example of how it's possible to lie with pictures."

"Is it? How so?"

"Well, you see this little rocky beach," Macdonald said, nodding toward it. "But in the film, Burt Lancaster wandered around on a rather impressive beach, and it was deserted."

"Yes."

"So they put the houses here in Pennan together with a beach in Morar," Macdonald said. "It's on the North Sea, just south of Mallaig. A ferry goes from there across to Armadale on Skye."

"Aha. That's your ancestors' neighborhood."

"Yes." Macdonald locked the car with the remote and started to walk. "They edited Pennan and Morar together." He whipped his hand around in the air. "An illusion."

"I remember that recluse in the film," said Winter. "He lived in some shack on the beach."

"Maybe we'll find him here," said Macdonald.

"I remember the inn, too, and the innkeeper."

"It's still here," said Macdonald.

They were standing outside Pennan Inn. Temporarily closed due to bad weather.

"We could have stayed overnight here," said Macdonald. He looked up at the sky. It was starting to grow dark.

Winter turned around.

"I recognize that telephone booth," he said, nodding at the red kiosk on the other side of the strip of road.

"I've never been here," said Macdonald.

A woman came out of one of the houses, seventy yards away. She walked toward them and greeted them as she passed. She was wearing a kerchief but was no older than they were. A few cars were parked beside theirs.

"Excuse me," said Macdonald.

"On a very clear day you can see Orkney," the woman had said.

"How about the northern lights?" Winter had asked.

"Oh, you've seen the film." It was a statement, for the most part. "You've come to see it for yourselves?"

"We're not here for that reason," Macdonald had said.

She had taken them to the next-to-last house in the row. Everything was closed and shut up as they walked along the quay.

In 1900, three hundred people had lived here, she had said. Now twenty people lived in Pennan permanently.

They walked past a construction site. Winter thought of Dallas.

"The first new construction in a hundred years!" said the woman.

They stood in front of a cottage. She knocked hard three times.

"Her hearing is bad."

After the fifth knock of her knuckles, there was rustling behind the heavy door, which still had its red base color.

"Mrs. Watt?" said the woman.

The door creaked open. The face of an older woman became visible.
She had small, sharp eyes.

"Aye?"

"Mrs. Watt, these gentlemen would like to ask you a couple of questions."

They climbed back uphill in the car. The dolphin house they'd parked in front of had been the inn in *Local Hero*. In the summer, dolphins played out in the water of Moray Firth.

Mrs. Watt had a memory that came and went. In addition, she had spoken a kind of Scottish that seemed to be too much even for Macdonald. Once she had nodded to herself and said, "Gie yehr ain fish guts to year ain sea myaves."

"What did that mean?" Winter had asked when they were standing outside again.

"'Give your own fish guts to your own seagulls,'" Macdonald had answered, "but I don't know what it *means*." He began to walk. "Maybe that you should take care of yourself and to hell with everyone else."

At the summit there was only sky and sea over the edge.

Mrs. Watt had spoken about "a stranger."

He had lived by himself in a little hovel next to the Cullykhan caves in the cove next to Pennan Bay.

"But there's nothing there now," she had said.

They had climbed over there, but there was nothing there.

"He was there and then he was gone," she had said.

"When was that?"

"The war. During the war."

"What did he do?"

"What everyone else did, I assume. Smuggled."

"Did you meet this stranger?" Winter had asked Mrs. Watt.

"No."

"Did you see him?"

"No."

"Where did he come from?"

"No one knew. Not that I know of. And no one asked. Not then." She had squinted her sharp eyes, which were like black stones. "They had probably checked him out and I guess he was allowed to stay."

"They? Who are they?" Macdonald had asked.

"The men in the village."

"Are any of them still here?"

"No."

"None at all?"

"Not from that time."

"What happened to the stranger?" Winter had asked.

"I guess he's just gone."

They drove west, toward Macduff and Banff.

"There were lots of people who came and went back then," said Macdonald.

Winter didn't answer. He looked out over the sea below the precipice. One quick movement of the wheel and they would be flying.

"What are you thinking about, Erik?"

"About something I've seen and yet not seen," said Winter.

"A common problem for a policeman," said Macdonald.

"Fuck."

"When? Where?"

"Recently," said Winter. "During this trip."

"Think back."

"What do you think I'm doing?"

There were some dark streaks across the sky. The sun disappeared. Macdonald thought about putting in a CD but he hesitated.

"It has to do with the photograph," said Winter. "Of Osvald."

Macdonald looked up at the sky.

"We'll have to find an inn to stay overnight."

Winter nodded.

"I know the place," said Macdonald. "The Seafield Hotel in Cullen. It's a classic. I didn't remember it before, but now I do. You can try Cullen skink there!"

48

He heard them talking behind his back. He wanted to know who they were, and why they were there. He didn't move. He had seen them arrive, and he understood.

She didn't say anything when they ordered.

Maybe she understood too.

It was only a small favor. He knew that he could ask her. A single conversation. A simple question.

But he didn't trust her anymore.

He had decided to tell everything. It was time. When had he made his decision? It had to do with the sea. The loneliness.

After all these years. It was easier at first.

When he was going to leave it all, it was harder. Not hard to leave; he had longed to do that. *Longed.* But he didn't want to do it alone, not now.

Who could believe it would happen like this? That the boy . . .

Take the car, the boy had said. I don't need it.

There was a shine in the boy's eyes.

It's all over now, the boy had said.

The boy prayed, he prayed all the time. His good sense seemed to disappear.

It had been tranquil by the sea. It was a peaceful beach.

Drive! the boy had screamed. He had hesitated.

Drive! The boy screamed again and his white hair stood straight up. His body looked old. It was old, but not as old as his.

The boy was blue in the face. His heart. The blue color disappeared. The boy walked on his own on the other side of the little lake, and he prayed.

Jesus!

A cry over the mountains.

We are all lost, he had said afterward. I will wash away our sins, wash us. I am glad that you sent for me. *Drive now!*

At night the dreams came back. Dreams of gold, of silver, of the money that destroyed everything.

How often had he sat with this pistol in his hand? First it was the threat, soon after. When he was staying hidden in cliffs, huts, on rotten ships. He had shot once.

Then there were the thoughts of doing it by his own hand. On his own.

He didn't know what would happen.

He carried it with him night and day.

He'd had it when he heard the voices in the Three Kings, when he saw them. They came from the other world.

Now his memories flowed on, flowed up. There was water everywhere; the sea washed over him. He had placed the dinghy in the shadow of the waves. The *Marino* had already begun to sink.

It was necessary. Egon had already been lost then. The trawler was lost.

He had felt Frans's face in his hands. Jesus! There had been no one to listen out there. God wasn't listening; not God's son. On the beach there were only stones. He made his choice. No, not then. It was long before.

There was still money in the oilcloth bags. The weapons were on the bottom or had been carried farther north, like the bodies.

The boy's boy hadn't asked any questions.

The boy's boy.

Here!

Bring it here!

They would never find him. Never! His face was different, his body. His name. His life, what was left.

He saw them out on the street, but it was a coincidence. They had been standing in front of the telephone booth, a coincidence. They had walked by.

None of them would find out!

49

Aneta Djanali was sitting in Halders's kitchen. She had wrapped a blanket around herself; she was freezing and the kitchen was the warmest place. Hannes and Magda were at a birthday party at a house three blocks away. It wasn't evening yet. Halders was making a quiche for some reason. A good smell was coming from the oven. Halders let Lucinda Williams sing from the living room in her cracked voice, lonely girls . . . heavy blankets cover lonely girls.

Aneta had had a short conversation with Anette Lindsten. Anette had been on her way down to the house by the sea, she said.

Was she running away again?

Everything about this was running away, sometimes invisibly.

This was part of the hell that struck the women, she thought. A horrid combination of guilt and fear and control and ownership.

She didn't want to think about it, but she couldn't stop.

It was about a woman's right to her own life. That was exactly what it was about.

Control over the woman's life. What it was about.

She didn't doubt for a second what it was about for Anette. Hans Forsblad wouldn't give up control, *would not* give up control. Nothing stopped him. He stayed hidden, but he was *there*. Aneta had seen his eyes. His eyes when he looked at her.

Two things were missing from her home.

She had discovered this while she was waiting for her colleagues from Lorensberg, or maybe it was after they were there.

The shell that had stood next to the telephone on the shelf in the hall. It was large and shimmered blue. It was almost transparent. Aneta had found it in a cove outside Särö, and it had been standing in the same place for two years and she hadn't even dusted it, as far as she remembered. The traces the snail left behind had been visible, a bare spot in a sea of fine dust.

And Kontômé. The Kontômé mask on the wall in the hall was gone. Who would want to steal that? It had no financial value.

Kontômé was there to show her the path through the future.

The person who had gotten into her apartment had taken these things with them.

She knew who it was.

Anette had sounded out of breath on the telephone. Aneta had heard the roaring sound of a motor.

"She's afraid for her life," she said to Halders, wrapping the blanket more tightly around herself.

Lucinda Williams sang in a broken voice about broken lives and broken words. "Can't you play something else, Fredrik? That's making me shiver even more. And freeze."

Halders was about to take out the quiche. He placed it on a trivet and walked out of the kitchen and Lucinda Williams was cut off in the middle of the song about the half sentences. After ten seconds of silence she heard beautiful vocal harmonies and a bright and gentle melody.

"Will the Beach Boys do?" Halders said from the door. "Is that warm and sunny enough for you?"

"At least on the surface," she said.

"Do you know your Beach Boys?" Halders asked.

"No," she said, listening again. "But you can hear that something is wrong with those guys, behind those sunny voices."

"That's absolutely right," said Halders, "but why not forget it for two and a half minutes? After that the song is over."

Aneta chose not to listen. She saw Anette's face in front of her again.

"She seems to be in constant movement between different addresses. On the run between them," she said.

Halders nodded.

"Isn't that a common pattern?"

"But she has her family," said Aneta.

"Yes?"

"But they don't seem to offer any protection. Or support."

"Well, she's not the only one keeping her distance there," said Halders.

"What do you mean?"

"Her father. We stumbled into his business through his daughter.

He hadn't counted on you getting stuck on this. Maybe not even on you showing up in his . . . Anette's apartment."

"Business?"

"He's sure as shit involved in this stolen goods ring. The theft ring. But how would we have known that if it weren't for his daughter?"

"Does she know, do you think? Is she afraid of *that,* too?"

"Maybe *that* is exactly what she's afraid of," said Halders. "That he might think that she will expose it." He put the quiche pan on the table. There was already a bowl of salad there, and a little bottle of dressing. "It might be her father's shady dealings she's running away from." Halders looked up. "He's sure as shit trying to keep us away from his daughter. And her problems. And her husband, Frützblatt. His sister. And so on."

"Yes," said Aneta, "but it's not her dad she's afraid of, not primarily. I'm sure. It's the threat from Forsblad."

"Why doesn't she say so straight out, then?"

"I think she is," said Aneta. "We're just not listening well enough."

"And now she's on her way to that cabin by the sea?"

"That's what she said."

Halders cut a piece of ham and cheese quiche and lifted her plate. "You sound skeptical."

"Well, I don't think she trusts anyone. Including me."

"Why the beach house?"

"Maybe it's the only place where she can feel safe," Aneta said.

That night she dreamed that she was driving on a narrow road that led her between low trees that were lit up by her headlights. Everything was black outside. Above her was the sky, but it was also the sea. How she knew that, she didn't know. It was the dream that told her.

Somewhere, a woman was singing with a cracked voice, or screaming. She heard the sound of waves from above. Even in a dream, where you accept everything, she thought that it was wrong. Why was the water above her?

In the light from her headlights stood her mother.

Her mother made a gesture she didn't understand. She didn't understand that her mother wanted to stop her, there on the road.

Her mother had never shown up in her dreams before.

Now she was driving on a beach.

Her mother was suddenly standing there, too, gesturing, raising both hands, standing in the way of the car.

Suddenly there was water all around! She tried to scream, scream. She couldn't *breathe*.

Her own screams woke her up, or her attempts to scream. She felt an arm around her shoulders. It was warm. She heard Fredrik's voice.

Macdonald parked on the square below the Seafield Hotel. The city sloped sharply toward the sea. Winter stood on the square with his overnight bag over his shoulder. It was twilight in the haze. Winter saw the enormous iron structures that were suspended straight across the upper part of Cullen. From a distance, the viaducts could be mistaken for horizontal cathedrals.

"Impressive," he said.

"I agree," said Macdonald. "But the trains have stopped running."

They had called from the car. There were two vacant rooms at the Seafield; more than that. The season was over.

The building was of white stone, an old inn. The lobby was done in polished mahogany, silver, gold, a tartan pattern that Winter guessed belonged to the owners' clan, the Campbell family. It had various shades of blue, black, and green, like the sea at the end of the road through Cullen.

Herbert Campbell discreetly asked them about the evening. Could he perhaps recommend the hotel restaurant? He could, and they reserved a table for eight o'clock.

They dropped into the bar for an ale before they went up to their rooms.

"Impressive," said Winter.

"It's famous even in Scotland," said Macdonald.

It wasn't only the shining wood of the bar, the leather furniture, the open fire, the heavy art on the walls. It was the bottles in a row at the bar and the shelves behind them. Winter had to ask.

"Two hundred forty-one kinds of malt whisky," said the female bartender.

"Think about that for a drink before dinner," said Macdonald.

Winter called Angela from his room. He stood at the window and saw the street below and half the sea and a group of small stone houses that flocked together down by the harbor.

"Found a good hotel?" he said.

"Sarah had a favorite and I agree with her," said Angela. "I can see the castle from the window right now."

"I can see half the sea," said Winter.

"How is the investigation going?"

"I don't know," he said.

"Are there any traces of John Osvald?"

"Maybe." Winter sat down and then stretched out on the bed. It was hard, but not too hard. Through the window he could see the upper portion of the stone house across the street. A seagull, or some kind of gull, was sitting above a window bay. "It's as though he's been here. Stayed here, if you understand what I mean. We've even spoken to an old man who knew him back then and claims to have seen him *now*."

"Well, there you go."

"I don't think we'll find him," said Winter.

"You can see the sights, anyway," said Angela.

"You too."

"We were planning to take the train tomorrow afternoon up to that place in the Highlands."

"We'll probably be driving at the same time. We should be there in time to see you for dinner. A reunion dinner."

"What are you doing tonight, then?"

"Eating dinner." He changed position on the bed. "I'm going to try that soup. Cullen skink."

"It doesn't sound good."

"Steve says it isn't good."

"Then I understand that you have to try it." He heard a sound behind her, a door opening, a male voice, a female voice.

"Oops, here comes room service." Winter thought he heard Sarah Macdonald's voice. Angela came back. "A bottle of good white wine."

"Have you talked to Elsa?" Winter asked.

"Only twice this afternoon."

"I called, but no one was home at Lotta's. And no answer on her cell."

"They're at the movies right now."

"Okay. I'll call later. See you tomorrow. Hugs and kisses."

He dropped the phone next to him on the bed. He saw Arne

Algotsson's face before him as the confused old fisherman said the word for the Scottish haddock soup.

He sat up and massaged his shoulder, which had grown stiff in the car. His body needed more massaging now that he was past forty.

There was a knock at the door.

He called out a "Yes?"

"Fancy a walk before dinner?" he heard Macdonald's voice say.

They walked south on Seafield Street, passed Bayview Road at the curve, and continued down a few stairways that led to the strange little houses, which formed a small, closely built neighborhood next to the harbor. Winter could see a beach beyond them.

This was Seatown. They walked along the narrow streets, which didn't have names. The numbers on the houses didn't make sense.

"I think the numbers show what order the houses were built in," said Macdonald.

They passed Cullen Methodist Church.

Farther down the street was a red telephone booth, as old as the one in Pennan. As Winter passed he listened for rings.

Hundred-year-old stairs had been carved out of the wall down to the docks. Smaller fishing boats were on shore now, during the ebb. Their bellies shone white, like fish on land. The sky had darkened and was blue on the way to black. The moon was faint, but it was there. The horizon covered everything the eye could see. The houses in Seatown were luminous. Children's clothes waved at them with short arms from a clothes-line.

"Where are all the people?" said Winter.

They walked back, past the church and the phone booth. A curtain moved in one of the windows of a house that looked like it would soon collapse. The house was black. The curtain moved again. Who wouldn't be curious?

They encountered a child walking along the western house walls with his eyes on the ground. It was a boy of about ten, in short pants and a cap. He could have been from the 1950s. All of this could have been from the 1950s, in some cases even the 1850s.

Winter thought of the smell that existed in almost every British building. It was a smell from the past.

They walked up the stairs again and took a right onto Bayview and walked in the shadow of the viaducts and took a left on North Castle Street. The Three Kings pub was there.

Macdonald looked at his watch.

"One for the long road back to the hotel?"

"Of course," said Winter.

Inside it was dark; the windows were small and couldn't let very much light in even on a brilliant day. There was a middle-aged woman behind the bar. Apparently all the bartenders in Cullen were women. A man was sitting at one of the tables by the windows. He had his back to them. There was a glass in front of him. He had a knitted cap on his head. A fisherman, thought Winter.

Macdonald ordered two glasses of ale. The woman tapped them up and served them. They remained standing on the bar as the ale cleared. The woman appeared to be looking out through the window where the man in the cap was sitting. He hadn't moved while they had been inside.

"Skaal," said Macdonald, raising his glass.

They drank. Winter couldn't help watching the man's back, which was thin and hunched forward. He still didn't move. The whisky glass in front of him was empty; the pint glass was empty. The man was like a frozen figure. One of many who'd frozen into place in these coastal towns and slowly crumbled away from wind and salt as the economy sailed away with the fishing industry. Macdonald drank again. Maybe he should be glad that his grandfather, or maybe it was his great-grandfather, had left the coast. Otherwise perhaps he would be sitting like that. At the same time, I'm from the coast myself. But I am from another world.

The tradition at Seafield was that dinner guests were shown into the bar while the table was prepared, and the headwaiter handed out menus and wine lists.

Winter and Macdonald didn't protest. They sat down in the two leather chairs by the fire.

Another female bartender came to their chairs to take their predinner drink order. Winter let Macdonald choose.

"What do you say to Springbank, the twenty-one-year-old, of course?" said Macdonald.

Winter nodded as he lit a Corps.

There was a gentle strain of a melody in the bar. Winter recognized "Galveston," Glen Campbell. It was probably a coincidence, or was the singer a distant relative of the owners?

Glen as in Glen Deveron, GlenDronach, Glen Elgin, Glen Garioch, Glen Keith, Glen Mhor, Glen Moray, Glen Ord, Glen Spey, Glen Scotia, Glenrothes, the unknown celebrities from the secluded distilleries.

The headwaiter arrived with the menus, handwritten and bound in red leather.

There were few other guests in the bar: a younger couple on a small sofa in front of one of the windows, two older couples sitting together around a coffee table in the middle of the room, a solitary younger man in front of a solitary glass at the bar.

The bartender returned with the whisky, two tumblers beside it, and a small carafe of water.

Macdonald poured a few drops of water into his malt whisky. Winter waited. They drank. It was good. A touch of coconut in the finish. Yes. Sherry, toffee, seaweed, grass, peat on the tongue. Yes. A complicated flavor.

Winter ordered Cullen skink as an appetizer. He thought he liked the taste of smoked haddock boiled with potatoes and milk and onion. Steve grinned behind his bouillabaisse. Winter thought of Arne Algotsson again. How could this still be in his crumbling brain? Why had the name Cullen skink gotten stuck there? Was it just Cullen, just the first part? Was that why? I've thought about it before. Why was it this strange little town that stuck with Algotsson forever? Did he even have time to come here? Did anyone else come here? Had someone mentioned the name to him recently?

The dining room was also done in Scottish colors and polished wood and offered innovative dishes in the Scottish tradition. Macdonald smiled a bit:

Grilled herring with pan-fried porridge cake.

Black pudding en croute with calvados and apple glaze.

Venison with black pudding.

Winter ordered grilled sole with pesto and garlic; Macdonald ordered a steak. They tried the wines.

"I thought Craig would have called by now," said Macdonald, putting down his glass.

"Mmhmm."

"Three calls," said Macdonald. "Two women."

"Well, we know that Johanna called him twice," said Winter.

"Craig ought to have been able to check that by now," said Macdonald. "And the third one."

"I don't think we can trace it," said Winter.

"Why not?"

"They probably thought of that," said Winter.

"Who is 'they'?"

Yes. Who is "they"? Winter drank the white wine. He smelled the scent of a charcoal grill.

Who is "they"?

A surviving fisherman and a woman who made his phone calls.

Or a former acquaintance of Axel Osvald. He had been here before. Or a new acquaintance.

The food arrived. They tasted it. It was good.

Winter noticed that the young couple from the bar was already getting up from their table in the dining room. The woman nodded shyly in their direction and Winter nodded back. The younger man turned around. Winter noticed his profile. It suddenly looked like John Osvald's profile in the photograph from Winter's thin portfolio, the photograph in faint sepia tones. The man over there was still standing, in profile like an Egyptian mural. Winter saw it. He saw the photograph in his mind's eye, he saw the stranger's profile, Osvald's profile, the hotel walls, he saw a red wall, a staircase that led . . .

"*God!*" he said loudly, and Macdonald gave a start with his fork halfway to his mouth and the other guests turned sharply around.

"I've seen him!" Winter said.

Macdonald lowered his fork.

"Have you suddenly been saved, Erik?"

"Osvald! He was there!" Winter said, and Macdonald put down his fork.

"Where was he?"

"What was that town called . . . Buckie, right? Where we were looking for the rental car?"

"Yes. Buckie."

"We had tea at the old hotel."

"The Cluny Hotel."

"We walked up the stairs."

"We walked down them, too," Macdonald said.

Winter moved his hand as though he were waving away Macdonald's comment.

"I think it was as I was walking up. I . . . we looked at all of those old framed photos that were hanging on the wall in the stairway."

"The photos of trawlers," said Macdonald.

"Not only that." Winter could see now, he could *see,* it was completely clear, completely certain. "One of those pictures showed a bunch of people standing around that war monument on the square outside. In memory of everyone, et cetera. And I remember that next to the picture I read that the picture was taken at the end of the war, after World War Two, and there are people everywhere, like I said, but in the foreground there's a guy in a cap, and you can see him in profile, and it was Osvald!" Winter leaned forward a bit. "It's the same face I have in the picture up there in my room, the same profile. Shit, I didn't see it then, but it's been lying there ripening in my wonderful subconscious." Winter looked to the side, but the young couple had left. "I realized it when I saw a guy here get up."

"The end of the war," said Macdonald. "Osvald disappeared four years earlier."

"It was him," Winter said. "I'm as good as positive."

"Well," said Macdonald, "it's a little late to go check now."

"We'll have to do it first thing tomorrow morning," said Winter.

He had left the window open, and his room smelled like the sea. Ringmar called as he was about to turn off the lights for the night.

"There's no trawler from Styrsö called the *Mariana*."

"I didn't think there would be," said Winter.

"And there's no fisherman on Styrsö named Erikson."

He had a restless night. He dreamed of many things, none of them pleasant. Everyone was scared in his dreams; he was scared.

He had called Elsa before dinner. He wished he had her voice recorded on tape. Next time he traveled. But he wasn't sure that he would travel without her again.

He dreamed of water, black water. He saw a face under the water. He couldn't see who it was. It shone with a dreadfully strong light, as though from within itself. There was nothing in its eyes.

It was someone he had known.

He woke at dawn and was thirsty. He pulled up the blinds a little bit and saw half the sea. He thought he heard it. He heard seabirds screaming. There was a black bus down there, on the other side of the street, next to the post office. He thought of his dreams again; a sense of fear remained in the room even now that he had been awake for a while. He drank a glass of water and considered a mouthful of whisky but refrained. It would be another day.

It wouldn't be like any other day he had experienced.

When he lay down again he thought about how this day that had now begun would be the last. Why did he think that? It was like a dream where truths that no one wanted to hear took form.

50

They left after an early breakfast. Macdonald hadn't slept well, either. Neither of them blamed the whisky. It was something else. It was this city. Something that had been here.

It could be called intuition. An impulse, sometimes immediate. To know without being able to present the evidence. That could be the most frustrating part. That could be the deciding factor: intuition. They both had it. A detective without intuition was doomed, doomed like a fish out of water.

It wasn't far to Buckie; it was shorter than Winter thought. They could have taken a taxi there last night, but he wanted to have a clear head. He wasn't tired now. It was gone now.

They drove along the coastal road through Portnockie, Findochty, Portessie. It was a calm morning. The sea was calm. The sun was hanging above the eastern mountains now, lighting up the horizon. Winter could see the smoke from a ship that was balancing on the line of the horizon. There were no clouds. It was one of the most beautiful mornings God had made.

The Cluny Hotel was half lit up by the morning. Macdonald parked outside of the Buckie Thistle Social Club. A small group of schoolchildren walked by. One of the children was carrying a soccer ball under his arm.

A maid in a gray apron was vacuuming the lobby. She had begun with the lowest tread and looked up in surprise when the two men nodded a greeting and stepped up the stairs.

Winter held the photograph in his hand, John Osvald's profile.

He walked slowly up the stairs, from frame to frame containing the city's black and white history. The fishing industry and fishing had been the present and future for this city of the past, Buckie. Now the past remained. The Cluny Hotel belonged to the past.

They walked in a staircase whose walls shone with red velvet.

Winter saw masts, forests of masts. Had he been wrong? Was it some-one else he'd seen . . . and somewhere else?

He looked at the picture of the young Osvald again, taken on an is-land in a Swedish archipelago. Winter could see the sea behind Osvald. It was also a calm day, a beautiful day. Maybe Osvald had turned his face away to avoid getting the sun in his eyes.

"Here we have a few thousand," said Macdonald, who was a step ahead. Macdonald pointed at another framed photo. He stood three steps from the restaurant level up above.

Winter studied the picture. The square, Cluny Square, was black with people. They were standing in a thousand circles around the monu-ment, the Buckie War Memorial, finally erected in 1925 in memory of the dead during the first great war.

Now it was 1945. Winter read the few words on the label next to the frame. The people of Buckie gather at the monument to celebrate the end of the Great War. There was a date on the label. It was a spring day. It was a beautiful day; the sun plowed shadows through the mass of people. Winter looked at the faces in the foreground. A man in a cap stood near the camera. He had turned his head to the side, as though to avoid the sun. It was John Osvald.

"Yeah, it's him," said Macdonald.

Winter looked at the two faces, back and forth. There was no doubt. Macdonald held up Winter's photograph, compared.

"Yeah," Macdonald repeated. "No question."

"But it doesn't tell us that he's still around," said Winter.

"Around where?" said Macdonald.

"Around life," Winter said.

They stood on the square. The letters on the stone of the pedestal were forever: Their Name Liveth For Ever.

Two elderly people were sitting on a park bench in front of the build-ing next to the square. They seemed to be the same couple Winter had seen last time he'd stood here. He walked over to the building. There was a sign on the wall: "Struan House—Where older people find care in housing."

They were two old men. Winter walked over. He asked the men if they were around when the end of World War II was celebrated. They looked at him. Macdonald translated to Scottish. They asked why he wanted to know that. Macdonald explained. Winter took out the photograph. They looked at it and shook their heads.

"Would you like to come along into the hotel and look at the photo on the wall?" Macdonald asked.

The two men got up after a minute.

Inside, they walked up the stairs without great difficulty.

"Has it been hanging here long?" one of them said, in front of the photograph.

They studied the picture.

"So I'm there in that sea of people," said the other, nodding at the sea of people.

"I can't see you, Mike."

"I don't remember where I was standing," said Mike.

"Do you recognize him?" Macdonald asked, placing his index finger on Osvald's cap.

"So it's the same guy?" said Mike.

"See for yourself," Macdonald said, holding out Winter's photo.

"Yeah," Mike said, comparing it a few times. "But he's a stranger to me."

Macdonald and Winter got into the car. The owner of the pub on the other side of the street rolled up the blinds. There were chairs on the tables inside the windows. A ray of sunshine lit up part of the bar. Winter suddenly felt very thirsty.

"We've gotten this far, anyway," said Macdonald.

"Don't you want to get farther?" said Winter.

"So where should we go?" Macdonald asked. "What should we do?"

"I don't know," Winter said. "And it's a question of time, too."

Macdonald looked at his watch.

"The girls will get on the train in an hour or so."

"We should probably start on our way up to those high lands ourselves," said Winter.

Macdonald studied the pub owner, who had started to take the chairs down from the tables. He was wearing sunglasses for protection from the sun, which shone intensely between the two houses behind Winter and Macdonald.

"I sense that we're close," Macdonald said, turning to Winter. "Don't you feel it too?"

Winter nodded but didn't answer.

"We've followed him. At least partially, we've followed in his old footsteps," said Macdonald.

"Or new ones," said Winter.

"New and old," Macdonald said. "We can drive through Dufftown so you can buy a few bottles at the Glenfarclas distillery." He turned the key.

His phone rang. He got it out of his leather jacket after the fourth ring.

"Yes?" Macdonald nodded at Winter. "Good morning yourself, Inspector Craig." He listened.

"Sorry it took some time," said Craig, "but it was like I couldn't convince the authorities of the penalty in this case."

"I understand," said Macdonald.

"It's not exactly murder," said Craig.

"Not technically," said Macdonald.

"In any case, I have the information now," said Craig. "Sure enough, two of those calls to Glen Islay B and B on Ross Avenue came from a landline in Sweden, dialing code thirty-one."

"The daughter," said Macdonald. "Johanna Osvald."

"Yes," said Craig. Macdonald heard the rustle of paper. Someone said something in the background. Craig's voice came back. "There weren't too many phone calls to Glen Islay during that time period. The off season. But one of them might be of interest. At least, it's a little odd. It's from the days when this Axel Osvald was staying there."

"Yes?"

"Someone called from a phone booth," said Craig.

"Good," said Macdonald.

Telephone booths were good. Cell phones were trickier; with those they could establish the area, but then it could be difficult. Telephone booths were not as mobile.

First they could tell that it was a phone booth, and then which one it was, and where it was. Sometimes they seized the whole booth for a technical investigation.

"It was a woman," said Macdonald, "according to the matron at Glen Islay."

"Whatever you say," said Craig, "The call came from a telephone booth up in Cullen. Have you ever been there?"

"Cullen?"

"Yes."

"I'm on my way," said Macdonald.

51

Aneta Djanali drove home. It was a brilliant day, really brilliant. Everything above the buildings was blue. There were sharp shadows all over Sveagatan. There was a fresh smell in the wind.

She walked quickly through the hall, after having checked the new lock, and she went into the bedroom and took off her blouse and the thin undershirt, and it was as she was unbuckling her belt that she froze.

She pulled the belt tight again and put on her blouse and felt her pulse. What had she seen? No. What had she *not* seen?

She walked slowly out into the hall.

The shell.

The shell was in its place on the shelf.

She approached it slowly. She didn't want to touch it.

She listened for sounds now, listened inward, backward. She turned around slowly, following the sound of bare feet.

"I didn't think you'd come back so soon," said Susanne Marke.

The woman was standing barefoot in her hall, in *her* hall!

Aneta could still hear hammering in her head, a sledgehammer between her eyes. She heard herself:

"Wha . . . what are you doing here?"

"Waiting for you," said Susanne. She had a strange expression in her eyes. "You were supposed to come home soon."

"Wh . . . why?" said Aneta. That was the most urgent question. Not how, when, what, who.

"You still don't get it?" said Susanne.

Aneta didn't think to move. Susanne was standing still. She had nothing in her hands.

"What am I supposed to get?"

Susanne suddenly laughed, hard, shrill.

"About Anette and me!"

"Anette and . . . you?" Aneta echoed.

Susanne took a step forward, and another. She was still a few yards away.

"Why do you think everyone is keeping so quiet about everything?" she said. "Including Anette? Why do you think?"

"I don't know what you want from me," Aneta said, and suddenly she could move. "You broke into my house. That's a crime, and now we—"

"I don't *give* a shit!" Susanne screamed, taking another step forward. "Just like I don't give a shit about anyone else. Why do you think my dear brother can't leave his dear wife alone, huh? Or why his dear wife's dad doesn't want anything to get out? Huh? *Huh*?"

"You've done the most to protect Hans," said Aneta.

"No, I haven't," said Susanne. "But I haven't been able to tell you *everything*. I had to think of Anette, too. Of what she wants. Her wishes."

"Where is she now?"

"Soon she won't have the strength to deal with it all," said Susanne.

"Who is Bengt Marke?" asked Aneta.

"He's my ex-husband. He has nothing to do with this."

"He owns the car you drive around in."

"That was a gift. Believe me. Bengt has nothing to do with this. He doesn't even live in Sweden."

"Where is Hans? Where's your brother?"

"He wanted to talk to her one last time. I tried to stop it."

"Where are they?"

"Anette wanted to make him understand. One last time."

"I don't believe it," said Aneta.

"But you believe this?" she said, making a movement with her arms in the form of a circle. "That someone can get in here whenever they want?"

"I see that you're here," said Aneta.

"And before?" said Susanne. "Who was it before? It wasn't me." She suddenly pointed at the shell that shone dully in the light from the naked fixture in the hall. "I brought that back. My dear brother had it. Do you believe me now?"

"I . . . I don't know what that explains," said Aneta. "I don't understand the logic of what you're saying."

Susanne continued to look at the shell. As though it would say something to them. It had a sound. Sometimes Aneta put the shell to her ear. It was the rush of the sea.

Aneta asked about Kontômé.

"There was a mask hanging here," she said. "A mask of a spirit from Africa."

She saw that Susanne didn't understand, didn't know.

"I got his special tools," said Susanne. "You can get in anywhere." She looked straight at Aneta. "Do you know who Hans got them from?"

"I can guess," said Aneta.

"They're down there now," said Susanne. She looked at Aneta. "It's wrong."

"Wrong? Wrong? What's wrong?"

"He shouldn't have gone down. And she shouldn't have gone down." She continued to speak in a small voice, like someone else. "Something could happen."

Aneta walked quickly through the hall, past Susanne. In the bedroom she first called the Lindstens' house in Fredriksdal but didn't get an answer. She called the house by the sea but didn't get an answer. She called Anette Lindsten's cell phone but didn't get an answer.

She had to make a decision.

Susanne was truly afraid out there; it wasn't just a disguise. They could solve the puzzle of everything that led up to this later, but right now Aneta felt that she had to act, act quickly.

She went back out into the hall.

"Are you really sure they're down there at the cabin?" she asked.

"They're there."

"Who exactly is there?"

"Hans and Anette."

Aneta took her jacket from the coatrack. Susanne was still standing completely still.

"Are you coming along?" asked Aneta.

"Coming along? Coming along where?"

"There," said Aneta, pulling on her short boots.

Susanne looked at her feet. She walked into the kitchen and came back with a pair of gray sneakers.

"I'm coming along," she said.

They walked quickly through the front door.

In the car, Aneta called Halders and explained.

"Stay home," he said.

"I believe Susanne," Aneta said.

"Doesn't matter. You could end up in danger."

"She's coming with me down there," said Aneta.

"Is she supposed to protect you?"

"I won't do anything stupid," said Aneta. "And I'm armed."

She heard him mumble something.

"What did you say, Fredrik?"

"Where are you now, Aneta?"

"On the highway. I can see the skyline of Frölunda."

"Exactly where is this damned place?"

Damned. Yes.

She told him.

"I'm on my way," said Halders.

52

Winter and Macdonald drove back, Portessie, Findochty, Portnockie. The day was still brilliant, larger than life. Cullen Bay was empty. Two months earlier, the dolphins had been there.

They drove under the viaducts, which cast long shadows over the city, like the arms or legs of a giant. Or like the cathedrals that cast their shadows over all of Moray and Aberdeenshire.

There was no movement in Seatown. The sun fell in such a way that the small houses seemed to lean oddly.

Macdonald had parked west of Seatown, next to Cullen Sands.

They could see the beach, wide open toward the sea. Winter saw a sign: water never failed EU tests.

There was a figure far away on the beach, only a silhouette.

They walked on the nameless street that cut through Seatown, past the Methodist church. Children's clothes were hung to dry in the yard of the house across from the church.

They couldn't see the harbor from there.

The telephone booth was still red and still there. The sun shone in the cracks of the red wood. The door was halfway open.

Winter and Macdonald looked in through the door. The telephone wasn't missing its cord. Macdonald lifted it and got a signal. There was a phone book. There was no graffiti. No telephone numbers of prostitutes. No smell of urine. No empty beer bottles. No broken glass.

"This booth is unique," said Macdonald.

"We're all unique," said Winter.

"What do you mean by that?" said Macdonald.

Winter didn't answer. He turned around.

"He lives down here," he said. "Here in Seatown."

"Mmhmm," said Macdonald.

"You could live a whole life here, being invisible," said Winter.

Macdonald nodded. It was completely true.

"Should we go door to door?" he asked.

Winter looked at Macdonald.

"He could be standing there with a Luger. Left over from smuggling."

Macdonald didn't smile. He didn't take it as a joke.

"Why would he do that?" was all he said.

"These are his secrets," said Winter. "We're a threat."

"Yes."

Winter looked at the phone booth again. It lay half in shadow. He could see half of his reflection in the glass. He turned around and looked south, up over the houses at the slope toward Castle Terrace and the viaduct and the plateau behind it. On the other side of the road there was a street. He remembered the pub at the crossing.

"The man who didn't move when we were in the pub up there," he said to Macdonald, gesturing. "Just a back. It was an older man. I remember he was completely motionless while we were there," Winter said. "Not a movement."

"Maybe he was sleeping," said Macdonald. "That's not unusual in Scottish pubs."

"No," said Winter. "I could tell he was listening, listening carefully."

Macdonald thought about what Winter had said.

"There was something about the woman behind the bar," Macdonald said after a little while.

"She snuck a look at that back one time too many," said Winter.

"You saw that too?" said Macdonald.

"Now that you mention it. But I don't know."

"Maybe it was his daughter," said Macdonald. "The back's daughter."

Winter looked at his watch.

"We can go there and ask. The pubs open at eleven."

Aneta drove south on an open road. The sun was strong and she didn't have her sunglasses. The sky was as blue as it could get.

"You know the way from here?" asked Susanne.

"I've only been there once," said Aneta.

"That goes for me, too," said Susanne. She flipped down the sun visor as the road turned. She looked to the side, at Aneta. "What are you going to do when we get there?"

"Make sure everything is as it should be."

They turned off of Säröleden and drove across the field, which seemed to be suspended in the sunshine. They would be able to glimpse the sea soon. Before that was the forest, and the hill that Aneta had climbed down earlier. She wasn't planning on climbing this time.

She felt strangely safe with Susanne by her side. Susanne was calm. She wasn't moving now.

Aneta drove between the trees.

Suddenly she saw her mother, her mother from the dream! Her mother was standing in the middle of the road. Aneta slammed on the brakes.

"What the . . . ," said Susanne, as she was thrown forward in her seat then caught by her seat belt. The tires squealed.

Aneta closed her eyes, then peeked. The road was empty. There was no black woman there, no hands held up as a signal to stop, nothing but a glimpse of sea between the trees.

Halders started to pass a vehicle at Skalldalen—Skulldale—and the damn truck he'd nearly passed suddenly skidded to the left, and Halders flew out across the shoulder and his car was thrown into a boulder that shouldn't have been there, absolutely not there, and the car flipped over but only once, and it ended up sitting as though it were going to keep driving, but Halders couldn't drive; he was stuck, and he thought, It's strange that I'm sitting here in Skalldalen with my skull still in place and filled with thoughts like these.

After that he was unconscious.

Aneta parked in front of the house. It was quiet everywhere. There were no seabirds screaming or laughing. There was no wind. The sea was like a mirror, but there were no boats out there to see their reflections, and no clouds above.

Susanne still hadn't gotten out of the car as Aneta stood in front of the door. She didn't feel calm, but she wasn't agitated either, as she had been recently. She saw her hand knock on the door, one-two-three times. She called out. She opened the door. She called out again:

"Hello? Is anyone there?"

She turned around, but Susanne was still sitting in the car. The car was half in shadow.

Something moved behind it, another half shadow.

Winter and Macdonald walked across Bayview Road. The door into the Three Kings was half open. It was quarter past eleven.

The woman who had stood behind the bar before was standing there now, too, drying glasses, or maybe polishing them.

She could have been fifty, or fifty-five. It was the same woman as yesterday. They walked across the floor, which shone. There was sun in the room, and it cut across the wood of the bar. The woman continued to rub a glass with a rag as she looked at them. There was no recognition in her eyes. She might as well be looking right through us, thought Winter.

Now she nodded.

"Yes?"

Macdonald looked at Winter. Nice and calm.

Macdonald pointed at one of the ale labels in front of the wooden handles that stood in a row of four.

"Two pints, please."

The woman put down the glass she'd been polishing and polishing and reached for two new glasses on a shelf behind her. She drew the fresh, cloudy ale into the glasses and placed them on coasters on the bar.

Macdonald paid. The woman took a few steps away.

"I wonder if you can help us," said Macdonald.

She stopped. Winter could see the tension in her face. She knew. She had immediately revealed something when she hadn't shown any recognition of them.

She knew, knew something.

"We're looking for a man," said Macdonald.

The woman looked at Winter, and back at Macdonald. Then she turned her profile to them.

"Oh?"

"An older man. A Swede. His name is John Osvald."

"John Osvald," Winter repeated.

"Oh?"

She was still standing in profile. A muscle moved in her neck. She didn't ask what it was about. What should we answer if she asks? Winter thought.

"We think he lives here in Cullen," said Macdonald.

"He might call himself Johnson, too," said Winter.

"We think he was sitting here yesterday afternoon when we were here," said Macdonald, nodding toward the empty table and the empty chair by the window.

That was the direction the woman seemed to be looking. The sun was intense through the window; it lit up half the table and half the chair. Everything outside the window was bright. The woman was still looking toward the window.

"I don't know any Swede," she said without moving.

She's afraid, Winter suddenly thought. She's afraid of this, afraid of us. No. Afraid of saying something. Afraid of someone else.

"He's lived in Scotland for a long time," Macdonald said. "He might not sound like a Swede."

She still didn't ask why they were asking. She looked. Winter could glimpse the corner of the house on the other side, and a little bit of the beach.

Winter walked across the floor to the table by the window. He could see more of the road and the houses and the beach, and he could see the sea. The roofs of Seatown. The beach was divided by the Three Kings rocks, and it continued on the other side. Winter could see the golf club next to the cliffs; the parking lot, which had a few cars in it.

Winter walked closer to the window to get a better view. He turned around and saw that the woman behind the bar also had a good view.

He saw a figure on the sand, on this side of the Three Kings cliffs. It could have been the same figure they'd seen when they'd parked down by Seatown. The figure didn't seem to have moved.

Winter turned around again and saw the woman's face, and he knew. He turned toward the window and the figure down on the beach, and back to the woman again, and everything became clear, he could read everything in her face, and Macdonald seemed to understand without really understanding and came up to the window and saw what Winter saw.

"It's him," Macdonald said. He turned to the woman. "That's Osvald out there, isn't it?"

She didn't answer, and that was an answer in itself.

They turned around and walked toward the door.

"I couldn't stand the lifelong lie anymore," she said.

They turned around again.

"Sorry?" said Winter.

"I couldn't stand Da . . . Dad's lifelong lie anymore," she said without taking her eyes from the window.

"Dad's . . . ?" said Macdonald.

"Couldn't stand it," she said. "And he couldn't stand it."

Winter and Macdonald didn't say anything.

"I sent a letter," she said.

"It arrived," said Winter.

She turned her head to them, suddenly.

"Be careful down on the beach."

When they had crossed Bayview Road and continued down the steps to Seatown, Winter could see the harbor and the breakwaters and the few local fishing boats, the very small ones, which were in a little row alongside the wall.

He could also see the trawler of steel that was just inside the harbor entrance. It was blue, blue like the sky and the sea on this day.

He saw the name.

Aneta stood facing the car and saw Susanne's silhouette in the window.

Last time, there had been a small plastic boat moored at the dock that belonged to the cabin. It was gone now. That meant something.

Someone moved behind the car.

"I didn't want you here," said Hans Forsblad, stepping into the sunshine.

"Where is Anette?" Aneta asked.

"Where is Anette? Where is Anette?" Forsblad mimicked her.

"She has the right to live her own life," said Aneta.

"Not as long as you keep interfering," said Forsblad. "You're always interfering!"

"I'm here with your sister," said Aneta.

"I'm aware of that."

There was a shine in his eyes; it wasn't from the sun.

Aneta took a step forward.

"What have you done with Anette?" she said, but she knew the answer.

Halders could move his head. He had regained consciousness some time ago; he hadn't been gone from the world for long. There were people standing around the car. He could see colleagues in marked cars and uniforms. I don't see an ambulance. They wouldn't waste an ambulance on me.

Someone had opened the car door without cutting the metal.

He could get out!

He did so, with some help.

"The ambulance is on its way," said Jansson or Jonsson or Johansson or whatever the fuck his name was, the detective from Frölunda.

"You can take it yourself," said Halders. "I don't need an ambulance."

He walked a few steps, and after a little bit, a few more.

"What time is it?" he said.

His colleague answered. Halders tried to focus on his watch, but he couldn't really see his arm clearly. He focused on the guy in the uniform.

"Can you drive me somewhere?" Suddenly he felt that it was urgent. He saw more clearly. "It's fucking urgent," he said, and fumbled for his cell phone but then gave up. "Can you make a call for me?"

Winter and Macdonald walked across the beach. Seatown was behind them. Winter could see the cars in the parking lot of the golf club. He thought one of them shimmered green, like metal.

They walked toward the figure. It was a man bent over, looking across the sea. They saw him in profile. He straightened up but remained in profile.

Winter knew who it was; Macdonald knew. It was the same profile.

He knew now. Here they came, side by side, one fair and one dark, suede jacket, leather jacket. As though they owned the whole world. But no! They didn't own a thing.

When he had seen their car over there an hour ago or so, he knew that they were there again. That they would come out here to him.

And he waited.

It must have been the telephone. He didn't think she'd said anything; she wouldn't dare. Was it possible to find out something like that? The telephone? Tracing, it was called. It was probably possible.

He didn't intend to answer any questions.

This was his beach, his city, his house, his *life*.

Don't answer, don't say anything

He could scare them, *scare* them. This wasn't where it was supposed to end. They couldn't do anything to him.

There was no one left who could say anything.

They had stopped ten feet from the old man. He turned around, toward them.

"John Osvald?" Winter asked.

The man looked through them as though they were invisible. He seemed to fix his eyes on something behind them, maybe his house. Or the viaduct.

"We only want to know if you're John Osvald," Winter said in Swedish.

The man didn't answer, continued to look with his misty gaze.

"Are you John Osvald?"

"Who are you?" said the man. In Swedish.

"I'm from home," Winter said. "I come with a message from home."

The marked car drove through the little grove of trees toward the sea. Halders saw the sea. His colleague Jonsson hadn't been able to contact Aneta. Halders had tried himself. No reply. Now he saw that there was no reception.

They cut across the beach and saw the house that had to be the Lindstens'. He saw the car that he knew was Aneta's. He didn't see any other vehicles.

He saw a woman on her knees next to the car. He recognized her. It was Susanne Marke.

He saw a man fifty feet out, bent over the water. He recognized him. He watched Hans Forsblad dive suddenly and start to swim away. Halders saw Forsblad's shoes kick the water.

He saw Aneta at the edge of the water. She was standing still.

*   *   *

The old man hadn't said anything more, hadn't moved. Everything was still. There were no birds, no fish, no people, nothing in between. They were alone in this northern world.

"What happened to your son?" said Winter, who had taken a step closer. "What happened to your son, Axel?"

The old man's gaze slowly became clear. It made him appear younger.

He was wearing a cap with a narrow brim. His face was sharp. He had a thick, knitted sweater under a tweed jacket. He was tall when he wasn't bent over. Winter saw a blue spot on one cheek.

There was a bulge in one of his jacket pockets.

"What happened to Axel?" said Winter.

"He washed himself," said John Osvald.

"What do you mean?"

"He washed away the sins. He wanted to do it. I couldn't do it."

"He wasn't wearing any clothes," said Winter.

"Only someone who God loves can do that," said Osvald. Winter thought the old man's gaze seemed to cloud again. "Whatever happens, good things will come to a man who loves God."

"Sins," Winter said. "What sins are you talking about?"

"My sins," said John Osvald.

"What sins are those?" Winter asked.

Osvald didn't answer.

"Does it have to do with what happened during the war?" Winter asked.

Osvald stared at Winter, or perhaps at something else. His gaze was clear again.

"Comes a time," he said.

"Sorry?" said Winter.

"There comes a time," said Osvald, who spoke Scottish English.

"A time for what?" said Macdonald, who was now standing next to Winter.

No answer.

"A time for what?" Macdonald repeated.

"A time to tell," said Osvald. He gestured with his arm, his hand. Winter looked at his jacket pocket again. It was . . .

"To tell what?" Macdonald asked.

He took a step closer.

"Stay away from me!" Osvald yelled.

"To tell what?" Macdonald repeated.

"Take it easy, Steve," said Winter.

Winter looked at Osvald's jacket pocket. He looked at Macdonald. He opened his mouth again to warn—

"Tell me what there is to tell," said Macdonald, who could almost reach Osvald now.

"*Nooooo!*" Osvald suddenly yelled, and he pulled a pistol out of his jacket pocket and shot it. Winter had time to register the Luger with his eyes, and he heard the bullet pass between himself and Macdonald. Winter was already moving to the side, a reflex. He didn't have a weapon. Macdonald didn't have a weapon. Winter heard another shot, and another; he didn't hear any bullets, but he saw Macdonald, ahead and to the side, get hit in the throat, he saw the blood start to spurt like a fountain, a gurgling sound from Macdonald, an open wound in Macdonald's shoulder where the other bullet must have exited, a slow movement as Macdonald began to fall, the taste of sand in his mouth, of horrid fucking sand that filled Winter's face, the image of the earth spinning around and around and becoming a blue clump of sea and sky, and then suddenly the sound of footsteps passing him but from the *other direction,* and through the haze of sand he saw Erik Osvald's profile, and he heard a scream up ahead, and another from a direction he couldn't determine, and he thought about how he had lured Macdonald into this, that *he* was responsible and no one else, that he would have to face Sarah and see her face, and she would have to face the children, the twins, and he pawed the sand out of his face and hurled himself up and forward and screamed and screamed, screamed like a madman.

53

When everything was over, Winter could look back. When everything was said and done, he saw that everything meant something else. Everything came undone.

Identity is a loan, a role, a mask. We cross the border between truth and lies and the light thickens into dark.

> *O, never*
> *Shall sun that morrow see!*
> *Your face, my thane, is as a book where men*
> *May read strange matters. To beguile the time,*
> *Look like the time . . .*

Winter had read Macbeth late in the evening, a paperback he'd found in the little book and stationery shop next to the entrance of the hospital in Elgin where Macdonald had received care for his gunshot wounds. In two or three days he would be transported to Raigmore Hospital in Inverness, but that was too risky now. But he would survive.

You could have said that Macdonald had been lucky, if that expression could be used in this situation. But it wasn't luck. It was something linked to everything that had happened, everything that had come to a head on the beach in Cullen.

It was John Osvald's daughter who had called the police even before the shots were fired. John Osvald's daughter.

Her name was Anna Johnson, and she had seen them walk toward her father on the beach. She had stood at the window with the view of half the beach, and it was enough for her to see her father, and then the men who approached him, and Macdonald, who got too close.

She had come rushing across the sand at the same time the ambulance screamed up from between the cliffs.

It had been nearby when the call came, on its way west from Macduff.

It took Macdonald to the nearest emergency room, twelve miles to the west on A96.

Macdonald's blood had been black in the sand. The large spot had looked like a stone. Suddenly there was a shallow wave, as the sea rose, and the blood had been washed away.

John Osvald hadn't moved.

They still had to talk to him. He was mute now.

He was sitting in the jail in Inverness. Chief Inspector Craig still hadn't spoken with him.

His grandson had been motionless on the beach, crushed. Winter had tried to talk to Erik Osvald even while Macdonald was still lying injured in the sand. Erik had bent over him. Winter didn't know whether Macdonald was dead. He had felt his heart pounding like the hammer at the shipyard at Buckie. He hadn't tried to *talk* to Erik, he had *screamed,* kept screaming as the sound of the shots was still echoing over Cullen; Winter had screamed his question to Erik Osvald, the usual old damned question: *Why?*

They would piece it together, stitch by stitch.

Erik Osvald had been in contact with his grandfather.

The grandson was still in a state of shock. It wasn't yet clear when they had first made a connection.

But the blue trawler, the *Magdalena,* that shining modern vessel, was in the harbor at Cullen as proof. Money had been put into it, lots of money.

It was a matter of penance, of guilt.

But in the end, that wasn't enough for John Osvald.

Night fell over Elgin. Macdonald was unconscious; he was in critical but stable condition. Winter could see Sarah at his bedside; half the wall was made of glass and for a second he thought of the walls around Jamie Craig's office at the police station in Inverness.

The light around Steve and Sarah was blue.

Angela held on to his shoulders.

"Let's go out for a while," he said.

The air was fresh and clean on the street, but the wind was mild.

Indian summer continued. Winter could see the silhouette of the cathedral above the buildings of the city. He couldn't help but think of the viaducts through Cullen. Seatown below.

He and Steve and Sarah and Angela had passed through Elgin when they drove to Aberdeen. That was only yesterday. Good God.

Macdonald had said that Elgin Cathedral had once been considered one of the most beautiful in Scotland, the only one that could compete with St. Andrews in beauty.

Now it was only a shell, but the façade was the same, and its beauty remained when the cathedral became a silhouette in the night. The darkness did what it could to maintain beauty.

They sat on a bench. Neither of them spoke.

Winter's phone rang. He let it ring.

"I think you should get that," said Angela.

He answered. It was Ringmar.

"How is Steve doing now?" Ringmar asked.

"He's going to make it," said Winter.

They had spoken during the afternoon, after the shooting. Ringmar had also had information, shocking information. It was a unique afternoon.

"Have you been able to talk to Aneta more?" Winter asked.

"No. She's still out there looking."

"Are there any traces at all?"

"No, not yet," said Ringmar. "We did find the plastic boat, but we haven't found Anette."

"And Forsblad still isn't talking?"

"No. Halders had almost started to hope that the guy would drown, but he turned around and swam back to shore and since then he hasn't said a word."

"It's so damned senseless," said Winter.

"When isn't it?" Winter heard Ringmar's tired voice. "Aneta is convinced he killed her. We just have to find the body."

"We just have to keep looking," said Winter. "And keep questioning."

"Forsblad's sister came up with a story about how she and Anette had become a couple, and that's what made the brother go insane," said Ringmar. "But Anette's father, Sigge, claims that's all a lie. It's just her way of making things better, according to him."

"Yeah, he's just the guy to tell the difference between truth and lies," said Winter.

"I believe him, in this case," said Ringmar.

"He's a swindler," said Winter. "And maybe more than that."

"He says he was only keeping her furniture for her in that warehouse on Hisingen."

"Well, good God," said Winter.

"Anyway, he's not getting away from *that* story," said Ringmar. "The man is a professional criminal."

"Where was he at the time of Anette's disappearance?" Winter asked.

"Well, we're not exactly finished with that puzzle now, but presumably he was with his gang at their very own Hisingen IKEA. In any case, they were there when Meijner and his guys came knocking."

"Say hi to Aneta," said Winter.

He sat with the silent phone in his hand. The darkness over Elgin was even denser now. The cathedral's silhouette had grown even sharper. It had three towers, the way there were three rocks, three kings, elsewhere. The cathedral could remind him of the three rocks on the beach in Cullen, if he wanted it to. The Three Kings.

Anna Johnson had come running down the stairs, through Seatown and across the beach.

It was our secret, she had said later, it was our secret, no, it was my secret.

"Couldn't we walk around a little?" said Angela, getting up from the bench.

Winter got up. Steve's brother and sister, Stuart and Eilidh Macdonald, came out of the hospital on the other side of the cobblestone street. They had only said a quick hello a few hours earlier. Dallas wasn't more than ten miles away.

Everything had been confusion then, and fear.

"Well, your bandages saved Steve's life," said Stuart Macdonald.

He looked at Winter's chest under the suede jacket. Winter had borrowed a shirt at the hospital. His clothes were still in the car since they'd checked out of the Seafield Hotel.

"They were extremely makeshift," said Winter.

"But very tight." Stuart Macdonald looked tired in the eternal blue light from the hospital, as though he were Steve's older brother. "They stanched it off, or whatever they called it in there. It helped him retain a little blood, anyway. Enough."

"The risk was that he could have strangled," said Winter.

"It's always a balancing act," said Stuart, and he actually smiled. "This time it worked."

"I was the one who brought him there," said Winter.

"Sorry?" said Eilidh.

"I was the one who took him there. If it weren't for me, this wouldn't have happened."

"You're feeling guilty, you mean?" Eilidh asked.

"Yes."

"Let me just say that Steve is a grown man with his own free will," she said. "He doesn't let himself be taken anywhere."

"I agree," said her brother. "And Steve is still alive, isn't he?"

Winter and Angela walked along the stone streets to the Mansion House Hotel, which looked like a castle from a distance. Winter stumbled. Angela caught him.

"I need a whisky," he said.

"You need to lie down," she said.

In the room, he poured a whisky and then lay down. Angela sat in an easy chair with her feet on his thighs. They had opened the window, and the mild wind brought in fresh air. They hadn't turned on any lights.

"What happened once upon a time out there at sea?" said Angela, whose face was half lit by the streetlight outside. He could see her face in half profile. "During the war."

"I can only imagine, so far," said Winter.

"What do you imagine, then?"

"A transaction," he said.

"What kind of transaction?"

"Well, it seems that John Osvald and his crew were involved in smuggling. That's what his grandson Erik said. But he hasn't learned anything about what actually happened."

Winter carefully shifted Angela's feet down to the edge of the bed, turned onto his side, and took the glass and sipped the whisky.

"But it wasn't an accident?" said Angela. "When the boat sank?"

"I don't think so."

"Will we ever know?" said Angela.

"I don't think so."

"But whatever happened was terrible enough that John Osvald switched identities," said Angela. "Become someone else, and leave your old self behind."

Winter nodded.

"Good God," she said.

"He tried to," said Winter. He drank again. The whisky tasted like the wind that came in through the window. "He must have wrestled with his God."

"Did he wrestle with his son?" said Angela, who had pulled her naked feet close to her body. She curled up in the easy chair, as though she were cold.

"John Osvald?" Winter changed position on the bed. "Well, that's the next question."

"I didn't mean physically," said Angela.

"No, no, I realize that."

"So what happened on the mountain, then? Outside Fort Augustus?"

"I have thought about that many times during the past few days," said Winter.

"I've started thinking about it now," said Angela. "It's hard not to." She shuddered. "And it's hard to." She looked at him. "Do you understand?"

"Yes, of course."

"And at the same time you think about Osvald and his unknown daughter."

"She wasn't unknown," said Winter. "She was unknown to us, but that doesn't mean she was unknown."

"Did anyone else in that city know about it, then?" Angela asked. "And who was her mother?"

"Her mother is dead, according to the daughter," said Winter. "And she says that she didn't know Osvald until a few years ago."

"But she believed him? Believed that he was her father?"

"Apparently he could prove it," said Winter. "But I don't have any details yet."

Angela shuddered again.

"Are you cold?" Winter asked. "Should I close the window?"

"No. The wind is nice."

"Do you want a whisky?"

"No."

"A little tiny one?"

She didn't answer.

"Angela?"

"I don't think I should," she said.

"Sorry?"

"I shouldn't drink alcohol," she said, leaning forward so he could see her face.

"Shouldn't drink . . . ," he repeated.

"That's all I'm going to say," she said.

"You don't *need* to say more," he shouted, hopping up out of the bed and spilling several of the ridiculously expensive drops.

"When did you know?" he asked. They were both lying on the bed now. The window was still open. It was still Indian summer in Elgin, or maybe it should be called *brittsommar* in October. "It must have been pretty recently."

Angela had a glass of mineral water in her hand. She drank it and placed the glass on the nightstand and gently bit her lower lip. She looked out through the window.

"What are you thinking about?" Winter asked.

"Still about what happened in Fort Augustus," she said. "Between father and son."

"Mmhmm."

"Do you have any theories?"

Winter sat up. He could smell the scent of the river outside. The evening was making way for the night.

"I think Axel Osvald dreamed of his father his entire life. That's only natural. And the circumstances were so dramatic. And this sense of loss got stronger and stronger." He turned to Angela. "I think we'll be able to find out much more about him now, from Erik, and from Johanna. Now that we know how we should ask. Why we should ask."

"But the dad, John, he made contact?"

"He must have, at least once Axel was here," said Winter. "And of course he also did indirectly, through Erik Osvald."

"He also had his daughter call?"

"Yes."

"Did he know what would happen?"

"When they met, you mean?"

"Yes."

"He didn't know his son," said Winter.

"What do you mean?"

"He didn't know him. He didn't know who Axel was. He couldn't anticipate that there might be an extreme passion, maybe an obsession."

Winter changed position again where he was sitting on the edge of the bed. "Do you understand? Something could give way. Something could give way very easily. The fact that he took off his clothes had to do with his strong Christian beliefs, his own strong beliefs. It had to do with cleansing, something like that. He wandered on the mountain and prayed and took off his clothes bit by bit. A cleansing bath. On the beach, John Osvald said that his son was washing away his sins. John couldn't do it himself."

"Do you think the father told?" said Angela. "Told Axel?"

"Told him what?"

"Told what he had done. What had happened out at sea that time." She pushed her hair away from one temple. "What his guilt consisted of. The extent of his crime."

"Yes," said Winter. "I think so. I think he told. And it ended in disaster."

"Did Axel Osvald really commit suicide?"

"I don't know," said Winter. "But I think so. Suicide. Yes. Lying there naked was suicide." He ran his hand through his hair. "But maybe in one way it was also murder." He took his hand from his head. "I don't know."

"Will we ever find out?"

"How would we find out?" Winter asked.

"Through John Osvald," said Angela.

"Maybe," said Winter, but he didn't think they ever would.

Later he thought about the sea again. A different sea, a different beach. This beach was on the other side of the North Sea, across from this city and this ancient landscape.

He carefully pushed Angela's arm off of his chest and slid out of bed. Angela was snoring, but very lightly, a relic of her polyp period.

He poured a finger of whiskey into the glass and stood by the window, which was closed. He opened it a few inches. The air was still fresh out there, but now it was cold. It smelled like water. He saw the sea and that beach in his mind's eye. He and Angela and Elsa were there, as well as another person he didn't know yet, a small person. They were all digging in the sand, and then in the soft earth on the plot of land above them. There was dirt in his shovel. He pushed a wheelbarrow filled with sand. He laid stones. He pounded a hammer against a wall.

It was a new era of life.

SIMON & SCHUSTER
READING GROUP GUIDE

Sail of Stone

INTRODUCTION

In Gothenburg, Sweden, Chief Inspector Erik Winter agrees to help an old girlfriend find her father, who has disappeared in Scotland under mysterious circumstances while searching for his own long-lost father, presumed to have died in World War II. With the help of an old friend from Scotland Yard, Winter finds himself on a journey through the Scottish coastline and gradually begins to unravel a web of secrets that stretches back across three generations.

Simultaneously, his colleague Detective Aneta Djanali senses there may be more to a domestic disturbance report than meets the eye and pursues her instinct. Like Winter, she is soon in over her head, and her missing persons case gets her caught up in a string of burglaries and a smuggling ring in a seedy part of town.

As they investigate their respective cases, both discover the difficulties involved in uncovering family secrets and the many intricacies of relationships, both their own and those of their clients.

TOPICS AND QUESTIONS FOR DISCUSSION

1. Discuss the novel's title, *Sail of Stone*. Why might Edwardson have chosen this title? What imagery does it conjure up for you?

2. The novel abounds with detailed descriptions of both the sea and the sky. Is there a particular passage that stood out to you for its vivid depiction of either?

3. Both Erik and Aneta rely more on their instinct than on concrete evidence as they doggedly pursue their respective cases. Is this what makes them good detectives? Why does Erik take the Osvald case—is he simply helping an old friend, or is there more to his decision? What motivates Aneta to delve deeper into the mystery surrounding Annette?

4. Both Erik and Aneta are reluctant to fully relinquish their independence, even though they are both in committed relationships. Why do you think this is?

5. Solitude, with its varying impact on individuals, plays a large role in the novel. Erik and Aneta both seek out solitude, holding onto their personal space even when it interferes with their relationships. Conversely, fishermen construct their lives around long periods of isolation as a necessity, and sometimes such a lonely life is said to drive them crazy. The Osvalds state that the silence is the most difficult part of being on a fishing voyage. What do you feel the novel says about seclusion?

6. The book is as much about relationship dynamics as it is about solving crime. How do the detectives' interactions with one another and their personal relationships impact the plot? Do you see parallels between their lives and those of the individuals they are investigating?

7. Erik Osvald says that storms are good for the sea, because they stir up the bottom, and Winter feels that the metaphor applies to his work, too (p. 111). Discuss the "storms" in the novel that stir up dormant problems. Are they beneficial? To whom?

8. Reread the passage on page 221: "Now here they stood, with a sudden sun over all the mountains that stuck up above the surface of the water. But that was only a small part of it, a tenth of a percent. Everything was below the surface. The iceberg effect. These weren't icebergs, but the effect was the same. That's how it was with good books. The simple words were only the topmost layer. Everything was underneath. Books, but also the work in their world. Their world was words, words, words." How does this iceberg metaphor apply to books, *Sail of Stone* in particular? How

does it apply to the detective work described in the novel? Do you find it an apt metaphor?

9. Discuss the pacing of the novel and the way in which events unfold. How do the concurrent yet independent plot lines relate to one another? Why do you think Edwardson chose to intertwine these two stories?

10. At what point did you identify the character whose reveries were interspersed? What did these flashbacks contribute to the story?

11. After reading the novel, go back and skim the first chapter. How does what you know now change that passage?

12. Discuss the culmination of the novel. Did it match your predictions? Edwardson leaves many questions unanswered; did you anticipate, or want, a more conclusive ending?

13. Ultimately, did either Erik or Aneta "solve" their respective crimes? What did their investigations contribute? Did they manage to clarify and clear up matters, or do you think they may have complicated them further in some instances?

ENHANCE YOUR BOOK CLUB

Familiarize yourself with the complicated areas around Gothenburg, Sweden. Go to http://maps.google.com/maps?q=gothenburg+sweden and search for places such as Kortedala, the neighborhood of Annette's apartment; Krokslätt, the site of the Lindsten family home; and Donsö, the island where the Osvald families live.

Similarly, look at a map of the Scottish coastline between Inverness and Aberdeen to help visualize the fishing towns Winter and Macdonald visit on their search for Osvald (Forres, Dallas, Buckie, Pennan, Fraserburgh, and Peterhead). Also check out www.VisitScotland.com for more information on the country. Be sure to look at the areas mentioned in the novel: Inverness and Moray in the Highlands Region, and the North East Coast in the Aberdeen City and Shire Region.

Try some traditional Scottish food, such as Cullen Skink (http://www.scottishrecipes.co.uk/cullenskink.htm) or haggis (http://www.worldburnsclub.com/begin/address_to_a_haggis.htm), or dine on the more common fish and chips.

Get a feel for an actual Scottish fishing town by watching the movie *Local Hero*, starring Burt Lancaster, which was partially filmed in Pennan, Scotland. The plot of the 1983 comedy/drama revolves around an American oil company representative who is sent to a Scottish village to purchase the town for his company.

Music plays a large role in the lives of the novel's characters—rarely do they take a drive or relax in their apartment without putting on a CD. Listen to some of the characters' favorite jazz, rock, and/or ethnic African music during your meeting. Try jazz legends like John Coltrane, Miles Davis, and Wynton Marsalis; classic rock bands such as Pink Floyd, Led Zeppelin, and Steppenwolf; and traditional African artists like Ali Farka Touré and Gabin Dabiré.

A CONVERSATION WITH ÅKE EDWARDSON

You have been a university lecturer, journalist, and press officer for the United Nations. What led you to become an author of detective fiction?
It was the only kick left in my life, so I decided to give it a go around 1993. Now it's been twenty-one books, roughly half of them crime novels, the rest "literary" fiction, some plays, too.

Who inspired the character of Erik Winter?
I was tired of the tired detective in mid-90s novels! I wanted somebody younger, more determined, possessed, on his way full throttle into the new millennium, without mayonnaise stains on a shabby jacket.
    The name? It's to show the complicated personality of Erik Winter: it's from the albino American blues guitarist Johnny Winter and the black Dutch soccer player Aron Winter.

Sail of Stone, **the sixth novel in the Erik Winter series, is now being published in English ten years after its Swedish publication. Do you think the story will be different for an American audience?**
An American audience is just as smart as readers in the rest of the world, probably smarter, so there will be no problem. Note that I have only intelligent readers; there are other books for the rest. The themes in *Sail of Stone* deal with the shadows of the past, the Good War, and the sea; those themes are larger than life and the passage of a mere ten years, or a hundred, makes no difference.

Do you have any advice for English readers just beginning the series with this sixth book? Is there any essential back story a first-time reader should know?

Erik Winter started out in the first novel as one of those arrogant dudes born in the early sixties (I was born in the humble early fifties), and as such he was (in the first couple of novels) very good at his work but pretty lousy at everything else, including relationships. I wanted him to grow, to learn something from his life: to learn the art of living, which is the hardest thing. When you get the hang of it you're pushing eighty.

So this is a *Bildungsroman* within the crime story; it's the only way to make it interesting I think. And when it comes to Erik, in the earlier novels he has married his girl, he has become a father, and he has matured a bit. He's on his way. He could almost be my friend in this one.

Why did you decide to set your novels in Gothenburg? This novel includes vivid descriptions of many towns along the Scottish coast as well; what drew you to set a large portion of the novel in Scotland? Did you visit the small villages Winter and Macdonald travel through?

Gothenburg is the second largest city in Sweden, with over one million inhabitants. It's by far the most dynamic city in the north of Europe; Stockholm, for instance, is just a prettily made-up corpse, dead and shining.

When I started out writing about Gothenburg in the early 90s, there was not much literature on the city, and absolutely no crime fiction. It was like no one had taken the city seriously, and I decided to do that, and I'm glad I did: the change here has been tremendous over the years, so the series on Erik Winter is really a saga of a big city changing from Workingman-land to Bladerunner-land. Even the crime is world-class now in Gothenburg; in 1995 I had to make that up.

Scotland and Gothenburg have old ties; streets of Gothenburg are named after Scots, and over the centuries there's been a lot of business between Gothenburg and Scottish ports, such as Aberdeen, which lies straight over the North Sea. Above all there's been that old fishermen's connection, which the novel takes its drama from.

I visited every one of them! On several occasions. So don't tell me being a novelist isn't hard labor.

The novel places a significant focus on the relationship dynamics of its characters, and their personal lives play a role in the evolution of the plot as well. How do you strike a balance between developing the personal side of your characters and still telling a compelling crime story?

Yes. It's the trick really. You can't have the one without the other, and you really can't tell a good story with hollow and shallow characters—everything depends on the people you put in the story. It's important for me to have my readers see that my characters have a huge backstory, even if I don't tell a word of it. I think you understand what I mean. This is the essence of writing, to make that *Gestaltung* of characters on the page. They are not alive, but if you do it right they could be any and all of the readers. That is the writer's duty. If it isn't done right the writer should work in other honorable professions.

You are a three-time winner of the Swedish Crime Writers' Academy Award for best crime novel. Congratulations! What do you believe makes a successful crime novel?
We all write the same story. It's like the blues: three chords. It could be wonderful and it could be awful; it depends on how it's done, by whom. It's the simplicity that does it. Simplicity exposes anyone in any field who isn't up to it.

The three chords in a crime novel are:
1. Mystery
2. Search for answers
3. Solution
That's all there is. Play on.

The detective work and department interactions are described in detail and seem very authentic. How did you become knowledgeable about such procedures? What type of research do you do to ensure accuracy?
Being a former journalist, I believe in research. Everything that happens in these novels *could have happened* in the real world, even if it sometimes seems strange. If you write a police procedural, the police procedural has to be absolutely right, like in any novel, about anything.

When it comes to the Winter novels, I'm fortunate to have my Chief Inspector friend Torbjörn, the head of Forensics Department of the Gothenburg Police, to read the whole manuscript in proof. That eliminates the last of my errors.

You include a variety of characters, yet all are well developed and play a specific role in the story. How do you create and maintain so many distinct personalities?

There is a clinical term for that, all those voices in your head . . . but seriously, this is what writing is about: to give voice and motion to the different personalities you carry—your masculine side, your feminine side, your violent side, your humble, your outspoken side . . . How could it be any other way? And writers are those who put it on paper.

Several of your books have been made into TV movies in Sweden. Were you involved with their production?
My only involvement in the productions was to condemn them afterward. It's a writer's absolute duty to pan anything done from his work regardless of quality. My motto: one single word says more than a thousand pictures.

Did you know how the novel would end before you began writing it? Did you have the Erik Winter series, and the evolution of his character, in mind from the beginning, or did everything develop continuously?

For me, that's the key question. I don't know that much when I start writing a novel, any more than the theme and idea of this specific book and a plot sketch on a single piece of paper, but I know one thing: the ending scene. I have to wait out that scene in my head before I can start writing, have to know where it will take place, who's going to be there (apart from Winter), what the motion and emotion are going to be. Sometimes it takes an extra month or two of waiting to get started. I believe that if I, as a writer, know where I'm going in the book, the reader will know too, and follow.

You concluded the Erik Winter series with the tenth book, which was published in Sweden in 2010. What made you decide Winter's story was completed?

I certainly didn't have a whole series of ten big books in mind when I started on the first Winter novel. My plan was to try and finish that one, and have it published! But after that was done I wanted to write another one. I was curious about this lead character I had created, and somewhere in the middle I decided to try and write the Decalogue, that classical number.

The tenth book, *The Last Winter*, was actually published in Swedish in 2008. I was proud of that final one, and I thought that if I just went on writing more Winter novels, the quality would drop. So I said, this is it. Nevermore a Winter novel.

But I was lying. I'm still curious about this guy, after all this time. We had twelve years together, and you just don't end such a relationship cold turkey. So this year I've decided to write a new big Winter novel, "Winter's Return," hopefully coming out in 2014.

In 2010, I published a "literary" novel (though I think my crime novels are just as "literary"), and in August 2011 came a thriller, *Meet Me in Estepona*.

What are you currently working on?

Currently I'm working on a young adult novel, *Indian Winter*, the third in a trilogy following *Samurai Summer* and *Dragon Month*, and I'm also writing stories for a big collection to be out in 2013, *Going Home*. So you can't say I'm only in it for the money.